Praise for *MELTING DOWN*

"This good versus evil thriller sneaks alot of good science into a wild and hopefully impossible plot. It will be hard for a reader to not absorb a few critical climate concepts along the way. And hopefully, it helps motivate society to wake up to the slow-boil crisis of our time."
—*Dr. Steve Running, 2007 Nobel Peace Prize co-recipient as part of the IPCC*

"Sheer weight of scientific data seems not to have gotten across the point about global warming; maybe a good old red-blooded American thriller can help do the trick!"
—*Bill McKibben, Author, The End of Nature and EAARTH; Founder, 350.org*

"Move over Dan Brown and James Patterson. Harvey Stone has written a page turner with multiple twists, turns and innovative international intrigue."
—*David Johnston, Author, Green from the Ground Up*

"This story is an action packed tale interwoven with real-world events that will grab and hold your attention. It's a must read for every policy maker, thought leader, media exec, CEO and the public at large!"
—*Hon. Claudine Schneider, Former Congresswoman, R.-R.I.*

"Harvey Stone's MELTING DOWN is one of those rare books where a fun and riveting fictional narrative is driven by high-stakes, real-world events. From beaches to boardrooms, readers will be discussing MELTING DOWN as they relate its story to events being reported in the news."
—*Nina Simons, Co-Founder and Co-CEO, Bioneers*

"MELTING DOWN is a page-turner. It is gripping, fast-paced fiction that takes off from real-world events. The story will continually surprise and engage readers. The male/female approach to protagonists is rare in action thrillers and fun to follow."
—*David Schaller, former US EPA Climate Change Analyst*

"Like strong medicine made more palatable by a teaspoon of honey, the realities of global warming are woven into an emotionally charged tale of action and intrigue."
—*Michael Mudd, Executive VP (retired), Global Corporate Affairs, Kraft Foods*

"It's entertainment of a high order."
—*Douglas Fischer, Editor, The Daily Climate*

"Take a couple hours refuge from the climate change headlines and dive into the action-packed world of Harvey Stone's Melting Down—with good gals and guys, evildoers, energy wars, and a surprising set of hostages. You'll come out feeling energized—and informed."
—*Eban Goodstein, Director, Bard College Center for Environmental Policy*

"MELTING DOWN is an extraordinary weaving of fiction, science, and real-world headlines. While reading the book aloud to each other, my husband and I were at times shocked and moved, distressed and heartened. Plus, in the tradition of Tom Clancy and other authors, we learned while we read."
—*Pamela Gordon, author, Lean and Green*

"MELTING DOWN is perhaps the first novel to bring climate change science, impacts and solutions to a mass audience in an entertaining, high-stakes thriller that appeals to a wide cross-section of readers."
—*Katherine Teter, former Sustainability Subject Matter Expert, U.S. EPA*

"Readers in Europe and around the world will be both utterly engrossed by this page-turner and chilled by its wake-up call to us all."
—*Mark Walker, COO, Streetcar (London)*

"2500 companies in 60 countries register their carbon footprint with the Carbon Disclosure Project. They understand the impacts of our changing climate. MELTING DOWN's fun, fast-paced plot will help individuals to understand those impacts as well."
—*Paul Dickinson, CEO, Carbon Disclosure Project*

MELTING DOWN

HARVEY STONE

3/14/13

Dan,
Thank you for all the great things you do in the world!

❖
The Way Things Are Publications
Los Angeles

PAPERBACK EDITION

©2010, 2011, 2012 by Harvey Stone. All rights reserved. Manufactured in the United States.

Published by The Way Things Are Publications, an imprint of Pacific Coast Creative Publishing, Los Angeles.

Jacket design by Pacific Coast Creative, © 2011.

ISBN-13: 978-0-9839641-4-8

Edited by Jennifer Havenner, Angela and Mark Hooper, and Julia DeGraf.

http://www.harvey-stone.com
http://www.meltingdownnovel.com
http://www.pacificcoastcreative.com

Printed on acid free paper. Interior pages are Sustainable Forestry Initiative (SFI) certified. Meets all ANSI standards for archival quality paper.

To those people who fight for a saner world - especially the ones who have an open mind, a wider perspective and a sense of humor.

Thank you, all. We need a few million more like you.

ACKNOWLEDGEMENTS

When the economy crashed in 2008, so did my environmental consulting business. With time on my hands, I started to write a non-fiction book about the increasingly unstable climate. But there was already a boatload of great books that weren't being widely read. At the same time, the campaign of manufactured doubt about the changing climate was succeeding, and the number of skeptics and deniers, including US politicians, was rising nearly as fast as greenhouse gas emissions.

Out of this sense that we are heading for the cliff, I decided to write a cliffhanger.

I'd never written a novel. I'd certainly never written an action thriller. But I figured we are all living in an environmental thriller with fast action, overwhelming obstacles and tremendous uncertainty about the outcome. So maybe it was time for a fictional work that would entertain people while it educated them. After all, how hard could it be?!

Two years later, I'm mortified at how naïve I was. Luckily, I had a ton of help.

Inspiration came from a lineage of writers (James Baldwin, Cormac McCarthy, Charles Dickens, Doris Lessing, John Steinbeck, Ayn Rand, Upton Sinclair, Elie Wiesel and many others) who write not only to describe their world, but also to change their world - whether I agree with them or not.

It came from the millions of people who try to make the world a better, safer, happier place — whether they are successful or not.

It also came from the long line of people who have articulated 1) the deep inter-connections in today's world and 2) the systems approach to both understanding and solving our problems. Amongst them, I have best known Gunter Pauli and have learned a tremendous amount from him.

I owe a great deal of gratitude for those people who helped me to speed up the action, deepen the characters, verify the science, clarify the impacts, refine contracts, research locations, meet scientists, connect with marketers and get rid of bombastic phrases and bad jokes. With apologies to anyone I overlooked, they include Michael Baldwin, Jim Balog, Leslie Barclay, Judy Berger, Sam Berger, Judith Christy, Richard Corriere, Paul Dickenson, Bob Felt, Martha Fielding, Andy Fogelson, Alison Gannett, Steve Garvan, Pam Gordon, Wendy Higgins, Jack Huckins, Sarah

Huckins, David Johnston, Adam LeWinter, Bob Mann, Dan McGrath, Bill McKibben, Michael Monroney, Jamie Morris, Michael Mudd, Mark Myles, Haggis Reeves, Steve Running, David Schaller, Harvey Simon, Nina Simons, John Steiner, Joni Teter, Zeno Tyrer and Mark Walker.

Bill Fritzmeier and George Mason pointed out the many holes in my grammatical education.

Max Regan was the perfect writing coach, who helped to unleash the part of me that enjoys creating bad guys, killing off people and blowing things up.

Jennifer and Mark Havenner at The Way Things Are Publications have been terrific publishers. At a time when the industry was contracting sharply, their risk tolerance in publishing a debut author should win them the Publisher of the Year award.

My daughter, Michael Greene, continues to be a light both in the world and to me.

My grandson, Dalton, is no less than a joy to be with — and a joyous being. I cannot forget that he will have to live with what we do - or not do - in the next few years. I pray that he and his generation will have the opportunities we've had in a world that is just as beautiful as ours.

Claudine Schneider and Erin Sanborn have been enormously supportive, as always.

Ginny Jordan is the living, breathing embodiment of friendship, support and encouragement. In so many ways, she has been with me every step of the way, as only true and loving friends can do.

And, lastly, I would have to be a far better writer than I am to adequately thank my wife and darling, Fleur Green. She has walked down the road of life with me for nearly forty years. She has shown me the very best of what it means to be a human being. And she has never rained on my insane ideas, including: "Honey, I'm thinking of writing an action thriller novel."

"I now establish my covenant with you and with your descendants after you and with every living creature... Never again will all life be cut off by the waters of a flood; never again will there be a flood to destroy the Earth."

—Genesis 9

"Today, the network of relationships linking the human race to itself and to the rest of the biosphere is so complex that all aspects affect all others to an extraordinary degree. Someone should be studying the whole system, however crudely that has to be done, because no gluing together of partial studies of a complex nonlinear system can give a good idea of the behavior of the whole."
—Murray Gell-Mann, Nobel Prize winner in physics

PROLOGUE

Washington, D.C.
Oct. 24, 2016

AT THIS MOMENT, Charley Breen would rather be a prisoner than the president.

President Breen sat alone in the US Capitol conference room. His tie was undone. He was coming undone.

He slouched farther into the high-backed chair. He put his hand on his heart and felt how fast it was beating.

He played with the fabric of his suit jacket. It could stop a .44 Magnum and was seven times more flexible than Kevlar.

The wedding band on his finger clanged lightly as he touched the metal dish covering his supper. The smells of medium-rare steak and fresh asparagus made him more nauseous than he already felt. His eyes blinked maybe twice a minute. Mostly, they stared at the "Twin Terrors," as he thought of them.

The left monitor showed the satellite images of the first nuclear attack since Hiroshima and Nagasaki. President Breen recoiled as the blast blew apart an enormous Pakistani glacier as if it was a house of cards in a windstorm. As much as anyone in the world, he knew that it also blew apart the illusion most people live under: namely, the idea that six o'clock supper or ten a.m. Mass could protect them from human stupidity.

God have mercy on their souls. He wasn't a religious man. But raised in a Christian home, religion was where his mind went as he watched the torrents of deadly water surge down a valley, carrying boulders the size of buildings and sweeping away animals, people, villages, and a whole way of life.

Finally, the screen went black. He wished his brain could, too. *They'll be coming for me very soon.* He forced his eyes to the right monitor and Terror number two. He aimed the remote and put his finger on the power button. He quickly took his finger off the power button.

In the distance, the president heard faint footsteps moving quickly across the marble floor. He imagined them passing the extra marines and Secret Service agents in the hall standing at attention, on alert.

Finally, as the steps grew closer, he rubbed his eyes. *If I can't do this, I can't do what I have to do when they get here.* As he pushed the power button, he wiped away a few tears before the first glacial images appeared.

There it was. As big as the Empire State Building. Breaking apart. Collapsing into the sea. As it hit the water, he curled his fingers so tightly into a fist that his fingernails hurt his skin. The hole the glacier left along the Greenland coast was almost as large as the hole it left in his heart.

Enough! The president shut off both monitors and sat upright. He stiffened as he heard the door open. He turned his head slightly as they came through the door.

Alex Sullivan, the president's chief of staff stepped forward. "Mr. President, we're out of time." Next to him, the secretary of defense, the chairman of the Joint Chiefs of Staff, and the national security adviser stood solemnly.

"The attack? Do we know who or why?"

"Not yet, sir." The president's national security adviser, or NSA, turned red.

"How many?"

"110,000."

"Do I have ten more minutes?" His request only deepened their fears about his state of mind and the state of the nation.

"I'm sorry, sir." The chief of staff held firm. "Like the planes, the networks are ready to go."

Slowly, the president knotted his tie. He raised his six-foot-three frame and looked at them. In doing so, he glimpsed himself in a wall mirror. *My God! I look ten years older than I did ten days ago.* "All right, gentlemen..."

The president buttoned his suit coat and walked directly to the secretary of defense. "Launch," the commander-in-chief ordered. Being in the air would save precious minutes when they finally knew who and where the enemy was.

"Yes, sir." The secretary turned and left. He took the chairman of the Joint Chiefs and the NSA with him.

One down. One to go. The president stepped over to the polished table. He looked down at the red, white, and blue memory sticks on the table. In descending order, they represented the degree to which he would risk the world's economies and people.

Finally, he picked up the red stick. He ran his long, thin fingers across it. *God help us.* Then he tossed it to his chief of staff.

Alex Sullivan arched his eyebrows. "Are you sure, sir?" The president nodded. "It'll be on the teleprompters." He raced out the door and made a cell phone call on the run.

The president of the United States walked purposefully toward the House of Representatives Chamber. He was about to deliver a Special Address to Congress just eight days before a presidential election.

Because he didn't know what he would say, media outlets were blacked out and stressed out.

Furthermore, from the United Kingdom to Chile to Russia, people were hoarding food, withdrawing cash, buying guns, and moving away from urban areas. How could this one man hold America and the world order together, when he could barely hold himself together?

As the president strode quickly through the oak doors, senators, members of the House, cabinet members, the Supreme Court, generals, admirals, and others dutifully rose.

He kept up the pace, making his way down the aisle. He glanced over at the statues of Hammurabi, Moses, Napoleon, and Jefferson. He tuned out the greetings that were as tepid as the applause.

"Feeling OK, sir?"

"Good luck, Mr. President."

Now, at the podium, President Breen looked up into the packed gallery.

The First Lady still felt like she had swallowed a pail of broken glass. A sedative had helped her. So had extra makeup. Proud as a peahen, she blew him a kiss. *Go for it, Charley. Swing for the fences.* She crossed her fingers and prayed he would do what she'd begged him to do.

The president beamed up at her. *I love you so much!* Then he thought of his closest friend, whom he loved far more than a brother. Right now, he sat in the White House Situation Room, watching global hotspots for more signs that the world was cracking apart.

Four years ago, the president had placed his hand on his grandmother's Bible and said, "I do solemnly swear that I will faithfully execute the Office of President of the United States, and will to the best of my ability, preserve, protect, and defend the Constitution of the United States."

Now he had to fulfill that oath against tactics that no previous president had ever imagined.

For a long moment, the president looked out from behind the podium. *Did Truman agonize about Fat Man and Little Boy? Did God agonize about the Flood?*

He started to speak. Then he stopped. He felt something working its way up his spine. *Where the hell have you been?* He took a sip of water to allow that primordial sense of "husband" and "protector" to flood his being. He had first felt it for his wife. But over the years, the feeling had rippled outward until it encompassed the only country he had ever loved and the only living planet anyone ever knew.

In this moment, he wouldn't be anything but president.

With a confidence he hadn't felt since his inauguration, the president of the United States began to speak.

The people of the world leaned forward to hear. In less than an hour, they would know how much of the world order he was prepared to risk.

PART ONE: GREEN

1

Colombian Jungle
Oct. 9, 2016

T EX CASSIDY HAD BEEN RUNNING like a gazelle with a lion on its tail for the past two hours. Through acres of coffee farms he knew. In mountain terrain he didn't know.

Even when he had lost the killers in overgrown ravines and muddy canyons, he still drove his legs forward.

Finally, he sat on a large, moss-covered rock and let his breath slow down. He took off his shirt and wrung out the sweat. He watched a gray squirrel climb a tall tree. He watched the tree's branches sway. He watched a bird circle in the wind that swayed the tree's branches.

On any given day, Tex would take the squirrel, the tree, and the bird over people. With a few exceptions, he had lost respect for them. But these men? They weren't even men. They were hyenas who had menaced and mauled Carlos, his friend. And they were not happy that Tex had stripped them of their guns and robbed them of their game.

For the moment, Carlos was safe. He himself was safe. But the line between "safe" and "dead" was thinner than the spider's web reflecting in the sunlight.

Tex patted his swollen cheek. It throbbed. He tried opening his half-closed right eye, but there were too many broken capillaries.

Tex looked around. *This looks familiar.* He was in the Santander Department in north-central Colombia, two hundred miles from Bogotá. He recognized a distant peak and remembered the Cauca River where he and Carlos had fished. If he could reach the river, maybe he could swim downstream until it joined the Magdalena River, find a road, get on a bus, make his way to Bogotá, and then back home.

Tex rose on his sore feet. Then he raced through acres of coffee bushes. He waded two miles in a cold mountain stream. Finally, sweaty and exhausted, he came to a familiar farm. He ran across a small garden and quickly knelt on one knee at the corner of a barn. His knee slipped forward in fresh cow dung. His jeans were already ripped, and the soft waste oozed across his leg. Instinctively, he brushed some of the dung away, but smeared it across his hand.

The sun was still fairly high. If he could lay low till night, he could make his way to the Cauca. He adjusted the brim of his old baseball hat to better look for birds rousted by any approaching men. He listened for crackling twigs nearby or engines farther away. All he heard was a loud wood quail in the distance and a quiet footstep behind him.

Then he felt cold steel press into the back of his neck.

Tex put his hands in the air. He thought of her, hoping she would be his last thought. These men didn't like having their punishment games interrupted, especially by a gringo. They enjoyed cutting up other men. They loved betting on how loud he would scream and how long he could take it.

"Stand up." Slowly, Tex rose up. The gun barrel followed him up. *Katie* . . . He braced for the stock of the rifle cracking down on the back of his head.

"Turn around." Even more slowly, Tex pivoted until he faced the man holding the rifle. "It's you."

The thin man was a fourth-generation coffee farmer. In the last ten years, his life had been sliced up like an apple. Not by men, but by markets. Anonymous markets that controlled most of the coffee supplies from Brazil, Vietnam, and a hundred other countries. While consumers paid more, farmers were paid less. "They offered me a lot of money for you, señor."

The farmer and Carlos were friends. Tex had met him, liked him, and taught him a little English. He in turn had taught Tex a few secrets about growing the bean.

Two years ago, Brazil's coffee production shot up while prices to farmers had hit bottom. The poor guy was forced to let his three workers go. He had no money, no help, and no hope. So Tex had bloodied his palms, helping him to pick coffee beans for a week. In the end, he took the scrawny carrots the farmer had given him, so the farmer could keep his honor.

"I wouldn't blame you . . ."

In the distance, Tex saw the farmer's three kids. One was skinnier than the next.

"I'm sorry, señor." The farmer hadn't wanted to grow poppies. He had learned Carlos's method. But then they had burned his house, chainsawed his bushes, and violated his fifteen-year-old daughter.

"Shoot me. Please." They both heard a truck approaching fast. "Tell them I tried running away. Tell them you had to kill me." Tex imagined what they would do to him. He would rather die by this man's hand than by theirs.

The farmer pointed his gun to the west. Tex turned. There was a small graveyard fifty yards away. "Not there. Past it. The goat trail." Tex saw the rutted path. "It'll take you to the river." Then the farmer pushed his rifle forward as far as his arms would reach. He grabbed the stock with both hands and jammed it so hard against his forehead that Tex heard bones crack. "Go . . ." he whispered, falling face forward into the same cow dung where Tex had knelt.

Now Tex was running toward the glacier-fed river. Sweat stung his eyes. Brambles stung his flesh. When he dodged a dwarf porcupine, he tripped over a root thicker than a hotel drainpipe, smashing his shoulder and cracking his knee, ripping two pearl buttons off his shirt. He forced himself up and took off again through the thick foliage. Then he saw her off to the side. *Katie!* His head turned, but he slipped on a mossy log and landed in the largest anthill in South America. Most of them scattered, but a dozen crawled across the bridge of his nose and into his hair.

Rising fast and brushing the ants away, he twisted his ankle like a propeller screw when he saw a coiled anaconda in a black oak tree, forcing him to veer off to the side. That last move cost him precious seconds. So did a thick vine slicing his cheek. So did running in cowboy boots. It beat running barefoot, but the passport he had stuffed into one boot and a little money he had stuffed into the other made the running harder.

Ahead was a small clearing where ranchers had burned the foliage away to graze their cattle. Three steps from reentering the forest, a leather bullwhip wrapped around his knees. Tex stumbled through ferns and orchids. His momentum vaulted his head forward into a tree trunk that hadn't budged in a forest fire and wasn't going to budge for him.

Barely conscious, Tex felt water splash on his face. He reached up to wipe it away, but his hands were tied and starting to swell. He smelled the three thugs before he saw them. One knelt and jammed his pistol way down inside Tex's ear. The second had worked his rifle inside Tex's pants. The third, holding the bullwhip, was on his cell phone. "We've got the gringo. Should we kill him?"

"If you do, I'll feed you to the vultures." The voice was deeper than the Marianna Trench and had an Eastern European accent. "He's a little bonus for Juan. Give him the phone."

The thug took his pistol out of Tex's ear and replaced it with the phone. Instantly, the American recognized the deep voice. "I wish I was there, Cassidy. I'd slow-cook you, like a pot roast."

They had met twice. The first time was in 2006, when, during an interview, the man had described his role in assisting Middle East terrorists. But three years ago, in 2013, almost a year after the American had arrived in the region, Tex had seen his methods firsthand.

At the time, the man on the phone was a private contractor on the open market. He was hired by the cartel to slaughter ten farmers in five days and to terrorize the rest from abandoning the poppies. Subsequently, he had hung four farmers from the trees that shaded their coffee bushes. He suffocated two farmers—one a woman—in pig waste. Three were dismembered and their body parts sent to members of the local coffee cooperative. The tenth had been strapped onto the large crucifix in the village church. Tex had found the poor man and, too late, had lowered him down with his own hands.

Three days later, on his way to the airport, the contractor had stopped to buy a cigar in the village store. Tex was there, getting supplies. The two Anglos in the small Latino village stared at each other across the bananas. The contractor smirked. Then he aimed his gun at Tex's head and said, "Adios, señor." Instead, he grazed Tex in the arm, laughed out loud, and left.

Now, captured, Tex knew he was dead meat. "Tell Juan to leave Carlos alone. It was me, not him." The method of farming that Carlos had developed, the single best alternative to growing cocaine, could be destroyed with a few bullets and matches.

As the sun moved across the sky, the thugs marched the stumbling American back toward the mountainous coffee region. One thug pulled Tex along by a rope tied between his wrist and the gringo's bare neck. Every time the thug wiped away sweat, Tex lurched forward. With his hands still tied, he was breakfast, lunch, and dinner for the mosquitoes.

Finally, they rested at a small stream. Two thugs went to relieve themselves behind some trees. The third one, holding the rope, pushed his captive flat onto the ground so he could have a drink. While Tex sucked in a little water, the thug put his rifle under his arm and lit a cigarette.

Tex heard the others finishing up. He pulled his legs up so his knees were under him. Then he grabbed the rope and yanked his captor down to him. He picked up a softball-sized river rock and smashed the cigarette into the stumbling man's mouth. The thug's teeth shattered. His nose broke. In another instant, he was unconscious as Tex cracked the man's head with the same rock.

While the others returned, Tex undid the ropes and raced west again. This time, he made it to the Cauca. But from the rocky cliff on which he stood, the river was 150 feet below—the equivalent of a fifteen-story building, with rapids swirling around rocks that could stop a bus. The height didn't bother him, but his lifelong dread of drowning forced his feet to grip the cliff.

Suddenly, a bullet whizzed by his cheek. Tex took a baby step forward and looked down. *No choice!* By the time the next bullet was in the air, he was too. His pursuers saw his body twist, turn, and tumble all the way down into the cold, raging water. They scrambled down the mountainside and raced along the water's edge, checking every eddy pool for a mile. They waded into the water to see if his body had been caught in tree roots along the shore.

Finally, empty-handed, the two men knelt on the ground and looked at each other. One pulled out his cell phone. "We can't find him, Juan. We're pretty sure he's dead." When Juan said the contractor wouldn't be happy, the thug was pretty sure he himself would be dead soon. Looking up, he saw four vultures circling.

2

Paamiut, Greenland
Oct. 10, 2016

"DROP EVERYTHING. Find the bomb." Three grueling years of work were at risk. Thus, the elite soldiers scanned the water's surface through the early morning haze.

Alpha was the leader. As a teenager, he had bullied the bullies. At age eighteen, when two creeps sexually threatened his fourteen-year-old sister, he broke all four of their arms and rearranged their internal organs. When he was twenty, he stumbled onto a fact that gripped him like a pair of steel tongs: of the estimated thirty million species on Earth, only primates use their eyes to threaten others. *Humans are primates.* Already able to throw a two-hundred-pound man across the room, he strengthened his glare in front of the cracked mirror in his mother's dirty apartment on the edge of Chelyabinsk, a crumbling industrial city in Russia.

"Over there!" Alpha pointed. "Four o'clock. Ten yards." As a soldier, Alpha was the Zeus of Russian Special Forces. He was trained using Soviet body science and extreme martial arts. Now, submerging his arm into the cold glacial waters, he remembered how the scientists had forced him to stand in a 55º water tank for a full hour. The electrodes showed the scientists that he could compartmentalize his blood flow, direct his body heat to protect his inner organs, and, after emerging, actually improve his performance time on an obstacle course. "Just driftwood. Keep looking."

Beta, the number-two man, was built like a tractor and just as strong. He wrapped his large, scarred hands around the powerboat wheel and steered it around the ice shards. His combat skills were legendary. So was his proficiency with poisons. When he was a kid, he had learned from his uncle how to build small bombs the way other kids build model airplanes.

In the distance, Alpha saw the town's red church through his high-powered binoculars. Nearby, as the dawning rays turned the low clouds pink, the first fishermen stumbled out of their A-frames and headed toward their rusted boats. Suddenly, Alpha heard a trawler chugging along as it made its way around a few small icebergs and headed out toward the fishing banks. "Catch that boat."

On the trawler stood a lone Inuit fisherman—the descendant of people who had first settled in Greenland way back in 2500 BCE. He leaned awkwardly at the wheel. His two arthritic knees ached. So did the bulging disc in his back. While those pains never left, the fish did. Sure, new fish were moving in. But they were a different kind. He didn't know their habits. He didn't have the right nets.

Keeping the coastline to his right, he headed north to find his old "fish friends." They were moving where the waters were cold enough to live. Most days, he had to travel farther out. Some days, he didn't find his friends.

The fisherman knelt down. He untangled his fraying nets. He saw the approaching boat. *Please don't be a police boat.* This year's catch had been especially poor. Instinctively, he looked at his commercial fishing license. It had expired in 2014.

"Good morning, sir." A master at mimicking voices and proficient in seven languages, Alpha sounded as Danish as Hans Christian Andersen. Along with the native Inuit, Danish was an official language of Greenland, and Alpha could easily blend in on the world's largest island.

"Special Services from Copenhagen." Alpha smiled, while flashing a badge in the fisherman's face. "May we come around?" A stickler for detail, he had spent the flight time to Greenland brushing up on the island's history. He now knew that Denmark had exercised control over the island nation for nearly three hundred years; that, in 1979, Denmark had granted Home Rule to Greenland; and that, since 2008, it only took responsibility for foreign affairs, security, and financial policy.

A minute later, Alpha questioned the old man. "A boat got smashed by an iceberg. It was smuggling weapons. Looks like a duffel bag drifted away. Have you seen it?" The fisherman's eyes darted to the shore before shaking his head. Just then, Beta held up a wet cloth strap.

Two minutes later, they rolled the fisherman in his own nets and dangled him in the icy water. "Where's the duffel?" Alpha poked him with a net hook. "Your lips and hands are turning blue. In five minutes, your liver and kidneys will start shutting down."

"The old blue house." The fisherman's teeth chattered so hard that he could barely speak. In seconds, the icy cold had soaked his clothes. Now it was penetrating his skin. Like the natural force it was, the cold would do exactly what Alpha had said it would. "Farthest north, along the point."

Alpha spotted the house with his binoculars. "If you're lying, every neighbor will die. So, the old blue house?"

"Y . . . y . . . yes." His brain was slowing down. Just before it shut down, he heard the two men climb into their powerboat and speed off toward shore, speaking Russian.

Sixteen minutes later, Alpha and Beta sped back to the trawler with the waterlogged duffel bag. They lifted the now-dead fisherman onboard and placed a high-powered explosive on the boat. Seeing other trawlers approaching, they towed the boat out to sea and out of hearing range. Finally, Alpha cut the towline. Making sure to keep the seawater from wetting and corroding his cell phone, he entered an electronic code. As they sped away, they heard the explosion. It ripped the trawler into a million splinters, cutting the man up into small pieces of fish food.

3

Minnesota Lake Country
Oct. 13, 2016

THE SHUTTLE DRIVER adjusted his Minnesota Twins baseball cap and arched his eyebrows. "You live here, and you don't know?"

"I'm an alien. What can I say?" The driver handed Tex Cassidy a newspaper. The headline read: "Do or Die for Twins!"

World Series! What a concept! After four years in South America, so much of what was normal before seemed extraterrestrial now. "What's happened to the ash forests?" It was dusk. All he saw was death.

"Beetles." The driver turned onto a dark, rural two-lane road. No streetlights. No people. A perfect location for films where tourists stand by the raised hood of their car and the pickup truck stops behind them. "With the drought, it's been a good couple of years for those suckers."

"But not so good for baseball."

"What do you mean?" This passenger was friendly, but weird. No luggage. Gashes on his face. Talking gibberish.

"Most bats are made from ash." After three flights, middle seats, and twenty-six hours, just being home reminded him that he was a human being. "What's it doing to the saw mills?"

The driver shrugged his shoulders and turned on his headlights.

"What about the state's tax base? Probably less money for cops and kids. Yes?" He knew the US was still reeling from the '08 financial collapse.

The driver was less versed than his passenger in the interconnections of things. "They'll just use some other wood, won't they?"

"Maple, probably. But they splinter. Players don't like them." Tex yawned so much that his jaw hurt. "Plus, can you imagine what it'll do to those hardwood forests? Hell, we'll be like Japan."

"Because they play baseball?" The driver slowed down. Except for starlight, the road was now pitch-black.

"Because they chop the forests down. Mostly for lumber. But for bats, too. And, bizarre if you ask me, also for fancy chopsticks."

"Really?" The driver cut his vocabulary close to the bone.

"Want to know what's worse? They cut the trees down to grow mushrooms. Hell, we just used a coffee waste substrate, and the fungi couldn't get enough of it." In the rearview mirror, Tex saw the driver's eyes glaze over.

The driver shifted to safer topics. "What'll you do up here?" They were in boonie-country, two hours northwest of the Minneapolis St. Paul Airport.

"Hell if I know." Tex leaned forward and grinned. "Cut wood. Read books. Watch the snow fall."

About a mile down the road, they saw the flashing red lights of a police cruiser. Tex put his hand on the driver's shoulder: "Some guy hit a deer?"

"Probably a security roadblock." The driver slowed down. "The president will be up at his summer White House in a couple of days."

"What do you mean 'summer White House'?"

This time, in the rearview mirror, the driver saw his passenger wince. *Guess he's not voting for Breen.* Before he could explain, he stopped in front of the barricade.

A tall state trooper sauntered over to the van. One hand rested on his holstered gun. The other hand held a dog-eared notebook. "Identification, please," the trooper told them both.

The driver handed over his license. Tex lowered his backseat window and stuck his head out. "What for?"

"Routine check. The president's coming. We need to know who comes and goes." The trooper shone his flashlight in Tex's eyes and held it there longer than he needed to. "If you live around here, you're familiar with the drill."

"I do live here, and I don't know the drill. By the way, whose authority are you operating under?"

"Secret Service." The trooper opened the notebook. "What's your name, wise guy?"

"Cassidy. Tex Cassidy. What's yours?"

The trooper leafed through the book. "If you don't can your attitude, you can read it on the arrest sheet." The trooper found the "C" page. "There you are. Show me a photo ID." He read aloud a notation next to Tex's name. "Friend of the president, huh?"

Reluctantly, Tex shoved his crumpled passport out the window. Except for Tex's reentry to the US the day before, the trooper found no entry after the Colombian stamp dated November 14, 2012. "You've really been gone four years?"

"My watch broke."

Ten minutes later, the shuttle pulled into a long dirt driveway. Tex paid the driver and walked up the creaky wooden stairs. *Home sweet home.* A sliver of moon was visible. So were a million stars. In the months before he had left, he had barely noticed the sky.

Inside, the shades were still drawn. Sheets still covered the furniture. It felt as if only dust, insects, and mice had been there during his four years away.

Tex flicked a light switch. *Solar electricity works. Amazing.* Instinctively, he avoided the photos on the living room bookshelves. Instead, he headed straight for the bedroom, where he took off his cracked cowboy boots and fell asleep in his clothes.

4

White House
Oct. 13, 2016

IN FOUR YEARS as president, Charley Breen had never gone to sleep without worrying about the collapse of Social Security, a nuclear attack on a US city, or something worse.

Tonight, he slept as lightly as a man on death row. He tossed. He turned. He was glad Ellie was off with their daughter, Mariah.

The problem wasn't sleeping without Ellie. It was the "something worse."

At 3:35 a.m., the president put on his bathrobe and plugged in the coffeepot. *Mariah. God love her!* One day, when she was still at the University of Michigan studying environmental science, she had yanked out the plug. "Waste of energy, Dad. More carbon emissions. Why? Because you're too lazy to pull the plug."

At 3:47 a.m., he poured himself coffee, sat in his armchair, and wrote in his private journal.

"October 13, 2016—dream sequence. *Tidal waves obliterating American coasts . . . food riots in Barcelona . . . African vigilantes terrorizing villagers . . . bodies washing up on Brazilian beaches . . . Tex in the Oval Office, wearing blue jeans and a Western shirt with snap buttons . . . Kansas tornadoes flinging silos into the air . . . Indonesians drinking salt water . . . half of Japan under water . . . lines of Israelis outside closed banks . . . abandoned cars along Vancouver roads . . . mobs ransacking the White House as mobs had ransacked the Czar's palace in 1917.*"

Finished writing, he closed the journal and closed his eyes. *God help us.*

A moment later, the president went to the sink and splashed water on his face. *If I get Tex, he'll go ballistic. Do I really need him?*
He glanced at the Campaign Summary.

- *Days until election: 19*
- *Average of polls: +1*
- *Swing states: Florida, Missouri, New Mexico, North Carolina, Virginia*
- *Main activity today: Miami rally*
- *Final strategy: (1) Be presidential (2) Focus on strong suit (national security) and Gov. Wilton's weak suit (climate change/energy)*

Then he picked up his Daily Briefing. As he had demanded, it was thick and thorough. In the Gulf War, he had lost seventeen men when he had been too young, pig-headed, and arrogant to gather enough intelligence. His self-imposed penance had been to visit the families of every one of them and apologize for the death of their child.

Opening the Daily Briefing, the president looked at the "Top Ten" items.

- *Up to a million deaths expected from new virus.*
- *China's foreign minister threatens to recall 25 percent of the $1.4T in Treasury bonds they hold.*
- *Iran is completing weaponization of nuclear energy.*
- *National Debt soars to record level.*
- *Vice president remains in critical care after stroke.*
- *Arizona vigilantes set to murder first of sixteen hostages by noon.*
- *Shortage of long-term care facilities worsens, as US population ages.*
- *Russians to hold sixth military parade in five years.*
- *Unemployment levels for Q3 rise slightly to 10.7 percent.*
- *Another massive glacier breaks free and drifts into North Atlantic shipping lanes.*

The president ran his finger down the page and touched each bullet point. They gave the illusion of separateness, as if each item was isolated. But he was acutely aware that, like a grove of aspen trees, they were all connected under the surface.

In fact, those events and virtually all events were interconnected ticking bombs. Only a handful of people really understood that this was the real worldwide web.

If one crisis went off, it could trigger others. If China, for instance, called in US Treasury bonds, it could raise US employment even further and put more strain on more individuals who might take more hostages. Internationally, it could embolden the Iranians to launch an attack. It could also encourage the Russians to do whatever the hell they were up to with their throwback military parades.

Order to disorder. It was the second law of thermodynamics applied to human institutions.

The president unplugged the coffeepot and unlocked his "Top Secret" desk drawer. As if he were pulling out a ticking bomb, his long fingers gingerly pulled out a three-ring binder titled "Arctic Region Update: For Your Eyes Only."

With each page, his breath got shallower. *This could be Humpty Dumpty.*

At 6:45 a.m., the president showered but barely felt the water.

At 7:23, he dialed his chief of staff. "I'm ready, Alex."

Fifteen minutes later, the president's staff stood up from the Oval Office couches to greet him. "Be seated and be brief. I've got Miami today."

"Sir, I'll start." Jane Harkle, the secretary of state, spoke up. "The Chinese aquifers are drying up faster than our own. Another drought, and a few hundred million people could be running through the streets."

An internal staffer held up the latest jobs report: "We'd better win the election," she joked nervously, as the president got out of his chair, went to one of the three south-facing windows, and looked out, "or we'll all be collecting unemployment."

The secretary of agriculture spoke last. "I toured six farms. I couldn't tell who's wilting more: the crops, the animals, or the people." The president kept staring outside. "What's the connection between all your reports?"

The staff members looked at each other. Finally, Secretary Harkle replied, "They're all top priority."

"What else?"

"They're election issues?"

"Anything else?"

Silence. Finally, the president turned. "Thank you for all your hard work." As they left, the president indicated to his chief of staff to stay behind. "I've changed my mind. Find him."

Alex tensed visibly. "Sir . . ." He paused, running ideas through his mind. "We talked about this. 'Tex Cassidy' is a four-letter word. If Wilton gets wind of him—"

"He won't." The president walked over to the Resolute Desk, which had been a gift to the United States from Queen Victoria. He stuffed his rally speech into a folder. "Look, Alex, I can tell you how 'William' turned into 'Tex' and who he first slept with. But for what I want, who gives a damn?"

The president watched Alex fingering the handkerchief in his breast pocket. He braced himself. "With all due respect, sir . . ."

"What's the burr up your ass, Alex? And how'd it get so big?"

The chief of staff gathered himself. "Cassidy was a mess when he left. Who knows how twisted he is now. I really think—"

The president stuck his hand up like a stop sign. "There's nobody else. You're wasting time. Find him."

5

Moscow
Oct. 14, 2016

TWO HOURS before dawn, Admiral Boris Sukirov finally got up. For the fourth time since midnight, he checked his computer. *Still nothing from Alpha!*

The admiral opened the fridge. He stared at the blini his housekeeper had cooked in honor of his big day. To him, it was better than caviar. *You could drop dead anytime.* The words of the Helsinki cardiologist he had secretly visited two weeks ago echoed in his mind.

A moment later, he stood at the sink. He turned the garbage disposal on and shoved the blini down it. He was willing to give up his favorite food. He was also willing to give up a friend. At this stage of Operation Noah, losing a friend was preferable to losing time. As he shut the disposal and the grinding noise stopped, he heard the *ping* of an incoming e-mail.

"Greenland equipment found. Mission secure. Operation Noah back on course."

The admiral replied to his chief operative. "Return to Amsterdam. Stay on full alert. Events will move even faster."

A few minutes later, he hummed along with Tchaikovsky's *1812 Overture* as he got dressed. His eclectic musical tastes ran from Rimsky-Korsakov's *Scheherazade* to Stravinsky's *The Rite of Spring*. But of all the magnificent Russian compositions, he always chose *1812* just before or after a victory.

He buffed his already polished black shoes in time to the music. Then he brushed his hair, taking more time than usual.

Finally, he went back to his dresser. He removed the false bottom from the middle drawer and took out the thin envelope, carefully letting the contents fall onto the dresser.

As *1812* reached its crescendo, the admiral pulled open the curtains. The early sunlight poured in. This was no time for a mistake.

Obeying Beta's instructions to the letter, the admiral opened the nail polish bottle. Holding the applicator steady in his right hand, he brushed the liquid on and around the entire middle finger of his left hand. Then he did the same with the two adjoining fingers and with his left palm.

Next, with the antidote in place, he picked up the tweezers. He grabbed the small piece of wood that was a half-inch long, less than a sixteenth of an inch wide, and made to look like a two-day-old scabbed cut. As he laid the "cut" near his fingertip, the resin on the underside bonded with his flesh.

Finally, the admiral put the special "Band-Aid" around the "cut" to cover it until he was ready.

By 7:30 a.m., he stared out the window, waiting for the limo. Three years of painstaking detail were about to deliver the world dominance that history had denied his Motherland.

The front door opened. "Good morning," he greeted his housekeeper. "The blini were delicious." She deserved to live in the world's most powerful country. He no longer fretted that her national pride would come through natural events and market forces rather than ideological struggle and military force. "Power is power," he had told the other Quartet members. "And at our age, I don't care how we get it."

"Thank you, sir." She had never seen him in his full-dress, white naval uniform with four rows of medals. "You look quite handsome."

"You're too kind..."

"If it's all right with you, I'll start in here." She gestured to an adjacent hallway door.

"Very good. I unlocked the library for you." Once a year, she feather-dusted his fifteen hundred books, including five hundred by Chekhov, Tolstoy, Pasternak, Trotsky, Lenin, and other Russian writers, philosophers, and political thinkers.

She turned the knob and saw the high birchwood shelves that were custom-made from trees in the Bikin Valley. A ten-rung ladder moved in its track along the shelves. The books were arranged alphabetically by author. "And your son's room?" She turned the knob, but it didn't open.

"No, thank you. It's fine." He looked down below at the approaching limo. At six-foot-two with a head of thick white hair, Admiral Sukirov resembled the Rock of Gibraltar with snow on top. The width from one shoulder to the other equaled the length from his neck to his waist. The shape of his large face and head was equally square.

"Watch the parade on my television, if you like." He walked out of the apartment, past the elevator, and quickly went down the four flights of stairs.

"Good morning, Admiral." The driver's hand shook slightly as he opened the rear door. "It's a beautiful day for the parade."

At 8:10 a.m., the limo pulled up at the staging area. The admiral got out and straightened his uniform. As soon as he had walked into the building to be briefed, the driver parked around the corner and sent a text message to his security handler.

6

Minnesota Lake Country
Oct. 14, 2016

ELEVEN HOURS later, with a "Breen '12" coffee cup in hand, Tex walked his property. This was his Taj Mahal. His Mont Saint-Michel. His Christ in the Desert. Every summer as a kid, he had notched his height against the large oak tree. As an adult, he had visited at least once a year. He fully expected to die here and have his ashes scattered along with Katie's.

In the garage, he started his 2010 Ford pickup truck. It cranked hard, but the engine kicked over. Wonderful memories of camping and hunting in this truck flooded back to him.

Outside, he walked through the overgrown vegetation. The Russian olive trees were way out of control. *Why not?* Tex put on leather work gloves. This felt right. And familiar. And who he was. Sustaining the land sustained him. It was also the perfect soil for his mind to wander and his emotions to calm down.

As Tex yanked the younger trees, he remembered being told that Russian olives were an invasive species, initially planted to stabilize the soil. As he tossed them into a half-rusted wheelbarrow, his mind drifted from the stability of soil to the loss of topsoil. As he dumped the pile for later use, when he would chip the biomass and spread the nutrients on denuded sections of his property, he thought about large-scale farming, mono-crops, and pesticides. As he returned the wheelbarrow to the shed, he thought about shareholders in agribusiness corporations who wanted higher returns on their investments.

As he walked back to his kitchen, he thought of his parents, who had relied on fixed income from corporate bonds to fund their retirement.

Inside, he sat at the wooden breakfast table he had made twenty years ago. Could he have gone on for hours with "controlled-wandering," as he called it: free association with a purpose? Easily. He had learned it as a kid and practiced it daily, the way people do crossword puzzles. Sometimes, he would start with a single word or phrase, like "Russian olive tree" and see where his mind went. Other times, he read a newspaper where he picked two disparate stories and tracked the links between them. *OK, time to get settled in.*

First, he made a list of groceries to buy. While scrubbing the kitchen counters, he remembered that Katie had once called him "the most curious man alive." From time to time, she would tell friends the classic "Tex" story. In college, he wondered about Henry Ford's statement that any Model T customer could have any color he wanted, as long as it was black. "Why black?" Tex hunkered down in the library until he found the answer: black paint dried faster, so Ford could produce more cars.

Finished with his grocery list, Tex took the sheets off the furniture and put them in a large plastic container under the house. Kneeling down, he saw the now-rusted recliner bed he had bought for Katie after there were no more reasons to be near a hospital and they had moved up here full-time.

Finally, he was ready for the lake. Like Tex himself, it was often smooth on the surface. It teemed with life. But it could be whipped up and, under the right circumstances, even take a life. Heaven was kayaking on this lake and soaking in the solitude.

Tex walked onto the deck, smiling. When he looked across the lake, he felt as if he had been run over by a tractor-trailer.

Directly in front of him, he saw prefabricated cabins standing where groves of aspen no longer did. He heard helicopter rotors starting up. He smelled gasoline. Right in front of his property, Tex saw a powerboat approaching. The driver scanned his property through binoculars. The other man held a rifle.

Suddenly, Tex was in emotional quicksand. He couldn't climb out. He couldn't touch bottom. This wasn't the world he had left or thought he was coming back to.

He ran back to the house and threw a few things into his pack. Then, moving faster than the wind blowing across the lake, he tossed his gear into the back of his truck. By the time the Secret Service agents were halfway up his dock, Tex was barreling down his driveway toward the road with his middle finger in the air. If the road weren't curved, both middle fingers would have been pointing toward heaven.

7

Hawaii
Oct. 14, 2016

THE OCEANOGRAPHER drove along the Ewa Beach coastal road at the end of his workday, though he was born and raised in Maryland. He slipped in his *Best of Hawaiian Music* CD. As his eyes followed a few roosters, hens, and chicks scurrying into bushes, he was lulled by the melodic chanting.

Shit! He slammed on the brakes. Too late. He had just flattened a chicken. The irony wasn't lost on him. *Why are these chickens crossing the road?* He answered his own question, when he saw a scrawny cat race up from the beach and burrow between thick tree roots. *Holy shit!*

The scientist made a U-turn and nearly caught his wheel over the side of the cliff. Then he gunned his car back up the windy Oahu road. His hands gripped the wheel. His eyes roamed the coastal water. *Please let me be wrong.* He drove past the Pacific Tsunami Warning Center sign and jumped out of his car.

"Forget your house key?" a seismologist in Bermuda shorts joked.

"The data. I need to look at it." He grabbed a chair. "Back me up, will you?" Together, they stared at four different screens. "I saw strange animal behavior, but there's no activity, right?" Then he saw his computer mouse move and water in a glass swirl. "It's a quake!" A few heartbeats later, the folding table collapsed, dropping the sixty-pound desktop computer and breaking the scientist's foot.

For the next fifty-one seconds, the chain of Hawaiian Islands shook like native hula dancers.

On Oahu, a ten-story parking garage collapsed. It crushed hundreds of cars, killing eleven people and setting off dozens of car alarms. Across the island, at Pearl Harbor, two seamen inspecting the hull of a ship cracked their heads on the dry dock below.

On Kauai, the espresso machine in a local business spit out hot milk that scalded the barista's arm. Nearby, the big sign for a convenience store crashed down and hit an empty baby stroller. Farther north, three hikers were thrown off the Napali Coast trail and onto the sea rocks.

On Maui, honeymooners had just made love. Tongue-in-cheek, the man sat up and announced, "I felt the earth move. Did you?" If she didn't then, she did a few seconds later when the building moved and the roof collapsed. The rotating fan above their head broke loose and severed the groom's carotid artery.

Within minutes of the 8.1 earthquake, scientists at the Warning Center were fielding calls with the recently elected governor.

"I'm sorry, sir," one scientist told him on the phone.

The governor was a native Hawaiian. He wore a flowered shirt to today's meeting with a professional hydrologist. They were at a resort hotel on Kauai's southern coast.

"Most quakes originate in Alaska or South America." The scientist rushed his words. "But this epicenter is only two hundred miles north of Kauai."

The governor's fingers trembled as he put the phone down.

"Wailuku?" the hydrologist asked. The governor's jaw dropped enough so that a small bird could fly into his mouth. "Destructive waters, isn't that what 'wailuku' means?"

"How do you know that word, Dr. Jansen?" Most haoles, or non-natives, only knew "aloha" and "mahalo."

Zavia Magdalena Jansen was the daughter of a Basque mother who had run off with a Dutch seaman. As a girl, she wanted to be both Princess Leia from *Star Wars* and Ripley from *Aliens*. Now, as an adult, she was medium height, snappily dressed, and uncommonly sure of herself. "I try to learn a few words . . ." She touched his arm. "Sir, sound the alarms."

Professionally, Zavia was in demand as the climate changed. A month ago, she had driven her travel agent insane, arranging her itinerary from Washington, to Tokyo, to Malé, to Lihue, to Washington, to Murmansk, to Amsterdam, and back to Washington.

Tokyo had gone beautifully. Killer typhoons pounded the country more often. The seas were eroding coastlines. Insects were dying off, affecting birds, crops, and the web of life. The Japanese government had been very generous in their contract with her.

In contrast, Malé, in the Maldives, had been awful. A tiny island country in the Indian Ocean, its average ground height was less than five feet above sea level. Seawater already contaminated their freshwater. "I'm sorry," she had told the leaders. "Barriers won't work. You'll have to evacuate everyone."

So far, Lihue had gone well. The governor had listened to her ideas for strategic barriers. At lunch, he had gotten a feel for her Hawaiian spirit, if not blood. "This is my eleventh time here," she had explained.

Now, at the resort, she squeezed the governor's arm. He seemed in shock, unable to comprehend that in less than half an hour, a tsunami would surge onto the land. "Sir, the alarms . . ."

"Maybe it'll miss us."

"It won't." Her full head of red hair swung from side to side. "It'll hit, and it'll hurt." She hesitated for a moment. "Pele. It's Pele." In Hawaiian culture, Pele was the goddess of fire who was as unmerciful in how she destroyed as she was miraculous in what she created. "Sir . . ."

The governor understood Pele. He grabbed the phone. Moments later, on Kauai and on the other islands, civil defense sirens pierced the air.

On the street, two tourists stopped. "Is that a construction whistle?" one asked the other.

Meanwhile, the locals knew what the tourists didn't: traveling as fast as a jet plane above the island, a giant wall of water was heading their way, underwater.

Around the island, surfers raced for land. People ran out of grocery stores, leaving food they had just bought. A motorcyclist was killed when a man ran a red light, heading for higher ground.

"Prepare for the worst!" The governor told each island's civil defense coordinator as he called them. He also took a quick call from someone he didn't like and was working against. "Yes, Mr. President, it may be a disaster. Thanks for your support."

Suddenly, the governor grabbed Zavia's wrist, almost breaking the shell bracelet she had bought at the airport. "Come with me!" Together, they raced out of the meeting room, heading for the helicopter in the back lot. They crossed the wide hotel lobby and saw guests running out of elevators and haranguing the valet crew to get their cars. Through the twenty-foot patio opening, they saw the ocean floor half a football field away, as the seawater was being sucked out of the small bay.

Then they saw an uninvited guest heading toward the hotel, right toward them.

The wall of water tossed small boats as far as a mile and a half up onto the shore. Then it smacked up against the beach and surged across the lawns and over the trees. It knocked over statues and turned the flowered, manicured landscape into a swamp. Moments later, it crashed up the marble stairs and into the lobby.

A television was on loud. The reporter spoke very fast. "In 2010, we dodged a bullet after the 8.8 earthquake in Chile."

Zavia and a new beau had been in Hawaii in 2010 and were evacuated to a hillside. When a teenaged girl asked how a tsunami worked, she explained that the top of the water surged forward, as the bottom hit land. Meanwhile, the beau had checked e-mails and checked out. His curiosity about her had dropped sharply. Sexy and smart? Yes, he was. But she had had her fill of self-centered idiots.

"Right now," the TV reporter's voice jarred Zavia back to this tsunami, "we're taking a bullet in the chest."

The tsunami roared across Hawaii and wrapped around the islands. On the Big Island, it flung palm trees into the air and tossed cars onto fences. Small houses were blown down or blown away. Rooftops floated in the ocean. Tsunami water cooled down the hot lava that flowed from Kilauea, arguably the world's most active volcano.

On Oahu's crowded Waikiki beach, the water drowned hundreds of snorkelers and swimmers, including three young boys who had raced to grab fish on the ocean floor when the water receded. If people didn't drown, the riptide dragged them out to deeper waters, where the sharks were waiting. In Honolulu, apartment buildings crumbled. Streets turned into canals. Bridges cracked, sending cars and their occupants plunging into the water.

On Maui, whole sections of the long, curved road to Hana were wiped away. Thirty-one passengers on a tour bus drowned. The forests were drenched. Hillsides became mudslides.

Closest to the epicenter, every Kauai beach was submerged. In Kapa'a, the waters swept away the espresso shop, the Italian restaurant across the street, and an entire shopping mall. From Hanapepe to Barking Sands, dead bodies floated everywhere, often colliding with each other.

At the resort hotel, the huge lobby chandelier crashed onto the floor. The front desk smashed up against the back wall. Zavia saw the governor being washed down the marble steps. She herself was thrown against a very heavy couch that had been carried by the water to the far end of the building.

Unable to stand in the swirling water, Zavia crawled across the slick lobby floor to a restroom around the corner. Once inside, she slammed the door shut. She leaned hard on one of the sinks. It felt sturdy. She climbed onto it and sat there with her feet in the basin, as the second tsunami wave struck the hotel and flowed under the bathroom door. Behind her, she heard the ten-foot mirror crack. She jumped to the floor and curled up under the sink, as the glass splintered around her.

Three more waves battered the hotel. Zavia barely moved a toe. Wet, cold, and hurting, she was still alive. The term "Mother Nature" always sounded so embracing. But now more than ever, Zavia understood what "Mother" could do to the human-built world.

She had no clue how all that understanding would multiply over the next few weeks.

8

Estes Park, Colorado
Oct. 14, 2016

By THE TIME he rolled into the small mountain town, Tex had stopped looking for state troopers who might be searching for him. His truck was full of fast-food wrappers and plastic bottles. But even paying $4.36 a gallon for gas didn't wipe the smile off his face. *This is God's country!* He walked out of a local health food store with a Denver Post, a razor, and two bags of organic groceries. "Thank you, ma'am," he'd told the store clerk, "and thanks for carrying healthy food."

A few miles later, Tex pulled up to a small guard station. "Welcome to Rocky Mountain National Park." The blonde, pony-tailed ranger slid open her window. "Been here before?"

"Many times." He handed her the entrance fee, brushing her hand with his. The last visit, four and a half years before, he and Katie had lain in a meadow holding hands, acting as if she weren't dying.

"Then welcome back." She scanned his features. *Caucasian, wide shoulders, early-to-mid 40s but maybe older. Brown eyes. Black cowboy hat. Two or three days' stubble. Recent facial bruises just about healed.*

He didn't look like a bank robber or a murderer wanting to hide out in the park. A glance at the "Wanted" photos next to the window confirmed her assessment.

The ranger also noted that his muscles were hard, but his eyes were sad and soft. "If you're camping, no open fires, OK? The park's drier than the Sahara." If it weren't against the rules, she would share a sleeping bag with him. Behind her, she heard a fax machine start up.

A few minutes later, Tex drove nearly four thousand feet up hairpin turns. He had every window open. The pine forest smell filled his nostrils. The wind howled against his eardrums.

Reaching the summit, he shut off the motor. He listened to the wind swirling over the short tundra grass. He watched marmots warming themselves on lichen-covered rocks. He let the peace he felt in places like this sweep through him.

Uncluttered by his usual thoughts, Tex felt in awe of the trees below. They were so different from the trees in Minnesota, Texas, or Colombia. But like all trees, they took in carbon dioxide, nutrients, and water; then they created sugars and exhaled oxygen. *How simple. What a miracle.* It reminded him of the open, concentric circles of life within the park: natural systems within natural systems within natural systems, all of that being a part of ever more-encompassing natural systems outside the park, up to and including the universe itself.

As the sun reached mid-sky, Tex saw his remote riverside campsite. Just then, the radio music gave way to "The One Minute World Round-Up."

"In India," the announcer said, "officials are bracing for the eighth anniversary of the Mumbai massacre. In Moscow, the Russians are holding yet another celebration to honor the Russian Revolution Centennial. On the home front, the Hawaii death toll is now more than 625. And President Breen is taking his reelection fight to Florida, where he will ..."

Fuck you, buddy! Tex practically punched the radio on/off switch. He gunned the engine and headed down the steep, rutted road. The half-bald tires skidded as much as they turned. The transmission bounced up and nearly whacked him in the ass. Finally, halfway through the small campsite parking area, he slammed on his brakes just three feet away from the river's edge.

Keep moving. Fast. At double-speed, Tex pitched his tent, set up camp, and put on his running clothes. For the next hour, he stretched, squatted, and sprinted. He ran up and down the hillsides like a mountain goat. He did isometrics against trees. In Colombia, he had done this regimen every day except Christmas and his birthday. Some days, like the anniversary of Katie's death, he did it twice. Over time, the regimen had rebuilt his speed, strength, and agility to a level damn close to where it had been in his twenties.

Back at camp, Tex felt calmer. But he hated himself for letting Charley get to him. Especially today.

9

Sanibel Island, Florida
Oct. 14, 2016

WEARING A THIN RED headscarf and thick dark glasses, Elena walked three feet to the side of the road. She felt like a human fish in an asphalt barrel. As best as she could, she watched the drivers' eyes and the direction of their car wheels. When a burly biker pedaled across the four-lane road toward her, she stepped onto a stranger's porch. Every thirty seconds, she peered into the thick, tropical vegetation for any sign of the hooded man who, in her boss's apartment, had jammed his hairy forearm against her windpipe until she was unconscious.

At age twenty-three, Elena already knew that monsters lived inside people.

She had first learned it in second grade. She had gone into the basement of her Miami slum and had seen her dead, shirtless father strapped up against the hot water boiler. A week earlier, he had been sick and left his bakery job early. When he found the local dealer free-basing with his wife, he threw the punk down a flight of stairs and tossed the coke out the window.

Four years later, Elena saw her mother, dead, standing at the sink. The neighbors assumed she had either overdosed or had an organ failure.

But this incident in Mickey's apartment? It had ripped out what little faith Elena still had in people. Partly, it was being choked. But really, who would want to hurt Mickey? He was the classic camera nerd: an underwater photographer and then a glacier video guy.

Furthermore, Mickey Logan rescued dogs from the pound. And although she sometimes saw a rise in his pants when he leaned over her shoulder to look at footage, he always kept his hands to himself. He had hired her three years earlier, when she had never seen snow and couldn't spell *glacier*. Now she was his assistant editor. And Mickey had trusted her enough to go into his apartment that awful night, so she could find a particular video and express-mail it to his next lecture location.

Six minutes later, Elena unlocked the studio's door. She opened it slowly and looked in. Turning the deadbolt behind her, she went about the deadliest part of her job: watching video feeds.

To prevent suicide-by-boredom, Elena turned her iPod way up and painted her nails with a maroon polish. Mostly, she stared at the rarely changing video footage. *Waiting for nail polish to dry is sexy compared to waiting for glaciers to calve.* Suddenly, she felt a hand pressing on her shoulder. She leaped out of her chair. "Jesus, Mickey, what are you doing here? You said dinnertime. Are you all right?"

He wasn't. He looked like he had just seen his mother run over by a garbage truck.

Mickey tossed a defective air valve onto the table.

Coincidence?

The night Elena was mugged, she had surprised the intruder, who was spraying black paint across Mickey's coral reef photos. Years ago, Mickey had documented reefs from Australia to Belize. Many were dead. Others were dying. Then he had linked "what" photos with "why" photos, juxtaposing images of agricultural pesticide runoff with images of half-dead reefs nearby.

Mickey sipped some water. "Sorry. I didn't mean to scare you."

A few minutes later, they distracted themselves in their work. "Where've you been today?" Mickey asked her. The question meant: "Which videos of which glaciers in which parts of the world have you looked at?"

"Alaska and the Andes. This one's Greenland."

Mickey was still lightheaded. "Any calves?"

"Lots. But no Petermanns." A year ago, Elena had visited her sister in Manhattan. The Petermann glacier in Greenland had broken off in 2010. It was four times the size of Manhattan.

First, they want to scare me. Now, they want to kill me. Not thinking, Mickey flung the valve over his shoulder. It smashed into the wall covered with citations from the Discovery Channel, National Geographic, Nature Conservancy, and Ducks Unlimited. And it cracked the framed poster for Mickey's 2013 IMAX film: *The Incredible Shrinking Glaciers.*

Mickey got up and swept up the glass with a dustpan and brush. "Any Sasquatches?"

"Sasquatch" referred to anything unusual from the low-res, direct-feed cameras that Mickey and his crews had installed in some of the most godforsaken terrains on earth. "Just this, from a few days ago."

Elena rewound some video. Together, they watched three small figures in white streaking along the edge of the coastal glacier. *People don't run on glaciers.* Seconds later, they knew why. They saw a glacier creak, crack, and calve. If it were a planet, it would be Jupiter. When it plunged into the icy waters below, it roiled those waters and set them in motion.

Suddenly, Mickey rewound the video a few frames. "What's that?" He jabbed his finger at a tiny speck falling off the calving glacier.

Elena wiped the screen with a cloth. "It's not dirt."

A moment later, Mickey almost ran to his desk. "That woman from the National Security Agency? Somebody Wolfe? We were co-panelists." He rifled through a stack of business cards. "They've got satellite images. Maybe they can zoom in."

Meanwhile, across the street, the burly biker leaned forward against the handlebars. He wiped sweat from his forehead and adjusted his earpiece.

10

Rocky Mountain National Park
Oct. 14, 2016

TEX WASHED in the river. He ate a ham sandwich. Then he opened the newspaper and confirmed the date: four years ago to the day that Katie had passed away. For the first time since then, he felt ready to wade into his emotional swamp.

As Tex put the newspaper down, a headline caught his eye. "Tsunami Rips Hawaii." He had been there twice with Katie. He liked the pace of the islands. It matched a part of him that had been undernourished most of his life. *Not now. Later.* He covered the newspaper with his pack, leaned back against a rock and waded into his memories of those last painful hours on the dock.

Katie's breathing had been scratchy. Sometimes she was in this world; other times, who knows where? He knelt by her and lay down next to her. He stroked her hair. He put washcloths on her forehead. But he couldn't keep her life from slipping away.

In a lucid moment, Katie took his hand. "Tex, it's fine with me, if someday you hold someone else's hand."

That was crazy talk. Really crazy. "It's you I love, sweetie."

Finally, as the sun sank over the lake, Katie opened her eyes: "I think it's time, honey." She passed into that place of peace beyond understanding. Tex remembered the geese flying south and how her life force seemed to go with them.

Suddenly, Tex was dragged out of the swamp. By what? *An engine? Coming this way?* The sound receded. So did his sadness, only to be replaced by the fury that still lived inside him like a parasite. Four years later, he still wanted to crack open the doctors' heads. He couldn't stop that feeling any more than the medical world could stop her organs from breaking down.

As a boy, Tex was a bonafide weirdo. In grade school, he announced during show-and-tell that he was going to count every leaf on every tree. In junior high school, he hung out at lakeshore pools rather than ballparks.

At his high school graduation, he cemented his bizarre image with a valedictory speech called "Because: The Most Destructive Word in the English Language." It was a diatribe against simplistic thinking that said "this occurred because of that."

Later, as a *Houston Chronicle* reporter, Tex linked the storm-vulnerability of Gulf Coast refineries, carbon emissions from electricity generation, the clear-cutting of forests for cattle grazing, the rise of obesity in developed countries, and the business opportunities for alternative fuel production from the capture of carbon emissions from coal-fired power plants. He had to sell the eight-part series to his editors, who thought there were too many dots for the *Chronicle*'s readers to connect. To their surprise, people were hungry for a perspective that linked economic, social, and environmental issues into a comprehensive story. And the story itself gave Tex the credibility that, in two years, earned him a nomination for the Pulitzer Prize for investigative reporting for a groundbreaking story about terrorists and assassins.

The very first day he had ever brought Katie up to the lake, he had taken her to one of the pools. As they knelt beside it, he had felt like he was showing her the world. "Look at this, Katie! It looks like just fish in water. But see those insects and those fallen leaves?" He had then moved his hand gently through the water, pointing out the complex interaction of fish, insects, birds, leaves, water temperature, bacterial action, sunlight, rainfall, and many other factors, all affecting and being affected by everything else. "It's a whole system. Everything's connected."

It was an approach that pitted him against the doctors.

"It may be a virus," they had said.

"What about the food she's eaten?"

"Could be a defective gene?"

"Have you tested her cosmetics?"

The process was grueling. Seventeen different meds. Fourteen different tests. X-rays. MRIs. Scopes down her throat and up her anus. Hope one day. Despair the next. Finally, the doctors had given up on Katie. And Tex had given up on the doctors.

A month after she died, Tex sat alone for hours by the lakeshore pool where he had first brought her. He momentarily capped the gushing well of despair inside himself by noticing all the interconnections in the pool.

Then lightning hit. It singed every cell. He saw the one interconnection he had missed.

The remodel: two years earlier.

When Tex got a pay raise at the *Chronicle*, they had put in tightly sealed windows and doors. They had bought new carpets, furniture, and paint. The off-gasses that were trapped in the house got trapped in her body. Her immune system got weaker. She was a fighter, but over time, she had no bodily defenses with which to fight.

For the next three months, Tex got only one haircut. His clothes fit looser. He unplugged the phones. He ate boxed rice and canned fruit. He drank cheaper whiskey. He put a note in his mailbox: "Return to sender. Cassidy moved away." He made thirteen marks on the wall, one for each time he called Charley, but didn't get through—or vice versa. He left messages on his own answering machine, calling himself a blind fucking asshole.

One night, Tex watched *The Deer Hunter*. Three times, he replayed the Russian roulette scene. Finally, he knew it was time to either end his life or to find a new one. Any life. A different life. A quieter life. A less painful life.

"Heads, shoot; tails, leave." It was heads. But he couldn't spray his own brains against the cabin wall. Instead, he closed the shutters, locked the house, cashed in his savings, flew to Bogotá, and hitched his way into the mountainous coffee region, where Carlos, a man he didn't know, was implementing a system of farming he had heard about.

Now, four years later, Tex's eyes were glued to the cell phone picture of Katie laughing. His experience of her was fading. His grief and guilt were not. *I'm sorry, sweetheart. I'm sorry. I'm sorry. I'm sorry. I'm sorry. I'm sorry.*

Tex put the phone down and watched a herd of elk. It helped. Then he lay on the ground. The earth under him and the wind circling around him helped, too.

Finally, Tex sat up. He grabbed his pack to put the phone away, when he saw the "Tsunami Hits Hawaii" headline again. He skimmed the story, and his heart skipped a beat when he read the fourth paragraph.

"At the time the tsunami struck, the governor was meeting with Dr. Zavia Jansen, a world-famous hydrologist. From Italy to South Korea, she has consulted with governmental leaders about protecting their coastlines."

Zavia! Decades earlier, they were a hot item at the University of Houston. Against his will, she had opened his heart and walked right in. She was Phi Beta Kappa smart. She spoke her mind. She had guts, studying for a profession in which women were nearly as rare as water on the moon. But when they weren't holding hands, they were balling their fists. She wouldn't take shit, especially from him. He wouldn't take shit, especially from her. Within a year, she broke his heart.

Spitfire! That's what I always called her! Over the years, at this conference or that symposium, they'd run into each other. They'd try to talk. But within minutes, they were running over each other and running away from each other. *Good for you, Zavia! You've really done something with your life that's meaningful.*

Tex put the newspaper down. He reached over to put his cell phone away, when he saw the icon for an unread text message. *Christ, Carlos. This better be from you.*

After Tex had arrived in Colombia, the gentle man had taught him the systems approach to farming that meshed with all Tex knew about natural systems. It had given him a slim ray of hope. People, small businesses, mega-industries: they could all make more money with less upstream devastation and downstream waste. Maybe humans wouldn't be the first case of species-suicide.

Tex opened the text message. "Charley wants to talk with u. FBI looking 4 u. Sorry. Ellie."

Tex's eyes bulged. His blood pressure soared as he reread the message twice more. He picked up a rock and heaved it into Wyoming. He stuffed food, water, and clothes into his backpack before sticking a note under a tent stake: "Gone fishing. Fuck you." He crossed the river with his hunting knife and rifle and clambered his way up the steep rock face.

A thousand feet higher, Tex looked down at his camp. *No!*

The FBI had faxed his picture to every ranger station. Eight minutes after receiving a phone call from the Rocky Mountain park ranger, FBI SWAT teams had zeroed in on his truck with satellite photos.

All Tex wanted was to be alone with the trees, the rocks, the sky, and himself. Instead, he had company. Lots of company. He watched four agents lower themselves on zip lines. He saw an armored Jeep race down the trail. He saw trained men with buzz cuts, earpieces, and firearms surround his tent, moving as quietly as lizards across a log.

"Mr. Cassidy," the team leader yelled toward the tent. "FBI. We need to talk."

Tex heard the words echo off the mountain. He slammed his fist against the rock. Charley was a pit bull. *Damn!* He ran down the mountainside. "Over here, you assholes. What do you want?"

"You, on a plane."

"Let's see your warrant."

"Sir, we're here on a presidential order. Maybe you're wanted for treason. Maybe you're wanted for dinner. Either way, we're taking you to the air force base in handcuffs or without them." Tex paced around. He calculated the greatest distance between any two agents and his likelihood of slipping by them. "Ten seconds, Mr. Cassidy. What's your pleasure?"

Tex stopped. He looked at the team leader. Then he got nose-to-nose with him. "My pleasure is that you tell the president to go fuck himself."

The other agents drew their weapons and closed in on him. One grabbed Tex's wrist. But Tex slipped his grip and cracked him behind the knees. The agent hit the gravel, face-first, with cuts on his cheeks and nose.

Two agents fingered their triggers. "Stop! Don't shoot!" The team leader drew his stun gun. He ran up to Tex. Any closer, and he could have cut Tex's cheeks and nose with his teeth. "Tell him yourself, or I swear, I'll send a hundred thousand volts up your asshole."

Tex pushed the stun gun away and stormed off toward the helicopter. "Believe me, I will."

11

Red Square, Moscow
Oct. 14, 2016

At 9:58 a.m., Admiral Sukirov stood up in the open limo. He felt the warm Moscow sun as he looked back at all the personnel carriers, tanks, and truck-borne missiles. Behind them, he also saw some of the eight thousand soldiers, sailors, and Arctic troops who would step across the cobblestones as if they were stepping across nations. *The French know how to do food. We know how to do military parades.*

This was the latest in a series of parades that were leading up to next year's centennial anniversary of the Russian Revolution. They were carefully designed to pluck deep chords in the Russian national psyche. They were beautifully executed. And they were wildly successful: national pride was at its highest point in many decades. National fervor was at the levels needed to support the government that would run the world after Operation Noah was completed.

The admiral faced front when the Russian Corps of Drums beat their sticks onto their drums. Everything was ready. The admiral glanced down at his finger covered with the Band-Aid. He was ready.

At precisely 10 a.m., the limo moved forward. As the warm breeze caressed his face, he put on the same harsh countenance that had served him so well during his years in the submarine corps, the Soviet Navy, and Russian politics. *This is better than I'd hoped for.* He waved at the half million Russians cramming the parade route. He called out greetings to children sitting on their fathers' shoulders.

A quarter mile later, the admiral saw a grizzled man in the front row glare at him and spit at him. He didn't care. *It's like it was back then.* He treasured the young boy's memory of peeking through a crack in the basement wall and seeing every man and woman, all two-thirds starved, swarm into the streets to celebrate Hitler's suicide. Today's wave of Russian pride was wiping away the terrible taste of glasnost, perestroika, the collapse of the Soviet Union, and all the other unbearable humiliations and unfulfilled promises in Russia's twelve-hundred-year history.

A few minutes later, he saw placards that the Quartet had arranged. One said: "I have a job. Russia has a future." Another said: "The Communists are gone. The sea ice is next." He saluted the man holding the second sign. He had been paid to show up with a similar sign at every parade. So had reporters who would "write" a pre-approved story and show a photograph of the sign. It was just one of the Quartet's ways of manipulating Russian citizens to understand the cornerstone of their future prosperity.

The limo turned a corner. Sukirov heard a voice scream louder than the military music: "Sledgehammer, rot in hell!" He also heard a chorus of hisses. He just smirked and waved in the direction of the sounds. For the admiral, the survival of the state had always superseded the survival of the individual. There were probably several hundred grandfathers, fathers, brothers, uncles, and sons of people along the parade route who lay in graves because the admiral had uncovered their individualist political thoughts.

The admiral soon passed the Reviewing Stand. First, he saluted the prime minister. If he could, he would exile the man. He had been a werewolf running the Soviet intelligence network. These days, he was worse than a eunuch.

There they are. The admiral saluted his coconspirators. General Igor Valikovsky. He was seventy-seven. He still stood tall and kept himself thin. The general had lost his right arm in the Afghan war but had found his life's meaning three years ago, when the two of them had conceived the Quartet. *You'll understand, Igor.*

Then the admiral made eye contact with Ivan Fyodorokov: scientist, researcher, explorer, the seventy-four-year-old with sallow skin and a full beard. "Sir Francis Drake of the North." Ivan had spent much of the Cold War under the Arctic. No one knew the region better. And no astronaut ever risked more than Fyodorokov did when he planted a titanium Russian flag on the seabed floor, nearly fourteen thousand feet straight down from the North Pole. *You won't like this next phase. But if your cancer slows down, you'll die a happy man.*

Reluctantly, the admiral also saluted Dimitri Bakov. The seventy-year-old director of the Northern Russia Shipping Company was nearly as big as the oil tankers he managed. He was a billionaire with no taste and less style. *Just go along, Dimitri, as you usually do.*

Finally, the admiral stared at the younger businessmen. None were alive during the Great Patriotic War. Many had never worn a military uniform. These days, they wore two-thousand-dollar suits and trusted the invisible hand that guided markets. *You think you're winning. Good.* As he rode past, he saw half of them reading e-mails.

The limo moved beyond the reviewing stand. The admiral looked back. A troubled look clouded his countenance. *Where are you, Sergei?*

A few minutes later, Admiral Sukirov joined the prime minister at a microphone. "Fellow Russians," the prime minister's voice boomed off the Kremlin walls, "today, we celebrate the ninety-ninth anniversary of the Russian Revolution. It is my great honor to introduce the architect of this centennial celebration: Admiral Boris Sukirov."

This time, no one dared to hiss the man who had twice played on Stalin's knee. Seventy-six years old, he was more physically flexible than he had been in his fifties, and more ruthless than he had been since the fifties.

"Fellow Russians," he bellowed, "Russia is the largest and proudest nation in the world. Today's event celebrates our leadership in the single most important cornerstone of economic progress: energy!"

Right on cue, the military band struck up the national anthem. Five hundred thousand voices sang loudly and proudly, as if they were one voice, one nation. Meanwhile, thirty-six truck-drawn floats began to pass. They carried replicas of oil rigs, natural gas vehicles, solar panels, wind turbines, hydropower dams, and a nuclear reactor.

The prime minister shook the hand of the man he no longer trusted. The reports he had been given set off his intelligence alarms. "Well done, Admiral. You sounded like you cared."

Just overhead, the Russian Knights, a six-plane aerobatic team, flew in tight precision. The admiral had barely sat down, when, under cover of the engine roar, Dimitri Bakov leaned over so far that he nearly tongued the admiral's ear: "Found the equipment yet?"

"Shut up," the admiral spat the words at Bakov. He then looked around furtively. *Damn you, Sergei. You can't be late for your own murder.* Ten rows away, he saw his friend coming over to congratulate him. Sukirov stood up and straightened his uniform. When Sergei was six feet away, the admiral bent over and coughed four times.

"Are you alright, Boris?" Sergei slapped him several times on the back.

The admiral stood up. He opened his arms wide. "I'm fine. It's so good to see you. I haven't had anyone to checkmate in a month." He gave his dear friend a Russian bear hug and a pat on the neck.

Sergei felt something. It didn't hurt. It didn't sting. "Can you play tonight, after the meeting?"

12

Glacier National Park
Oct. 14, 2016

THE FIRST LADY, Ellie Breen, kept sneaking glances over her shoulder. She knew they were sitting ducks out here on the open trail. She just wanted one lousy hour with her daughter in total privacy. In this moment, as they walked along in blue jeans, hiking boots, and half-zippered parkas, she didn't care that a small plane could swoop down and pepper them with bullets.

At twenty-six, Mariah was thin, trim, and average looking. She wore little jewelry and less makeup. But her eyes shone as bright as Venus in the early night sky. Ever since her first breath, she had loved life and lived it like it mattered.

"Mariah, I'm your mother. Just tell me what happened." The First Lady wanted to kick herself. *She's not fifteen.*

Mariah stopped and pivoted. Her hands landed on her hips. Strapped to her wrist, the video camera banged against her thigh. "Mom, I told you: he was too much like a brother. But don't worry. You and Dad will have grandbabies."

Ellie felt like she was looking in a mirror. "I'm sorry. You're right. I'll keep my mouth shut." She went over and put her arm around her daughter as they continued walking back. "Tell me about this place, sweetheart." Ellie gestured toward the jagged mountains lightly covered with snow. In doing so, she noticed the Secret Service agents standing on top of their limos, scanning the valley with binoculars.

Mariah pointed toward the tallest glaciers off to the left. She loved them as she loved all glaciers. Plus, it was a lot easier to understand their melting away than her last boyfriend's melting away. "Well, as I told you last Christmas, glaciers are rivers, but rivers of ice. They expand. They contract. They cut through land just like rivers of water. And these days, they're the most obvious sign that the climate's warming."

Ellie was the proud mama bear. Mariah had been fascinated with photography since she was five. She deeply wanted to help the world. Now, she had found a way to combine both passions. "How many glaciers are there, honey?"

"Millions." Mariah sipped from her water bottle. "Maybe a hundred thousand major ones." Mariah had videoed many of them in Alaska, Washington State, and now here in Montana. Ellie knew she would soon leave the national nest and head for glaciers in more distant and dangerous areas. Worried sick, she had even ordered a pair of amulet earrings to protect Mariah, but they hadn't arrived in time.

"Mom, remember that job I applied for? Well, they offered it to me."

Oh, no. Just what I was afraid of. Indeed, Ellie remembered the six-week video shoot to document the disappearing glaciers in Chile, Peru, and other South American countries. "Wow! Congratulations! Have you accepted?"

"Just got the call." Then she turned to look at her mother. Her hands were back on her hips. "You know Dad will go crazy. He'll win the election in a few weeks, and he'll want me to be a two-term Rapunzel. I can't do that, Mom. I've got my own life to live. And, I swear: the day after the election, I'm telling him."

Ellie saw the Secret Service cars in the parking lot. "Can I tell you two things? You'll like both of them."

Mariah was skeptical. "First?"

"There's nothing to tell Dad. After November 1st, it's over."

"No way!" Mariah stopped in her tracks. "Are you serious?"

Ellie held up her "honest-to-God" hand. "And by the way, it's his idea. I'm just the official messenger, relaying the deal." Over the years, father and daughter had negotiated many deals. "Are you ready for the terms and conditions?"

In typical "Dad" fashion, Charley had couched the deal in a humor that conveyed a deeper wish or fear. Ellie counted off each term and condition on her fingers. "One: while he's in office, you can't get kidnapped. Two: you can't fall in love with a Head of State. And three: you can't do a nudie layout for a men's magazine. Other than those things . . . and keeping the same level of Secret Service protection . . . you're a free woman. Agreed?"

Ellie loved the joy in her daughter's face. It was more than the deal. It was a father who saw his daughter, and a daughter who felt seen. In Ellie's life, there hadn't been many moments like that with her own father, an emotionally conservative man who had held together his small farm long enough to pay for Ellie's college.

Tears filled Mariah's eyes. "You're serious, right?" She knew her mother was. Neither parent toyed with their daughter's feelings. When her mother nodded, Mariah noticed the agents opening the limo doors. "What's the second thing?"

"Uncle Tex. He's back. In fact, he's probably with Dad now. And I'm sure he's jumping out of his skin to see you." Tex had been at Mariah's first twelve birthday parties. In high school, when Mariah got dumped by her boyfriend, she went to her godfather for "guy" advice. For one of Tex's birthdays, Mariah had had a T-shirt made. On it was a likeness of the cover of the book *The Godfather*. The words stenciled above were: "My Godfather is better than your Godfather."

"Wow!" A smile spread across her face. "I'll come see him."

"Don't book your ticket yet. If they can stop acting like Hatfield and McCoy, Hatfield's sending McCoy to the Arctic."

"The Arctic? I'm going!" Then she got very quiet. "But if he's going before the election, Dad won't let me."

In another minute, they would be with their respective protection units. "Uh-uh. He wants you to go, sweetie. Just depends on whether Uncle Tex agrees to go." Mariah's smile turned into a grin, and she bounced along the trail on the balls of her feet.

"But can I be Mom for another minute?" Ellie's face became taut. "Call Dad more often. He needs to hear your voice. It's been a really tough campaign."

13

White House Situation Room
Oct. 14, 2016

"TEN MINUTES, General. Maybe less." The president's dapper chief of staff, Alex Sullivan, was escorted into the White House Situation Room in the basement of the West Wing. He was impatient and irritable. "Why are we meeting here?" With the election less than three weeks away, he was barely sleeping three hours a night.

"You know Emma Wolfe and Dave Dunn—our senior analysts." General Leonard Mason, USMC (Ret.) was the president's national security adviser. He wasn't in a picnic mood either. A White House reporter once described him as "the reincarnation of General George S. Patton." And that was at a time when he hadn't been woken up at 4:16 a.m. to review glacier videos.

The five-thousand-square-foot conference room contained secure communications equipment, including the large-screen monitor they were watching. It was replaying a satellite video of the Moscow parade earlier that day. The general turned to Emma. "What do you have, Emma?"

The prim woman had fled Russia with her mother forty-one years ago. "As you know, Mr. Sullivan, the Russians are rolling out this '100th anniversary' celebration."

"Leave it to them to celebrate a failure." Alex removed his suit coat.

"They don't see it that way, sir," Dave Dunn chimed in. Over his career, he had been a nuclear weapons specialist. "To them, it's a success-in-progress."

"Who's in the reviewing stand?" Alex pointed to the video, where the Russian leadership looked painfully bored.

"Mostly Centennial Committee members," Emma responded, "which is a front-group for something, but we still don't know what."

"And the navy guy next to the prime minister?"

"Admiral Boris Sukirov," she answered, more sharply than she would have liked. "Aka 'the sledgehammer'—his favorite interrogation tool." Emma looked away and squeezed her hands. Then she continued. "He's a second-generation *zampolit*. Political officer," she explained, "assigned to a military unit responsible for rooting out bad thoughts. Stalin, Brezhnev, and Khrushchev: they all cut their teeth the same way."

General Mason looked over at Emma. His serious voice got more so. "Years ago, Emma's father was on B-59 with him."

"Do you know B-59, sir?" Dave Dunn knew they only had a few minutes with the chief of staff.

"I assume it's not a multivitamin."

"Russian sub," Dave explained. "During the Cuban Missile Crisis, they lost touch with Moscow. Sukirov and the two top officers were authorized to launch a nuclear weapon if all three thumbs pointed up. His did. One of the others didn't."

"A gripping story. But Russia's not a swing state. What's it got to do with today?"

General Mason signaled a technician, who turned on a separate monitor. "We've got satellite photos and a video from a guy on Sanibel Island who knows Emma. Looks like a couple of men in camouflage dropped some equipment off the Greenland Ice Sheet. Could be Russians."

Alex took off his glasses and rubbed his eyes. "Are we talking toaster or something that wipes out civilization?"

"We're not sure."

"Well, General, I'm glad you told me. That's a lot worse than Governor Wilton surging in Virginia." He got up and bolted for the door.

"It will be," the general added, "if it's connected to all that Russian activity in the Arctic. You better tell the president."

"Call me when you know something." Alex strode out of the room. *Pray to God it's a toaster. As it is, there's way too much the president has to deal with.*

14

Miami, Florida
Oct. 14, 2016

PRESIDENT BREEN Breen walked through Air Force One, chatting up to the press. He had rolled up his sleeves and rolled out the charm. "That's right. Creating jobs is still Priority Number 1." "Why climate change today? Talk to my speechwriter. She said I had to." "I want good stories about this rally, or you're taking the bus home."

Somewhere over Georgia, he sent a text question to his chief of staff. He spent ninety seconds eating a salad and reading through his speech. Then, while brushing his teeth, he decided the FBI report was wrong. Dead wrong. Three rallies. Three brawls. That was no coincidence.

When the plane rolled to a stop, the president quickly descended the staircase. He entered the presidential limo, and the twenty-five-car motorcade sped away.

Down on the street and up on rooftops, Secret Service agents double-checked both their earpieces and their weapons.

Inside the vehicle, President Breen smiled at Lynn, his young aide. She was a distant relative of Marian Anderson, who broke a color barrier in 1939 when she sang at the Lincoln Memorial. "First time in the limo, isn't it?"

"Yes, sir." She reminded him so much of Mariah.

The president looked out at the crowds. The September 11 attack was fifteen years ago. The financial collapse was eight years ago. Still, so many millions were out of work and out of hope.

Suddenly, the president's private phone rang. "Hey, Alex. What's up?"

"Those ice-breaker numbers you just asked for? The Russians have at least a dozen and a half. We've got two."

"Two? Well, let's hope they're good ones." The Arctic Report had chilled his blood. This took it down a few more degrees. The motorcade slowed a mile from the stadium. "What about Tex? Any luck in finding him?"

"He's in the Rockies. We've . . ."

Suddenly, less than a block away, the president heard a volley of sharp sounds. Simultaneously, a barrage of objects slammed against the limo, streaking the window red and yellow next to his head. He recoiled. Lynn screamed. The agents shoved them onto the floor. The driver accelerated onto a side road.

15

Moscow
Oct. 14, 2016

ELECTRONICS SPECIALISTS swept the ornate Kremlin conference room. They knelt and looked under chairs. They stood on ladders and checked above ceiling tiles. Before exiting, the man in charge told the prime minister, "No explosives, cameras, or listening devices, sir."

A moment later, the prime minister watched the sixteen Centennial Committee members enter. He saw the younger ones scuff their wingtip shoes on the floor, entering together, enthralling each other with 'market' facts and stats. And he noticed that the older cadre walked in silence, nursing something he still couldn't put his finger on.

"Gentlemen," he looked out at both factions, "enjoy your meal. Our meeting will follow." He needed to hold them in check until the power plant was finished and the climate was warmer. But over the years, he had become a political Buddhist who knew that everything changes, including people and their loyalties.

As usual, the prime minister picked at his food, while eavesdropping on conversations. Nothing he ate or heard upset his stomach.

"That new underwater drilling rig?" An entrepreneur from Vladivostok made two fists and moved them up and down like pistons. "Fast. Very fast. We've never filled a tanker that quickly."

"You love the technology," the former financial officer of a natural gas corporation joked. "I love the year-over-year revenue growth."

"The Americans think they have God on their side," Ivan Fyodorokov bantered with the younger businessman next to him. "But we've got nature on ours. She's doing all the hard work!"

"If there are natural cycles that operate over many thousands, if not millions of years, why isn't the warming due to those cycles?" Sergei Galin asked Dr. Melnikov, the former Soviet chief scientist. He sponged his forehead with his linen napkin.

"Some of it may be." Dr. Melnikov dipped his meat in a mustard sauce. "But who cares if it comes from those cycles or from cars, factories, dead forests, live cows, full landfills, or thawing tundra? What counts is the total accumulation."

When the prime minister turned to Admiral Sukirov, his stomach lining felt irritated. *Why does he keep brushing his hand against his pants pocket?*

The prime minister thought back to 2011. His ratings had dipped even more than Russia's GDP. "You have balls," the admiral had said, "but no vision." He laid out a map that showed how much of the Arctic landmass was Russian, running his finger from just north of Russia, across the North Pole, and down toward Greenland. "Here is the Lomonosov Ridge, underwater. There's a century of oil and gas around it. Fyodorokov's already claimed it for us. Think ahead a decade, at most." If geopolitics were a roulette wheel, the prime minister had placed his bet on the admiral's number. *What is that clouded look on his face this morning?*

The prime minister stood up. "Let's begin, gentlemen. First, our Resources Review." He nodded to the chair of Russia's Natural Resources Division, whose report wouldn't stir controversy. As he did so, he noticed Admiral Sukirov pull out his cell phone and listen to a message that was less than five seconds long.

"Offshore, onshore, altogether," the chair exuded optimism, "we still produce more energy than anyone. And the more the climate warms, the stronger our position becomes."

"What about the Middle East?" Sergei Galin asked, loosening his tie.

"Even the super fields are running out."

"And the Americans?"

"More dependent than ever. Their Alaskan pipeline produces half of what it used to. And they're scared to drill in the Gulf of Mexico."

The prime minister thanked the chair. He wanted more things the committee could agree upon. "Dr. Melnikov . . ."

The former chief scientist pointed his laser pen at a screen. "See this figure?" The red light settled on "350 parts per million of CO_2 in the atmosphere." "That's what scientists say we should be under." Then he moved the red light up to "410." "Give or take, here's where we are."

One of the younger businessmen laughed. "Isn't it ironic? What we couldn't do with ICBMs, we're doing with greenhouse gasses."

The prime minister didn't laugh. He saw Dimitri Bakov lean all 295 pounds onto the oak table. "Let me say it again. It's dangerous to wait. Other countries could get serious about switching to . . ."

The prime minister was torn. If he cut off this crap, he risked bruising their egos and losing their support. If he let it go on, he risked the committee fracturing even further.

"Oh, come on, Dimitri," a different businessman interrupted. "The sun could also rise in the west." He fingered his thick binder with color-coded tabs. "Relax, we track the production numbers for alternative energies."

General Valikovsky was irate. "You're naive, Comrade. The Americans are developing thin-film solar. The British are harnessing the tides. China's turning out more wind turbines than the Danes and more solar panels than the rest of the world."

"Drops in the energy bucket," the younger man retorted.

"Gentlemen!" The prime minister stood again and quickly looked around the conference table. "Enough." He needed to short-circuit the "gradual versus accelerated" argument that underlay this sniping. "The timetable remains as it is. General Valikovsky?"

"Mr. Prime Minister . . ." The general squeezed the mouse in his left hand. ". . . we have to confront the differences . . ."

"No, we don't. Not now." The prime minister's taut face grew tauter. He wished he had a gavel. Or a gun. "We are closing in on what we want. I won't allow any of you to threaten that." Then he turned to the general. "Now if you don't give your report, I will."

The general shook his head, but he displayed a map of Kazakhstan, a country larger than western Europe. He announced to the group that Russia had just signed a contract with Kazakhstan to codevelop its oil reserves. The prime minister nodded. He knew the agreement better than he knew the general, who seemed like a man with a very deep secret.

"Thank you, General. Ivan . . ."

Since he had mapped much of the Lomonosov Ridge, Fyodorokov's stature in the committee had risen. He used that stature to defuse the situation. "I'm pleased to tell you that the submersible rigs are now drilling, and we're starting to extract the gas and oil from below the seabed."

The whole committee applauded. The prime minister relaxed slightly. This was a milestone they had all agreed upon and celebrated. Indeed, the younger businessman with the binder had attended the underwater ribbon cutting on a submersible, along with his top analysts, who verified the energy projections. And Admiral Sukirov had brought along two staff engineers, who had inspected the geological placement of the pipes down in the seabed floor.

Finally, the prime minister stood. "Gentlemen, the last update is mine. The '2020—2025 Climate Change Impact' reports you asked for? We'll have them next meeting."

"In what areas, sir?" the younger businessman asked.

"The amount of climate-related destruction the European countries, the United States, and other major countries will suffer. Also, the energy volumes they'll need to buy to rebuild their economies. The percentage of energy revenues Russia should realize from Climate Energy

Sales. And the 'high/medium/low' dependence each major country will have on Russia."

The younger businessman stood and raised his glass. "To your leadership, sir." The others stood as well, clinking glasses and repeating the toast.

"Meeting adjourned." The prime minister dismissed the committee. He allowed himself a thin smile. He had been able to hold the committee together. And it would be several months until they reconvened.

A moment later, the members headed for the door, all except Sergei Galin, who grabbed his chest, vomited on the table, stumbled forward and, pulseless, smashed his face into the carpet.

16

Miami, Florida
Oct. 14, 2016

WHILE THE PRESIDENT'S limo sped to safety, the major TV network used blimp-based cameras to reveal the long Miami coastline. Viewers saw skyscrapers, homes, and boat-filled marinas butting up against the Atlantic.

Anchorman Phil was vamping. "The president needs a home run today. I'm not sure he's going to get it. This climate change talk is a real gamble. Cindy, what do you think?"

The senior reporter spoke into the camera. "You're absolutely, right. This city . . . this whole state . . . could be devastated by hurricanes. As the climate warms and sea temperatures rise, hurricanes get more force. But still, it seems that—"

"Cindy, I'm sorry to interrupt." Phil's voice quaked. "The president's motorcade has been attacked. Do you have any information about that?"

"Oh, my God! Could be St. Paul, St. Louis, and Phoenix all over again."

Behind her, people wildly waved signs with the president's campaign theme: "Let's Finish the Job." Others waved signs saying: "Let's *Start* the Job" or "Cut Taxes—Not Emissions." Police with batons struggled to keep the protesters apart.

The anchor paused as someone whispered into his earpiece. "Listen, we just learned the president is safe. Someone set off firecrackers in the crowd and threw food at his limo. Weird. What do you make of that?"

"They're trying to humiliate him, not hurt him."

Just then, in the background, a guttural chant rose steadily. "Four more years . . . four more years!" A young girl on her father's shoulders covered her ears.

A counter-chant spread through a different part of the crowd. "No more years! No more years!" The little girl squeezed her ears tighter.

The anchor quickly cut in. "Thanks, Cindy. I think you're right. The president just got to the podium. Let's listen." Behind her, the cameras zoomed in.

"Ladies and gentlemen," the president looked out at the huge crowd, "it's a great honor to be here in Miami. Let's get right to what matters. Do you want national security?" he asked rhetorically, launching a "yes" the size of Florida from his supporters. "How about economic opportunity?" The response was even louder. "Well, that's why I'm here!"

The president pasted on his campaign smile. First, he made a statement that would have made George Washington look like Pinocchio. He praised "the progress in fighting the world's number 1 common problem—the shifting climate that threatens everything from the quality of Miami's water to its property values," when, in fact, there was precious little progress.

Next, he came out swinging. "And let me add that Governor Wilton is no friend of Miami, no friend of Florida, and no friend of the nearly seven hundred coastal counties across the nation."

He aimed for the chin. "Do you know that those seven hundred coastal counties include nineteen of America's twenty densest population areas? One hundred and sixty million Americans, more than half of us. And do you know that a warmer climate means stronger storms, which means greater devastation to those of you who live on America's coasts?"

He went for the knockout. "Can you believe it? Governor Wilton doesn't think the changing climate is a threat to Florida's citrus and tourist industries. Either he doesn't get it, or he doesn't care."

Then, sensing the tension in the crowd, he looked toward the Wilton supporters. "Personally, I think the governor's a good man. I like him. But, folks, he wouldn't recognize a twenty-first-century reality if it kissed him on the cheek: namely, from Afghanistan to Zimbabwe, we're all in the very same climate change boat."

Finally, the president waved and smiled. "God bless you. God bless America. Get out and vote." Before he put his hands down, he saw a dozen protesters crashing into his supporters. That was all he saw as four Secret Service agents immediately hurried him down the platform stairs and back into the limo.

Meanwhile, the TV camera caught two men in steel-toed boots kicking a college student in the chest. Behind them, a young, dark-skinned woman with saucer eyes covered her face. Next to her, a burly man wearing bike shorts swung his metal pole against a senior citizen's shoulder. Inside the departing limo, President Breen stared into space. *What the hell*

is going on? Who's behind this?
 Then he turned to his young aide, Lynn. She gingerly told him, "Sir, they've got Mr. Cassidy. Where should they bring him?"

17

Summer White House
Oct. 15, 2016

BACK AT THE LAKE, Tex was escorted to his home by a Secret Service agent with a thick New England accent. "I know you're the president's friend." The agent worked hard to keep up with Tex's pace. "How long you lived up here?"

In the best of situations, Tex liked chitchat about as much as menopausal women liked heat. He didn't answer. He sped up. Finally, he made it home and slammed the door. He sat in an old armchair with the lights out, nursing a beer and cursing the world. Two hours later, he heard an owl hooting and fell asleep, sitting up.

Rising with the sun, Tex walked the quarter-mile path to Charley's property. This time, the New Englander kept his mouth shut. Along the way, Tex saw two deer and five Secret Service agents. *You guys have been here four years. I've been here nearly fifty.*

The president had flown directly from the Miami rally. Tex sat in a deck chair, waiting. A minute later, he stood up, paced around, sat down, stood up, paced some more, and kicked one of the four-by-fours holding up a staircase. He was hot enough under the collar to raise the global temperature another degree. And then he got hotter.

Glancing out at the lake, he spotted a lookout platform in a grove of trees where he had once helped Charley bury his dog. He saw honking geese disturbed by belching boats. His fists tightened when, looking over at the ridges surrounding both their properties, he spotted ugly steel communication towers.

A moment later, Tex heard hiking boots clomping toward him. Charley's mother used to say that Charley had learned to march before he learned to walk. Now his stride seemed even more purposeful. "Don't worry," he heard the president say to the agent standing guard, "I've known Tex longer than I've known my wife."

"Hello, Tex." The president extended his hand. The other hand clasped a white three-inch binder.

"Go fuck yourself, Charley." Tex ignored the hand and sat down.

"You've said that a million times. This time I had it coming." The president brushed his sandy brown hair aside. He leaned forward, lowered his voice, and morphed into the guy who had hunted rabbits and insulated water pipes with Tex. "I need your help. But first, I need to tell you something, whether you help me or not: I'm ashamed, and I'm sorry. It was election week. There was a rally the day of Katie's memorial. I did what I had to. But not calling until I reached you . . . ?"

The knot in Tex's gut loosened, but only slightly. Many times, the two friends had locked horns and torn flesh. But Charley's callousness had cut to the bone. "Why didn't you?"

"I don't know, Tex."

"You don't know?" Tex grabbed Charley's shoulders.

Instantly, the agents drew their weapons. One ran toward them. One aimed at Tex's head. Charley pulled away. "It's fine, I'm fine." They backed away slowly, without turning around.

Charley then whispered to his friend, as if he were giving away a state secret. "If they handed out medals for being a dumb jackass, I'd have won it." He stopped and looked at Tex, who was looking at a knot in the weathered deck floor. "Can we get back to Jesse and Frank?"

One summer, Charley's parents took the boys to Northfield, Minnesota, for the annual "Defeat of Jesse James" festivities. It celebrated the time when, in 1876, townspeople stymied the James-Younger gang's attempt to rob the First National Bank of Northfield. Jesse and Frank James were brothers. For years afterward, the two friends called each other Jesse and Frank when they set out to hunt for treasure, deer, or girls.

Tex looked up. "Not now, Charley. Maybe never."

"That's fair. We'll see. But right now, I want your help, not your friendship." The president raised the binder so Tex could see the title: " Arctic Meltdown."

At that moment, an aide interrupted. "Sorry, sir, we need your signature." Tex stared out at the lake while the president scribbled his name and the aide left. He remembered Charley, Ellie, and Mariah helping him winterize the lakefront house after he and Katie had moved up here. He knew that Ellie wouldn't have minced a single syllable with her husband.

"Old news," Tex noted, returning to Charley's face. "Any kid in junior high knows about it."

"Trust me: they don't. Two weeks ago, I didn't." Just then, another aide walked onto the deck and waved a cell phone. He looked like he was hailing a cab on his way to a Yankees game. The president shook his head. The aide stuck a finger in the air indicating the priority level. "Sorry, Tex. I need ten minutes."

As the president stood up, Tex asked him, "Is Ellie here?"

"On her way, just to see you." In the distance, they heard a helicopter. "That's probably her."

"Mariah?"

"In Montana, filming. She hates missing you."

Tex watched Charley step away. *He walks like a president.* For the very first time, Tex saw "President Breen." This man wasn't just his lifelong friend. He was also his commander-in-chief.

Just then, Charley pivoted. "Why don't you take one of the kayaks. I'll come find you."

18

Summer White House
Oct. 15, 2016

TEN MINUTES after he left the president, Tex lifted his paddle. *The water's at least a foot lower than four years ago.* In the distance, Charley's kayak splashed into the water—a sound that carried Tex back to all their childhood summers.

Again and again, Charley's father had harangued them about water safety and water realities. "Nylon rope stretches when it's wet." "If you drop your cell phone in the water, it'll corrode the circuits." "Water is life, but water can take your life."

Two years before they enlisted in the army, Tex and Charley forgot those warnings when they mixed whiskey and testosterone.

"Let's race! Last one to Mackenzie's Point cleans camp." Moving fast in the starry night, Tex smashed against a very large submerged rock. The front of the kayak splintered. The rest turned over. Tex was upside down and drunk. His legs were trapped under the seat.

Without thinking, Charley jumped out, dove down, found a wrist, grabbed an arm, and saved a life. Back on land, shaking with fear, two summer friends became lifelong brothers. In each, a psychological cornerstone had been laid. For Charley: a confidence to act decisively. For Tex: a terrible fear of drowning.

Now, back on the lake, a thin fog closed in as Charley glided next to his friend. "Tex, the Arctic: the climate's the easy part to see. But trust me: there's a lot more. Go and be my eyes."

Tex shook his head. "You signed on to solve the world's problems, Charley. But I signed off." Indeed, Charley knew how hard Tex had worked. He also knew how crushed Tex had felt when the world got worse.

"Well, sign on again." Charley leaned forward. "Ten-day contract. That's all I'm asking."

Tex slapped the water with his paddle. "Why me?"

"Because you see things others don't."

Tex looked down and shook his head from side to side. Across the lake, they heard the speedboats heading toward them. "Charley, I'm way out of touch."

"Fewer preconceptions."

"But it's one big screwed-up circus."

"Help me unscrew it."

Tex just sat there as the speedboats got closer. He thought of Carlos's farm. *That's the unscrewing model. The only one I know.*

"Tex, you don't see parts; you see wholes. You make connections. You think upstream. You think down—"

"Charley," he looked harshly at his friend, "stow it."

"Tex, look," Charley framed his words carefully, "you don't take a damn shower without thinking about where the water comes from, where it goes, how much energy it takes to heat the water, whether the pipes are lead or plastic, how the towels are made, how far they've been shipped, and a dozen other things that nobody else on the planet would think of."

Indeed, during his investigative reporting days, Tex's nickname had been "Doctor Dots." When he had been nominated for the Pulitzer, the announcement letter had referred to him as "a man who makes connections as well as Mozart made music."

"I just got back, Charley. I need time."

The president moved his kayak closer and lowered his voice. "That call I just took: the Russians want to float a nuclear power plant in the Arctic to power their drilling."

Tex turned his head away and cursed under his breath before paddling back to shore. Minutes later, they knelt on the dock, tying up their kayaks. "Ok, I'll go, but here's the exchange." Tex stared into Charley's eyes. "First, my friend Carlos, in Colombia: find out if he's all right."

"Give the details to Alex, my chief of staff. What else?"

"Two things." Tex's whole demeanor softened, as he looked up at a flock of honking geese. "The day Katie died, I made a promise to her. If I do this for you, I can do that for her."

"Of course." Charley felt both their knots coming untied. *My God, I've missed you!*

"Last thing: when I get back, you get off my back." The president put his hand out. This time, Tex shook it. "Give me a day to prepare."

"How about four hours, buddy?"

PART TWO: BLUE

19

Summer White House
Oct. 15, 2016

ELLIE BREEN RAN up the stairs to Tex's house. On the deck, she nearly tripped over his pack. *Thank God, he hasn't left.* She tossed her hair back, walked inside, and heard him on the phone with Alex. Seeing him, her heart opened like French doors on a Mediterranean villa.

In college, Ellie had been a psychology major and Katie's sorority sister. Tex fixed her up with Charley when Charley was home on leave from the Gulf War. A year later, Tex was best man at their wedding.

Now, waiting for Tex, Ellie looked inside the empty fridge. She plugged in a few lamps. She blew dust off photos, mostly of Katie. There was one photo of the two couples at Mariah's high school graduation. A fading photograph of Tex in military uniform caught her eye.

"An officer and a gentleman, wouldn't you say? Just shows you how life takes its toll!" Tex put his phone away and gave her a full-bodied hug. Then they sat together on the sheet-covered couch. By mutual, unspoken consent, whatever sexual feelings they had had for each other had long ago been put into deep freeze.

"All right," she teased him, playing with his hair, "you didn't come back to the States just to vote for Charley. So why did you?"

"Pepperoni pizza." He smacked his lips. "You just can't find it in the Colombian mountains."

"Smartass. Well, what did you find there that you couldn't find here?"

"Not much. Peace of mind. A saner way to live. A whole different way to farm food, make products, and build a world."

Ellie had talked with him every few months. At first, he was an emotional quadriplegic. Gradually, feeling came back into his voice. Six months ago, he had sounded like Tex again, pontificating about how the last hundred years had been "one goddamn chemistry experiment, and we were the mice."

Ellie walked over to the sink. She poured herself a glass of water. "Then why give that up?"

"I missed that marvelous daughter of yours. How's she doing?"

Ellie flicked water onto his face. "You're lying. But I'll let it pass, for now." There was too much emotional distance to cover and too little time. She saw Tex glance at the clock. "She's a woman, Tex. Her own woman. And she's really, really excited to see you."

"Ten days, as soon as I'm back."

"I can speed it up. In fact, I'd really like to." Ellie's tone dropped an octave as she filled him in on the deal between Mariah and her dad. "Greenland's a lot farther than Georgetown. I'd feel better if you were keeping an eye on her."

"Are you kidding? I'd love to." Tex got up, closed a few curtains, and locked up the house. "It gives me another reason for making this damn trip."

Then he grabbed his pack, and they walked slowly along the dirt path that connected the two properties. "Tell me the truth, Tex. Will Mariah be in danger?"

"She'll be fine. We'll be on some tour boat with flush toilets and guardrails." His step was lighter as they approached the summer White House. "By the way, thanks for your text message about Charley sending the FBI."

Ellie stopped. She took a deep breath. "There's something you should know." She took him by the arm and walked him to a large cabinet in Charley's study. She opened the cabinet doors. And she watched Tex's eyes widen, as they wandered across every newspaper story and journal article that he had ever written. "He had them gathered a year ago."

"Why?" He had never seen all his writings in one place.

"Because nothing else makes sense."

"And that's why he hauled my ass here?" Tex rolled his fingers into a fist.

"Uh-uh." She pointed a finger toward herself. "I'm really scared."

Tex took her arm. He walked her over to Charley's standing globe and pointed to the Arctic. "Because of what's happening here?"

With her finger, she traced a large circle around the whole globe. "Because of what's happening everywhere."

20

Murmansk, Russia
Oct. 15, 2016

A DMIRAL SUKIROV got out of the cab at the Northern Russia Shipping Company offices. He entered the gray-on-gray conference room and checked the clock on the wall: 6:40 a.m. *Twenty minutes. Enough time.*

Scanning the room, he still felt relieved that Russian intelligence officers hadn't hauled him off the day before in Moscow. Evidently, the prime minister hadn't made the connection between the admiral's love tap on Sergei's neck and Sergei's face on the carpeted floor. Or he didn't care.

Deliberately, Sukirov placed his coat at the head of the conference table and sat down. Then he checked the small puncture- and leak-proof bag in his coat packet. Beta's vials and needles were ready to go. He was prepared to "Sergei" anyone who steered the group off-course.

He heard a car door close outside and quickly put the bag away. As the others entered, he greeted them, looking for any signs of fear, doubt, or betrayal.

"Dimitri, good morning to you."

Bakov was a man driven by three loves: Russia, power, and money. He had bankrolled Operation Noah in exchange for a ten-year exclusive contract shipping oil and gas across the Arctic.

"Ivan, welcome. I hope your cough's better."

Fyodorokov's eyes had misted over when he first heard about the operation. He knew so much about water, glaciers, tectonic plates, and underwater mountains in the Arctic. "To use it this way . . . to restore Mother Russia . . ."

"And, General Valikovsky, I look for your guidance today," he lied.

They had known each other for decades. Three years before, the admiral had risked treason. "The prime minister sold us out. He stacked the committee. Those corporate yappers will sabotage Russia unless something happens."

In response, the general confessed treason: the 1991 heist of more than one hundred tactical nuclear devices. Relative to the thirteen-kiloton Hiroshima bomb, these were small, ranging between one and five kilotons. But they could be carried by men and placed anywhere. "It was a chaotic time. A collapsing empire always is." Then he put his one good hand on the admiral's arm. "Back then, I only wanted to protect Russia. Today, they could be used to elevate Russia."

Outside the room, the sun rose. Inside, the tension rose.

Normally effusive, General Valikovsky was subdued. "I'm worried. It's Alpha and Beta . . ."

"I am, too," the square-faced admiral lied again. He knew Alpha and Beta from Russian military operations, before they had sold their services on the open market. Since then, they had crossed a dozen borders and disposed of fifty to sixty contractors, freelance soldiers of fortune whom they had personally recruited. At this stage of the operation, he trusted and needed Alpha and Beta far more than the general, Bakov, or Fyodorokov.

As the others took their seats, Sukirov launched right in. "Gentlemen, two items: first, these ridiculous events, the meeting with the American woman, the press conference, and the tour. But the prime minister insists. Anything to say about any of them?"

There wasn't.

"The second item is why we're here. Operation Noah's final stage starts today. We have to agree on the final steps."

General Valikovsky fidgeted. "Beforehand, we need to discuss the last step." His one hand was balled into a fist. Every snuke burial had gone flawlessly until the Greenland mess. "Alpha and Beta: are they distracted? Burned out?"

Instinctively, the admiral patted his coat pocket. "I don't think so. The Kangaroo team was burying the package when the glacier calved. It was a coincidence, not a screw-up."

"He's right, General," Fyodorokov coughed his way through his comment, "if there's more warming, there's more calving, and there's more chance something will go wrong. Besides, look: the other Kangaroo burials went perfectly."

"So you'd still put Russia's future in their hands?" Bakov asked. The jowly director shifted uncomfortably in his extra-wide chair.

"I would. But judge for yourself." The admiral looked at his watch. "We'll hear from Alpha very soon."

"To explain what happened?" The general sounded suspicious.

"And to get new orders if you agree to the following change." Admiral Sukirov pulled out a calendar and circled October 19, October 22, and October 25. "I want to move up the detonation dates." He then drew a black circle around November 1, 2016—US election day. "And this date for the 'Big Bang' finale."

Ivan sat on the windowsill, rubbing his forehead. "Why this change? Sergei's death? You're not afraid of dying, are you?" At this stage in his cancer, he himself was.

"At our age, it could be any one of us, any day."

"They're too soon, Admiral." General Valikovsky slapped the table hard, hurting his knuckle. "We've still got snukes to bury in the Andes and Antarctica."

The admiral imagined a slip-and-sip scenario. At dinner, he would slip a vial of something or other into the general's drink. The general would sip it and die in his sleep.

"General, let's think this through. We don't need . . ." Suddenly, the admiral jumped up from the table. "I apologize, gentlemen. One minute till Alpha reports in. Yes or no to the new schedule?"

Bakov and Fyodorokov nodded their agreement, as the admiral watched the encryption code unscramble on his computer. "Alpha, your report."

"As you instructed, sir, we hid the Greenland snuke after we got it back. And we disposed of the Kangaroos in the usual manner."

The admiral looked at General Valikovsky. Reluctantly, the old soldier nodded. "Excellent. Now, listen closely." He laid out the accelerated timetable. "With all the programming, can you meet it?"

"Yes, sir. The programmers only need three more days to input the codes. The question is the Lions team. Whether you want to accelerate the first detonation." Alpha and Admiral Sukirov had talked this through off-line. "The team is in place right now. They could do it manually."

"Give us a minute." The admiral looked at the others. "Why not? We've been planning this for three years. We're ready. Let's light the match."

The room got very still. None of the others were ready for this decision. But none opposed it. "Authorize them, Alpha."

"Right away, sir. Anything else?"

"The US operation. Are you still nervous?" For the conspirators, this was the most dangerous and dubious side of the whole operation.

"Less so. Our key operative takes orders well, and her rehearsals went well."

A minute later, Alpha was gone. The admiral smiled. "No turning back now, gentlemen."

21

Summer White House
Oct. 15, 2016

THE PRESIDENT sauntered into the room with his bowl of yogurt and berries. His step was light. The meeting with Tex had gone better than expected. Tex was heading to Alaska, his first Arctic stop. He himself was off to Albuquerque to whip Governor Wilton's ass. "Good morning, gentlemen, let's make this quick."

Tex leaned forward on the old couch. Alex Sullivan was in a stuffed chair. The president sat down and put his half-eaten breakfast on the old coffee table between them all. "Uh-oh, Alex, what's up? Your arms are crossed. That's never a good sign."

The president's chief of staff could charm senators and bludgeon White House staffers. Or vice versa. His cheery nature had carried him through two divorces and a 1987 bankruptcy, as well as the daily hennypenny crises at the White House. "I've got a bad feeling about this mission, sir."

"Is it the mission? Or me?" Tex had sensed Alex's hostility from the moment they had met.

"Mostly you."

"Ka-ching?" Tex picked up the president's breakfast and took a spoonful. He had been doing that for decades.

Alex nodded, acknowledging the five-part exposé of military cost over-runs. Tex had titled it with the sound of a cash register. "You grabbed too many lapels." A US senator had lost his seat, a general lost three stars, and four companies lost a billion dollars.

"Including your friends?"

"They were friends to a lot of people."

"For God's sake . . ." The president's temple veins enlarged. "He's not up for the Supreme Court, Alex. He's just a special assistant evaluating a special situation."

Alex pressed his arms tighter against his chest. "There's also Colombia. Right or wrong, 'Colombia' means 'drugs.' If the press or Wilton gets wind of this, they'll . . ."

Tex put the bowl back onto the table. He turned to the chief of staff. "You know I wouldn't let you pack my parachute, or my lunch for that matter. But in this case, you are absolutely right." Tex stood up. He grabbed his pack and turned to the president. "I can cost you a lot more than I'll get you."

"Tex, sit down! I brought you here. I'll tell you when to leave." The president went to the window and looked out at the lake. "There's a lot of smoke. I need someone to look for fire. So here's the deal. You go. You look around. You ask politely. You come back. Can you do that?"

"Sure." He shrugged. "But, really, why?"

"Because I want you to. And, Alex, you'll help, because I'm telling you to." Tex shook his head in disbelief. Alex nearly crushed his sternum, pulling his arms in farther. "For Christ's sake. Both of you. Stop acting so damn self-important." He looked at his watch. "I've got eighteen minutes. Alex, tell him what we know."

The chief of staff let his arms go. For the first time this morning, he looked at Tex. "It's part Tom Clancy, part Stephen King." Behind them, a Secret Service agent entered, carrying a box full of thick boots and down jackets.

For the next four minutes, Alex methodically described Russia's planting polar flags, building ice-breakers, and rolling out military parades. Tex listened, got up, sat down, then walked around, trying on the clothes. By the time he had chosen the best fit, Alex had also outlined the Russians' oil and gas deals with former Soviet countries and their long-term contracts with big European customers.

The president narrowed his eyes. "Alex, you never forget a man's favorite cigar or a woman's perfume."

"Sir . . . ?"

"The Russians' drilling? Farther north than ever before? Does that ring a bell?"

"Sorry, I'm distracted."

The president filled in Tex on the rigs and drilling equipment. Tex felt the president's eyes boring into him.

At the end, the president picked up the yogurt and berries bowl. "Tex, you don't mind if I finish my own breakfast, do you?" He went on to list the topics and geographies he wanted Tex to check out. "You may have your own. Work it out with your new best friend."

Tex turned to Alex. "I'll call you later." He picked up his pack and headed out the door. "By the way, do I get frequent flier miles on military jets?"

The president put his glasses on and gathered up a few papers. "You don't have to like him, Alex. Just work with him. Any reason you can't do that?"

22

Indus River Valley, Pakistan
Oct. 15, 2016

TWO HUNDRED FEET below the glacial moraine, Lion 1 and Lion 2 peered up at the enormous lake in this remote part of Pakistan. "It'll be our pleasure," Lion 1 had told Alpha over the secure radio about the manual detonation, "and the extra $50,000 is a nice bonus."

Each member of the burial teams, including the Lions, had endured a three-day glaciers training. "Some are as small as a football field," Alpha had told them. "The longest is more than 250 miles long. Each team is assigned a strategically important glacier for reasons that are none of your business."

For professionals who typically operate in urban, jungle, or mountainous terrain, the $200,000 paycheck was for a very different kind of assignment. "Just cut holes in the ice and bury equipment. Sounds easy, doesn't it?" He had displayed graphics of everything from glacial crevasses to rotten ice: dangerous weak spots that occured when glaciers retreat. "The cold temperatures, thin air, and glaring sunlight will be as dangerous as any surveillance camera or armed guard."

In the end, nothing prepared them for the hardships.

Lion 1 and 2 had slowly made their way up the glacier. They had labored under the weather, altitude, and their load, including ropes, shovels, ice picks, and a fifty-pound suitcase nuclear device on each of their backs. Twice, they had to use a snow ladder to cross deep crevasses.

"There he is." Lion 1 pointed his gloved-finger toward the local Pakistani making his way up the glacier. The man was carrying the added equipment. After they checked that it was all there, they each grabbed him by an arm and tossed him down a thousand-foot crevasse.

"Let's keep going," Lion 2 announced. During the last steep quarter mile into this high-altitude Hindu Kush-Himalaya area of Pakistan, they followed a three-phase routine: step-stop-breathe. During one stop phase, close to the moraine lake, Lion 2 looked through his polarized goggles at the glacier they were on. He remembered Alpha's words: "You guys are chaos junkies. That's why you'll love your assignment. The glacier irrigates tens of millions of farmland acres. It provides electricity to hundreds of millions of people. When you're done, the region's done."

An hour later, Lion 1 and 2 rested. They sat on one of the thousands of boulders that had been pushed along by the advancing glacier thousands of years ago. They looked around at the silt-like glacial flour that was especially apparent these days, when the glaciers were retreating so far and so fast. "I'd say over there." Lion 2 pointed to the weakest-looking section in the moraine wall. "Big explosion. Huge hole. The water rushing out will do the rest. What do you think?"

The hard ground made for hard digging. But finally, the nuclear devices were in place, and the Lions climbed to their detonation point. "Ten seconds. Cover your ears." They heard two deafening explosions rip apart the moraine wall.

Seconds later, they watched boulders tossed high in the air like marbles, along with a cloud of silt, ice, and snow. They saw the first sheets of water rush through the hole. Gravity did the rest, as the water headed down the valley, picking up speed, force, and debris.

Lion 1 radioed in. "Confirm detonations."

"Congratulations, gentlemen," Alpha replied. "Make your way to the rendezvous point. We'll meet you there."

The two men descended. From time to time, they slipped on the ice or scree. At one point, they got close enough to the valley to hear the screams below. Less than a half hour later, they reached a rock overhang and looked at the impact of their handiwork. "I've never seen anything like this," Lion 1 said. "Let's enjoy it for a minute."

They stared at the fast-moving river that carried houses, livestock, crops, and trees downstream. They watched hundreds of men and women screaming, crying, not knowing which way to run. Some waded through chest-high water with children on their shoulders. One woman carried a lamb on her head, when the body of a dead boy floated into her, knocked her over, and sent the bleating lamb to its watery death.

In the distance, Lion 1 saw where the river had spread out over the entire valley and submerged everything. *Looks like the edge of the ocean.*

Several hours later, they changed into the trekker clothes they had hidden in a small cave. Then they headed down the mountain and ran the last mile to catch an overcrowded bus. In Karachi, they walked separately to the rendezvous apartment.

Lion 1 arrived and was let in by Alpha and Beta. Before they could finish a light lunch, they greeted Lion 2.

For the next few minutes, the four men cheered at the fast-moving television scenes, where thousands of Pakistanis ran through the streets of Islamabad, screaming, "Death to India." They had their fists in the air, waving weapons.

Alpha got out of his chair, opened a bottle of champagne, and poured four glasses. While images of Indian troop convoys moving to the border crossed the screen, he proposed a toast. "To your skill, success, and safe travels." He drank up. The others did, too.

Finally, Alpha shut off the television. "Time to go, gentlemen. Here are passports, tickets to your destination of choice, and ten thousand dollars in local currency. Now, why not check that the final $100,000 plus your bonus was deposited into your account?"

Lion 1 stepped forward to Beta's computer. He entered a web address, user name, and passwords. "It's there," he said, not noticing that Alpha and Beta were sipping from other glasses.

Lion 2 did the same. "Let's go. I want to spend my money."

Three minutes later, the Lions stuffed a few personal belongings into their packs and felt the first wave of abdominal pains. Both men vomited up their guts. Their body temperatures increased, and their blood pH decreased. Their hearts slowed down and then sped up. Their muscles twitched, and their brains swelled. Their seizures intensified. Finally, they made sounds that weren't recognizable as human.

Alpha held up a small vial of concentrated water hemlock. "This is an easy way to end these operations," he joked, "but the antidote still tastes bitter."

Beta laughed, manipulating computer keys and watching the screen. "All the money is transferred back."

Before leaving, Alpha placed an explosive on each body. "Let's get moving." Later, they drove south out of the city. While Beta dodged delivery vans, stray dogs, and people, Alpha entered the detonation code into his cell phone. In the distance, he heard the explosions that ripped apart the Lions, the apartment, and much of the street below. Then he dialed a secure line. "Mission complete, sir."

At the other end of the line, Sukirov raised his glass. "Contact me when you're back."

23

Murmansk Harbor
Oct. 15, 2016

TO THE WORKERS in Murmansk Harbor, the presence of an armed naval patrol boat was about as novel as snow in winter. What would have raised their eyebrows were the four people on it.

The three Quartet members—Admiral Sukirov, Ivan Fyodorokov, and Dimitri Bakov—arrived twenty-one minutes late. They had said good-bye to General Valikovsky, who returned to Moscow. They had taken their sweet time because they knew it was an epic waste of time. The Centennial Committee wanted it to show the world how Russia was combatting the terrible impacts of climate change and to distract the world from Russia's energy grab. If the meeting hadn't given them a cover, the Quartet members would never have volunteered.

The fourth person, Dr. Zavia Jansen, paced anxiously, waiting for them. Aside from professional reasons, this meeting was important to her. She was a single woman. If she got this contract, she could remove "retirement" from her Worries List.

"Gentlemen," she said crisply, as the patrol boat pulled away from the dock. Her red hair blew across the harbor. "I've got a few questions."

Since getting the call from the prime minister's office two months ago, Zavia had read every Murmansk-related hydrological report she could find. She researched the Russian and Soviet histories of the harbor. She made comparisons with other harbors similarly exposed to climate shifts.

"What's the average depth of the harbor?" she asked. "Tell me about storm surges. How much do the tides swell with spring run-off? Those closed-off areas: are they where nuclear subs are decommissioned? My research turned up hundreds of nuclear accidents around this peninsula, including the intentional sinking of nuclear reactors. Is that right? Those ships, are they storing spent nuclear fuel?" She pointed toward a dozen vessels where flakes of rust fell into the water.

Each question bored like a mite under Admiral Sukirov's skin. At a different time and place, The Sledgehammer might have dumped her into the contaminated waters. Instead, mite-for-mite, he went after her. "What about Three Mile Island? Why are you Americans so phobic about nuclear energy? Why can't you develop a nuclear waste storage facility?" Zavia didn't flinch. "Admiral," she leaned toward him, "I'm truly sorry if I offended you."

When she was growing up, she often heard her father say, "You've got a mind, girl. Tell us what's in it." In the thirty years since then, she had given a piece of her mind to a lot of people, especially men who thought they were something special just because they stood up to pee.

But here was a new twist. *He's Russian. He's male. He's in his seventies. He's been in power. He's lost the Cold War. His wife probably cooked his meals and raised his kids. It would grate on him to be questioned by an American. Or by a woman. But to be questioned by an American woman?*

"But before you spend Russia's money," she continued, softening her voice but not her position, "you better know if barriers will work and what they'll cost. That's why you're paying me to do a feasibility study. If you give me answers, I can give you answers."

Zavia had gotten under Ivan's skin as well. But ever the peacemaker, he offered her a cold drink. "The prime minister will land in a few minutes, Lara. What's your preliminary evaluation?"

"It's Zavia, sir," she corrected him, as they headed back toward the harbormaster's office. She stood up, grabbed the railing tightly with one hand, and swept her hand in the direction of the coastline. "In a nutshell, Mr. Fyodorokov, I see factories but no forests. You've replaced inlets with roads. You've built an economy, but it's unprotected."

"Which means what, Zavia?" Fyodorokov took pains to get her name right. Most people had trouble with her name. She didn't care. She loved that it was part of her Basque heritage and that Zavia meant "new house." To her parents, she was a reminder of the new house in America that they had come to when their old house in the Netherlands was washed away in the massive 1953 flood.

"Mr. Fyodorokov," she leaned forward toward him, "Murmansk is 125 miles north of the Arctic Circle. This harbor is fed by the Barents Sea and links directly to the Arctic Ocean, which you know as well as anyone in the world." Some days, she felt like an oncologist, giving terrible news to communities or governments. "So if the climate continues to heat up . . . and the seawater continues to heat up and expand . . . the harbor will flood over. I'm sorry, but the three hundred thousand people who live up here? Are they at risk? I'm afraid so."

The Russians, including the admiral, put on their "concerned" faces. But Zavia's evaluation wasn't anything the Centennial Committee hadn't already discussed in agonizing detail.

"But that's decades away. We've got plenty of time to build barriers." Bakov sounded like he cared.

"You've got other problems." She pointed to thunder clouds. "Ever lived through a once-in-a-hundred-year storm like Hurricane Katrina? If it hits, Murmansk could be your New Orleans."

Fyodorokov sat with his head closer to his knees. As a young boy, he had survived the nine-hundred-day Nazi siege of Leningrad. Afterward, his mother shipped him off to Murmansk to live with her shipbuilder sister, who still had a job that paid and a stove that worked. "And what are your preliminary recommendations?"

"Do what everyone needs to do. Reduce your energy use. Cut your emissions. Switch to renewables. At the same time, build your defenses. If you do it right, you'll save the city."

"Like New Orleans?" The admiral was trying again to get under her skin.

"More like the Dutch," she parried, speaking louder because of the noise from an approaching plane. "Half the Netherlands is below sea level. So, defending against the sea is a national priority. Russia could learn a lot from the Delta Works in particular." Indeed, Zavia probably knew more about that complex of dikes and barriers than anyone outside the Netherlands.

Suddenly, Admiral Sukirov stood over her. His facial veins were engorged with blood. Zavia raised her arms, not knowing if he was going to give her a piece of his mind or the back of his hand.

"Admiral, is there . . ." Suddenly, the square-bodied man stumbled back a step, when the patrol boat banged up against the pier. Two sailors jumped off and tied it down. "That's the prime minister's jet," Bakov volunteered, thankful for a way to end this tour. "Be ready in an hour, Dr. Jansen. A car will pick you up."

24

Summer White House
Oct. 15, 2016

ELLIE AND TEX were doubled over laughing when the president strode into the room. "Ah, two of my favorite people." Tex noticed that his friend touched him on the arm, but didn't touch his wife.

At that moment, the chief of staff stuck his head out. "Sir, the press conference . . ."

"You should hear this, Tex." A moment later, they watched the Russian prime minister move to the podium. The room was packed with people, cameras, tape recorders, and plainclothed police.

"Ladies and gentleman," the former interrogator began, "I am pleased to announce Russia's latest activities in regard to the world's common danger: global warming."

"Mr. Prime Minister," a reporter interrupted, barely beating a dozen others who were wildly waving their hands, "the nuclear explosion in Pakistan, what's your comment?"

The prime minister just glared at her. "For now, let me point out that it was Russia's signing of the Kyoto Protocol in 2004 that made it international law. But, since then, not a single nation has decreased its greenhouse gasses. In that regard, I am announcing that by 2025, eight percent of Russia's energy will come from renewable sources."

"That's pathetic," the First Lady said. *Not that we're much better.*

"Sir," a BBC reporter chimed in, "was the nuclear device Russian?"

The prime minister looked up. "If I have to stop again, this press conference is over." Meanwhile, the plainclothed police moved closer to the reporters.

"Second point," the prime minister continued. "As you know, the world's weather patterns are changing. The changes first occur in the Arctic, before spreading to every other part of the globe." A third of the reporters closed their notebooks. They wanted to know whether the nuclear explosion was an attack or an accident; who did it; what the prime minister thought it meant; and would there be a second one? Instead, he babbled on about events that would wreak a lot more havoc, but not before today's deadline.

Alex looked at the president. *Do I tell him about the "equipment" in Greenland? Is it related to Pakistan? Much too speculative for now.*

"And lastly," the prime minister let himself sound worried, "every coastline is vulnerable to rising seas. Therefore, Russia will build storm barriers to protect Murmansk . . ."

"Who's paying for that?" Alex asked. *We should be doing it for Washington and New York, at the very least. But it'd cost billions.*

". . . and to that end, we've contracted with one of the world's most recognized hydrological engineers: Dr. Zavia Jansen from the United States."

The camera zoomed in on Zavia. Tex nearly levitated out of his chair. He mouthed her name and followed it up with a silent "Wow!"
As the prime minister wrapped up, the president turned to Tex. "See what I mean. This should have been a press release, not a press conference."

Ellie had had enough. She went outside to wait. A few minutes later, a car pulled up. Tex sauntered out, carrying his pack. Ellie put her arm through his and walked with him. "Your time with Charley went pretty smoothly, yes?"

"Smoother than you and Charley. What's up, Ellie?"

She looked over at Tex. He was the only person in the world she would say this to. "The presidency changes the man. It also changes his marriage."

"Are you rooting for him to lose?" In the distance, the driver had the trunk and backseat door open.

"Only on Mondays, Wednesdays, and Fridays. Now," Ellie switched the subject, "tell me about your friend on Russian TV."

Tex laughed out loud. "'Mr. Oil and Ms. Water.' We dated a little. But if I said 'apples are red,' she'd tell me that some apples are green."

"And your part?" They both knew that like everything else, relationships were a system, and all parties contributed to its successes and failures.

"The usual: I asked too many questions and answered too few. She wanted my heart and got tired of waiting."

"When did you last see her?" While Tex thought for a moment, Ellie pulled a small gift-wrapped box out of her pocket.

"Five years ago. At a conference. But we did better. It was at least ten minutes before we pissed each other off."

"You like her, don't you?" She had prayed that Tex might meet someone.

Like most men, Tex could neither ask for directions nor see the water spots on a glass. But unlike most men, he respected the hardwired, feminine approach to life that was surprisingly different from yet equal to the masculine approach. Plus, he knew how to cherish a woman. And as unpolished as he was, he didn't fear intimacy.

Tex chuckled. "She's sassy as hell, which I love, when it's not directed at me." He knew what Ellie was thinking. "Believe me, I'm not ready. But thanks for keeping hope alive." They were at the car.

Ellie gave him a big hug and the gift-wrapped box. "Earrings for Mariah, OK?"

"Of course." Tex carefully placed it in his pack.

"Safe travels." She pecked him on the cheek. "And have a great time with Mariah! Tell her to call as soon as she's back in the country."

Tex drove off. Ellie turned back and blocked her eyes from the sun. Given the angle of the sun, a bedroom window had become a mirror. In the mirror reflection, she saw Alex watching the limo driving away.

25

White House Situation Room
Oct. 15, 2016

S ITTING IN HIS OFFICE with Dave Dunn and Emma Wolfe, General Mason was more furrowed than usual. He even smelled worried. "What's the story, Captain White?" At the other end of the speakerphone was the pilot of the WC-135 Constant Phoenix, the detection plane developed under President Eisenhower for nuclear verification purposes.

"We're over the valley, sir. No doubt about it, there's radioactivity. I'd guess a couple of kilotons."

Dave whispered. "Suitcase."

"Other observations?"

Captain White spotted the lateral moraine walls. They were the side edges of the glaciers, as the ice rivers advanced and retreated over time. He also saw remnants of the terminal moraine, through which all the glacial melt in the lake had poured out. *If the Hoover Dam ever blew up, this is what would happen.* "One thing," he said, "the force of the explosion plus the intense heat, it's pretty dramatic, sir."

The general ended the call and turned to Dave. "If it was a snuke, doesn't that rule out India and Pakistan?"

"Unless they bought or stole it."

"Work your networks. Find out." When they left, a few minutes later, the general spoke to the president on Air Force One. Carefully, he separated fact from speculation. At the other end of the line, the president rubbed his eyes. "For the time being, General, let's keep this between us. When I'm back from New Mexico, I'll see what I can find out."

26

US Embassy, Bogotá, Colombia
Oct. 15, 2016

M<small>EXICAN</small> BY HERITAGE and American by birth, Lou Mendoza put on his best suit, best shirt, and best tie. He kissed his wife on the lips and headed out of their apartment. It was early, but the streets were already loud and steamy.

At seven, Lou entered the ambassador's office. "Good morning!" She shook his hand and guided him to two chairs. "As you know, I've only been here a few months. Tell me a little about your background."

Despite the air-conditioning, the foreign service specialist was sweating. "My first assignment was in Honduras, when Hurricane Mitch destroyed the country." He then gave her a thumbnail of his other postings over the last eighteen years.

"Then you know how important it is for the Foreign Service to be very visible at times, and very discrete at other times." He did. "What I'm asking you to do, informally of course, since we're just chatting, is to be as discreet as you've ever been."

"Yes, ma'am." He was sweating even more, staining his best shirt.

"Then here's what I'd like you to do." She explained that she needed information about a particular campesino, a coffee farmer. "You will visit him as part of a Market Research program we have in the embassy."

Lou listened. He nodded. His ears perked up when she told him, "There is some danger. We don't think much. But you'll be in cartel country. I know you just got married last year. So it's not a strike against you if you decline."

"I'll take the assignment, ma'am." He liked a little danger now and then. He wondered why the ambassador was giving it to him rather than to his section head. Fifteen seconds later, he knew why.

"It's a direct request from President Breen. It's unusual. It's informal. It's evidently more personal than diplomatic. And it's not formally part of anything the embassy does. You understand, of course, that you can't mention that it's the president's request to anyone, including your new bride. I'm only telling you so you understand the need to be thorough."

"I do understand." *President Breen!*

"Good. Then here are the specifics. Primarily, you are to determine whether Señor Gomez, who now limps, is healthy and whether his coffee farm is doing well. Secondarily, you are to determine any information you can about an American, Tex Cassidy, who worked with Señor Gomez until recently. I know that's vague. Sorry. It's all I know."

Lou nodded as he stood. "I'll put it in my schedule right away."

The ambassador shook his hand again. "It's already in your schedule. For today. I suggest you change clothes before leaving for the mountains." As he walked toward the door, she asked him, "So, is the assignment clear?"

He stopped and turned. He looked puzzled. "What assignment?"

27

Canadian Air Space
Oct. 16, 2016

Two hours into the flight to Alaska, Tex was mentally beating himself up. *What a mistake! Screw this mission.* He would give up his eyeteeth to go home, chop wood, and listen to the loons on the lake. But he had committed to Charley. And in both their codes of conduct, "commitment" meant "no choice." You gave your word. You went to the end of the line to keep it. There was no "trying"; "reasons" were bullshit.

"Ready when you are, Mr. Cassidy." Lynn sat like a West Point plebe in front of a high-speed computer. She cracked her fingers, ready to play it like a concert pianist.

"Must be awful for you, being exiled to this mission." By instinct, Tex tracked how events affected people. He also knew he was projecting his own feelings onto her.

"It's fine," she lied, opening a new document: "10.16.16.Cassidy-Overview.doc." Two days ago, she was with the president in the middle of a photo-finish presidential election. Now, in the middle of nowhere, she was with a guy who couldn't sit still.

"This could be the longest wild goose chase on record." Tex spread a large map on the table and put a callused finger on it. "We start here," he pointed to Alaska, "and end here, a million miles away." He dragged his finger eastward across Canada, the Atlantic Ocean, and western Europe, finally stopping at Samso Island, a part of Denmark where folks harness the wind for 100 percent of their power.

"Here's the first report, sir." Tex took the folder from her. Still irritated that he'd agreed to this mission, he wanted to open the plane's door and scatter the pages. Instead, he sat on the table and flipped through the eight carefully stapled "Trans-Atlantic Pipeline" sheets.

On page one, he stared at a map of the eight-hundred-mile pipeline that zigzagged its way from Prudhoe Bay on Alaska's North Slope to Valdez in the south. *Eleven pump houses. What if one of them is burned down or blown up?*

On the next few pages, he scanned facts and figures. "Jesus, eight billion dollars to build that sucker—and in 1977 dollars." A minute later, he asked Lynn, "Why is it half above ground and half below?"

"That's on the next page, Mr. Cassidy. But to answer your question, there are a lot of factors."

"Tell me." Tex looked up at her. She was older than her years. She could organize the material, but could she articulate the material?

Lynn gave herself no more than a few seconds. "The underground part is because permafrost covers 80 percent of Alaska."

"But why bother if the 'perma' in 'permafrost' stands for 'permanent'?"

"Because it can still move and shrink." There was an edge of "isn't it obvious?" in her tone. "And these days, it even melts. So burying sections underground keeps the struts from moving and the pipeline from breaking."

Tex kept reading. His investigative reporter side was surfacing. At one point, he whistled. "Production today is about half what it was in the late seventies."

"Yes, sir. But that's still about twenty percent of our country's domestic production."

"This is a good beginning, Lynn. Very good." *Can she do better?* He pulled out his laptop and found two images that captured his view of reporting and his view of life. He'd shown them many times. The first one had about a hundred dots, a third of them connected. "What's this?"

"No clue." The second one had all the dots connected. "A radio-telescope, like the kind used to look for extra-terrestrial life."

"Right, but the take-away? It's the Rule of Links." Tex moved his hands up, down, sideways, in the air, on the floor, every which way. "The more dots we connect, the clearer the picture."

"So you want me to drill down, as they say?" Behind them, the conference room door opened.

"Broader information. Different kinds of information, including unintended consequences." The copilot entered. He watched Lynn take notes as fast as Tex talked. "As a beginning: get me figures on both world oil production today and projected reserves for the future. Plus timelines for when oil might run out and a couple of unintended consequences when it does."

"By when?"

"Half hour."

Lynn stared at him. "Thirty minutes. Sure. If you'd like, I can also compose an Italian opera." Before he could respond, she was out the door, walking faster than normal. "What's up, Major?"

"Alex Sullivan, sir, the president's chief of staff." Tex swiveled to take the call.

"Hey, Alex. Any word on Bakov, your Russian buddy?" He took

the plane's portable phone and wandered around. Stranger than strange: he was now looking forward to meeting this guy.

"Dimitri will meet you in Churchill. He's a big-time Russian businessman. Years ago, we did a few joint ventures together."

"What should I know about him?" Tex felt like he was back at the Chronicle.

"He defected in the seventies to England, where he fell in love with money. Then when the Soviet Union went kaput, he got the patriotic virus and went back to help rebuild."

"Is he smart?"

"A few billion dollars smart. And by the way, smarter than he looks. Wouldn't you agree, General?" Alex had patched in General Mason. "I understand you two go way back."

"I wouldn't say it's good talking with you again, Cassidy, but it's good you're helping the president." Ten years ago, when he had worked on his "ka-ching" investigation, Tex had interviewed the general. Halfway through, they were glaring at each other. "Bakov's on this 'Centennial Committee.' Get me information about the committee, and it'll help me forget what an asshole you were."

"Fuck you, too, General. But thanks. I'll do what I can."

Tex put the phone back. All this adrenaline made him antsy. Plus, all he had done was fly and talk, talk and fly. He got on to the carpeted floor and did push-ups and sit-ups until Lynn returned with charts, graphs, and bulleted notes. "Tell me what you found."

As the plane headed northwest, Lynn pumped out background facts. "The world's first oil pipeline was in Baku, under Russia's control. Today, Russia's oil industry is second only to the Saudis'. And a lot more."

Before she was finished, Tex was finished. He had had enough. "So, by the time they get the Arctic reserves, they'll have a lot more and we'll have a lot less. Is that a fair summation?"

She nodded.

"OK, then let's go to the next phase."

For the next two hours, elbow-to-elbow, they pored over her notes and graphs. Twice, she asked, "Enough for now, sir?" And twice he gave her withering looks.

At one point, they projected an Arctic map on a large screen. "Wow! This is night and day from Antarctica, isn't it?" Tex stood with his hands on his hips. "Have you got a slide of Antarctica?"

Lynn put the two polar regions side by side. Tex stepped closer to the screen. He loved to learn, and he was learning a lot.

At the bottom of the earth, Antarctica was the fifth-largest landmass, a continent bigger than both Europe and Australia. And it was 98 percent covered in ice.

In contrast, the Arctic was a vast oceanic region. It extended from latitude 66° 33' north to latitude 90° north. The landmasses within the Arctic region were primarily parts of Russia, Canada, and Norway, as well as Alaska in the US and Denmark-controlled Greenland.

Furthermore, the Arctic's cold was critical to maintaining the interlocking system of weather patterns, temperatures, plant life, and animal species all over the world. In turn, the Arctic was affected by what happened all over the world. These days, it was particularly impacted by heat-trapping particles that were released anywhere on earth, trapped in the earth's atmosphere by gravity, and wind-distributed throughout the atmosphere like sugar in a cup of tea.

"Sir, we just crossed into Alaska." The copilot's voice came over the intercom.

Tex looked out the window. He saw white everywhere. How ironic! Three hundred million years ago, trees, ferns, and plants died. Nature pressured them into fossil fuels. Then, more recently within geological time, snow and ice covered over the fossil fuels in this part of the planet, as the earth's climate, oceans, and landmasses shifted.

In preparation for landing, Lynn gathered her paper documents and closed the electronic ones. She felt his hand on her elbow. "One other thing, why is knowing about systems important?"

Lynn was startled. They sat and buckled their seat belts as the plane descended. "So we can solve a problem?"

"So we can solve multiple problems at the same time. Think about that." He turned to her. "Maybe you'll be president someday. Knowing about systems could make you a great one."

The plane touched down. As it taxied, Lynn and Tex didn't look at each other. They said nothing to each other. Separately, they mulled over the last few hours.

For Lynn, Tex had blown open two doors. First, thinking in systems. It was as different from her habitual, narrower way of thinking as speaking Chinese would be different from speaking English. And second, Tex's off-the-cuff remark that she might be president. *A black woman in the White House? Not a prayer.* But whether it happened or not, something frozen inside herself started to melt. "Not a prayer" was radically different from a deep, unconscious belief that it was impossible.

For Tex, it was a return and a renewal. *It's good you're helping the president.* General Mason's words were like round pegs that just fell into round holes. What he would tell the president would be transformed into action. How the president acted could bring a little more sanity to an insane world.

The plane stopped. Lynn and Tex undid their seat belts. They nodded to each other, thankful for each other. Then she went back to her research, and Tex headed into the Arctic.

28

Colombian Coffee Region
Oct. 16, 2016

LOU SNAPPED his fingers to music on the embassy's car radio. Three times, he had read the one-page backgrounder that focused on the Colombian coffee industry: "Five hundred thousand farms, mostly very small, maybe 1.5 hectares. Mostly on the edge economically, some crossover with cocaine production. Important ties to American coffee brokers, roasters and retailers."

After three hours on the road, Lou felt like he had passed two-thirds of the coffee farms. Virtually every house needed paint. Most kids were thinner than the farm animals. Every ten minutes, he rolled up the windows because the smoky air from the burning coffee bush waste singed his nostrils.

Finally, Lou drove up a long, dusty driveway. Except for one badly charred building, the sheds and barns smelled of fresh lumber.

In the distance, protected by a grove of guamo shade trees, he saw workers harvesting coffee beans on hillsides. That was familiar. But something was different. He couldn't put his finger on what.

He waved to the middle-aged woman beating a rug on the porch railing. "Ola, señora. Carlos Gomez?" She pointed toward a pond where green algae grew and a man was limping along the edge. He was shoveling algae waste into a metal tub next to a pickup truck.

A moment later, the two men shook hands awkwardly. Lou said, "I'm Mr. Mendoza, I'm here as part of a market research program. Are you well, sir?" The campesino stared at Lou. He nodded nervously, not liking the presence of any American on his farm these days. "And your coffee farm? Is it successful?"

"Señor Mendoza, I'm busy, and this isn't a coffee farm. Please, what do you want?" Carlos knelt to lift the tub.

"But I saw coffee bushes." Lou knelt to help him. The algae waste smelled strong. It reminded him of what was different: there wasn't the smell of burning coffee waste in the air. Together, they hoisted the tub and placed it on the truck bed.

"Gracias, señor." Carlos could have done it by himself. But he was grateful for the help. "We grow coffee. We also grow mushrooms." He pointed to the sheds Lou had seen driving in. "We raise algae." He pointed to the pond behind them. "We raise fish." He pointed to another pond about twenty yards away. "This is an integrated farm."

"I see," Lou fudged. "And does that help you in the market?"

Carlos stood awkwardly. His bad leg ached. "Which market, señor? We sell in local markets. We sell in your country and in Europe. We sell in Asia." He got into the truck, reached across the seat, and opened the door for Lou.

Lou got in. He opened his mouth, but nothing came out. He had worked on two dozen economic development projects, including fair trade projects. But selling this many products to that many markets? "Do you make money?"

The integrated farmer struggled to stay gracious. "Always with some products. But it depends on supply and demand. Too much coffee . . . not enough mushrooms. You know how markets work." Slowly, he drove to the fishpond. Once there, he got out. "Can you help me again, por favor?"

Together, they lifted the tub off the truck and carried it to the edge of the fishpond. Carlos picked up a shovel. He waved to three workers on the far side, harvesting fish. Then he reached into the tub and threw some of the algae waste into the pond. Immediately, tilapia came to the surface to eat.

Lou held off introducing his next topic. "Is this how you always do it?" He knew his question was as lame as his host's foot.

Carlos chuckled. "This is how nature always does it." He gave Lou a one-minute summary of nature's design principles, including, "The waste of one kingdom of nature is food for another. That's how we run the whole farm." He explained they used the coffee bush waste as a substrate to grow mushrooms; the mushroom waste to feed the pigs and cows; the animal waste to generate heat in a biodigestor to be used in the algae farm; the algae waste to feed the fish; and the fish waste as fertilizer for the coffee bushes. "We just copy how natural systems work."

Carlos got back in the truck. So did Lou. The campesino handed Lou a few mushrooms. "Try these. You'd pay ten to twelve dollars in your country for a pound of them."

Lou ate one. Delicious. He ate several more. "Let me ask you one other question, Señor Gomez." Carlos started the truck and drove slowly across the rutted roads. "You had someone working here. An American. Tex Cassidy. Can you tell . . ."

Carlos slammed his good foot on the brake. His gentle smile

turned into a snarl. He looked in the rearview mirror then in the sideview mirror. "You must go."

"Why? I'm just trying . . ."

"Now." He checked the mirrors again, terrified his cousin, Juan, would drive up. As a young man, Juan had been in the Medellín Cartel and was a personal bodyguard for Pablo Escobar. Juan now worked for the local cartel. Juan had told Carlos, "No calls with the American. No e-mails. Any contact and you're a dead man with a dead wife."

"Cassidy was here, wasn't he?"

Carlos looked twice toward a mountain road near a large grove of Erythrina fusca trees. His face was full of fright as if the devil himself might come roaring down the road. Then he headed back toward the embassy car. "Yes, he was here."

"What did Cassidy do here?" They passed the bamboo shed full of mushrooms.

"Everything." Carlos's lip quivered. "He built that shed. He cut the bamboo himself."

Lou was being bounced around in the truck. "Can you slow down, señor?"

They passed the fishpond at the same speed, if not faster. They could now see Lou's car. "He also built this pond. Every shovelful. As a thank you."

"Why did Cassidy come here?"

Carlos quickly turned and stared at Lou. He gripped the wheel tighter. "Why did you come here?" He suddenly feared that Juan was testing him.

"I told you that . . ."

"You told me nothing. And I'm telling you nothing. I don't know where he is. I haven't had any contact with him since he left. I swear."

"Señor Gomez, I'm just asking about the past." They were less than a minute from Lou's car.

"He came because he loved what we did."

"Is that the only reason?"

Carlos swerved to avoid a pig. "His wife died. He was unhappy. He couldn't stop her from dying." As he swerved, he saw the road coming down from the mountain at a different angle. He also saw two trucks on it, barreling toward the farm. Carlos was flooded with fear. It was contagious. Lou caught the fear. "Who is that?"

Carlos pushed his gimpy foot harder on the accelerator. He yanked the steering wheel to the left. The truck almost tipped. Then he drove straight across his vegetable garden, mowing down rows of tomato plants. "Let me talk. You're here surveying coffee farms. That's all. No more. Do you understand?"

Carlos slammed on the brakes in front of Lou's car. He grabbed

Lou so hard that he nearly broke his forearm. "Don't mention Tex Cassidy!"

Before Lou could protest, the trucks roared up the driveway, kicking up a mini-Sahara. Six armed men with automatic weapons jumped out. A seventh man with a bullet belt and body odor walked toward them. "Carlos, you have an American guest and didn't invite me over?"

"Juan, Lou Mendoza, from the US Embassy. He's doing market research. Mr. Mendoza, my cousin Juan."

"Market research? Very nice. I'm a businessman. In fact, I'm helping Carlos shift his business model." He pointed toward the arch of Carlos's right foot.

Lou looked over at Carlos, who explained, "An accident. I shot myself in the foot."

In fact, one minute before Tex had taken out the thugs, Juan had given Carlos a gun and a choice: "Shoot yourself in the foot, or my men will shoot two of your workers in the head." It was payback because Carlos's model of farming worked. Farmers who did it made money, but they weren't growing poppies.

"I'd better start back for Bogotá." Lou stepped toward his car.

"Very nice. Cotton or silk?" Juan put his dirt-covered fingers on Lou's white shirt and rubbed them together. When he didn't respond, Juan continued. "Here's an easier question. Tex Cassidy: do you know him?" He let his fingers ride up to Lou's throat. Lou shook his head. "Think carefully," Juan said.

Lou shook his head again. He soiled his pants. "You smell, señor. Stand by your car. It would be good for you to see market forces at work."

Carlos tried to intervene. "Juan, please . . ."

Juan turned back to Carlos. "I'm sorry, cousin. Apparently, one foot and one building aren't enough."

In the next few minutes, Juan's men poured gasoline on the mushroom sheds and lit matches. They shot holes through the bio-digester pipes. They tossed grenades into the fishpond and watched the carcasses fly onto the banks. They pulled chainsaws out of the trucks and cut down Carlos' coffee bushes. And finally, they threw bags of coca seeds in front of Carlos. "Welcome back to the family business."

Lou saw Carlos fall to his knees, praying. Then he felt Juan whack him across the shoulders like he might whack a cow. "Go write your market report before my men set your car on fire with you in it."

Lou raced back down the driveway. Juan's men fired at his car, laughing. They were seeing how many times they could hit the car without killing the driver.

29

Alaska
Oct. 16, 2016

"YOU'RE NOT THE USUAL Washington dickhead." Eddie Meeker had one hand on the steering wheel and the other on his thermal mug. After twenty-eight years, "Mr. Pipeline" knew the Trans-Alaska Pipeline System better than he knew his wife.

"Thanks for the compliment." They drove along remote access roads. Tex was bundled up like Nanook of the North. *Be my eyes. See what's going on.* The president had particularly wanted Tex to go to Alaska. It was America's only presence in the Arctic. Its oil was a vital part of America's security.

Suddenly, Eddie shoved his coffee mug into a cup holder. The car was sliding into a ditch. "I hate mud!" There were only three wheels on the ground when Eddie shifted into four-wheel drive and got back on the road. He stopped the truck. "All right, Cassidy, enough nicey-nice. Why did Breen send you? And, by the way, I'm voting the other way this time."

"He wants to know what's real."

"He's got all the facts."

"Facts are different than real. You got any interest in telling him what's real to you?"

The engineer shifted into first gear and started driving. "What does he want to know."

"Let's start with me. I'm a Houston guy. And this isn't Texas flatland." He unzipped his parka halfway. He was in more danger of suffocating than freezing.

"I don't take anything from the folks who dug the Panama Canal." Eddie looked over at Tex like a proud father. "But, mister, we laid this sucker across three mountain ranges, earthquake fault lines, and over eight hundred rivers and streams. Some of the land is frozen forever. Some of it thaws every year."

Thirty yards farther, Eddie passed an eighteen-wheeler hauling construction equipment and sections of pipe. The driver honked at Eddie, who waved back.

"Where we going?" Dickhead or not, Tex didn't like being out in nowhere with a man he didn't know.

"Relax. Breen wants to know what's real. Sometimes, you gotta see it to know it." Eddie smirked as he picked up his coffee mug again.

"OK, tour guide. But tell me: building the pipeline, was the cold the toughest part?" Tex needed to steer the conversation.

"The heat." The engineer swerved onto a different road and stopped. "The oil can be 140 to 145 degrees. You wouldn't want it spilling down your pants." Eddie got out of the car, went behind a boulder, and returned. "Sorry. My plumbing doesn't work like it should. But back to the heat: the oil could melt the permafrost. So could the outside temperature. That's why we use a zillion heat exchangers."

Tex rolled down the window halfway. "So, melting permafrost: should the president worry about it?"

Eddie shook his head. "In the last thirty years, do you know how many permafrost leaks we've had?" He held up two fingers. He pulled out his wallet and showed Tex a photo of his one-story home. "I lose a lot more sleep over this." The frame building tilted down to the right.

"And the next thirty, say, between now and 2050?"

Eddie shrugged. "Whatever happens, we'll adapt. That's what people do." He held his body in a weird, tight way.

"Are you alright?"

"For another minute or two. What are you really asking?"

Tex took in the engineer's discomfort. Eddie indicated with his hand for Tex to speed it up.

"Look, the president's trying to figure out what's going on in the Arctic. A big part of it's due to melting. Glaciers, sea ice, permafrost. What if the models are right? Alaska could lose eleven feet by the end of the century. Then what?"

Eddie climbed out of the truck. "Alaska won't be Alaska." He went behind a tree. A few minutes later, he climbed back in. "Sorry. I'm paying for my two beers last night." He turned the ignition on again and drove off.

"That's poetic, Eddie, but what does it mean?" Tex noticed that they had entered a narrow canyon. He could almost reach out and touch the mountains.

"Compared to today, I wouldn't recognize it."

Tex rolled the window down all the way. He needed more air. He also needed more answers. "You worry at all about the Russians?" Eddie stared over at him so long that Tex got nervous. "The road . . ."

"The Russians? What? Firing missiles at Anchorage?"

"Drilling oil in the Arctic."

Eddie gripped the steering wheel more tightly. "I don't worry they'll put us out of business. I worry they'll screw up the Arctic."

"Like the Gulf?"

"And like here." At that moment, Eddie drove out of the canyon and pulled into a lookout area. In front of them was a wide open body of water. "Prince William Sound. Does it ring a bell?"

30

Polyarny, Russia
Oct. 16, 2016

POLICE, MILITARY, and intelligence officers swarmed around the motorcade. They wore black suits or blue uniforms. They carried shields, batons, and firearms. It wasn't just who was in the limos; it was also where they were going.

Polyarny, a town on the western side of the Murmansk Fjord, was hardly a tourist spot like the south of France, given its location and its radioactivity. Its claim to fame was its shipyards, especially Shkval, shipyard number ten. In some ways, it was like Los Alamos, New Mexico, during World War Two. It was a place where secrets were kept and devices were built.

In one car, Admiral Sukirov whispered to Dimitri Bakov: "If we were sticking to the Centennial Committee's timetable, I'd find this interesting."

In another car, the prime minister was prodding and pricking. Who knows? Maybe there would be a funny look or a slip of the tongue. "You'd tell me, wouldn't you, if you knew anything about Pakistan?" Fyodorokov avoided the prime minister's question by coughing phlegm into his white cotton handkerchief.

Finally, armed guards waved the motorcade through the last security post. They drove up in front of a seventy-eight-foot-by-sixty-five-foot structure with a massive wind-and-corrosion-resistant door. The prime minister and the others stepped out. Bodyguards ushered them through a steel-plated access door where soldiers held submachine guns and short-leashed attack dogs.

Once inside, the entourage marched through the assembly area that was several soccer fields long. Walking with Fyodorokov, the prime minister took in all the cranes, cables, chains, and catwalks. *There it is!* He pointed to the nuclear power plant that was in the final assembly stage and spoke loudly over all the hammering and welding. "Power for the drilling

31

Alaska
Oct. 16, 2016

"Yeah, it rings a bell. A loud one." Tex tapped his fingers on the side of the truck. He wasn't fond of stupidity. But he went ape-shit when it was mega-stupidity that led straightaway to mega-pain and mega-suffering.

Until 2010, the Exxon *Valdez* oil spill had been the daddy of America's ecological mega-stupidities. It had occurred in this peaceful, if no longer pristine, body of water. Both men sat in silence, as if they were paying their respects. Finally, Tex pointed across the Sound. "Columbia?"

"That's her. Or what's left of her." The Columbia Glacier was part of the Chugach Mountains. It was the world's fastest-moving glacier, retreating a third of a football field every day. "Could say the same thing for them." Eddie aimed his finger toward small, commercial fishing boats hauling in their nets. "The fleet's about half what it was in '89."

Tex turned sideways to face the engineer. "Why'd you bring me here?"

"You said he wanted to know what's real." Eddie turned to face Tex. "You know what happened before the spill? The safety regs got loosey-goosey. Everyone knew it. But nothing breeds complacency like a great track record." He sounded equal parts mad and sad. "Till ten million gallons of crude covered eleven million square miles of water."

"You were here when it happened?"

"And afterward. Clean-up foreman. For three years. You ever held a bird covered with oil? Not a picture of one. The real thing?"

Tex hadn't.

"I probably held a few thousand." Eddie held out his hand, as if he were holding something. "How 'bout a mutant fish? Two heads? One gill?"

"And the people?"

"Couldn't tell you how many folks on the crew are dead. Or dying. But want to know what happened to their brains and their body organs?" He paused. "I'm one of them. Screwed up my kidneys, big-time."

Tex got quiet. He debated whether to tell Eddie about Katie. But before he had made up his mind, Eddie cranked the engine hard. They headed for Valdez, where the pipeline's southern terminal was located and where the Exxon Valdez had taken on the oil. "Listen, my kidneys can handle one beer. Got time to join me?"

Eddie drove into town. He drove around oil storage tanks to an out-of-the-way bar with no windows and two cop cars parked out front. It was a dive. But an alive dive. Full of tough men and tougher women, able to brave the cold in winter and the black flies in summer. They drank. They danced. They whooped it up. They sang along with old Johnny Cash songs on the jukebox.

A dozen high-fives and handshakes later, Eddie led Tex to the only empty table in the place. They had their beer. Tex figured they were done talking. He was wrong.

Eddie had a load. "I've had three wives, and I had a kid die in a car accident. But that spill?" He took a long swig of beer and noticed a cop at the front door. "Hardest thing in my life. And, in case you're wondering, that's why I'm not voting for Breen."

Suddenly, at a table next to them, three cops surrounded a guy with a big belly and a thick accent. "Vlad, we need to talk." The guy crashed into one of the cops and broke for the back door. The second cop drew his gun. People screamed as they dived for cover. The third cop caught Vlad around the ankles, before cuffing him and hauling him away.

"Russian," Eddie said. "Worked for me on the clean-up. Always stealing. Needs money for painkillers."

A moment later, Tex swigged beer and ate nuts. "Tell me, again: why aren't you voting for Breen?"

The bar was loud, and people danced again. The place smelled of sweat. Eddie looked at Tex with mad eyes and a scowl. "Actually, two reasons."

"First . . ." Tex braced himself.

"He's out of the same mold. Carter, Reagan, all the rest. They talk about 'energy independence' like they're talking about the Virgin Mary. But actually do something? Come on. They've all been liars or incompetent or both. And before too long, you won't have cheap oil for your car."

"And the other reason?" Tex downed a few more swigs.

"The whole country's Prince William Sound. Breen still mouths that 'greatest country' crap." Eddie pointed his beer bottle at different parts of the crowd. "They know what's happening to the weather. They know there won't be a 'Next Big Disaster.' There'll be a wheelbarrow full of them. And it'll be a lot uglier than birds dressed in oil."

Tex just listened. He couldn't argue. Wouldn't argue. "You're as bleak as I am. Got any predictions?"

Eddie had that tight look again. "You wait: when people can only turn their lights on three times a week? When their supermarkets look like Japan's in the fifties? You asked about the Russians: we'll be bending over for them with our pants around our ankles." Then he bee-lined to the men's room.

32

Renesee, Netherlands
Oct. 16, 2016

T HE TRAIN SPED through the Dutch countryside. Zavia stared blankly at the tulip greenhouses and the new windmills. She closed her eyes before putting on eyeshades and earplugs. But she could no more sleep than she could fly.

Maybe I'll read. Usually, Zavia devoured at least one science fiction book a week. She pulled Robert Heinlein's *Stranger in a Strange Land* out of her purse. When she couldn't remember the three paragraphs she had just read, she switched to music. When she had switched from classical to country and then to jazz, she shut the player off and filed her nails with an emery board.

She was as emotionally all over the map as she had been geographically.

For starters, the Maldives situation had sapped her hope. The Hawaii tsunami had drenched her in fear. But worst of all, she couldn't get the lousy 'admiral' taste out of her mouth. And the Arctic storm that had delayed her overnight flight from Murmansk to Amsterdam had her skin crawling.

An hour later, exhausted, she stepped out of the taxi in front of her great aunt's old stone house. Suddenly, all the angst . . . all the bitter tastes . . . all the worries . . . were blown away by the North Sea air and the sight of her Dutch family. The people on the wooden porch waved wildly, as if the princess had just arrived. The younger kids jumped up and down. "She still doesn't know I'm coming, right?" Zavia asked a cousin, who was kicking around a soccer ball.

Now that Zavia was finally here, the guests put on party hats and sang 'Happy Birthday.' Dagmare's great-granddaughter wheeled out a cake with eighty candles. When the little girl said, "Make a wish, Grandma," the elderly woman closed her eyes. When she opened them, she saw her American niece and burst into tears.

For the next few hours, Zavia drank wine and held court, bantered back and forth with her curious relatives.

"How is your new apartment in The Hague?"

"Zavia, have you taken any more science fiction writing classes?"

"Do you think they'll close the barriers, because of this storm?"

"I just got a great two-week job with Climate Trackers," her twenty-two-year-old cousin, Ingrid, said in the bathroom, where they tried each other's lipstick. Ingrid was even more radiant than usual, as she brushed back the short blonde bangs that framed her large blue eyes. "Guess what? We're programming software to activate cameras on glaciers. Isn't that cool!" Altogether, these people were the loving, extended family Zavia never had in the US.

Finally, after the last guest was gone, Zavia plopped down next to Dagmare on a porch swing. She listened to a tile banging in the wind. On the radio, she heard a calm voice issue an "extra high tide" warning and add nonchalantly, "The Storm Surge Warning Service recommends a dike watch in the following sectors . . ."

Dagmare turned off the radio. "It's only a Level 1, honey. Nothing to worry about."

"Do those warnings ever bring back memories?" Zavia asked.

In 1953, a massive North Sea storm had drowned the Netherlands. Like a water serial killer, it filled lung after lung after lung. Two thousand pairs of lungs. One pair belonged to Zavia's grandmother. She had jumped from the roof of her two-story house into the raging water, when Zavia's mother, at age five, had slipped on wet shingles. Carried along by the raging water, Zavia's grandmother grabbed her baby child by the arm and held her soaked, shaking body. Then, feeling her strength sapping, she heaved her into the arms of an old man in a rowboat less than a foot away. Seconds later, the water smashed Grandma's head against the windshield of a car floating by.

"Oh, once in a while, sweetie," Dagmare replied. Living along this raw Dutch coast, she could read the drops of rain and gusts of wind. "But hardly ever after they built the Delta Works."

They sat quietly, Zavia gently pushing them back and forth on the swing with her feet. Ever since Zavia had been old enough to read and write, she and Dagmare had exchanged a letter each week. When Zavia graduated high school, Dagmare had sold a cow and bought a plane ticket.

Finally, Zavia let out a soft sigh. She shifted both her weight and the conversation. "Well, tell me this, Wise Old Aunt: what have your eighty years taught you?"

Sometimes, life is a shredder. In those times when she was being chewed up, Zavia turned to her aunt. In fact, nine years ago, when Zavia had come home early from a business trip and found her husband in their bathtub with another woman, she had yelled, kicked the son-of-a-bitch out, and then called her aunt.

"Stay close to this." Dagmare stretched her hands out. "People may disappoint you. The natural world never will." She half-turned to Zavia. "You sound worried, dear. Are you?"

"A little." She nodded. "I still love my work, Auntie, but I'm really tired of working at love." Since her divorce, she had dated, she had mated, but she always walked away deflated.

Dagmare took Zavia's hand in hers and stroked it a few times. "Want to know something else eighty years has taught me? Love is just one second from now."

Zavia shrugged her shoulders and stood up. Some people lose faith in God. She had lost faith in love. Or was it men? Or was it herself? She leaned over and kissed Dagmare on the top of her head. "Good night, Auntie. It's lights out for me."

33

Rockville, Maryland
Oct. 16, 2016

"CHRIST, DAVE," General Mason zipped up his jacket. "I'd have guessed a laundromat. Maybe a punk disco. But this place?!"

Every four months, the NSA and his two top aides did something fun. And different. They rotated choosing an activity. Usually, it had nothing to do with saving the nation. Sometimes, it did.

The Rockville ice skating rink was packed. The police league hockey game would start in a few minutes. Emma Wolfe shivered as they took their seats. "You said this was more than fun. I sure hope so." She remembered the cold, when, as a kid, she watched her father play outdoor hockey back in Russia.

"The reason's in front of you," Dave Dunn teased. "Think about ice. Look at this ice. Look closely," he said, as the teams lined up for the face off. "I'll tell you in-between periods."

As soon as the first period ended, the general, Emma, and Dave raced down to the crowded food court. They bought beer and Polish sausage from a Middle Eastern woman with round eyes and a beautiful smile. They found a small, raised table that they stood around. "So here's the deal," Dave said, leaning closer to them and using the crowd noise to cover his words. "The rink owner's a neighbor. Two days ago, he told me about a new gizmo that takes air out of water before it makes ice."

"There's a point here, right?" Emma checked her cell phone, hoping for a national emergency that would cut this night short. General Mason, meanwhile, was trying to avert a national emergency.

"Patience," Dave chuckled. "Anyway, he told me how this gizmo uses less electricity, which means it cuts his costs. Plus the ice is clearer, so he charges more for ads under the ice. Plus . . ."

General Mason shifted from one foot to another. He was eating a sausage, but something was eating him. "Dave, sorry, later. We need to talk about Aleksandr Lebed."

After the Pakistan detonation, the general had been manic. "Facts! Rumors! Confessions under torture! Get me anything, and get me everything." One nugget was the September 7, 1997, bombshell that Boris Yeltsin's former head of National Security had dropped on the world. Appearing on *60 Minutes*, Lebed announced that up to two hundred small nuclear devices had been lost when the USSR fell apart.

"What about Lebed?" For six years, Dave had been in the US Small Ammo Munitions Device program. Just yesterday, he had replayed that interview.

Emma asked, "Did you believe him?"

"Still do. If Lebed was half right . . . a quarter right . . ." He washed down the rest of his sausage with the rest of his beer.

The general shook his head. "I better tell the president," he whispered mostly to himself. Suddenly, he headed toward the exit. "Let's go." He took the stadium stairs two at a time. Then he practically ran through the parking lot to their car. Dave climbed into the driver's seat. "Put the siren on," the general ordered.

Cars swerved out of the way. Dave swerved around the ones that didn't. Holding on tightly, Emma leaned closer to the front seat. "This isn't for the president, but the FBI's looking at photos from his last few rallies. If they find anything, they'll want our help."

Dave pulled into the White House driveway. The general's seat belt was already off, and he had the door open. "Quick, finish the rink story."

"That ice machine? It's made by a Swedish company. Remember Zavia Jansen, the woman at the prime minister's press conference? Well, she's on the company's board, and she's been to Russia eight times in the last two years. She even speaks some Russian."

"Just don't tell me she's on Langley's payroll."

"Not the CIA's, but the Army Corps of Engineers. In New Orleans, three years before Katrina, she'd raised a holy stink about the dikes. They tried to shut her up by sending her to East Nowhere. She quit and went out on her own."

The general opened the door. Racing toward the White House, he yelled back. "Find her. See what she knows."

34

Churchill, Manitoba
Oct. 17, 2016

THE WINDS OFF Hudson Bay shook the rivets and rattled the doors. The whole plane bounced around like a Ping-Pong ball in a hurricane.

In the cockpit, the pilot barely read the vibrating gauges. If he weren't under direct orders, he would have bagged this third landing attempt and headed south to Winnipeg.

In the back of the plane, both civilian passengers struggled to keep down their dinner.

One minute, Lynn's stomach was in her throat. The next minute, it was below her knees. Under her breath, she whispered the Lord's Prayer.

Tex stared out at the churning whitecaps that, each autumn, turned into a humungous sheet of ice stretching thousands of miles up to the North Pole. His prayer was that if his time was up, the plane would break apart in midair rather than plummeting under the water. Death was bad enough. Death by drowning was a lot worse.

"Are you all right?" he asked Lynn, who had her head between her knees and obviously wasn't. Tex wasn't much better. He couldn't ignore the turbulence, so he tried to focus on why the hell he was descending through the turbulence. Oh, yeah, the Russian. Frosting on the cake. Katie was the cake itself.

As they descended though the clouds, he remembered the year before she died. *What a great time!* They had spent many a happy hour with maps, airline schedules, ticket prices, picture books of polar bears, and a bottle of wine. "This'll be great! The trip of a lifetime! Oh, God, what if we don't want to come back?"

But nothing Tex felt in this plane ride compared to what she went through. First, the migraines that wouldn't stop. Then the nausea that wouldn't leave. The week before they were due to fly to Churchill, she couldn't keep down a salad. For four days, she lay motionless. She wore a blindfold. She used a bedpan. Every cough turned the room into a centrifuge. Every touch felt like an acid burn on her skin. "Cancel, Tex," she finally whispered.

Tex swore to her, "We'll go next year." But as her immune system broke down, so did their hopes for the trip.

Finally, two days before she died, Katie asked him, "Will you go yourself and spread my ashes up there?" He couldn't say no. He didn't want to.

Suddenly, the plane jammed hard onto the tarmac. It rolled forward and taxied to a stop. Tex was brought out of the past and into the present. "Do you know when Bakov gets here?" he asked Lynn, while he stood up to get his parka and fur hat.

She couldn't talk, so she just shook her head. "Are you all right?" Tex sat back down next to her.

"Are we in heaven, or are we in Churchill?" She was doing better.

"Churchill, I think." Tex stood again. "Last chance? Want to come along?"

"That would be no, but thanks for asking."

Tex descended the stairs toward the snow-packed runway. On the bottom step, he called out. "Lynn, find out what you can about Bakov." Then he stepped onto the snow. *This ain't Houston.*

The town of Churchill was a short car—or dogsled—ride from the airport. A thousand people lived up here on the remote northern tip of Manitoba, just below the Arctic Circle. Some were white; most were Inuit. During the next eight weeks, they would be joined by a few thousand tourists who paid big bucks to see Hudson Bay polar bears before there were no more polar bears to be seen at any price.

Twenty minutes later, Tex's cab slid down ice-covered Kelsey Street like a curling stone. Finally, it skidded up in front of the Iceberg Inn, a small clapboard hotel that shared a waiting room with the Sears catalog store.

Tex checked in. "Do you have an end room, please?"

The clerk looked at Tex's name on the register. "I'm sorry, Mr. Cassidy. We're sold out. You're in 114."

Tex went to his room. The bed was a cot. The mirror was cracked. The faucet dripped. The phone was funky when he called Alex to review the itinerary. If there were lovers in the next room, he would hear every kiss.

Suddenly, his mobile phone rang. "Please hold for the president."

Tex put a few clothes away. But he didn't take off his coat. He wanted to see what a town with no traffic lights was like.

"Hey, Tex, got everything figured out?" Charley joked from his limo.

"I do, except this guy Bakov. Why am I meeting him?"

"Hell if I know. Talk to Alex. They go way back."

"Charley..."

"Hell, Tex, the guy's on that weird Centennial Committee. Do your 'Tex' number on him. Pry a few secrets, OK?"

"Yeah, sure." Tex pulled the phone away from his ear. He wanted to hang it up. "Where are you?"

"Pittsburgh. What'd you learn in Alaska?"

"If the warming continues and the pipeline collapses, the economy's fucked and so is the country."

"Depends on what you mean by 'collapse.'" Charley became the president. "A few days, we've got reserves. A few weeks, we've got other sources. A few months, you're right, we're fucked."

"Charley, if you know all this..."

"I'm looking for new connections, Tex, not new facts. Talk to the Russians. Talk to the Europeans. Then talk to me."

Tex rolled his eyes. "Coming right up. In the meantime, is the world running out of oil?"

"The easy-to-get, easy-to-refine stuff? Yes. But, boy, with these new platforms and drills? We can pull it out of of the earth's asshole if we have to." Outside, an aide held up two fingers.

"Including the Gulf of Mexico?"

"Don't go soft on me, Tex. It was the mother of all accidents. But do you know where 65 percent of today's oil is?"

"In places where they'd like to boil us in the stuff, right?"

"Or they're as stable as a three-legged dog." Charley saw his aide, now wildly shaking a lonely index finger. In the distance, he heard the ramp-up music to *Hail to the Chief*. "Got to go. It'll be fine this afternoon, Tex. Later, buddy." Suddenly, the line went dead.

Something was eating away at Tex. It wasn't just Katie. That would twist him in knots. But at least he knew the emotional hellhole he was heading into. *This talky-talk about oil and wind...*

Tex zipped up his parka, placed his pack over his shoulder, and headed down the street. He walked fast. He stumbled on the ice twice. He slipped once near the train station, when he landed hard on his butt, but he managed to keep his pack off the ground.

Limping slightly, Tex saw the massive grain elevators in the distance. In this place of flat land and one-story clapboard buildings, they looked very out of place. Nevertheless, he meandered over to the Port of Churchill. He wanted to check out the port before his meeting with Bakov in the morning. Plus, he was feeling queasy and checking out the port was a better distraction than alcohol or television.

From Lynn, he knew that, years earlier, the first Russian shipment from Murmansk proved the Arctic Bridge concept: goods could move across the Arctic and then by rail down into North America. Now, would Churchill ever be Los Angeles, Rotterdam, or Shanghai? No way. But higher temps and less sea ice would bring in a hell of a lot more money from shipping than polar bear tours.

Tex checked his watch. *Thirty minutes.* He felt even queasier as he strolled by the loading berths, tugboats, and storage capacity for thirteen million gallons of petroleum products and 150,000 tons of grain and fertilizer. *This is why Bakov's here. This is what the Russians are up to. At least part of what they're up to.*

35

Oosterschelde Barrier, Netherlands
Oct. 17, 2016

Z AVIA WAS UP with the sun. She packed her clothes, left her roller bag by the front door, and headed for the nearby beach.

For the next half hour, she strolled barefoot along the shore. The sand was damp from last night's rain. Lost in thought about the training she would deliver in a couple hours, she stumbled into a sand hole and fell. Red-faced, she looked around. The beach was deserted. *Love may only be a second away. But not the next few seconds.*

Back at the house, Dagmare served her homemade muffins and jam. "Before I forget, sweetie, your cell phone rang twice." Zavia checked. The two missed calls said the number was blocked.

When the plates were cleared and the cab was out front, they hugged and said their good-byes. It was teary for both women. "I'll come next summer, Auntie, I promise."

The ride to the nearby Oosterschelde Barrier didn't take long. Once there, they drove over the highway constructed on top of the barrier. "The museum at the other end? Drop me off there, please."

The driver slowed to make a right turn. In the rearview mirror, he saw something he had never seen before: a passenger's face light up at the sight of the barrier towers and gates. Awe? Yes. But joy? Never.

Everyone has places they deeply love. Places where they feel at home. Maybe the ocean. A cabin in the hills. A patio garden. For Zavia, this was one of her places. It had been compared to the Great Wall of China in scale and the moon landing in complexity. It was considered one of the seven engineering wonders of the world. Zavia liked all that. But in the same way that people feel kinship to the Lincoln Memorial or the Eiffel Tower, she felt kinship to this very large hunk of concrete and steel.

The cabbie rode past the gates with the towers in between them. *The monsters are still there. Hey, guys!* She gave them a little wave. She noticed that, as usual, the gates were raised so the tides could nourish the marine ecosystem. *I'm glad your mouths are open.* Lars's software only closed their "mouths" when a storm threatened to flood the inland side of the barrier.

Years ago, on just her fourth internship day, she had decided the gates were mythical monsters. She named all the gates, from number one, whom she nicknamed "Leviathan," all the way up to gate number sixteen, who was "Jabba." By the time she became a full-time employee, her Uncle Lars and the rest of the staff said things like "Jabba needs a paint job." When they gave public tours, they would amuse folks: "Oh, Typhon . . . you wouldn't want to steal his supper. He's forty feet tall, a hundred and forty feet wide, and weighs three hundred to five hundred tons."

The driver pulled up in front of the museum entrance. Zavia paid him and walked a few steps. The gentle wind carried the happy sounds of a gentle man. "Zavia! Zavia! Zavia!"

Nearly sixty-five years old, Lars Jaeger, the lanky, gray-haired chief software engineer, ran toward her with a grin as wide as the barrier itself. Though he had worked on other sections of the Delta Works, this was his "Barrier Baby": two hundred thousand lines of software code and computer programs linked to weather, tide, and sea level data. "You can't stay away this long!"

"Lars!" He was her uncle, Ingrid's father. He grabbed her and hugged her tightly. During her early years at the barrier, he had mentored her. Now, with her experience in New Orleans, Singapore, Venice, and other climate-vulnerable places, she often mentored him.

Arm-in-arm, they walked along the access road toward the training room. Zavia turned her head to the right to talk with her uncle. Then she would turn her head to the left to take in the water and the nearby land. In her cells, she felt again the powerful juxtaposition of a tiny nation seated up against a gigantic ocean of water that ran all the way to the top of the world. It was a constant reminder to her and especially to the Dutch: humans were a part of Nature and not its master.

"Ingrid's a gem, Lars. The acorn didn't fall far from the software tree."

"Believe me, I told her to go to medical school. Become a tattoo artist. Be anything but a coder. It was all wasted breath."

They passed gate number twelve. Zavia stared at the tenting around the gate. "What's up with Cyclops?"

"Painting, scraping, routine stuff before winter. We'll be tenting the gates on either side in another few days as well." He squeezed her arm tenderly. "Now, we've got a few minutes. What's up with you?"

In the distance, Zavia saw people entering the barrier on their way to the training room. She gave Lars the quickie version of her travels and adventures, including the Murmansk trip.

"Well, that's a coincidence." Lars's face crinkled. "Six weeks ago, some Russian spent the whole day here."

Zavia's ears perked up. "Who? An engineer?" Suddenly, Zavia's cell phone rang. She saw it was an unknown number. "I'll get it later."

"Definitely not an engineer. Was an older guy, about as technical as a tulip. He spent a lot of time walking the access roads and nearby beaches."

They were close to the training room. People could hear. She stopped and turned Lars sideways. "I'm curious, Lars. Did he ask a lot of questions?"

Lars lowered his voice. "No. But, three times, he asked what would happen if there was a big storm and the gates didn't close."

36

Churchill, Manitoba
Oct. 17, 2016

AFTER A SLOW WALK back into Churchill, Tex's heart skipped four or five beats. He saw the private helicopter Alex had arranged. It was ready to go. He wasn't.

"Great day for flying," the chirpy pilot said. Tex climbed into the front seat, set his pack between his feet, and put his headphones on. "If it's OK with you, we'll sightsee for forty-five minutes. Then you'll have fifteen minutes personal time."

The helicopter swooped over the land and sea. The rotors were like a very loud white noise. All of it helped Tex feel better. Expanded landscapes like this allowed him to feel personally expanded.

"My wife loved the bears." He saw the tundra buggies down below. "Know a lot about them?"

"Used to hunt 'em, when we still could." The pilot pointed down at an eight-hundred-pound male, pacing back and forth at the water's edge. "Been there every day for two weeks waiting for the ice. Poor guy, he shows up on time, but the water freezes later every year."

"Looks skinny. Is he?"

"Auschwitz skinny." The pilot pointed to the bear's ribs. "Less ice means less hunting, which means less food, which means fewer cubs."

"Will they make it?"

"Not in these parts." The pilot checked his watch. "Nothing anyone can do about it."

Tex gripped the seat. Katie would have gone ballistic if she were here and heard him say that. *Funny, it feels like she's here.* "You don't believe that, do you?"

"No offense, mister, but people are people." The pilot turned east and headed back toward the spill area. "They'll change their lightbulbs. But change their lifestyles?"

"You know it's not just the bears." Tex sketched out a few dots.

]"The warmth will drive the krill away. The fish will go. Then the seals. The bears will starve or leave. So will many of the natives. So will many of the businesses, including yours."

"Whoa! Hold your horses." The pilot climbed another hundred feet. "First of all, the ecosystem won't go. It'll just be different. Maybe even better." He pointed toward a red fox on the ice. "New kid on the block. And there'll be others. Probably new trees and plants. And new opportunities. Hell, if Churchill booms, we might even get a Chinese restaurant." The pilot pointed to his watch. "Sorry to cut off this conversation," he lied, "but it's time."

For the last little while, Tex felt Katie more and more. At first, distantly. But now it was as if she had her arms around him, smiling at him, loving him up. *You're here, sweetheart. I can feel you. Jesus, I've missed you.* He felt her soft hand in his. They were together again. They were one heart again.

The pilot slowed the helicopter. Tex eased Katie's picture out of his pack and placed it on his lap. Tenderly, he did the same with the urn that held her ashes. The pilot, looking the other way, did not see him close his eyes and whisper, "Good-bye, my darling. We'll always have the lake. We'll always have each other." He opened the side window, unthreaded the urn cap, reached outside, and spilled the ashes.

Below, Tex watched two polar bear cubs scampering with their mother. He hoped a few ashes would settle on their thick hair and they would carry a piece of Katie far into the wild north.

37

Oosterscheide Barrier
Oct. 17, 2016

LARS AND ZAVIA walked through the inner corridors of the barrier. They passed the massive concrete piers and the engine room that powered the hydraulic gates. Then, as he pushed open the door to the orientation workshop, Lars whispered, "Full house today."

Zavia walked in. She was distracted thinking about the Russian. But she loved to teach. And she was delighted to be asked to deliver a module on water again.

This was day three of a five-day program. Each day, the new employees and contractors visited two barriers, getting the bowels tour of everything from the control rooms to the storage rooms.

"Zavia is a hydrologist," Lars introduced her, "who was a Delta Works employee for six years."

Zavia looked out at the mechanical engineers, software engineers, welders, security personnel, and others. A few had white collars or cotton dresses. Most wore overalls and hard hats. Two men in the back row had kept their safety glasses on.

"She's also my niece, so applaud at the end. And she's an American, but don't hold that against her. Please welcome Dr. Zavia Jansen."

For the next ninety minutes, she told anecdotes, jokes, and horror stories about water. She gave them facts and pointed out fiction. She referenced everything from Noah's Ark and the Old Testament flood to the Australian myth about the huge frog that drank all the water and caused a drought. She talked about the death of her grandmother in the '53 flood within a discussion of the dynamics of surging water. Carrying the discussion to the present, she made links between the warming climate, dying coral reefs, depleted fishing industries, and the migration of young people to big cities.

Zavia glanced at the clock. Time to wrap this up. She noticed a civil engineer with her head down. "Something's on your mind, isn't it?"

"Oh, nothing." A tear perched on the edge of her eye. "I just get afraid the sea will win."

"Do other people think the same?"

A young security guard spoke up. "I think the opposite. I think the sea will die."

Behind the guard, a middle-aged accountant chimed in. "Oh, God, stop watching those enviro-horror movies."

Zavia stepped over to where they were sitting. She liked controversy. But it saddened her so deeply when people didn't see or care that living in an unstable climate was like flying in an unstable plane.

Out of the corner of her eye, she saw Lars charging toward the front of the room. "I'm sorry, Zavia. The control room tour starts in four minutes. Any final words?"

Zavia turned to the group. Most were stuffing computers into bags. The "goggle guys" were laughing. "Just congratulations on your new jobs. If the predicted floods happen, the Netherlands has a defense system as good as they come."

The people applauded politely and headed for the barrier control room. Ten minutes later, Lars drove Zavia to her train. "Thank you. You did a great job, as always."

"The last few minutes felt off. And who were those idiots in the back?"

At the station, they hugged and Lars left. Zavia boarded the train before checking her cell phone. She saw a slew of "unknown caller" messages. *Why don't they leave a message?* Then she put her head back on the seat.

Instead of drifting into sleep, she drifted into memory. She saw scenes from the film *Judgment at Nuremburg*, which she had watched in college. The soldiers' defense, "I was just carrying out orders," had riled her for weeks.

Years later, driving to work in New Orleans, she heard a retired vice admiral being interviewed on radio about the national security implications of a shifting climate. "Hard to imagine. Impossible to plan for."

The interviewer posed a question. "Fifty years from now, if the worst happens, old people, including you and me, will be living in shacks and growing most of our food. What do you think people will say when their grandkids ask them how they'd been so stupid?"

The vice admiral needed no time to answer. "We didn't know. That's the lie people always tell after predicted but unheeded disasters rip away their savings, their homes, their futures."

When Zavia had heard that response, she ran a red light and nearly hit a school bus. Her mind had been locked in on an idea. "We didn't know" was the civilian equivalent of "I was just following orders."

Now, as the train lurched forward, she heard echoes of "We didn't know" in the accountant's comment. She knew it wasn't "We didn't know anything" but rather "We didn't know how bad it would be."

The conductor took her ticket. "Thanks." Then she closed her eyes. She had just fallen asleep, when the cell phone rang. "Unknown Caller."

"Zavia Jansen." After listening to the thick Russian accent, her eyes popped wide open. "Well, yes, I am a little surprised. You're fast. Thank you."

"The contract will be waiting for you when you get home, Dr. Jansen. In the meantime, do you know an American named Tex Cassidy?"

Zavia gasped loudly. The man sitting in front of her turned to see if she was okay. "No, I don't know him." Both her jaw and her shoulders tightened. "What I mean is, I did, many years ago, though I did see him five years ago, and sometimes, I read what he writes."

38

Churchill, Manitoba
Oct. 18, 2016

AT 5:00 a.m., Tex bolted upright in bed. The room was dark. *Katie. What were you doing?*

Tex laid his head back onto the pillow. He relaxed his body as much as he could. He scanned his mind. Nothing. Then something. It was a feeling more than an image. Something large. *A large building. An airport. You're at an airport.*

Then, suddenly, he recalled another piece of the dream. And another. It came back to him. He saw it. He felt it. He clung to it like a child clinging to a teddy bear.

Katie, you're getting on a plane. By yourself. You're giving the ticket to the gate agent. I'm there, watching. You turn around. You're smiling at me. You're waving to me. I feel scared. I want to go with you. I can't move. The gate agent won't let me, anyway. Your eyes are so clear. You're so beautiful. I feel empty, alone. You say something. What is it? What is it?

"Time for me to go, Tex. Bye-bye. I love you." Then you smile. You turn. And you disappear down the jetway.

Tex lay in bed for twenty more minutes. Gradually, the dream faded. A shroud of pain inside him shifted a little, lifted a little.

Tex sat up. He rubbed his eyes so hard that his pupils hurt. *Katie . . .* He got up and took a long, hot shower. He felt lighter, as if more than dirt and sleep had washed off him.

39

Churchill, Manitoba
Oct. 18, 2016

6:08 a.m. *Less than two hours till the meeting.* Tex needed to clear his mind. That meant coffee.

Though it was still dark, he made his way down Kelsey Street. The dream fragment was still with him. But walking took concentration. The tail of a snowstorm whipped through Churchill. His eyes were like slits. The wind-driven snow stung them like paper cuts.

Finally, Tex stomped snow off his boots in the foyer of Gypsy's Café. Tex put his fur gloves in his pocket. But, still cold, he walked in with his parka hood up. He looked like the Abominable Snowman in search of breakfast.

The clerk at the Iceberg Inn had said, "It's like Rick's café in Casablanca. Everybody goes there." Indeed, it was the town hub. In the front of the store, tables were reserved for the van, bus, and dogsled drivers, who traded road information and tourist jokes.

Tex went up to the counter. He breathed in the smells. *A Parisian bakery just south of the Arctic Circle.* Espresso drinks. Croissants. Fancy egg dishes. "Large coffee and an almond croissant, please."

Tex waited while the young woman got his order. He leaned over, almost drooling at the pastries.

"Have you seen this man?" Behind Tex, a man with a thick accent asked one of the drivers.

"Wasn't on my tour."

"How about you? Does he look familiar?"

Tex half-turned and saw the man holding a picture of him.

"Yeah, I saw him yesterday, wandering around with a pack." Another tour guide, was chirpy helpful. "Who is he? Some movie star?" The drivers all laughed. Most hadn't seen a movie in years.

"So he's here. You're sure?"

Tex paid for his food. Then he turned and said, "I'm sure." He put his hand on the man's shoulder. It felt like an ox's shoulder. Tex felt a strap under the man's wool sport coat. "Who wants to know?"

"Mr. Cassidy . . ." Tex turned toward the sound. It came from a Slavic-looking man at a nearby table. He was wider than his chair. "Will you join me?"

Tex walked over. He passed two other bodyguards with straps under their sport coats. "Dimitri Bakov." He stuck out a fleshy hand for Tex to shake as he sat down. "Was that strange? Must have been, seeing your photo passed around. I apologize. But you weren't on the commercial flights. And I wanted to know if you'd arrived in lovely Churchill."

Tex sipped his coffee. Alex had described Bakov as "smarter than he looks." But chatty? Traveling with bodyguards?

"I understand, Mr. Bakov. Thank you for meeting me." His almond croissant tasted better than this first encounter. "I look forward to talking with you in an hour."

"Perhaps we can begin now. And end earlier. I'm meeting the mayor for lunch."

"Of course, if it will help you. So tell me: how do you know Alex?'

The Russian laughed. "Twenty-five years ago, he was the chief financial officer of a large multinational, if you can believe that."

Tex could. Easily. "And you did business together?"

Bakov laughed harder. "We called it 'meals and deals.' A lovely dinner at a five-star restaurant. By dessert, terms and conditions we could both live with."

"And you became friends?" Tex probed, gauging how much Bakov might reveal later that morning.

"A bit. I was glad to help when he was in trouble." Tex didn't know what the Russian was referring to. "You can Google Alex and read about his addiction. It was a long time ago. He owed a few dollars. I helped my friend, just as you're helping your friend, the president."

Tex wrapped up the rest of his croissant and put it into his pocket. "That was very generous of you." He stood up to leave. *And smart.*

"We send Christmas cards and do favors for each other. Like today, with you. I'm at your service. Ask anything you like. Except my weight and my net worth; the two things most people seem to care about."

Tex stepped out into the cold morning. He headed back down Kelsey Street. *Of all the stories he could have told me, why that one?* It was light outside. Vans were warming up. Tourists were waking up. Tex headed toward the Iceberg Inn with his coffee, the rest of his croissant and, finally, a strategy for his meeting with the Russian.

40

Murmansk, Russia
Oct. 18, 2016

ACROSS THE ARCTIC BRIDGE in downtown Murmansk, Ivan Fyodorokov walked slowly along the busy streets. He got winded easily and rested often. Before, he rarely looked at the buildings, shops, parks, and people. These days, the eyes of a dying man looked a good deal more closely.

It was lunchtime. The streets were crowded. People ate, shopped, and chatted incessantly about the new Russia and the new Murmansk.

Many people actually had hope. Several times, Fyodorokov had sat in a restaurant and heard people talk. "I don't trust it," a man with a carpenter's belt around his waist and a Northern Russia Shipping Company cap had told his friend. "This is still Russia. And this is Murmansk, not Moscow. But I can't remember shorter winters. Even better, I'm making money."

Others looked through a different lens. History was bearing bitter fruit, especially one that Fyodorokov himself had eaten. Across Russia, the cancer rates were higher than in the Soviet area, and Murmansk had one of the highest rates of all. As Fyodorokov entered the Murmansk Medical Center and rode the elevator, perhaps he more than anyone else understood the parallels between cancer and climate change: both took a long time to develop, both were painless until the symptoms broke out, and if unchecked, both would devastate its host, be it person or planet.

The cancer ward waiting room was crammed. He knew half the people by sight, since they were on the same chemo schedule he was. "Please have a seat," the receptionist said, as Fyodorokov signed in. Fifteen minutes later, he was in the treatment room. Afterward, passing through the waiting room, he noticed a woman whose shoulders shook and lips quivered. *I know her. Who is she?*

Fyodorokov headed for the elevator. The doors opened, but he didn't get in. Instead, he went back. He stood over the woman, who was removing hair that had fallen out and landed on her blouse. She didn't look up, until she heard him ask, "Weren't you the director at Shkval?"

The woman looked up. She recognized Fyodorokov and put her head right back down without a word. A moment later, her name was called. She brushed by the researcher, and he took her seat.

"May I talk with you?" Fyodorokov asked, when she returned from treatment.

"No." She put on her scarf and headed toward the door.

Fyodorokov stepped in front of her. "Please, I have to know something. Just between us. I promise. Do you drink tea? Let me buy you a cup."

She was tired, and she felt sick. But she heard the warmth in his voice. She knew that he was also sick. And she was a private person, not a cruel one. "For a few minutes."

They sat on metal folding chairs in the hospital cafeteria. Neither felt well. "I know you were led out of Shkval." Ivan shared his pastry with her. "You were forced out of your position. I think I know why. But could you tell me why you think it happened?"

In the back of the cafeteria, two hospital workers argued loudly. Fyodorokov turned. In that moment, the project director raised her weak arm. She threw the pastry right at Ivan and headed out of the room.

Startled, he went after her. She walked faster. Breathing hard, he kept pace. The elevator she got into was crowded. He jammed the doors with his arm, forced them open, and backed himself in.

On the ground floor, she pushed him aside and walked outside onto the crowded street. Fyodorokov made himself run a little. With his last step, he grabbed her arm, nearly doubling over, exhausted. "The nuclear power plant . . ." He struggled to catch his breath. "The safety checks. You were behind schedule, weren't you?"

She pushed his arm away and shrugged. "There's no treatment for political stupidity."

Fyodorokov raised up enough to look at her. "Please, there may be something I can do."

Has the chemo affected his mind? Nearby, three shoppers approached, chattering loudly. The project director grabbed Fyodorokov's hair and pulled his ear close to her mouth. "When it came to safety, we were never on schedule, and never would have been." Then she stepped into the crowd and was swallowed up by it.

Fyodorokov got into a cab. He looked out the window. On a government building, he saw a Russian flag. For the first time, he turned his eyes away. *Can I really do this?*

41

Churchill, Manitoba
Oct. 18, 2016

AT 7:58 a.m., Tex shivered his way toward the tundra buggy launch platform. At the bottom step, he grabbed the railing to navigate the icy steps. He looked up at the partly cloudy sky. He felt partly cloudy.

On the one hand, he was clear about why the Russians wanted shipping routes across the Arctic. It was like the Dutch developing transatlantic shipping routes five hundred years ago. The competitive edge was huge, maybe a game changer. Maybe a military edge as well.

But did the Russians have a plan? If so, how well developed? What did it include? How broad were the goals? How far along was it? To help Charley, these were a few of the areas he needed to probe.

Now, crossing the platform, Tex saw the white buggies, up close. *They're like extra-wide school buses, for God's sake.* He stopped for a minute and looked down at the five-foot-high tires.

Walking inside one of them, he saw the uncomfortable seats, a heating stove, and a pit toilet. He noticed that, for photographers, all the windows slid halfway down and there was a viewing platform out back.

"Hi, good morning." The driver was very cheerful and very curious. This was her "Christmas season" for making money. The longer the bears were around for the tourists to see, the more she made. But in six years, she had never had a gig like this. *Two passengers. No cameras. Just drive around. Don't bother pointing out bears. Weird.*

"Good morning again, Mr. Cassidy." Wearing a business suit, an expensive overcoat, and a fur hat, Dimitri Bakov entered the buggy. Alone.

"Good morning." Tex settled into the very last seat. He scanned the platform and saw the ox-man in another buggy.

The Russian took the seat in front and folded his big arms across his chest. He had followed Tex's eyes. "I hope you're not worried. He's a bit of a cannibal," Bakov chuckled, "but he's very discriminating as to who he eats." Tex didn't laugh. "Pardon my humor. Alex will tell you it can be inappropriate. Now, he said you wanted to know about sea routes across the North Pole, what we call the Arctic Bridge. But he didn't say why."

"Actually, Mr. Bakov, it's President Breen. He wants to know the future of shipping."

"Why?" The Russian shrugged. "In a few weeks, it could be someone else's problem."

Tex checked to see if the Russian had a holster bulge. *Probably not. Coat's too thick . . .* "If I may be blunt: the president's opponent is Governor Wilton. To him, global warming's a plot."

Bakov chuckled again. "He seems to think that gravity and the laws of physics don't apply to the United States." These days, the suitability of Governor Wilton for Russia's purposes was one of the few topics the whole Centennial Committee agreed on.

"So the president wants to exploit his differences with the governor. Plus, if the president wins, Russia wins."

"Really?" Bakov arched his eyebrows. "How so?"

"We saw the press conference. Russia could lose a lot of coastline. Your prime minister is worried. If you help the president frame this issue, he'll help Russia protect those coastlines." The Russian broke out into a long, loud chuckle. "Is that funny, Mr. Bakov?"

"Please . . . the United States has many traits that Russia envies. But protecting its citizens from the changing climate?" Bakov tapped his window. He expected that Cassidy would have a different motivation than gathering information. But he hadn't expected this motivation. "Nevertheless, Mr. Cassidy, I'm honored. How often can a Russian citizen assist an American president? So, ask me your framing questions."

"Thank you, sir." Tex put his hands on the metal handrail above the back of Bakov's seat. "In ten years, there won't be any sea ice in the Arctic. First time in seven hundred thousand years. Russia knows that, I assume."

"Of course. American leaders don't?"

Tex didn't take the bait. "So you're building a Murmansk-to-Churchill shipping route over the North Pole to capitalize on the open waters."

"Mr. Cassidy, if an earthquake cuts a road through a mountain, only a fool would not use it. Why is it different if the changing climate cuts a route through the Arctic?" Bakov shifted position. "Your shipping companies: today, if they trade between Europe and East Asia, they use the Suez Canal. Imagine if they went across the Pole and chopped 50 percent off their travel time."

"And your company is preparing to take advantage of those time savings?"

"We prepared years ago. We're already saving time. And by the way, we're also saving money and greenhouse gasses."

"So your plan is well along."

Bakov saw three bears outside his window, standing on their hind legs. He tapped the window with his fingers, teasing them. "Compared to your country, yes, it's well along."

Tex glanced over at the bears. He saw ox-man's buggy just ten yards behind. "So, if I might test an idea on you, the president could point to Russia's leadership in Arctic shipping. He could frame it as a great danger to American interests. And he could point out Governor Wilton's total failure to recognize that danger."

"I suppose," Bakov scoffed. "But aren't Americans bored with making Russia the enemy? That's so twentieth century. Why us when you've got your War on Terror?" He made faces at the bears. "Besides, do Americans really care about shipping routes?" The more he talked, the more he stared at Tex for clues.

Tex nodded his head in agreement. "But what if the president used Russia and shipping just to get people's attention? But then he brought out the real boogeyman? The one that would get Americans to wet their pants?"

Bakov looked puzzled.

"Oil and gas."

Bakov glared at Tex. "Is that why I came to Churchill early? Because your president wants to know about oil? Energy is not my area. Perhaps we should just enjoy the bears." *What's he after? What's he know? Not that it matters with Operation Noah.* A moment later, Bakov's jowls bounced around in laughter. "He's worried, isn't he?"

Tex leaned forward again. "Look, Mr. Bakov. The president could get a lot of mileage out of this. You can hear him, can't you? He matter-of-factly describes Russia's claims to the oil and gas. Then he speaks faster, louder, more intensely: 'Russia's drilling in the Arctic will devastate America and destroy the Arctic.' And finally, he sticks the dagger into Wilton by accusing him of being blind to the Russian threat and deaf to the voices calling for America to do something about the threat."

Up front, the driver maneuvered the tundra buggy through a foot-deep rut. The buggy lurched as if it had missed a few stairs. Tex and Bakov each saw the launch platform only half a mile away. "If Americans are that gullible . . ."

"Is there anything the president could add to that story?"

Bakov arched his eyebrows as if to say, "Like what?"

Tex leaned forward again. "Like Russia building a nuclear power plant to run the rigs."

Bakov froze in his seat. His whole body stiffened. *How does he know that?* Then he burst forward and grabbed Tex's head between his hands, as if he were going to smash his head into the metal handrail. "Is this why Alex arranged this meeting? I'm afraid he won't get a Christmas card this year."

"Let go of my head."

"What else is inside your head?"

They were a few hundred feet from the buggy platform. Tex's skull was ten inches from a bar that could crack it open. "Speaking of nuclear, does Pakistan belong in the same sentence as Russia?"

Bakov's right hand shifted from the side of Tex's head to the back. He pulled Tex's head down. It landed hard against Bakov's left hand that he had slipped over the metal bar. Then he let Tex go. Tex looked up. Bakov was watching the ox-man's buggy pull into the platform alongside theirs.

The driver set the parking brake. The Russian stood. He reached quickly inside his coat pocket. Adrenaline shot through Tex. He dove onto the seat across the aisle. The Russian looked at him, rolled his eyes, and laughed out loud. He then handed Tex a business card. "If you want to talk more, contact me. Please give my best to Alex."

Tex got up. *What the hell.* He stood eye-to-eye with the Russian. He zipped up his parka. "If the sea ice melts, Russia's coastlines will be under water. So will a lot of people. Is that really why you hired Zavia Jansen?"

"You should be precise, Mr. Cassidy. If the sea ice melts, the sea levels won't rise. Think of ice cubes melting in a glass of vodka. Now, fresh-water glaciers... they're another story, aren't they? And Dr. Jansen, she's yet another story, isn't she?"

Bakov walked to the front. Tex followed. They thanked the driver and shook hands. "I wish you luck, Mr. Cassidy. Where else will you visit?"

Tex walked down the platform stairs with Bakov. "Unfortunately, no place as cosmopolitan as Churchill."

Tex had the cabbie drive to the airport faster than he should have. Once onboard the plane, he got Lynn. "Here's what I need." He spelled it out. "In half an hour." Then he went into a private area of the plane and made a secure call. "It's worse than I thought, Charley. They've thought this thing through." Tex summarized the conversation with Bakov.

"That's what I was afraid of. Thanks, Tex, I'm racing. Are we done?"

He hesitated. "Almost. Years ago, Alex dug a hole for himself at the tables. How deep was it?"

"Enough to bury himself. Why?"

"Probably no reason. But you know me: no dot's too small..."

Bakov, meanwhile, took a cab into town. Before his meeting with the mayor, he stopped off at his hotel to make a secure call. "I just left the American. He's fishing, that's all." He listened for a few moments. "Good night, Admiral."

42

Illulisat, Greenland
Oct. 18, 2016

TEX STEPPED carefully into the motorboat. The wood was rotting, and the engine leaked. The boat seemed older than its driver, a sullen man with a full beard and a large belly. He looked like Father Christmas.

Illulisat was about 40 percent up the west coast of Greenland and way the hell up above the Arctic Circle. It was also just north of the Illulisat Icefjord, the largest outlet whereby calving glaciers and melting ice on the Greenland Ice Sheet reached the sea.

Sitting down, Tex scanned the town of five thousand people, mostly Inuit and some Danes. For every person, there was at least one sled dog. There was not a collie or a lab in sight or out of sight. In fact, this far north, it was against the law to have any dog other than a sled dog. And if a sled dog got around another breed, both dogs were put down.

As they moved away from shore, Tex glanced over at some fishermen and dock workers. Nearby, he saw workers at the fish processing plant and almost had to cover his nose from the smell. He even saw a few tourists on hotel decks, mesmerized by the icebergs parading by.

All seemed clear. And Tex felt very clear about his purpose for this phase of the mission.

Initially, it was to get information from Mickey Logan, the videographer, about links between the world's melting glaciers and the world's fragile economies.

Now, especially after the conversation with Bakov, he was no longer doing a favor for the president. He shared Charley's gut instincts: the Russians were playing in the shadows. But what game? Why? And to what end?

That was why he needed Mickey to do what Mickey wouldn't want to do.

As the driver gunned the engine, they rounded a medium-sized iceberg. Tex squinted. The afternoon sun glinting off the berg hurt his eyes. Then, seventy yards away, Tex saw the SS *Pilgrim*. Lynn had told him that, with the sea ice disappearing, tourist ships had formed a new "see-the-glaciers-while-they're-still-here" industry. With eighty passengers, the *Pilgrim* was one of them. It was heading north up the Baffin Sea, just west of Greenland. Eventually, it would reach the US Thule Air Force Base a few hundred miles away. Just a few years ago, this trip at this time of year would have been suicide.

Tex eyed the deck where people crowded the railings. Some gazed at the barren, coastal hills. Many took snapshots of the icebergs in the harbor or the brightly painted A-frames on land.

What he didn't see was someone in a below-deck stateroom taking rapid-fire snapshots of him.

Nor did he see Mariah.

Now, twenty yards away, Tex overheard an elderly Italian woman. "It's like an iceberg garden, every shape, every size," she gushed at the hundreds of them floating by. Indeed, they were like three-dimensional clouds. Often dripping, they periodically broke apart or rolled over. Sometimes, you could see dirty streaks on them, where they had done a somersault, hit bottom, and righted themselves in a different position.

He also heard an American, who crossed himself and said to no one in particular: "Mother of God! Look at the size of that one!"

Tex turned his head. *The man's right.* The iceberg looked like a small white mountain range floating between the mainland and the long, narrow Disko Island, a few dozen miles to the west. It had peaks and valleys, and long, winding streaks of bright blue, where melting water had frozen in a small crevasse.

He also knew from Lynn, that, like the many hundreds of others along this section of coast, the iceberg had crossed over the huge underwater moraine of rocks and dirt and sand at the mouth of the ice fjord. According to scientists, it was likely that the iceberg that sunk the Titanic had come from this ice fjord.

Behind the moraine, bergs were trapped because they were up to 90 percent underwater And they banged up against the moraine. As a result, on the surface, they were packed in and jammed up. Indeed, Tex had seen the ice fjord when flying in on the military jet. They were like rush-hour cars kissing bumpers on a freeway. Ultimately, there were only two ways over the moraine. First, to be forced over the edge by the pressure of the ice backed up for thirty-five kilometers. Or, second, to melt enough so they could float over the moraine.

Finally, the motor boat pulled up next to the *Pilgrim*. Tex clambered aboard. He greeted the first officer. Then he spotted her.

Mariah ran down the deck, dodging passengers and deck chairs. She was laughing and crying at the same time. She ran right into her godfather's outstretched arms. "God, I missed you!"

Mariah stepped back. She looked him up and down. "If Dad had let me, I'd have gone to Colombia to see you."

Tex looked her up and down. She had transformed: the college girl was now a young woman. *You've got your mother's eyes. Her hair. Who are those people watching you?*

"Can we go inside?" Mariah didn't like people looking at her. Like most presidential kids, she was a ghost to the American public. Of the twenty-odd Americans onboard, none had a clue that the pretty lady who kept to herself was the First Daughter. But that could change on a dime. And would.

"Anywhere you want, honey. But I need an hour. To shower and find myself. Can I have it?"

"Of course." She looked at her watch. "Let's meet at four-thirty. The presentation's at five. Then we can talk over dinner."

Tex started to walk away. He turned. "Mariah," he whispered to her, pulling her to the rail so the wind would cover his words. "That couple over there. One of them is always watching you."

"They're supposed to, Uncle Tex. They're my protection unit," she whispered back.

Relieved, Tex nearly bumped into the gushy Italian, as he ran too fast down the stairs to his stateroom. Finally alone, he stretched out on the bed.

Tex closed his eyes. He had to. He was trying to manage the sensation of being pulled in two different directions by wild horses.

The first was his "Ben Gunn" nature. Katie used to call him a hoodless monk. For him, solitude was right up there with air and water. The Minnesota lakefront wasn't just a lake: it was a deep, deep spring that fed him. So was his alone time with Katie. So was the simplicity of Carlos's farm. And so was the quietude of the Churchill tundra and Hudson Bay, one of the few areas in the world where—like a classical Japanese or Chinese painting—the human presence was relegated to a few small strokes amid the water or trees or mountains.

Mariah knew Tex's loner part and loved it. He took her to the top of mountains. He introduced her to wilderness parks. He gave her Thomas Merton books to read. On her sixteenth birthday, he took her out for a three-day silent, fasting retreat in the desert.

But Mariah also knew the second wild horse: Tex's schizo relationship with the world.

Sometimes, he would come to visit. Two in the morning, Tex would be snoring with a government manual or an economic report floating up and down on his chest. Then, he would wake up at six, gulp coffee, and research the interconnections that he suspected.

On the other hand, mention most political campaigns or foreign policy or anything else that smacked of the world, and he would groan. "People . . ." Usually, he would stop there. Sometimes, when someone was bitching about how they were treated by a hotel clerk or a boss, he would ask in his most serious, archaeological voice, "Were they human?"

What Mariah didn't know was that place in his mind where the two wild horses ate oats out of the same bag. How could she? She was twenty-six, for God's sake. And so she didn't really understand that, for her godfather, that place was connecting dots and making connections.

Making connections demanded stretches of quiet time. Time to widen the lens and see much more of the connective tissue between what companies say, nations do, and the degree to which people either succeed or suffer from unintended consequences.

Now, with his eyes closed, Tex struggled to connect the dots on this mission for Mariah's father.

After thirty minutes, nothing. He got up and showered quickly. *We import more oil than ever. We're running out of Alaskan oil. We're screwed sometime soon. That's clear.*

Then he put on the one Western shirt he had brought, his old jeans, and the cowboy boots he would trade in for hiking boots tomorrow. *The Arctic is melting. The Russians are building shipping lanes. That's clear, too.*

Going up to meet Mariah, he took the stairs two at at a time. *What was Bakov hiding? What am I missing? Why are the Russians hiring Zavia Jansen, and what the hell is the Centennial Committee really about?*

He walked into the Happy Hour lounge, where the passengers were schmoozing, boozing, and looking at each other's photos. They were happy and getting happier. Jokes were flying. A few couples were dancing. Invitations to stay at someone's house in Vancouver or Dublin or Istanbul were being passed around like a platter of cheese. *Mariah, where are you? Mickey Logan, how do I convince you?*

Now, Tex was arguably the world's worst at small talk. He would rather go to a tax audit than a cocktail party. Typically, he would find a good strong wall and lean against it. Using the same MO here, he found a great spot near a floor lamp. Until Mariah showed up, he could be all alone with a soft drink in one hand and a small party plate of food in the other.

"What do you think?" An attractive woman in her mid-thirties slipped in between Tex and the lamp. She aimed her sky-blue eyes at the meatballs. "Think they were flown in?" Her voice was light. Her gaze was direct. She was the only woman wearing a dress.

Oh, God, here we go. "Given that they're soggy, 'floated in' might be more accurate."

"Bernice Johnson, environmental sciences instructor at the University of Stockholm." She stuck out her hand and spoke in a voice that wasn't obviously Swedish. "And you're . . . ?" There was a tinge of familiarity in her voice, as if she knew him. Or knew of him.

"Tex Cassidy." He shook her hand. "Researcher. From the US." Her arms and legs were sculpted, more like an acrobat's than an academic's.

Bernice's face contorted into something midway between a smile and laugh. "Tex Cassidy. Are you a cowboy?" In the background, the band ended one tune and began another, slower one.

"Half a cowboy. I can ride and shoot."

"Can you dance?"

He shook his head.

"Good, I don't either." Then she took him by the hand, led him onto the dance floor, and put his hands in dance position.

"Listen, Bernice . . ." Tex felt weirder than weird. He hadn't put his arm around a woman in a very long time. "My goddaughter, she'll be here any minute."

Before he could pull away, she started them moving around the floor. "Tell me about your research, half-cowboy."

"You don't want to know." She did. "Arctic shipping routes." He looked around. People were staring at them. No Mariah.

"Really?" She smiled, leaning back a little to see his face. "You must be talking with the Russians."

An alarm went off. "Why do you ask?"

Bernice stopped dancing. "Maybe you can help me." She took him by the hand to a quiet corner of the lounge. "Ever owned antique porcelain plates?"

"My wife did."

"Then you know. They're extremely fragile, a lot like the Arctic."

Tex stared at her. *Who are you? What do you want?* "So's the whole planet."

"Yes, but the Arctic's like one of your wife's plates with a hairline crack. That's why—" Suddenly, the *Pilgrim* lurched. Then lurched again. People stumbled. Bernice was one of them. A few fell down. A couple glasses were knocked off a table and broke on the floor.

"Ladies and gentlemen," a calm, authoritative voice came over the ship's intercom, "this is the captain. That was a just a moderate-sized iceberg that broke apart nearby. Happens all the time. Nothing to worry about."

"To finish my thought," Bernice continued, regaining her balance, "I'm here to study the Arctic."

Tex snuck another glance. Still no Mariah. But at least the conversation had some juice. "What specifically?" He didn't know whether to believe her.

"Comings and goings. These days, the Arctic's like an airport. Animals, fish, plants, leaving all the time. New ones coming in. Another decade or two, it'll be night and day from now. So I'm trying to gauge what that'll do to the Arctic and what the Arctic will do to the rest of the world."

"Leaving, as in dying off, like the polar bear?"

"Or migrating. But, yes, like the polar bear. By the way, if you want my hunch, it's the killer whale that'll take the polar bear's place as the dominant species up here. Not nearly as cute. But with all the open water up here now, they're moving in."

"So why are you only hunching?"

"Oh, it's a longish story," she said. "Tell me about the Russians. Who did you talk to? What did you ask? What did they say?" She lowered her voice. "They're doing something up here. And, to make a bad joke, they're like a bull in a porcelain shop. I'm worried."

"Well, tell me what you . . ." At that moment, a cell phone in her dress pocket went off. "Want to get that?"

Bernice shook her head. "It's just my brother. I know his ring. You were saying about the Russians . . ."

Tex relented. "They're moving in like the killer whales and taking advantage of the open seas. That's all." At that moment, Tex saw the female Secret Service agent coming toward him.

"Excuse me," she said to both of them. "This is for you, Mr. Cassidy." Tex opened the note from Mariah, as the agent walked away. "Talking to Dad. Will be a little late."

"Sorry for that. My goddaughter's delayed. So, now, that longish story. I've got time."

Bernice also relented. He wasn't going to talk. "Here's the short version. The whales are coming, but up to 40 percent of the plankton's disappearing. So will they survive up here? Who knows?"

Tex was intrigued. Plankton made up the bottom of the food chain. If they were disappearing, it would be like the first floor of the Sears Tower in Chicago falling away. "Why are they disappearing?" He started running the economic downstream consequences in his head.

"You know, I should call my brother." Bernice started to get up. Behind her, Tex saw Mariah entering across the room and looking for him.

"Sure, but give me the ten-second version."

She ran her hand through her hair. "They don't do well in warmer water. So, when the ice melts and the water temp goes up, their numbers go down."

As Bernice turned to leave, Mariah reached them. She looked so happy. She wore a purple silk blouse and a pair of brand-new jeans, along with her hiking boots. "I'm so sorry, Uncle Tex. When Dad gets going . .

."

Mariah stopped. "Mariah, this is Bernice Johnson. Bernice . . . my goddaughter, Mariah." He deliberately avoided her last name.

"Nice to meet you, Mariah. What a beautiful name. Unusual." She looked very closely at her. "Your godfather's a very interesting man." She then pivoted and made her way quickly across the dance floor and out into the hallway.

"A new friend . . . ?" This was thin ice. But they had always been able to walk gingerly through thinly iced areas.

"Uh-uh. We started with meatballs and ended with why declining plankton levels may keep killer whales out of the Arctic. Hardly Romeo and Juliet."

"Sometimes, it's not the words, but the music under the words." She laughed. She really missed Katie. But she knew how much Tex loved women and needed to be with one. "By the way, she's got the question wrong. Killer whales eat meat, not plankton." In college, Mariah had had a yearlong course on whales.

"You're sure?" She nodded. Another alarm sounded. He looked across the room and saw Bernice in the hall on her phone.

"Oh, honey. I've missed you. Fill me in. How are you? What are you doing these days? Are you in love?"

At that moment, Mariah saw a long-haired man in his late thirties entering. He walked with a purpose. He greeted a few people. The chandelier light reflected off the stud in his left ear.

"Mickey Logan?" Tex asked.

"Whoever he is, he's cute." She loved teasing her godfather.

"Mariah, we're here for the message, not the messenger." He didn't tell her about his other purpose. She would find out soon enough. And she wouldn't like it.

43

Fairfax County, Virginia
Oct. 18, 2016

GENERAL MASON rarely worked at home. Today, he needed to.

He ran four miles on the treadmill. He emptied the French press coffeemaker and filled up an ashtray. But the white board in his office was as blank as his mind. The events around this Pakistan detonation remained as opaque as a lead shield.

Finally, dressed in a dark-green work shirt and jeans, the general pushed the screen door open and walked onto the porch. He put one foot on the railing and looked out at his three-point-three-acre wooded parcel. *Hell, it's worth a try. Desperate times call for desperate measures.* He went into a large metal storage shed and came out with a hunting bow and two arrows. Then he posted a paper target on a raised hay bale.

His friends called him General Bowhunt. Turkey . . . elk . . . he loved crawling through brush to get a clear shot. It was fun. He ate what he killed. Sometimes, like now, target practice was a source of insight.

The general paced off thirty yards. He raised the bow and aimed. First shot: bull's-eye. Second shot: bull's-eye. He pulled both arrows out, laid one on the ground and broke the other in half across a large field rock. *Damn! Could that be?*

Ninety minutes later, General Mason put his feet up on his White House desk. He stared at both the good arrow and the two halves of the broken one. Dave Dunn came into the spacious office in the northwest corner of the West Wing. "What's up, General?"

"Two things; first, this Pakistan detonation is no broken arrow." He held up the broken arrow pieces. In military terms, a "broken arrow" designated nuclear accidents that didn't lead to nuclear destruction. "But, terrain-wise, doesn't Pakistan smack of that 'broken arrow' in Greenland? You were there. Tell me what happened."

"Jesus, General, I can't remember breakfast." With that disclaimer, he remembered one of the most formative experiences of his life when, as a junior member of the investigation team, he got his nose way deep in the shit that had come down.

It was in 1968. The Cold War was sub-zero. Every day, B52s flew out of Thule Air Force Base with nuclear and conventional weapons. If the Russians even looked at their ICBM triggers, the bombers would turn Moscow and St. Petersburg into Armageddon.

"But what was the broken arrow? Wasn't there a fire on a plane with A-bombs?"

"Hydrogen bombs." Dave held up four fingers. "Some retard put cushions on a heater. They caught fire. And the plane crashed."

"But the bombs didn't blow."

"The conventional ones did. Plus . . ." Suddenly, Dave got what the general was saying. ". . . the jet fuel exploded. A quarter million pounds of it. And it melted a glacier down to water level."

"Okay, then here's the second thing. Imagine you're some lunatic. You get a hard-on thinking about a nuclear blowout between India and Pakistan. Where would you set off a bomb to get the war going?"

"Calcutta. Bombay. Islamabad."

"You wouldn't haul a snuke up some glacier?"

Dave jumped to his feet. "Nobody would. So there's got . . ."

Suddenly, there was a muted ring. It was from a dedicated phone on the general's desk. Dave headed for the door. "Twenty bucks," the general raced his words, "says it's tied to that Greenland weirdness."

"I'll watch the tape again." As Dave closed the door, he heard, "Mr. President, what can I do for you?"

44

Illulisat
Oct. 18, 2016

TEX WAS TORN. He and Mariah hadn't really talked.

Passengers had drifted toward the seats the crew had set up. And Mickey Logan, with a Rasputin look in his eye, already had his title slide up: "Greenland Ice Cap: A World in Transition."

Alex Sullivan had confirmed his willingness to talk with Tex. But would he do more?

"Thanks for coming on this trip, folks," Mickey began, strolling between the circular tables. "We'll get lots of great photos. But I'm also hoping you'll be ambassadors for the glaciers. After all, if they disappear, many of us will, too."

Tex looked around. Jaws were dropping. *Thirty seconds in, and the guy is shoving reality down our throats.*

For the next ten minutes, Mickey bombarded the passengers. "This is Kilimanjaro twenty years ago. Here it is now. How many of you have been to Alaska? If you were there in '84, this is what the Columbia Glacier looked like. Now, it looks like it spent a few years under a heat blanket."

Tex watched the crowd. It was as if the chairs were wired, and someone was turning up the voltage. People squirmed this way and that way, as Mickey showed them how Peru was running out of glacial water, Tibet was looking very un-Tibet-like, and the US Department of the Interior was going to change the name of Glacier National Park in Montana or look profoundly stupid.

During all of this, Bernice Johnson was paying attention, even more so when Mickey clanged his digital cymbals together for his climactic final sequence: a series of photos of the Greenland Ice Sheet.

"Here we are, folks," he said, showing an old 2010 National Geographic cover that said "Greenland—Ground Zero for Climate Change."

"If it was true then, it's super true now."

For the next five minutes, Brother Mickey gave his flock a visual tour of climate hell: roaring rivers of meltwater flowing down ever-widening crevasses; whole meltwater lakes that disappeared down moulins in a matter of minutes; illustrations that showed how surface water eventually reached the very base of the Ice Sheet, where, through "hydraulic jacking," it forced the Ice Sheet to bulge, to crack, and, at lightning speed for a glacier, to move toward the sea.

Mickey sucked the air out of the room. Then he sucked out more. "We've planted time-lapse cameras out on the Ice Sheet. They take a photo every hour of sunlight. We just got the computer chip from one of the cameras. Let me show you what our own eyes can't see."

For two minutes, people saw mountains of ice breaking free from the Ice Sheet and moving down the thirty-five-kilometer ice fjord. Like all time-lapse photos, it was herky-jerky. If Nature were a reality TV show, this would win an award.

Finally, Mickey backed off. But just for a moment. "Now, why are they disappearing? Because we ship things from East Jesus to West Texas?" A white-haired German couple got up and left. "Because we go to work and leave three lights on?" So did a family of eight from Turkey. "Because we cut down Indonesian rain forests to grow palm oil so we feel better about what's in our dishwashing soap? Yes, yes, and yes, but it's mostly because we're stupid." Tex counted six other couples or families who headed for the exits, complaining out loud and bumping into tables.

Mickey glanced at them. But his sugar-coating days were long gone. "Think about it," Mickey held up a cup from a table near him. "We've turned the atmosphere into the world's biggest sink. We dump greenhouse gasses into it like they were one of these."

By now, a quarter of the passengers had gone. Finally, the dam burst apart for an American. "You bastard! You've got no right to scare my family like that." Built like a lumberjack, the man walked right up into Mickey's face and then got closer.

You could almost hear the rats running around the ship's hold. "Scare people? I'm trying to wake them up."

The man tightened his fists. Mickey stepped back. The man stepped forward. "You flew here, right? You put jet fuel into the clouds, right? But you're getting your paycheck for lecturing, so it's okay, right?"

Mickey flared back. "Name one thing I said that isn't true."

"It's what you didn't say." He jabbed a finger into Mickey's chest. "How about all the fossil fuel it takes to make the concrete that holds up your precious windmills?" He jabbed Mickey again. "Or to extract the lithium for the batteries in your precious hybrids?" He jabbed Mickey a third time. Tex moved to the edge of his seat. This was getting out of control. And he couldn't afford for Mickey to get hurt.

Suddenly, an Irish schoolteacher yelled, "Hey, enough. Sit down. We want to hear Mickey, not you."

The American scowled. Years of being pissed off by righteous environmentalists came pouring out. "I don't hear an ounce of compassion for people who feed their families planting those palm crops." Mickey started to speak, but no words came out. "Or who send their kids to college working on tankers that ship the palm oil. Or pay doctor bills by making the containers that hold the palm oil." Out of the corner of his eye, the man saw three thick-armed crewmembers heading toward him. He spat in Mickey's face. Then he turned and signaled his wife. Together, they marched out into the hallway.

The room was stone silent. Mariah handed Mickey a napkin. He wiped off the spit.

"Tell us about your project," she said.

"Another time." He started to walk away. He got halfway down the aisle, when the Irish schoolteacher called out again. "The Pakistan glacier? What do you think about what happened?"

Mickey stopped. He was between Tex's table and Bernice's table. "It makes me ashamed of my species."

An accountant from Syracuse popped up from his chair. "Mickey, any comment on Breen's speech in Miami?"

"I was there. It made me ashamed of my government. I understand we're ten days from the election. But ten months ago? He was just as gutless."

In the back of the room, the chief steward gave Mickey the "cut" sign. "Dinner's in half an hour," Mickey said. "Thanks for coming. If you want to talk, I'll hang out for a few minutes."

Sitting in silence, Tex and Mariah tapped their fingers on the table, as an Aussie reporter double-checked facts; as Bernice Johnson oohed and aahed about Mickey's dedication and upcoming plans; and as the Syracuse accountant told Mickey his own opinions about President Breen. Finally, they all left. Tex walked up to Mickey. "Alex Sullivan called you. I'm the president's special assistant. Do you know who this is?"

Mickey stared at Mariah. *Oh, Christ!* "If you are who I think you are, I apologize if I offended you. Your father's a good man. I just wish he did more." On the table, he saw a notebook with papers in it. Behind Mariah, he saw Bernice walking back down the aisle.

Mariah whispered for effect, "So do I."

Tex put his hand on Mickey's shoulder. "Help me help the president. Take me with you to the Ice Sheet tomorrow."

Mariah's jaw nearly hit her knee. "He means take us."

"Excuse me. Forgot this." Bernice took the notebook and headed back. It slipped out of her hand. Some papers fell under a chair. She knelt, gathering up the papers and putting them back into the notebook. At the same time, she took something out of her pocket.

Poor Mickey, meanwhile, endured a dueling five-word family feud. "You've got to take me" versus "It's too dangerous out there." Finally, Mickey threw up his hands. "Look, I'm not taking either of you. If anything happens, the project dies."

Tex grabbed Mickey's arm. "The president wants to know what's real. He'll listen to me. But I've got to see it myself."

Mickey turned to Mariah. "It's true. Dad will listen to Uncle Tex."

Mickey brushed Tex's hand from his arm. "Work it out. The zodiac leaves at 7:00 a.m.—not 7:01. The helicopter goes up at eight. We're looking at $3,000 to $5,000 an hour. I wouldn't wait for God."

Mickey walked out. Tex tried to joke his way out of this family mess. "You know, sweetheart, patience is one of —"

"Don't patronize me!" Mariah was heartbroken. This was what she wanted to do with her life. And Tex had cut her out. "And don't call me sweetheart." She stormed away, looking a lot like her mother.

"Mariah, wait. I've got something from your mom."

She stopped and came back. Tex pulled the gift-wrapped box out of his pocket. She opened it and took out a pair of gold amulet earrings. Each had a miniature engraving of a bear. "She said it wards off bad things, like stubborn godfathers."

Mariah put the earrings on, dug a small compact mirror out of her purse and primped for him. "Like them?"

"Love them. Have dinner with me, and I'll love them even more."

Mariah tossed the box on a table and headed for the door. "That hurt, Uncle Tex. A lot. So, maybe tomorrow, when you're back, and it's safe enough to do so."

45

Illulisat
Oct. 18, 2016

THE HOTEL ICEFJORD dining room was empty except for two men drinking beer out of bottles.

One was a burly foreigner with money to spend for information. From time to time, he looked out the window across the small harbor to the SS *Pilgrim*.

The other was Father Christmas. He knew everyone in Illulisat, including their sled dogs. "His wife's sick. He needs money to get her to Copenhagen. He'll help you out." Then his old cell phone rang. "In an hour? Sure. I can pick you up. Call me when you're ready."

The burly foreigner passed an envelope across the table. "One other thing: the American this afternoon. Did he say anything?"

"Thanks, and keep the change."

"That's all?"

Father Christmas nodded. When the stranger headed up to his room, the motor boat Captain put the money envelope in his pocket and went out to gas up his vessel.

46

SS *Pilgrim* Cabin
Oct. 18, 2016

NO ANSWER. *Shit*.

Tex put the phone down. Once, when Mariah was still in pigtails, he had bought her a third ice cream cone because he couldn't say, "You've had enough, sweetie." Now, he had just smashed to smithereens what her heart was set on.

Yawning, he walked over to the porthole and looked out past the coast. Maybe a mile or two inland, the Ice Sheet began. *It was the right decision. A lot can go wrong out there.* He felt good about protecting Mariah and keeping his promise to Ellie.

A minute later, Tex piled up two pillows and leaned back against them. He yawned again. He felt his mind playing with dots. To slow it down, he picked up Lynn's "Glaciers and Climate Change" report and started reading.

What is probably the least discussed aspect of climate change are the core principles that children learn in science class.

1. Energy from the sun, what we call sunlight, passes through the earth's atmosphere. Some of that energy is absorbed by green plants, the oceans, and so forth. Some of that energy is reflected back into space especially from the world's ice sheets and glaciers.

2. Matter, i.e., anything with mass is trapped within the earth's atmosphere by gravity. Except for a few single-atom hydrogen molecules and, these days, materials on spaceships, nothing gets out of the earth's atmosphere. The earth is a locked box when it comes to matter.

3. Carbon dioxide, methane, and other greenhouse gasses are composed of atoms, have weight, and are trapped in the atmosphere. The more of those gasses that humans release through burning fossil fuels and other methods, the thicker the heat blanket that surrounds the earth. It is no different from closing all the doors, windows, and chimneys in a house and then lighting candles and smoking cigarettes. The carbon dioxide by-products of burning those candles and cigarettes will gradually fill the house and . . ."

Tex put down the report. He picked up the phone. He dialed Mariah's room. While he listened to it ring, he felt a small berg brushing against the *Pilgrim*. Still no answer. *Are you not there or not picking up?*

He went back to the report.

4. Heat melts ice. Therefore, of the many different impacts of the atmosphere warming up, the most obvious is the melting of (a) continental ice sheets in Antarctica and Greenland and (b) glaciers around the world.

5. Less than a decade or two ago, the Greenland Ice Sheet covered more than 80 percent of Greenland. Today, it covers about 78 percent. The assassin I interviewed. The one who killed those people in Colombia and wants to slow-cook me. He was Russian.

6. Positive feedback loops speed up the melting, e.g., the more the air temperature warms, the more sea ice melts. With sea ice gone, the sea absorbs more heat from the sun, and sea temperature rises. The warmer water leads to the faster melting of sea ice and coastal glaciers, which in turn raises the sea temperature even more. This positive feedback loop, along with others, means that the melting of the glaciers will happen in a nonlinear fashion. There is a point where breakdown will accelerate. Similarly, when a person gets a fever, i.e., the overheating of the bodily system, symptoms occur as the bodily temperature rises. But when the temperature reaches a critical point, e.g., 104° Fahrenheit, the body breakdown accelerates dramatically, often leading to death.

Last try. Tex dialed Mariah again, but got the same result. He knew he should read through the rest of Lynn's report but couldn't. Instead, he got out of bed and opened his pack. He pulled out his warmest clothes for tomorrow's trip. He also pulled out his Walther P99 semiautomatic pistol. *Bakov had three armed bodyguards. Why?*

Tex held the gun and stared at it. *Won't need it*. He put it back into his pack.

From the small stateroom bureau, Tex got out the chips he had taken from the ship's lounge. He crunched away. Out of nowhere, he remembered a college sociology class. The professor had a "Six Degrees of Separation" exercise. The goal was to connect any two people on the planet. Tex and Zavia Jansen had been paired together for the exercise. It was right after their "hot item" status had cooled off. To say it was awkward was like saying brain cancer was a summer cold.

A few years later, pre-Katie, Tex shifted the exercise to "Six Degrees of Connection." The goal: connect any two events or people in six moves or less. As an olive branch, he had sent Zavia a description of the exercise and a "maybe we can be friends" note. The response he got was "thanks" and "maybe someday." *What are you doing these days? You'd be interested in all this glacial stuff.*

Just then, a single noise broke the stateroom silence. "Ping." An e-mail. But not an ordinary e-mail. Eyes wide, Tex stared at a weird-looking, fast-swirling icon that finally stopped and announced: "Message decoded."

Tex clicked on the icon. Seemingly random letters formed into words.

"It's urgent we communicate."
—*Zhivago*

Mariah? Are you messing with my head? Twenty years ago, he had read Pasternak's novel about the doctor/poet/idealist who was horrified by the chaos in Russia, both before and after the Revolution.

He hit reply and wrote:

"Urgent? Why? Who are you?"

The message encrypted and shot back out. Three minutes later, another shot back.

"Because we are on the brink. And you are in danger."
—*Zhivago*

<*Is this the NSA's office? Is it a Russian? Is it a setup?* Tex splashed water on his face. He couldn't decide whether to laugh or pull out his gun. Back at the computer, he responded.

"What brink? What danger?"

A few minutes later, he heard the beep.

"Keep your door locked and your mind unlocked. Good night."
—*Zhivago*

Before, Tex couldn't stay awake. Now, he couldn't sleep. He

slipped out of bed and got his Walther. He disassembled the gun, spread the parts out on the bedspread, and cleaned each piece. Then he reassembled the gun and placed it under his pillow.

He dialed Mariah again. Still no answer. Scared for her, he walked around the entire deck. The sun was setting. To the east, he saw the Pilgrim's eerie reflection along the bottom of a massive iceberg. Then he went into the lounge. No sign of her. But in the corner was a member of her protection unit eating a quick dinner.

"You know who I am?"

The Secret Service agent stood up. "Yes, sir. You're Chickadee's godfather." She referred to the code name they used for Mariah. "I'm afraid you're in her doghouse right now."

"Is she in her cabin?" The agent nodded. "Just not wanting to talk with me?"

"Or anyone, sir."

"Is she safe?"

"Is there a reason she might not be?"

In a low voice, he told her, "Maybe." He explained the e-mail a few minutes ago. "Watch her closely, okay? And can you get a message to General Mason, the president's NSA?"

Tex went back to his stateroom. After brushing his teeth, he double-checked the deadbolt on the cabin door.

47

Greenland Ice Sheet
Oct. 19, 2016

T EX FELT LIKE he had eaten an infected fish that had eaten an infected fish.

First, there was Mariah. To have her not pick up the phone cut him deeply.

Second, he was sitting very low in the backseat of a cab, next to Mickey. "You're shitting me? Sixty-five thousand people in all of Greenland?" He sounded more cheerful than he felt. *Why am I acting like there's a guy with a rocket launcher on the side of the road, and if I'm low enough in the car, maybe it'll pass over my head?*

They were driving from Illulisat to the airport. The road, five kilometers long, was the second longest in the country. Mickey put his hand in the air, as if taking an oath. "May the lens of my camera crack.... But, if you think that's desolate, wait till you get on the Ice Sheet. It's like being on an ice planet."

And third, Tex had been an investigative reporter. He knew the standards for a credible story. This didn't add up.

How many bodies had been found? None.

How much money was missing? Not a dollar.

Was a twelve-year-old kid being held for ransom? Uh-uh.

No story.

Plus, this Zhivago? If Tex saw a movie about a presidential special assistant who got deep-throated by the namesake of a book title whose author was once on Stalin's execution list, he would ask for his money back. *Who are you, Zhivago?*

Another two minutes, and they pulled into the airport. Outside, near the hangar, the small helicopter sat on a wooden pallet. They left their packs by the helicopter and walked into the hangar.

The pilot greeted them. He was thin, white-haired, and three months from retiring. He took the GPS coordinates for where they were going. Then he marched into the office and filed his flight plan with the airport administrator.

Tex looked around. "Where's the cameras . . . the batteries . . . ?" All he saw was another helicopter sitting idle.

"On the Ice Sheet. Mac's my tech. He took them out two days ago."

The pilot returned. "Let's go. We're ready. The weather's good."

Tex and Mickey went outside and climbed into the back of the helicopter, buckling their seat belts and putting on headphones. Mickey had a radio for communicating with the pilot over the rotor noise.

The helicopter warmed up, and the pilot lifted it off the pallet. As they rose in altitude, Tex scanned outside. He didn't see anyone with binoculars tracking them, never mind aiming a rocket launcher. He leaned back against the seat and let himself be awed by the barren coastal mountains and, in a few minutes, by the edge of the Ice Sheet.

For the first time that morning, he didn't feel like throwing up.

48

Illulisat
Oct. 19, 2016

A BURLY MAN in an airport employee's uniform watched Tex and Mickey take off. As soon as they passed over the foothills, he went inside the hangar, entered the administrator's office, and pulled down the shades. He had a gun holstered in his boot. He handed over an envelope with five thousand US dollars. The administrator handed over a handwritten piece of paper with the GPS coordinates the pilot had given him.

Three minutes later, the burly man made a secure call to the Netherlands. "They just left."

"You're sure the Breen girl wasn't with them?" Alpha asked.

"I'm sure."

"And it was the video nerd with Cassidy?"

"Same guy I tracked in Florida."

A moment later, Alpha hung up and speed-dialed Moscow. "That's right, Admiral. They're on their way."

The admiral hung up and dialed Washington.

Alpha hung up and dialed a secure global cell phone that could be accessed anywhere.

Meanwhile, the burly man went back into the administrator's office. He broke the man's windpipe and put a lit cigarette in the man's mouth. Then he went into the hangar, stuck a tube in the gas tank of the parked helicopter, applied the right fittings, and siphoned out the gas. He put the end of the tube inside the administrator's office and ran at full-speed back to his car. In a few minutes, he was off the airport grounds, as the fumes reached the flame and all of Illulisat heard the hangar blow up.

49

Greenland Ice Sheet
Oct. 19, 2016

A THOUSAND FEET ABOVE the Ice Sheet, Tex stared at what happened when ice interacted with the sun, water, and wind. Ice moved. It cracked. It bubbled. It broke. It melted and froze again and again.

Staring at the horizon-to-horizon expanse of ice, Tex saw more crevasses than he could count. Some were covered with yesterday's snow, the second storm in two days. Others had streams of meltwater running through them either in narrow, shallow crevasses, or in wider ones that were hundreds or even thousands of feet deep.

He thought about a point Mickey had made. Namely, at some impossible-to-predict moment, a crack would break open in the bottom of a crevasse. The water would drain out and head downward through a vertical moulin. The water would find glacial plumbing; in other words, holes, channels, or sluices in the below-surface ice. If it didn't find them, the pressure of the water would create them. Eventually, the water would make its way to the bedrock below the Ice Sheet. At bedrock level, the water would accelerate the Ice Sheet's death march to the sea, where freshwater would dilute the ocean saltwater and impact the coastal ecosystem.

The volumes of water could be greater than the volume of water going over Niagara Falls. Four years earlier, two Canadian graduate students were in a rubber boat, taking scientific measurements. The ice cracked. The water rushed out. They were sucked down like drops of soap in a bathtub drain.

The force of the water could smash down against the bedrock and, through hydraulic jacking, bounce back, pushing the Ice Sheet upward. On the surface, the ice would bubble. If the bubble broke, huge blocks of ice would fly across the surface. Two years before, an ice block, shaped like a slice of pizza and weighing many tons, decapitated a Norwegian scientist.

Tex turned to Mickey and gave him a double thumbs-up. I hope heaven is this beautiful.

On this Ice Planet, in this quietude, in this moment, Tex touched something holy inside himself. It wasn't religious in the usual sense. But Tex knew religion came from the Latin lignio, meaning "to connect." His connection was with the whole process of earth's evolution and of life itself.

Tex lost himself in the amazing changes the earth had undergone. For a billion years, asteroids rained down and lava oceans covered the surface. It was so hot that life couldn't exist, and it was so cold that life barely existed. By earth's standards, the last ten thousand years has been balmy, allowing for more than 7 billion people, wheat farms, the Silk Route, and the World Cup.

Suddenly, Tex felt himself disconnected again, as Mickey tapped him on the arm. Since talking over the rotor noise was too hard, Mickey mouthed, "Survey Canyon," as he pointed toward eleven o'clock. Tex followed his finger and saw the supra-glacial meltwater lake Mickey had talked about the day before.

It was bigger than many Minnesota lakes. But unlike those lakes—many of them thousands of years old—this one was living on borrowed time. Today, tomorrow, next April, sometime, a crack would open and the water would drain down.

For Tex, it triggered very mixed emotions and a memory. Twenty years ago, he had interviewed an astronomer. On her office wall was a photo of the sun as it would appear five billion years from now. It was a red giant with a diameter a hundred times greater than its current state. "Beautiful, isn't it?" she had asked, "except it signals the end. Just a short time later, in galactic terms, it will collapse."

Tex imagined a framed photo of this meltwater lake. It, too, was a stunningly beautiful sign of a coming collapse. *This much meltwater this far up the Arctic Circle in the middle of October?* He looked away. Then he looked back. Then he looked away again.

Ground zero for climate change. Mickey's words. Yesterday, he had understood them. Today, he felt them. It was as real as the dirt in his garden and the blood in his veins.

If Charley gets a second term, we're coming back here. If he sees this, he'll get it, too, and he'll have four years to do something. A smile crossed Tex's face. *And we're bringing Mariah.*

As the helicopter descended, Mickey tapped Tex again. This time, he pointed toward an area at two o'clock. It was a mile and a half away, but Tex saw two snowmobiles, equipment crates, and a man waving his arms wildly. "That's Mac," Mickey mouthed, as the pilot headed straight for the technician. "This is his sixth trip out to the cameras."

As soon as the rotors stopped, Tex and Mickey clambered out with their gear. The pilot took off.
Mac hugged Mickey and shook hands with Tex. "Welcome to the edge of the world."

50

Greenland Ice Sheet
Oct. 19, 2016

"It's almost hot." Mickey checked all the crates. "Hell, I'll bet it's twenty above."

"Should have been here yesterday. It was whiteout time. In fact, I stepped into a crevasse covered with new snow. Lucky for my girlfriend, it was only waist deep."

"Tex, give us a hand. But move really slowly. This is precious cargo."

The camera they lifted onto the trailer behind Mac's snowmobile took two years to develop. The photographic part was easy. But a computer circuit had to be developed. Both the solar panels and the battery had to function in temperatures that would reach 50 to 60 degrees below zero Fahrenheit. And the whole unit had to be drilled into rock with bolts and guide wires that could withstand katabatic winds that swooped down the glacial inclines at speeds up to a hundred miles an hour.

"Are you all right?" Just as the unit was loaded, Tex slipped and banged his knee.

"Got any ice?" he joked, as he got up on his own and leaned against Mac's snowmobile. "Where's the gas gauge on this thing?"

"It's electric," Mickey said. "Quiet as a mouse and zero emissions."

"That's the difference between us. You know why I love driving it?" Mac asked Tex. "The speed, the acceleration. Ever gone sixty on a snowmobile? Wear your jock strap." Dressed in black from helmet to boots, Mac looked as natural on his snowmobile as Roy Rogers looked on his horse.

Mickey stood up. The crates were OK. He nodded to Mac and turned to Tex: "He's going east. We're going south."

Mac buckled his helmet. "Stay warm, stay calm, stay alive," he yelled, as his vehicle sped off.

"Ready, Tex? I want to show you a few things that might be helpful to Breen."

"Almost." He squatted and signaled for Mickey to do the same. "Listen, something's happened. I can risk my life, but not yours." He told Mickey about Zhivago's warning. "And there's other stuff, but nothing I can put my finger on. Anyway, call Mac, if you want. Get him back here. We can call this off."

Mickey looked at Tex. Rasputin was back. "Someone played tornado in my house and fucked with my air hose." He pulled a rifle out of his duffel. "It's for bears. But it'll work for humans." Mickey got up and on his snowmobile. "Let's go."

Mickey drove along, slowly. He read the ice and threaded his way between the hummocks—tufts of ice—and the crevasses that dotted the landscape. The ride was brutal on his tailbone. But plunging a few thousand feet into a crevasse would be brutal on all of his bones.

Tex sat behind Mickey. His hands were around Mickey's waist. His range of vision was very small, so he closed his eyes. *Something's off. Is it me? Him? Us? Being here? At least Mariah's safe. That was the right decision.*

The sun was higher. Tex put his visor up and his sunglasses on. He figured he wouldn't need them very long, since there were low clouds off in the distance heading their way.

Mickey turned his head and raised his voice. "Was I an asshole last night?"

"You pissed some folks off. On purpose?"

Mickey got quiet again. Tex saw his hands gripping the handlebars. "Moshe the Beadle? Know who he is?"

Tex didn't.

"Ever read *Night* by Elie Wiesel?"

He hadn't.

Moshe was a Jew in a small Polish village. One day, he went to the big city and saw Germans rounding up Jews and throwing them into ghettos or cattle cars. When he got back, he told everyone.

"Know what they said?" Mickey's voice was both incredulous and sad. "That can't be happening. And, if it is, the Germans have a good reason."

Tex felt Mickey take a deep breath. "Sometimes, I feel like Moshe."

Tex took one hand and squeezed Mickey's shoulder. *Good guy shoots videos of glaciers. Someone messes with his air hose. Another dot?*

Ten minutes later, the clouds covered the sun. Mickey pulled over alongside a crevasse that snaked around. It was new—maybe three feet deep with stream-level meltwater running through it. "First stop. We're going over there." He pointed to a bend in the crevasse, as he pulled a thirty-foot rope out of his duffel. He double-knotted one end tightly around his waist and told Tex to do the same. "Stay back. Keep the rope taut. Step in my steps. If you wander, we could both die."

Thirty steps later, they stood as close to the crevasse edge as Mickey dared go. "Do you know what cryoconite is?"

This time, Mickey indicated an area under the water, right where the crevasse bent. It was dark and stood out against the color of the water and ice. Much like sediment that piles up in a river eddy, the cryoconite coagulates in the elbows of the crevasse.

As if he were defusing a bomb, Mickey put one knee gently on the ice. Then the other knee. Then, almost in slow motion, he scooped up a gloveful of the gooey mixture. It had a soft, quicksand feel to it. "Some of it's residue from burning oil or coal."

"From up here?" Tex put the cryoconite up to his nose.

"From anywhere. Boston, Buenos Aires, Berlin. . . . The winds carry it, along with the rest of the shit." He explained that it also contained everything from Asian desert sand to particulates released when forests are burned down in South America. Explorers first reported it nearly a hundred and fifty years ago. Today, researchers find pockets of it all across the Ice Sheet. The cryoconite's dark color absorbs sunlight, which triggers more melting.

Mickey looked at Tex. "Breen doesn't need another 'smoking gun.' But if he did, the cryoconite proves human involvement in climate change." He stood up abruptly. "The temp's dropping, and the wind's rising. Let's keep moving."

The two men retraced their steps. Mickey was fifteen feet from the snowmobile; Tex forty-five. Tex looked east toward the clouds moving in. Before he looked back, he heard a crackle and lurched forward.

Mickey was dropping. Tex was being pulled along. He reached out but found nothing to grab onto. He dug his boots into the ice, but they wouldn't hold. The closer Tex got to the edge, the lower Mickey dropped. The lower Mickey dropped, the more his weight pulled Tex to the edge. He was now ten feet from the edge. Five feet from the edge, he nearly crashed his head into the snowmobile. At the last second, he dropped down, squeezed his arms and shoulders and legs as tightly as he could. He felt his ribs on the edge of cracking, as he absorbed the jolt.

"Mickey!" He held the rope with both hands and crawled to the edge. He looked down and saw Mickey dangling in open space with nothing between him and the crevasse floor three hundred feet below. Tex's heart beat faster than the speed of light. "Mickey, say something!"

The voice was weak. "Can you get me up?"

Tex tried to lean back. Nothing. Mickey was a dead weight. Then he leaned against the snowmobile. *Might work.* Very slowly, Tex started untying the rope. When it came undone, he lost some slack. Mickey dropped a foot, as Tex held onto the rope for Mickey's life and probably his own. "Hold on!"

With his last bit of strength, Tex wrapped the end of the rope around the snowmobile ski and tied it. Mickey dropped yet another foot. His weight pulled on the vehicle, but it weighed enough to hold. Tex jumped up, got on, and started it. He didn't know if he would be heading down into that crevasse or another crevasse. As he moved forward, Mickey moved up. Soon, he was out of the crevasse, lying on the ice, shaking, coughing, and breathing hard.

Tex sat Mickey up and held him until his convulsions passed. Slowly, the fear did, too. "You've been working out." He nodded deeply to Tex. "And I'm grateful for it."

Tex got a thermos out of the duffel and poured Mickey some tea. "Drink this. It'll warm you up."

A few minutes later, they were back on the snowmobile.

"Want to go back?" Tex leaned forward so Mickey could hear him.

"It'll be hours before the pilot's back. Let's keep going." They drove into an area with jagged cliffs, where ice quakes had blown open the ice and created frozen foothills. "That cryoconite? Seeing it. Is it helpful?"

"It is." Tex wasn't sure whether he was convincing himself or Mickey. "But give me your opinion on something else, will you?" He told Mickey that, after Greenland, he was going to Europe. He didn't think there was much value in seeing the impact on the Alps. He thought that seeing what the Spanish were doing with solar or what the Germans were doing with wind or what the British were doing with tidal waves would be more useful to the president. "Do you agree?"

Mickey nodded as he stopped the snowmobile. His body went rigid. His eyes concentrated on every square inch of the ice he was looking at. "Be right back." He maneuvered one leg over the snowmobile, so Tex didn't have to get off. This time, he got a ski pole out of his duffel and poked around the snow. "I think it's okay." He inched the snowmobile forward. Finally, he accelerated and drove south with the sun now to his right for another few minutes before he killed the engine.

Tex started to get off.

"Stay," Mickey ordered. "We're just looking from here." He pointed to a spot about twenty-five feet away. "There. See that little rise in the ice?"

Tex saw the bulge. He gauged it was about eight feet across, six feet wide, and six inches off the surface.

"Know what it is?"

"A contact lens? Hell, Mickey, what is it?"

"Cigarette lighter."

"Wish I smoked. And speaking of smoking, what are you talking about?"

"Methane bubbles."

"You mean like methane in landfills?" He was referring to the gas released when decaying organic matter is captured and turned into electricity. "I understand the cryco-whatever-the-hell-it-is getting up here. But where's this methane come from?"

Mickey eased the snowmobile forward another two feet. "Think dinosaurs. That period. Worldwide, it was a time of forests and ferns. When the vegetation decomposed, it gave off enormous amounts of the gas. Ten thousand years ago, it got trapped under ice. When scientists take ice core samples to determine the climate's history, they find the methane."

"What's the bubble part?" Tex zipped up his parka the last quarter inch.

"When the ice melts, the gas rises. When the ice refreezes, it's like plastic and gets pushed into a bubble."

"And the cigarette lighter part?"

The clouds were now lower and closer. "I met an Inuit hunter. He swears that if the wind ever got too strong, they'd shoot the bubble, set the gas on fire, and light their smokes."

"It's a great story. But why are you telling me all this?"

"Because there's a methane time bomb. Breen's got to know." Rasputin took off again. "Methane is a less common greenhouse gas than carbon dioxide. But as a heat trapper, it's Super Gas: twenty times more potent. It's in everything from natural gas to cattle farts. But the time bomb: all that melting permafrost in Alaska, Russia, and other areas? It's where Nature trapped enough methane to make this planet a few shades more like Venus. The stuff's leaking. All over the world's tundras and even up here." Ominously, scientists had detected methane chimneys in the Arctic: columns of gas rising to the surface as the sea ice disappeared.

"Trust me, Mick. He knows most of that."

The videographer's shoulders tensed up. "Get off the snowmobile!" He was half-screaming at Tex.

"Why?"

"Because I fucking told you to." He was yelling now. Tex backed off the vehicle. His boots barely touched ground before Mickey's did, too. He looked Tex in the eye. "Why'd he really send you?"

"I told you. He—"

"Come on, Tex." He pushed Tex back a few steps. "He knows this. He knows that. You're no more up here to find out details than I'm up here to get laid."

Tex couldn't tell him about the Russians and floating nuclear power plants or the other things going on. "Look, Mick, you've got to—"

"Fuck you. Do you know what it costs me to come up here? The time...the money...the hassle....If you're really just after details..." Mickey stormed away twenty feet, then came back. "Get back on." He perched himself on the snowmobile. "I'll show you one more thing. It's on the way to where Mac is. If the fog doesn't close in, that's where we're going afterward."

"Mickey..." The videographer waved him off with his hand.

Twenty minutes later, they were at a higher elevation: more snow, along with jagged cliffs and valleys. Tex's ass was really aching now. No horse had ever bruised him to the bone. His fingers felt like popsicles. Plus, he was at the mercy of this guy, who was pissed at him.

Mickey shut off the ignition. Slightly calmed down, he pulled the thermos out of his pack and poured them each a cup. "Take your helmet off and put it next to mine on the seat." Then, he set off. "Follow me, and keep your ears open."

A dozen yards away, Tex heard a low roar. Twenty yards later, it was a cover-your-ears roar. "It's a moulin. They're all over glaciers."

Tex half-yelled, "How deep?"

"Could be thousands of feet."

"Has anyone ever gone down to—"

"Maybe I can really help him, Tex."

"You are helping." Tex knelt. He sipped his tea and pressed his cold gloves against the hot cup.

"You're lying. Maybe you have to. Let's go."

Only two sounds broke the silence on their way back to the snowmobile, wind and boots on ice.

Then a third sound shattered the silence: the bullet that shattered the thermos in Mickey's hand and cut his cheek.

51

Greenland Ice Sheet
Oct. 19, 2016

"GET DOWN!" Tex screamed. "Get down!"

Both men dove onto the hard ice. They slid under the volley of bullets that cut through the air, Mickey's duffel bag, and the sleeve of Tex's parka, just missing his elbow.

When the bullets stopped, the men heard engine sounds coming closer. Tex held up two fingers. Mickey confirmed. Then they inched their heads up over the snowmobile. Where are they?

Mickey saw one snowmobile off to the right, barreling toward them. The killer was working the throttle with his right hand. He held a gun with his left.

Tex saw the other assassin heading toward them at twelve o'clock.

Mickey's hand trembled as he laid his rifle across the back of his snowmobile. For all his tough talk, he had never shot a squirrel, never mind a bear or a human.

Tex's hand was steady. He held his pistol in it. They took their gloves off. "Thirty seconds!" Tex yelled. "They'll be in range. Fifteen seconds!" Their fingers were on the triggers.

Suddenly, a bullet crashed into the ice from the left. They looked. They froze. They understood. A third snowmobile. But no engine sound.

"It's Mac!" Tex screamed.

Tex looked up. The assassins were splitting up. Like wild dogs, they were surrounding their rabbits.

"Mickey, listen to me." He laid out a plan. "Put your helmet on." He did likewise. "On three . . ." Mickey whipped onto the seat, Tex a second behind him. Then Mickey gunned the accelerator and kamikaze-like, they headed straight at the closest assassin. Tex gripped Mickey's waist with his left arm. He screamed over the noise, "Keep your shoulders steady."

Mickey drove. He knew the chill factor was probably down to fifty below. He screamed back to Tex. "Couple of minutes . . . frostbite!" Tex couldn't hear him through the now-howling wind.

Twenty miles an hour. Thirty miles an hour. Tex steadied his gun on Mickey's right shoulder. He held it there as two bullets whizzed by. Then he squeezed the trigger. Missed. He squeezed it again. Missed. But his third bullet shredded the assassin's visor and left eye. His blood gushed onto the gauges. The vehicle flipped and rolled over three times. The man's blood emptied out of his veins and streaked the snow red.

Mickey veered off. Tex almost fell off. His hand was going numb from the cold. Hanging on was tough. Shooting was becoming impossible. He spotted a narrow trail snaking along the backside of the jagged ice hills. "Go there!" With only one rider each, the two assassins were gaining ground. Fast.

The road narrowed. "Mickey, stop!" Tex pointed to an indent near the hills. Mickey pulled in, and they jumped off. Tex pulled out the cable. He gave one end to Mickey. "Can you do this?"

"We'll find out." Mickey sprinted across the snow to the other side of the trail.

They brought the cable down to ice level and hid it in the snow as best they could. Then they hid themselves as best they could.

Finally, engine sounds. A hundred yards away. *We'll find out.* "Count of three," Tex screamed at the top of his lungs. "One . . ." Then they heard the muted sounds of the electric vehicle a dozen yards away. No time to think. Tex stood up fast and raised the cable. So did Mickey. Mac saw the cable a millisecond before it ripped open his throat.

Meanwhile, nearby, the third assassin saw both men out in the open. The driver turned toward Mickey, who looked for a weapon. Something. Anything. Nothing. Frightened, he ran, zigging and slipping, zagging and sliding.

Helpless, Tex watched as the assailant closed in on Mickey. Twenty yards. Ten yards. Tex screamed louder than a public address system. "Dive sideways! Now!"

Mickey heard him. He flung his body to the left and onto the ground. He banged his ankle badly. Two seconds later, the snowmobile crushed it.

Mickey's screams rolled down a glacial valley and up the glacial walls before they were smothered by the wind.

Tex heard Mickey's screams. He flipped out.

Somewhere inside, those screams got all mixed up with the screams of people he had interviewed after heavy rains flooded down treeless mountains and killed their kin; the screams of terrorized farmers in Colombia; and the screams of the person he loved the most, when her pain was stronger than she was.

He shook his fists in the air and took his turn to scream. "I'll kill you!"

Tex had killed dozens of pheasants, eight deer, and one man. He was prepared to double the number of men. Multiple times, he opened and closed his fists. "I'll kill you!" he screamed again.

Quickly, Tex took off. He had his gun in his pocket as he ran toward the jagged cliffs. He slipped. He got up. He slipped again, this time landing flat on the icy ground. The gun fell out of his pocket. When he turned to pick it up, he saw the snowmobile turn and head toward him.

Tex got up on one knee and aimed the gun. But he saw the assassin crouched low behind the windshield. And just seconds away. *The cliffs!* Tex jumped up. He ran, crisscrossing left and right. The assassin accelerated. Tex veered. The snowmobile nearly kissed his boot. Tex turned and fired. The assassin turned and headed back toward him.

Tex felt the icy ground. It was rougher. He was closer. He ran even faster. Seconds later, he heard the snowmobile just seconds away. He saw the edge of a cliff. He lunged, landing inches behind the cliff as the snowmobile passed just behind him.

Tex looked around. He could hide in the jagged cliffs. But he would freeze. It's my only chance. Instantly, the prey turned predator. He looked over an edge but didn't see the assassin. He listened but didn't hear the snowmobile. His fear that the assassin had gone away was blown away by the three bullets meant to blow him away.

Tex inched his way around the cliff until he came to a lower area, an ice mound. He crawled up the mound and peeked over it. Below, he saw a narrow, snaking crevasse. When he turned his head, he saw Mac's snowmobile nearby. *I've gone in a circle.*

Tex had no idea where the assassin was, but he had to do something. He tucked his body in close and rolled down the mound. Gauging where he was, he threw his arms out on the ice and stopped himself a foot from the crevasse.

Lying there, he saw nothing but ice and heard nothing but wind. He was closer to the vehicle.

Tex crouched. Gingerly, he stepped toward the crevasse. He crawled onto a lip of snow, pulled out his sunglasses, and waited for a lull in the wind. When it came, he threw the sunglasses as hard as he could into the crevasse. He barely heard it hit bottom, but now he knew it wasn't deep. Then he lowered himself into the crevasse. Afraid to move and break the ice, he lay on the crevasse's slope and peeked over the snow's lip.

If the assassin didn't come soon, death would.

A minute passed. Two minutes. Tex fired a shot, hoping the assassin would return the gunfire and provide some clue as to where he was. Nothing.

Finally, Tex knew he had to do something. He squatted. In one minute, he would break for the snowmobile.

Here we go. But behind him, he heard a faint noise. Someone coming? He fired. Two bullets fired back. He moved down the crevasse, away from the shooter. He heard the assassin coming toward him. He only had three bullets left. He had to reach the snowmobile. He fired once and took off over the ice.

Behind him now, the killer took aim. To get a better shot, the killer took two steps to the right but landed in a pool of cryoconite that gave way under the weight.

Tex heard the killer fall. *Now!* He dashed for the electric snowmobile. It was lying on its side with the engine still running. Tex got up and threw his helmet off to the side. Then, with aching arms, he stood the snowmobile up, jumped on, and took off. Dazed and half-crazed, he didn't know if Mickey was dead. He didn't know where he was going. Maybe he would run into someone. Maybe there would be an igloo out here. Maybe the pilot would come back early.

Then he heard an engine. *The helicopter? The snowmobile.* The assassin was behind him. He gunned the electric vehicle and it accelerated. It was fast, like Mac had said. For the next thirty seconds, Tex opened a little distance between himself and the killer. *Maybe I'll escape. But I'm lost, I'm cold, I'll die. If I go back, maybe we'll die together.*

Then he did a U-turn.

Let's play chicken.

Tex opened the throttle all the way. The wind and snow blew in his eyes. He went on sound more than sight. He didn't give. The assassin didn't give. The distance between them kept halving. Finally, just before the point of no return, the assassin swung the vehicle to the right. Too late. The vehicles crashed into each other with the screeching sound of fast-moving metal against fast-moving metal; a split-second after Tex had barrel-rolled away.

Tex crawled over to the collision point. One snowmobile ski was lying four feet away, along with drive belts and motor mounts. The assassin's body was sprawled lifelessly in the snow, face-up. Tex picked up a gun lying next to the body. Then he pulled off the driver's helmet. *Bernice Johnson!*

Minutes later, Tex found Mickey. He was barely conscious, but he could sit up on the ice. "Can you get us back to the pickup site?"

Mickey shivered. His teeth chattered. "Don't move." Tex took a knife and cut the snowmobile suit off Bernice, covering Mickey with it. Slowly, Mickey raised his arm and pointed toward the northwest. Then he passed out.

Tex put Mickey over the front of the snowmobile and headed to where he had pointed. The gas gauge read "1/8." Worse, on the horizon, he saw a dozen men dressed in camouflage whites with automatic weapons on their backs. They were on cross-country skis, racing down a glacial hill toward them.

52

Greenland Ice Sheet
Oct. 19, 2016

TEX COULDN'T SEE where he was going. The fog had moved in and obscured the glacial valley. He stopped the snowmobile. Carefully, he laid Mickey down on the ice and waited.

Who are these guys? What do they want with us? What will they do to us? Tex had been captured a few weeks ago. He wasn't going to be captured again. He only had two bullets left. One was for Mickey. One was for himself.

Tex pulled out his gun. He could barely see it. Thirty seconds later, he couldn't see it at all. He couldn't see anything at all.

The Ice Sheet fog was a cloud shroud. A total gray-out. Scientists feared it. Pilots died in it. Anyone could lose their sense of direction and sense of balance. Up was down, and down was up.

Tex moved ten steps away, hoping the fog would be thinner. It was thicker. He thought he heard a sound to the left but saw nothing. He thought he heard sound above but saw nothing. Whoever they were, they could be close enough to shake hands without knowing it.

For twenty minutes, Tex knelt in place. His knees hurt. Everything hurt. He was hot and cold. He was hungry and thirsty. All he could see were shades of gray. He was ready to die. He ran down the list of who had meant the most to him.

Mariah: what a beautiful human being. Thank God she's safe.
Ellie: a magnificent mother and a better friend.
Charley: more than a brother; a bond stronger than blood.
Carlos: a simple man using a simple model who had restored his faith.

And Katie: they had had seventeen years. They should have had seventy. She had taught him that a human relationship was the chance to know something so very precious: who another person is and who one's self is.

And he thought of himself. He smiled. *To die in the fog. If that's not a metaphor for human existence!* Tex had been born curious. He longed to know life. It had taken him decades to believe it was a mystery and to live with uncertainty.

Then the fog started to move away.

Tex now saw the thin sheet of white snow on the valley floor. He saw the dark blue snowmobile and Mickey behind it. He saw the top of a cliff just twenty feet up.

Kicking toeholds as he climbed, Tex made it to the ridge. He heard voices on the other side. Ever so carefully, he peeked over. Down below, he saw this new group of killers, who had reassembled and were making new plans. He also saw something else that stirred his blood.

Tex slid down the cliff the way he had come. He rolled the last few feet, got up, and raced back to the snowmobile. He saw that Mickey was still alive. Then he took Mickey's rifle, raced back, and scrambled up the cliff again.

Tex waited a few seconds until his breath slowed down. Then he lifted his body onto the top of the ridge and aimed his rifle. He had been quiet. But not quiet enough. The men below heard him. They turned to fire. Tex beat them to it by a single shot that left the barrel of his gun, spiraled through the air, and found the cigarette lighter.

The bullet tore through the bubbled ice and set off the methane under it. The explosion blew away four of the killers. The others regrouped and headed for Tex, who retreated to the snowmobile and Mickey. He reloaded the rifle and made sure there were two bullets in the chamber of his handgun.

Cassidy's Last Stand would be a good one.

The killers came quickly. Tex's first shot punctured an attacker's lung. His second shot punctured a forehead. The others took cover and moved in. They had rifles with specially designed Arctic triggers, so their gloved fingers could fire the weapon more easily.

Tex fired a few more shots. He heard a click. The rifle was out of bullets.

This would have to be quick. He heard the attackers move closer and felt three bullets pass by. He picked up his handgun. He placed it on Mickey's temple and started to pull back on the trigger, when he he heard two clasps of thunder fly low across the glacier, firing rockets.

The attackers turned. They fired up at the helicopters that had been circling above the fog, desperately trying to find Tex and Mickey. They had moved away in their search. When they heard the explosion, they roared back, strafing the valley.

Tex heard at least four bullets strike the landing skids and the fuselage, one of them right next to the fuel tank. In seconds, though, the helicopters had silenced the attackers forever. Half a dozen men jumped out before the helicopters touched down.

"Cassidy? Captain Sykes from Thule Air Force Base. Let's get you out of here."

Several soldiers put Mickey on a stretcher. The others checked the attackers. They turned several of them over and checked for distinctive clothing, boots, or labels. The one with the bullet in his lung was still breathing. They strapped him on a stretcher. They left the rest, lifeless, on the ice.

"We've got Cassidy and Logan," the captain radioed. "Confirm: the president's daughter is not here. Repeat: Mariah Breen is not here."

Back at the White House, General Mason, Alex Sullivan, and the National Security staff had been tracking the rescue by satellite. "Great work," General Mason said, as Alex raced off to tell the president. "Now, get Mariah off the *Pilgrim*."

The captain's voice broke through the radio static. "On it, sir. We just talked with her protection unit: the *Pilgrim* is secure."

"Excellent. Now, those troops; who were they?"

There was a pause. "A few of them look Russian. But there are no identifying marks. If the survivor lives, we'll find out for sure."

53

White House
Oct. 19, 2016

THE NAVAL STEWARD the plates. He noticed that the president and the First Lady had only picked at their dinner. The president compulsively turned a tennis ball round and round in his palm.

"Sir, Mrs. Breen." Alex entered, out of breath. "Tex is safe. So is Mariah. She wasn't with him. She'll be on a US naval boat in less than an hour."

Thank you, God! Thank you! Charley breathed for the first time in hours. He saw tears streak his wife's mascara, as she squeezed his hand. "And Mickey Logan?"

"A leg injury, but alive."

"That's great news, Alex. Tell us as soon as Mariah's on the naval boat."

The president tossed the tennis ball to his chief of staff. "Cancel the Missouri rallies. Set up a full cabinet meeting in two days. Cut Tex's trip short. I want him there, and I want someone else as well."

Alex arched his eyebrows when he heard the name.

54

Dulles International Airport, Washington
Oct. 19, 2016

WHEN THE OFFICER SCANNED Zavia's passport, a notice appeared. "Detain. Notify Supervisor." Two men in dark suits were already heading toward her. "Dr. Jansen," the older man flashed an FBI badge. "I'm Agent Harris. This is Agent Brewster."

A few minutes later, they entered a drab conference room. Zavia put her purse and coat on the table. Behind the one-way mirror, Emma Wolfe sat with Dave Dunn. The Russian-born analyst had just ordered a database search for any Russian with a "Zhivago" connection. She listened to Zavia being questioned while she scanned the sheet of photos in her hand.

"You've been to Russia eight times in two years. Why?" Agent Harris asked, sipping from a water bottle.

"Business." Zavia folded her arms. "I'm a hydrologist. I find ways to use water that save money, energy, and jobs. What's this about?"

"For example?" Agent Brewster ignored her question. She ignored his. "Dr. Jansen, we're prepared to be here all . . ."

"Where did that water come from?" she asked suddenly, pointing to the bottle. "Probably from another state or watershed." Clearly, they didn't get the point. "We move lots of water in this country. But it takes energy. What's the energy source? Usually a fossil fuel. If we cut the energy, we cut the costs, and we cut the emissions. Now, can we cut the crap? What do you want?"

Inside the soundproof room, Emma stared at surveillance photos from the Detroit, St. Louis, and Miami rallies. In each set of photos, she found one of a pretty young woman with eyes like saucers. *Who are you?*

Agent Brewster was a rookie. Zavia had rattled him. He would rattle her. "Dr. Jansen, the prime minister personally chose you for the job?" He leaned forward. "Were you sleeping with him?"

Zavia stared at the agent as if he were an archaeological relic from some era when people used stone axes and men said those things to women. "Of course I was." Abruptly, she got on her feet. She swept her coat and purse off the table and onto the floor. "Take your pants off, Agent Brewster. Lie down. You're next."

Brewster froze. This wasn't a situation they covered in FBI school. "Dr. Jansen, your career is at risk. I suggest you—"

"Risk?" She walked around the table and stood over the FBI agent. "In China, three hundred million people are at risk. In Japan, it's most of the population. How about the Maldives in the Pacific? Do you know that a few years ago, the cabinet held a meeting underwater, wearing scuba equipment to dramatize that a coroner could soon write a death-by-drowning certificate for every citizen?" By this time, she was leaning over him. He could smell eggs and breakfast sausage on her breath. "And by the way," she concluded, "I'd include the three hundred thousand people in Murmansk. Believe it or not, I was brought in by the prime minister because I can help reduce that risk, you idiot."

Agent Harris tried to cover. "It is odd, Dr. Jansen, that a government with a lot less money than ours is talking about a very high-ticket item like dikes. The head of the government introduces you on television, but you're a foreign contractor who works by herself. And your harbor tour guides are all members of Russia's Centennial Committee."

Behind the mirror, Emma had had enough. "Let's go." She and Dave marched into the conference room. "Dr. Jansen, we're with the National Security Agency." She turned to the agents. "New developments. Sorry." Then, woman-to-woman, she pulled her chair up next to Zavia. "I need to apologize for my colleagues. But style aside, we need to know what was said between you and the Russian authorities on your most recent trip. Trust me: no detail is irrelevant."

Zavia sighed. She had been to several World Science Fiction Conventions. They attracted strange people and stranger plots. But this felt far weirder than anything she had ever heard at those conventions. *Okay, okay.* She gave them a fifteen-minute recounting of what had transpired.

"On this trip, or any trip, did anyone make reference to 'Zhivago'?" Emma pressed on.

Zavia shook her head. "I'd have remembered. I've read the book twice."

"Dr. Jansen," Dave threw her another curveball. "What's your relationship with Tex Cassidy?"

"Tex Cassidy! About the same as my relationship with him." She hooked her thumb at Agent Brewster.

"Cassidy is a special assistant to the president." Emma stepped in. "Someone is trying to kill him."

Kill Tex? He's a son-of-a-bitch, but . . . Zavia took a deep breath. "A hundred years ago, in college, we dated. Nothing serious. From time to time, I hear about him because he's one of the best at what he does. Who's trying to kill him?"

"Did any of the Russians mention him?"

"Not in Murmansk. But I got a call from Dimitri Bakov yesterday. He had just talked with Tex in Canada. I told him what I just told you."

Emma leaned closer to Zavia. "When it comes to national security, I don't believe in coincidences. Do you?"

55

Amsterdam, Netherlands
Oct. 19, 2016

IN HIS ROOM at the Golden Tulip Hotel, Alpha stared into the mirror. First, he inserted his blue-tinted contact lenses. Then he put on his custom-fitted blond wig. Satisfied that he looked Dutch again, he walked out of his third-floor room and rode the elevator down. He walked across the lobby to get a newspaper, checking each employee, guest, and visitor as he did so.

A few minutes later, Alpha exited the hotel and started walking down Nieuwezijdskolk Street. It took him twenty-four minutes to make the ten-minute walk from the hotel to the Climate Trackers office. During those extra fourteen minutes, he sauntered with his umbrella pointed backward, so that the camera in the tip could relay images of people behind him to Beta. He entered a large café, bought two cappuccinos, and left by a different door. On the street, he intentionally set the hot cups on top of a mailbox and grabbed them from a different angle, an action that allowed him to survey the street.

Finally, Alpha entered the alley next to the office building. He passed the two programmers' unlocked bicycles next to the door. He leaned over and smelled the small blue and yellow flowers that were delicately tied to Ingrid's handlebars. Alpha then adjusted his blond wig one more time and bounded up the back stairs to the fourth floor.

"Good afternoon," he said, cheerily. "I brought you cappuccinos to make the work go faster!"

Ingrid was tall, like her father, Lars, with short blonde hair framing her blue eyes and maiden-fair skin. "Good afternoon to you. And thanks for this," she said, smiling and reaching for one of the cups.

Christian, Ingrid's coworker, was twenty-four—two years older than her. He drove her crazy because he whistled while he coded, and he preferred to work in a "coffeeshop"—the Dutch term for a bistro where marijuana was legally sold. Like Ingrid, Christian gave a damn about the world. On any given day, he would bemoan the billions who survived on less than two dollars a day. As of seven weeks ago, he was the father of their embryonic baby.

"Nice to see you again." Christian smiled at Alpha. He liked his boss, who had lied so passionately about the importance of fighting whalers off the Icelandic coast.

For the next quarter hour, Alpha bit his lip, asking website questions he didn't care about. Then, putting his hand on Ingrid's shoulder, he asked the only question he did care about. "And finally, are all the latitude and longitude coordinates in so we can activate the cameras at the same time?"

"Christian's coordinates are done. I'll finish mine in the morning," Ingrid said, opening a new computer window and pointing to a set of coded commands.

As soon as the two programmers left for the day, Alpha locked the door, lowered the shades, and logged onto a secure website. From there, he video-conferenced with Admiral Sukirov, who was sipping brandy, though he felt like swigging it. Alpha's disguise didn't faze him, since they were like changes of clothes. "Alpha, you're worrying me. First, it was the lost snuke; then the botched mission on the Ice Sheet; and now the Americans have one of our contractors."

"I'm sorry, sir. We've located him, and he'll be dead by midnight." Alpha looked up, hearing a familiar whistle. It came from the street below and was getting closer.

The admiral put his glass down. "You sound strange. Are you all right? Is there anything I should know?"

The operative immediately sprung to attention. "No, sir. Nothing you should know." *Nothing you need to know.*

"That contractor. He'd better be dead. Next: Greenland. Can we still get the result we discussed?"

"Yes, sir. Your 'submersible' idea was genius. Otherwise, we wouldn't have the firepower." Alpha heard a key turning in the front door.

"I'm counting on that, Alpha." There was a menacing tone to the admiral's statement. "Get back to me when the codes are all done."

Just before they terminated their call, the deadbolt turned, and Christian entered. "Sorry. I forgot my cell phone." He caught a glance of a strange icon on Alpha's screen.

"That's okay." Alpha shut down his computer. "I was just talking to one of our funders. Hey, if you're going over to the coffeehouse, I'd love to join you."

In no time, they were at the Melting Pot. It was crowded, and the sweet-smelling smoke hung in the air. "Anything you'd recommend?" he asked Christian, looking at the chalkboard with today's featured joints. Alpha then paid for the White Widow that they smoked in a back booth. When the joint was gone, Alpha went to the counter. He noticed a section of wall with a dozen photos draped in black cloth of unnamed young adults, mostly men, with a date under each photo. One of them, a man in his thirties with a geometric face, caught his attention.

Alpha paid the woman behind the counter. He pointed to the photo. "Who is that? Do you know?"

"Sorry." She looked at the date under the photo. "He died way back in February 2001."

Alpha returned to their table and offered a second joint, Dutch Dragon, to Christian. "What's the story on those photos?"

Christian held the sweet smoke in his lungs. "Regulars here who overdosed on one drug or another." Then he exhaled.

Alpha toked as well, though he knew how to minimize its effect. "We just don't know when life will be over, do we?"

When they left the Melting Pot, Christian was orbiting somewhere beyond the Milky Way. "Those cameras? It's wonderful how you're trying to save the glaciers." He was hungry for skewered lamb and led them down one of Amsterdam's many alleys toward a Moroccan restaurant.

"If everyone doesn't do something," Alpha philosophized until they were away from the street, "everyone will suffer." Alpha nudged Christian away from the streetlight. "Do you know that 99 percent of animal species have gone extinct?" Alpha pulled his serrated knife out of the sheath strapped to his forearm underneath his loose-fitting shirt. "Hopefully, that won't happen to us." He put his hand on Christian's shoulder. He nudged the young man slightly, until they were face to face.

"I sure hope—" Suddenly, Christian saw Alpha's knife. Stoned as he was, he stuck out his arm to defend himself. Alpha cut his arm and slid the knife between Christian's ribs. He lifted Christian's body and heaved it into a nearby Dumpster. He closed the top, stuffed his blond wig into his pocket, and headed back to the Golden Tulip.

56

SS *Pilgrim*
Oct. 19, 2016

DOZENS OF PASSENGERS stood along the Pilgrim's deck rail, bitching. "Damn, those jets are flying low." One passenger covered her ears. Another spit into the sea. "This is ridiculous. I can't get a decent photo." He pointed to the helicopters whipping up wind and water.

"What's that?" A young woman was looking through her binoculars.

"It's a naval patrol boat," a crew member said. "American. Coming fast." A few minutes later, the bitching turned to gossip when the passengers realized that President Breen's daughter was onboard.

Mariah herself was a keg of dynamite with a very short fuse. Her godfather had abandoned her. Now her Secret Service protection unit wouldn't let her on deck. To calm herself, she set up a tripod by her porthole and videoed coastal glaciers. She felt better when she heard a loud cracking sound. *Finally, some decent audio.*

Out on the deck, passengers jostled for places along the railing. "My God, that glacier's as big as the Empire State Building," a New Yorker told his teenager.

"Look, Dad, it's moving!" By the time the boy raised his camera, the glacier had crashed into the sea and set the sea in motion.

The whole boat shook. On the bridge, the captain's insides were also shaking. He had seen hundreds of medium-sized and large glaciers calve. Very few were even half as big as this one. "Sound the alarm!"

The SS *Pilgrim*'s emergency siren blared. Over the public address system, the passengers heard "This is the captain speaking. We are in an emergency situation! Clear the deck IMMEDIATELY! Go to your cabin or the dining room. Hold onto something solid. The waves from the glacier will rock this ship. Repeat: clear the deck IMMEDIATELY!" Before he finished, the crew was shoving people through doors and down stairs.

Down below, Mariah and the Secret Service agents all grabbed bunk legs. But the very first big wave knocked them all loose. "Chickadee!" The senior agent saw a night table slam into the president's daughter. The lamp and the amulet earrings fell on top of her as the agent crawled over to help.

"I'm okay, I'm okay." She held her injured arm. Then, one after another, very large waves, some ten feet high, began to hit the *Pilgrim*. Each was bigger than the last. And the swells now carried hunks of glacial shards that crashed into the boat's hull. Mariah and the agents were flung around the cabin like shirts in a dryer. Mariah screamed as her head hit a wall.

Suddenly, the boat lurched thirty degrees to starboard and started taking on water. On the bridge, all the electronics failed. The rudder was useless. The captain couldn't turn into the waves, and the defenseless *Pilgrim* was smacked broadside again and again. "Mayday! Mayday! Mayday! SS *Pilgrim*!" the captain yelled into the ship's radio, seconds before ordering his crew to lower the lifeboats.

Meanwhile, in one of the helicopters, the pilot saw a third chopper approaching fast from the Ice Sheet itself. His attention, though, was on the water rushing through a large hole in the *Pilgrim*'s hull. He saw screaming passengers fall into the icy, roiling ocean, where the water poured over them and the ice shards smashed their bones and sliced their arteries. A few stumbled to the higher end of the boat only to lose their footing and slide under the railing. The pilot saw the *Pilgrim* become an overturned vehicle. He screamed into his radio, calling the patrol boat still a quarter mile away. "OTV! OTV! Speed up! It's sinking!" Then he tried reaching the protection unit. *Answer, Damn it!*

Looking down, the pilot saw the Secret Service agents frantically waving to him. They had Mariah on the deck. "Prepare to jump," he told the Navy SEALs onboard. Immediately, the para-jumpers moved to the door and opened it. "See her? Purple parka under her life vest!" The others prepared the cables, slings, and baskets.

The pilot lowered a cable and harness. It swung wildly in the wind a few feet from the agents. One of them leaned over the railing as the water pounded her face. On her fourth try, she grabbed the harness, pulled it down and started wrapping it around Mariah. The pilot was about to lift the cable when another massive chunk of ice crashed into the ship like a trailer truck smacking a Volkswagen. Horrified, the pilot watched the *Pilgrim* rise farther up on its stern and begin to capsize. Helpless, he watched the president's daughter and her two guards slide into the freezing water.

"Free entry jump!" The pilot alerted the para-jumpers. The wind was less than five knots. He brought the chopper down less than ten feet from the surface and as close to Mariah as he dared, fearful of churning up even more water with the rotors. Moments later, the SEALs jumped. They were in the water. One of them swam toward the *Pilgrim* and banged on the hull, listening for other passengers trapped inside. Two of them headed for the purple parka.

Inside the third helicopter, Tex was near delirious. Two hours ago, he was nearly killed. Mickey might lose his ankle. And now Mariah! "Get as low as you can!" he yelled to the pilot.

The chopper dropped as close to the surface as it dared, and then some. Tex wrenched the cargo door open. Scanning the water, he saw Mariah bobbing up and down. *Where are the SEALs?*

The waves were less intense now. Tex saw Mariah dog-paddling with her arms, frantically trying to stay above the waves. In one instant, her body was tossed around and her face turned up to the chopper. Their eyes met. He saw the fear in hers.

A half second later, Tex jumped out the door and hit the water, thirty feet from Mariah. The water was frigid. Instantly, he felt his body go numb. He was an average swimmer at best. His waterlogged clothes made each arm stroke and leg kick an ordeal.

Luckily, the force of the water carried him closer to her. He screamed, "Mariah!" when the wave trough gave him two seconds of clearer sight.

He heard her faint yell back, "Help me!" as she was pulled under the waves.

Tex swam harder, but he couldn't swim hard enough. *Oh, God, Mariah! No! Mariah! Mariah!* Then, when the next wave passed, he saw that one of the SEALs had his arm around her.

"Anything broken?" the SEAL yelled over the sounds of the chopper. She shook her head. Then, in seconds, he checked that she wasn't bleeding and that her airways, breathing, and circulation seemed okay. Finally, he put a thumb up to the technician SEAL in the chopper.

The tech started to lower the basket. When he heard the parajumper yelling, "Sling, just the sling," he pulled it back and quickly lowered the horse-collar on a cable.

In the churning water, the SEAL put the horse-collar around himself and the semi-conscious Mariah. He wrapped his legs around her and contained her arms. As the tech lifted them, he rotated his body and protected her head so the tech could guide her inside.

As Tex bobbed around, he saw Mariah and the SEAL entering the helicopter. Then it turned north and sped away. *Thule! The hospital. Thank God!*

Moments later, Tex's chopper sent a cable down for him. His fingers were so numb that he could barely close the harness buckle. Finally, he lay on the chopper floor. He was shivering, as his chopper also sped toward the base.

Before the helicopter fully landed, Tex jumped out and raced across the ice. The air was colder. The wind was stronger. With his clothes still soaking, he pushed the emergency room doors open. Immediately, two medics grabbed him and threw blankets around him. "Where's Mariah?"

She was on a table. In the distance, he saw the medical staff racing equipment to the room. Others were alternately giving her mouth-to-mouth resuscitation and pounding her chest. "Sir, they're doing what they can. She's coming around. We need to go to another room."

Tex struggled but couldn't get away. As they moved him down the hall, he saw the heart monitor next to Mariah. The signal was weak, but okay. He let himself be walked to an open door and warm clothes.

In the treatment room, the medics got Tex into hospital clothes. Quickly, they checked his pulse, pressure, and pupils. "I'm all right." He calmed down. They calmed down. Until they heard running in the hallway.

A nurse yelled, "She's failing!" Tex broke away from the medics and ran down the corridor with his hospital gown flapping. He saw six, eight, ten medical people around the table with Mariah. He saw the heart monitor signal get weaker. Three soldiers raced toward him. Seconds before a nurse slammed the door shut, Tex saw the doctor applying shock to his goddaughter's heart.

PART THREE: YELLOW

57

President's Private Residence, White House
Oct. 19, 2016

"**O**W!" THE PRESIDENT GRABBED his left knee and nearly fell over. The pain was searing. But he didn't mind. It was the price he paid for doing the silly little jig his father had taught him. He only did it at times like his wedding, the day Mariah was born, and the night of his Inauguration. Ellie rolled her eyes as she always did, loving her husband's silly celebration.

"They're safe," he said softly, mostly to himself, aware of how frightened he had been for both his daughter and his friend. He sat next to Ellie and took her hand, brushing his shoulder against hers. He took another sip of wine. "Tell me again. How did she react? Did she believe that going to the Arctic was my idea? I want the blow-by-blow."

Ellie let his happiness sink into her pores. She missed these moments. Long ago, she had accepted that, like estrogen, they diminished with age. But the presidency had sucked them out the way the Arizona sun sucks moisture out of skin. They would die knowing that these were the most interesting days of their lives, but not the happiest. "Forget cloud nine. She was on-the-moon happy."

"And she called me twice in three days! She hasn't done that since she was fourteen." Charley beamed. "Even better: she said she'll celebrate with us election night." Charley filled both their wine glasses and lifted his. "To our amazing daughter . . ."

Ellie's arm froze mid-lift. Her head turned forty-five degrees in the direction of racing footsteps in the corridor. *Even when there's a crisis, people don't run.* She felt something at the bottom of her spine. It was cold like December. Then, as the steps got closer, it was January and February. By the time Alex Sullivan and General Mason burst through the door and caught their breath, hers was gone.

"Tell me she's all right." She started to stand.

Both men shook. The general looked at the president and then back at the First Lady. His lips trembled. "I'm so sorry, Mrs. Breen. Her boat was capsized by a glacier. They airlifted her to a hospital. The doctors worked on her for more than an hour..."

Ellie imploded. Her skeleton couldn't hold her upright, and she collapsed on the floor.

"Get a doctor!" the president yelled, now sitting on the floor with her, detached, almost disembodied. He put his wife's head in his lap. He couldn't get her sobs to stop. He couldn't breathe right. He couldn't get the jackhammer on his heart to slow down.

58

En Route To Washington
Oct. 19, 2016

TEX FELT LIKE he had drunk a gallon of Novocain. And he was thankful for it.

Twenty-four minutes after the nurse had closed the hospital door, the doctor opened it. He stepped out, shook his head, said, "I'm sorry," and went to call the White House. Behind the doctor, Tex saw Mariah's body covered by a sheet, head to toe.

Within an hour of Mariah's death, Tex was back in the air. "Sir, the president's still not available. Neither is the First Lady." Major Bowden stood over Tex in the back of the plane. Tex didn't look up. He hadn't touched the food Lynn had brought him nor would he talk with her. The hot coffee and ice water were now at room temperature. "Are you okay, sir?"

Tex's eyes seem fixed, as if they had stopped blinking. The major pulled a pen-sized flashlight out of his pocket and shone it into Tex's eyes. Tex grabbed the major's wrist. "Keep trying," he said.

Ten minutes later, Major Bowden called over the intercom, "Sir, the president's chief of staff . . ."

Tex picked up the phone. "Alex . . ."

Alex's voice trembled. "I'm so sorry, Tex. I know she was like a daughter. And I know you tried to save her."

"I need to talk to them." There was no timber in his voice. No anything in his voice.

"The First Lady is in bed. Sedated. The president's with her."

Tex didn't say anything. Alex understood. Finally, he blurted out, "I need to tell you something, Tex. But I can wait till you're here."

"Tell me now. I won't be there long. I'm going home to Minnesota."

Alex loosened his tie. Then he spoke very deliberately into the phone. "Tex, the president . . . maybe he'll pull out of this, maybe he won't. But we can't wait to find out."

"Why are you telling me this, Alex? I just told you I'm going home."

"Tex!" The chief of staff suddenly got very loud and very intense. "Do you understand? We've got a real crisis. The president may be done. The vice president's in a coma. The Speaker of the House is from the other party and a different planet. So we've got to know about the president. We need your help. You've got to stay at least one more day."

Tex pulled the phone away from his ear. His heart pumped blood, but he didn't feel anything. Katie was dead. Mariah was dead. Carlos might be dead. He was in psychological free fall. As fast as he could, he had boarded up his emotions like plywood on broken glass. Zero emotion is better than chronically being kicked in the gut by an emotional pile driver. "Alex, anything else before I hang up?" In that moment, he just didn't care about national crises or whether his friend remained his president.

Alex suddenly looked up. The door to his office flew open. General Mason flew in. Alex indicated with his eyes: "Help." He held out the phone. "Cassidy says he's going home."

"Tex, it's Mason. Listen to me. I get it. Life's kicking you in the balls. It really is. With steel-toed shoes. But there's millions of people who'll get the same treatment or worse if we don't do this right."

Tex felt nothing and said less.

"Tex, damn it, you want to go home? You want to go Colombia? You want to go to the fucking moon? You have my word. I will personally arrange it. But first, help us. Please, help us."

Tex was silent. Then, dead man talking, he barely mumbled, "What kind of help?"

"The cabinet needs to know what you found up there."

"You mean other than my dead goddaughter?"

The general gripped the phone tighter. His voice softened. "Yes." He took a long inhalation. "And something else: after you see the president, how you think he is." The less Tex said, the more the general did. "You know the president. Better than anyone other than his wife. And his wife's out of commission." The general hesitated. "I shouldn't tell you this . . ." He looked at Alex, who held his jawbone and nodded slowly. "The cabinet has to decide whether or not the president's too far over the edge."

"If you pile on him, General, I'll—"

"Tex, he's your friend. But he's also the president." The general's tone softened. "He may resign. That's happened before. But the cabinet may ask the president to resign. That's never happened before."

59

Washington, D.C.
Oct. 19, 2016

ZAVIA STEPPED OUT OF THE FBI CAR and watched it drive away. She waved, but Agent Brewster didn't wave back. She folded down four fingers and left the middle one up. Then she rolled her suitcase through the revolving door.

"Welcome home, Dr. Jansen." The lobby guard gave her a wide Zimbabwe smile. "Good trip?" He was a friend, of sorts. Like so many others, he was part voyeur, delighted to spend twenty minutes looking at her photos but not caring the slightest about who she was or whether she preferred Italian takeout to Chinese.

Once inside her apartment, Zavia hung her coat in the hall closet and looked around. The apartment was cleaner than a hospital, just as she had left it. The silk flowers hadn't shed their leaves. The pillows on the couch hadn't moved or been moved.

Zavia opened the fridge and saw the box of baking soda, two unopened wine bottles, and half a brick of moldy cheese.

In the bedroom, she sat on her queen bed. The corners were tucked in. The answering machine told her that her dry cleaning was ready, and a girlfriend wanted to know if she could babysit.

Time was her ever-present enemy. Usually, she didn't have enough of it. Occasionally, like now, she couldn't fill it up. Desperate, she rummaged through her purse. She tossed out old boarding passes and stuffed restaurant and cab receipts into an envelope. She thought about going out for groceries but decided she wasn't that desperate.

Slowly, Zavia took off one earring. Then the other. Then the bracelet she had bought in Hawaii. The more she settled in to being home, the more unsettled she felt. During the long shower, the water ran off her back, but not the desire to slap Admiral Sukirov across the face and give him a very large piece of her mind from the reptilian section of her brain.

Can't go there.

As she shampooed and conditioned her hair, she saw the frightened faces of the Maldives leaders when she gave them the answer they dreaded. *Don't go there.*

She put her foot on the edge of the tub and picked up her razor but put it right down, as her cells again felt the tsunami waters surrounding her. *Christ! Where can I go? Retirement. Thank God, it's set. Thank you, Mr. Prime Minister! Thank you! Thank you! Thank you!*

A few minutes later, Zavia sprawled on the couch in her bathrobe. She sipped a glass of Merlot from one of the refrigerated bottles. By the second sip, gravity forced her eyelids down. The last thought she had before she fell asleep wasn't about Dagmare's birthday party or the FBI interrogation. *Why is someone trying to kill Tex?*

An hour later, Zavia rubbed the sleep out of her eyes and lotion into her skin. She put on a pink silk blouse and blue jeans. "Amanda," she said into the phone, "I'm back, and I'm starving! Can you meet me at the deli, and I'll tell you everything?"

"Oh, Zavia, I'm sorry. I've got the kids. I'll call you next week, and we'll get a pedicure."

Three voice mail messages later, Zavia sank into her desk chair. She stared up at her framed degrees and her nineteenth-century hydrological charts. She loved them. But they were lousy conversationalists.

Next, she saw the three-foot-high painting of a drop of water that she had been given when she was named Hydrologist of the Year. She looked over at photos of her parents and of Dagmare. There was one photo, taken two years ago in Reno, where Zavia, another woman, and twenty-six men pretended to be having the time of their life. They were at a hydrology conference cleverly titled "Climate and Water: Place Your Bets." *Maybe it's time to get a dog.*

Zavia tried one more person, a friend from her Army Corp of Engineers days. But she was also away from her desk. Zavia didn't leave her name, number, or time she was calling. Instead, she reverted to her number-one emotional defense: doing.

Zavia opened her computer and keyed in the Murmansk Harbor data about tides, radiation, and seasonal storms. She even sketched out a few preliminary storm-surge barrier designs.

It worked, hallelujah. Time passed. So did her ache to talk. When she looked up, it was three in the afternoon. Zavia shifted to her number-two defense: distraction. She traded in her computer screen for the television screen.

"A massive glacier has broken off from the Greenland Ice Sheet." The young news anchor looked ashen beneath her studio makeup. "The resulting waves capsized a tour boat carrying twenty-two crew members and seventy-six passengers. One of the passengers who tragically died was Mariah Breen, the president's twenty-six-year-old daughter. At this moment, we have no details, other than she fell into the sea."

Zavia felt her insides capsizing. Young people are killed every day by cars and stray bullets. But the president's daughter? By a glacier? It was the straw that cracked her emotional dam. Weeks of tears . . . years of tears . . . they just poured out of her. She bent over. She sobbed. She whimpered. But she couldn't stop them . . . she couldn't even slow them . . . until two hours later, she was out of tears and half out of her mind.

Finally, she lay on the couch. She reached over for a tissue. That was when she felt the volcano in her belly. Mt. St. Zavia. As fast as she could, she covered her mouth, ran into the bathroom, slipped on the dark-blue throw rug, knelt by the toilet, and threw up the little food in her stomach and the emotional bile in the rest of her.

When the volcano stopped, Zavia pulled herself up and changed clothes. She moved through TV channels faster than she moved through the long line of immature men she had encountered.

When she couldn't find any more real news about Mariah, she punched the "off" button.

When the phone rang, she looked at the caller ID for three rings. "Is this a joke?" she finally asked.

"No, it isn't, Dr. Jansen. Nor is the request I'm about to make." The president's chief of staff spoke very slowly. "It's tragic . . . He's still the president . . . We've run into a set of circumstances . . . We need your help . . . Can we count on you?"

"Yes, sir, you can count on me." She had a thousand questions, but couldn't get one of them out.

Zavia put the phone down. She sat down. She got up. She paced around her apartment. *The president wants me there in two days. It'll never happen. He's in mourning. I'd better be ready.* She sat back down in front of her computer and opened a new folder: "Cabinet Presentation." She had thirty minutes to present and thirty hours of material.

Forty minutes later, she was drafting her eighteenth slide. Suddenly, an error message appeared: "Your computer will shut down in one minute." Frantically, she moved to save her material. Meanwhile, the phone rang again. *I knew it. He's canceling.*

She hit "save" with her left hand and grabbed the phone with her right hand. "Yes, sir?"

"Zavia, it's been a month, but I haven't changed that much." The voice was feminine. It was also strong; what you would expect the senior epidemiologist at the Centers for Disease Control to sound like.

"Deb . . . !"

They had shared a house during their last year of college.

"I'd love to hear about your trip. But why don't you adjust your meds and call me back!"

"No, don't hang up." Zavia explained about the presentation. "What do you know about dengue fever?"

The senior epidemiologist had had more than a few three-in-the-morning heart-to-hearts with Zavia. They talked about men, mascara, and methods of scientific inquiry. Her friend could gossip with the best of them. But Deb knew that Zavia was the poster girl for On Purpose. "It's carried by mosquitos. But they make lousy pets. Why do you care?"

"Do we have them in the US?"

"A few in the south. But if the temperature keeps getting hotter, they'll come north like ants to a picnic."

"What's the likelihood—"

"Zavia," Deb interrupted, irritated, "come on: my life is full of dull things like viruses that can destroy humanity. But yours? Oh, my God, Zavia: you're my very first friend to nearly die in a tsunami and, before your clothes dry out, be introduced on TV by the head of Russia. Tell me the truth: did he invite you up to see Lenin's writings?"

Eight minutes later, Zavia had sworn to give a full account of everything. But not now. Not till after her presentation to the cabinet. Before the receiver settled into its cradle, she was back to her slides. *Do I include the health impacts? No, it's too much.* Then she deleted that entire set of slides. Fifteen seconds later, she hit "undo typing." *They've got to know . . .*

Suddenly, she felt another volcano inside her. It was residual disgust from standing in Katrina's waist-high water, when the pesticides, paints, and other everyday poisons had swirled up against her and seeped into her skin.

Zavia needed to calm herself down. She stepped onto her patio. She felt the breeze on her cheeks and remembered Dagmare's comment about the natural world. She didn't notice the limousine with the Russian flag on the hood as it pulled up outside her building. Three minutes later, she was at her front door, shaking hands with a humorless man in a somber suit who handed her a sealed letter. "I'm instructed to stay until you've read this."

Dear Dr. Jansen,

Please be advised that all conversations and interactions involving you and the Russian government are strictly confidential. If this confidentiality is violated in any way, the Russian government will prohibit any future visits to Russia and terminate any commercial contracts currently in force or under discussion.

Regards,
Igor Kranig
Chief Commercial Officer

"Is the letter clear?" he asked.

She turned her back on the man and closed the apartment door. She went over in her mind what she had already told the FBI and might tell the cabinet. There goes the contract. There goes my security. She flashed on her father. He dropped dead at age seventy-three, slicing ham behind the grocery counter to make a few dollars.

Zavia plopped herself down in front of the water drop painting. Under the graphic was the line "Water is Life." If she had just broken up with a lover or had more work to do than time to do it, she would take comfort from the beauty of the graphic and the simplicity of the message. Nine times out of ten, it calmed her down. Apparently, this was the tenth time.

60

Kremlin
Oct. 19, 2016

ADMIRAL SUKIROV WALKED BRISKLY down the corridors, quietly humming the Russian national anthem. Looking at the paintings, a smile crossed his face. His chest swelled. He pointed to a bare spot along the south wall and imagined his own portrait hanging there one day.

"You're late," the prime minister's red, tired eyes followed the admiral as he crossed the conference room. "A full two minutes."

Blood engorged the veins in the admiral's forehead. They doubled again as he sat down at the small table, banged elbows with Dimitri Bakov, bumped knees with the two younger Centennial Committee businessmen, and locked eyes with the man he no longer respected.

"Gentlemen," the prime minister addressed them all, "Breen's daughter is dead. And so are our plans if your factions can't work together." His face was redder than his eyes. Up until now, he had ignored the Centennial Committee split. But that split was wider than the Great Rift in Africa. It pitted the committee's factions in a way that would sink Russia's last chance at destiny, as well as the prime minister's last chance at redemption.

Instinctively, the prime minister rubbed his thumbs back and forth against his index and middle fingers. "Fingers," as he used to be known, had been a maestro at using those fingers in prisoners' noses, eyes, ears, and testicles.

The four committee members sat like stones in the Kremlin walls.

"I know we're moving too fast for you," he looked at the younger businessmen, "and too slowly for you," he addressed Bakov and Sukirov. "The 1917 Revolution wasn't picture-perfect. Neither is ours."

The prime minister hit the intercom on his nearby desk. Six armed soldiers entered. "The climate's doing its part, gentlemen. Will you do yours?" All four men nodded. "Any problems working together?" When none were expressed, he dismissed the meeting. "Admiral, before you go, a word."

The prime minister sat opposite the admiral. "Boris, you broke the cell phone rule at the Centennial Committee meeting. I assume it wasn't your mother." He leaned forward, almost nostril to nostril.

"It was a detail about the meeting with the American woman." He felt the man exhale. "I wasn't thinking."

"I see," the prime minister said, his fingers now back at work, dangling at his side. "And speaking of Dr. Jansen: you, Ivan, and Dimitri missed her big moment at the press conference."

"Mr. Prime Minister, with all due respect," the admiral leaned back against his chair, "it was a waste of time. We're never going to build those barriers."

"I see," the prime minister said. But seeing wasn't believing. "One last question, Boris. Have you learned patience?"

The admiral looked up, puzzled.

"Remember the Black Sea? Our conversation? Your certainty of a quick road to Russia's power?"

The admiral shrugged as if he had just learned that a restaurant was out of his preferred entrée. "I can live with baby steps."

"Let's both hope you can."

Sukirov left the prime minister's office with a terse "Good-bye." He went to a private restroom, locked the door, and splashed water on his face. Just above a "Conserve water" sign, he took a long look in the mirror. *He knows something.*

Sukirov pulled out his cell phone and started to make a call. Then, he put it away and made a decision. He left the water running and walked quickly down the corridor, past the paintings, past the area where he had envisioned his own painting, and down the Kremlin steps, where his car was waiting.

"Take me around Victory Park," he said, not waiting for the driver to open his door.

Later, he ordered the driver to circle Gorky Park, Neskuchniy Garden, and other parts of Moscow that were like churches to him.

An hour later, the admiral opened his apartment door and sat in his library, staring at the newly dusted books. He walked over to the writings of Anton Chekhov, for whom his son had been named. He removed *The Cherry Orchard* and half a dozen others and placed them on a nearby table. Then he moved the tumbler lock back and forth on the safe. Finally, he removed a number of objects, closed the safe, spun the tumbler, and replaced the books.

Minutes later, Sukirov spoke with Alpha over a secure line. "Last time, we discussed four detonation dates. With the death of the Breen girl, we're combining them," he lied, making it sound like a Quartet decision. "First, we'll detonate all the Greenland snukes and issue the terms of capitulation. If they refuse, the Big Bang is forty-eight hours later."

"Understood. We'll be ready."

"And the personal touch for the Netherlands?"

"Frankly, sir, it's been a burden." He explained the hundreds of hours wasted. "We could easily launch the codes from Santorini or Rio."

Admiral Sukirov sneered. He knew it was a lot of time. But he was as vengeful as he was patriotic. "Stay with it, Alpha."

"In that case, sir, do you know what 'spring tide' is?" He explained that it was a monthly alignment of the sun, moon, and earth that maximized tidal heights. "The October spring tide coincides with this part of the operation."

"How very nice. And what's the personnel situation at the barriers?"

"Skeleton. They mostly use software."

"And security?"

"Couldn't be thinner. Beta and I were joking that it's an insult to our profession."

"You're not getting cocky, are you?"

"Just bored with these classes and tours. When it's time to go live, seven minutes is all we'll need."

"Excellent. Then, one last change: I leave in two hours to join you." He fingered the black hair dye, color-coated lenses, and six passports on the table in front of him. He stuck the Finnish passport in his pocket. "Other than Beta, no one else knows about this local operation. Let's keep it that way."

61

White House
Oct. 20, 2016

TEX RESTED HIS HAND on the doorknob. Ten seconds. Twenty seconds. Thirty seconds. He rehearsed again. Finally, he turned his wrist and slowly opened the door. He entered the living room next to the presidential master bedroom. He smelled pain and death. It was just like entering Katie's room during her last weeks.

"Ellie . . ." The First Lady wore black, head-to-toe. She sat on a couch, motionless. Any movement was too much movement. She sat with her back to the windows, staring toward the Center Hall. Across the hall was the Blue Bedroom that had been set aside for Mariah's visits.

Tex sank to his knees and took her hand. "Ellie, I'm so sorry. I'm so sorry!" He was brilliant with written words. But not spoken words that connected his deepest pain to the deepest pain in another. Everything he had rehearsed seemed shallow and stupid.

Ellie didn't respond. She didn't pull her hand away. But it lay in his palm like a dead person's hand. They stayed that way for more than twenty minutes. Twice, Alex entered, saw them and backed out of the room like the family butler.

"What happened out there, Tex?"

"What, Ellie? I'm sorry. I can't hear you."

The First Lady made an effort. "What happened out there?"

Tex looked into her eyes. He knew those eyes. They wanted to know. So he told her, stroking her hand, letting his own tears drop onto both their hands. Finally, he looked at her but didn't say anything.

Ellie saw that there were words trapped inside him. "What is it, Tex?"

"I want you to know something, Ellie, to really hear it, okay?" The First Lady nodded slightly. "Mariah was the daughter you raised her to be."

Ellie's face softened. "She was, Tex. I know that. I'll always have that." She fought hard to keep from crying. She was partly successful when she said, "Now I want to ask you something. Why did somebody want to kill you?"

"I think they were after Mickey. I just—"

"A guy who videos glaciers?"

"... who makes it real to people." All that seemed on the far side of Pluto. "How's Charley?"

"We can't talk about this yet." Behind them, the partially opened door from the master bedroom opened wider.

"Is he okay? Alex wants me to help the cabinet find out."

Charley quietly entered. "You'd better. They can't trust me. Neither can I."

Tex stood and hugged his friend for a very long time. Then Charley pulled a chair up close to the couch and his wife.

"Where have you been, Charley?"

"In a meeting," he said, stroking her arm. "Planning our strategy. All I want is to go to bed."

For the next fifteen minutes, they hunched together, talking about Mariah. Ellie told the "broken finger" story, when Mariah had punched a fifth-grade bully. Tex recounted the time she had come up for a week to help him take care of Katie. Charley described the time she soloed the rapids in the Grand Canyon.

The knock startled them. Alex entered, head bowed. "The protocol staff ... they're here."

Ellie recoiled. "You go, Charley. Just keep it small and private, okay?"

Ellie walked toward the door to their bedroom. Then she stopped and turned to her husband. "The strategy meeting: what did you decide?"

"Later, sweetheart ..."

"Now, Charley." Something had returned.

He took her hand and looked her in the eye. "I'm staying in the race. We're playing to win."

"You're going to use Mariah's death, aren't you?" Ellie pulled her hand away, put it in the pocket of her mourning dress, and walked into their bedroom.

62

White House
Oct. 21, 2016

A LEX SULLIVAN LOOKED OUT THE WINDOW of his large, first-floor, West Wing corner office. He saw the flag at half-mast. *Should be a slow day.* Aside from federal flags, all fifty governors had ordered state flags to be lowered. And both Governor Wilton and the media had issued a one-day moratorium on political attacks. *But it won't be.* Off to the side, the news anchor yapped away on a muted television.

"You're sure?" Alex's face was chalky white. It looked even whiter against his black mourning suit. He opened his desk drawer, pulled out a plastic bottle, and downed another migraine pill. "No chance she was murdered?"

The national security adviser had walked down the corridor from his own office. He sat across Alex's desk and picked up the pill bottle. "What's in these? LSD?"

"Give me a break, General. I've got to ask."

"Why?"

"Everyone's asking me."

"Tell them to call me."

"Bakov wouldn't."

General Mason looked at him strangely. Alex caught the look. "Christ, General, I set him up to meet with Cassidy."

"But why'd he call you?"

"He's close to the prime minister, who . . ." Alex made a disgusted clicking noise with his tongue. He rubbed his temples. The pills were helping, but this conversation wasn't. "Tell me about the Thule doctor." He opened a manila folder. "Pieter Skov."

"You're pushing it, Alex. Who's pushing you?"

"Skov sounds Russian." Alex glanced over at the TV.

"He's a Dane."

"Did he do everything he could? Did he not do something he could have?"

"Is it Jane?" The general glanced over at the television, too.

"If you're keeping something from me . . ."

"It is Jane, isn't it? The secretary of state would have to know, because the cabinet has to know."

"Oh, shit!" Alex turned toward the television. Earlier, there were six video cameras. One morbidly looped a satellite image of the calving glacier that had killed Mariah. The others were funerals in North Dakota, Virginia, Vermont, Georgia, and Michigan, where the president and First Lady were burying their daughter's ashes. "Can you bomb that goddamn station?"

Now, instead of tight-lipped, slow-walking mourners, Alex and General Mason saw parading climate-change protesters. In Atlanta, thousands of them were chanting: "Two, four, six, eight, the changing climate will seal our fate."

In Washington, outside the White House fence, about a hundred evangelicals walked by with a thirty-foot-long banner: "Love the Creator? Don't Mess with His Creation."

Suddenly, they saw scenes of Big Ben and Parliament buildings along the Thames. They heard the anchor's voiceover. "Of the hundred rallies, this is the biggest."

The anchor droned on. "London. A coastal city. A vulnerable city where, today, 250,000 Brits braved the heat to tell the world: either we get our act together or our act falls apart."

General Mason smirked. "If we can't bomb them, can we at least get them new writers?" He picked up his laptop and headed for the door. "If you don't contradict me in ten seconds, I'll assume it's Jane."

Twenty seconds later, the general didn't open the door. He locked it. "Bakov. Tell me about him."

Alex's body got rigor mortis. "Don't insult me."

"You owed him. Did he call in the chit? Did you make an innocent remark that turned deadly?"

The chief of staff walked over to the door and unlocked it. "Get out, General."

The two men glared at each other.

"We're not done, Alex." The general left.

Alex popped another pill and muted the television. This day can't get any worse. That was when he heard fast-moving high heels outside his office.

For Donna Dean, the president's chief political strategist, the "Please Knock Before Entering" sign could have been written in Farsi. "What's up? I almost got flattened by Mason. Have you seen this?" She pushed his door open and held up a one-page fax.

"Nice to see you, too, Donna."

"Read this." She shoved the fax under his chin and sat facing him at the conference table. "It's tomorrow's lead editorial. We've got two hours to comment." Reluctantly, Alex picked up the fax and read.

CAN HE GOVERN?

More often than not, this newspaper has supported President Breen. If this election were solely about his policies, we would shortly endorse the president. But the tragic death of his daughter gives us pause.

Does the president's grief cloud his judgment? Americans will have between now and Election Day to answer that question. Our pause speaks to a far more complex question: Will President Breen suffer emotional after-shocks over the loss of his beloved only child? At a time of national, international, and environmental upheaval, will this country be led by a sometime commander-in-chief and a sometime parent-in-pain?

No one, including this newspaper, can gauge the impact of losing a child. Our only endorsement today is that voters keep that in mind when they vote for their next president in ten days.

Alex put the fax down. He didn't know if the president or his wife could take another body blow. "You predicted this."

"Yeah. From a fringe blogger, not the LA Times."

Alex crinkled the fax and slammed it into the wastebasket. "Tell them: no fucking comment."

63

White House
Oct. 22, 2016

"**I**T'LL BE TWO HOURS before the president can see you." The staff member, Mariah's age, escorted Tex to a first-floor conference room. "We'd gone for a drink a couple of times." Tears leaked from her eyes. As she left, she added, "Oh, FYI, General Mason, the national security adviser, was asking where you were."

Tex got a mug of water from a side table. Then he sat down. He ached to be at the lake, where every species was preparing for winter. *I should be, too.* Then he took a deep breath, opened his laptop, and checked the so-called news.

Mariah's picture was plastered everywhere. The news sites, sure. Understandable. But sports sites had photos of her playing soccer. Hell, he found a dance site that had an archived photo of Mariah in a tutu. The more he looked, the more he felt like someone was driving nails into his soul.

Ironically, one news story featured her high school honors thesis: "The Non-Linear Nature of Climate Change." Suddenly, Tex was back in the Breens' kitchen eight years before. Together, he and Mariah had heated water on the stove and put a thermometer in it. "Notice the temperature, Mariah. It's going up a degree at a time. But when it gets to 212 degrees Fahrenheit, suddenly, there's a shift from water to steam. At some point, the steady rise in greenhouse gasses will suddenly shift the atmosphere."

With other stories, he slapped the table and swore out loud. "Was the Pilgrim's captain drunk?" "Were the Secret Service agents inexperienced?" "Twilight Zone: the president gives a major 'climate' speech one day, and his daughter dies from a major 'climate impact' the next." *Jesus fucking Christ!*

Tex once lectured at a university journalism class. "What's the difference between a parrot and a reporter?"

A smartass in the back yelled, "Parrots get crackers from their owners. Reporters get shit from their readers."

Tex had laughed, adding, "Parrots repeat what they've been told. Reporters make connections for their readers."

Evidently, none of these reporters had been in that class. Not one story connected the dots between the SS *Pilgrim* disaster, energy-hog refrigerators, federal subsidies to fossil fuel industries, energy practices in large buildings, heat island effects, and a thousand other factors.

Disgusted, Tex slammed his ceramic mug on the table. Some water spilled. As Tex closed his laptop, he heard a new e-mail ping. And the conference room door opened.

64

White House
Oct. 22, 2016

"**M**AY I COME IN?" General Mason stepped into the conference room. "Even better, walk with me. There's something I want to show you."

A minute later, Tex followed the general through back corridors. He worked to keep up with the national security adviser. Emma Wolfe approached from the opposite direction. "Emma, Tex Cassidy. Tex, Emma Wolfe, one of our top analysts." They shook hands. As Emma walked on, General Mason called out, "I need a minute with you. Meet me downstairs."

A moment later, the general and Tex entered a private elevator. "By the way, the year you were nominated for the Pulitzer? I thought you should have won."

As they exited the elevator, the military guards snapped to attention and saluted the general. At a thick security door, the general placed his hand against one bio-scanner and looked into a second one. A disembodied female voice preceded several clicks. "Thank you, General Mason. Please enter."

"You've seen Situation Rooms in a thousand movies." The general swept his arm to indicate walls of video screens and communications equipment around a large conference table. "Here's the real deal."

Tex felt like he was stepping into a holy chamber. This is where the presidential pope and his national security cardinals made decisions. He gawked at enormously magnified images from satellites in space. On one screen: a terrorist training camp. On another: Russian shipyard workers. "Switch to the Ice Sheet," the general told a technician.

While the tech keyed in a set of codes, Emma Wolfe joined them. General Mason walked her a few steps away and spoke under his breath. Seconds later, Tex saw himself and Mickey being pursued by the assassins across the ice. *This is surreal. I'm watching someone trying to kill me!* Startled, he took two steps back. As he did so, he heard a muffled, "Yes, Sullivan."

"These images saved your life." The general was back. Emma was gone. "No images. No cavalry." He then ordered the tech to rapidly move through five more sets of images. "There are more of these hotspots than flies on horseshit. We can't cover them all."

Back in the elevator, the general pushed the stop button. "Cassidy, a thousand years from now, America won't be here. And some historian will write a paper about how America disappeared. Do you know what the paper will say?"

"Do you?"

"Not a clue. But I'll tell you the Great Conclusion will come from one of three categories. It could be some lunatics that took a potshot at this country. It could be natural forces like an earthquake that blocked out the sun for a year or two, or a climate that supported some kind of life-forms, but not ours. Or it could be some kind of economic collapse because the world had more people than it had food or water or oil for them."

"Brilliantly said, General, but why are you saying it to me?"

"It isn't brilliant."

Tex looked puzzled.

"Because none of those categories includes a president who's sliding off his saddle." The general softened his voice. "Take a few days. Help us. Then go be a hermit."

Tex stared back. "No. Anything else?" He stuck his finger out to release the elevator.

The general grabbed his arm. "Stay."

"Let go of my arm."

The general turned away from Tex. Then he turned back. "Who knew you were going to Greenland?"

Tex looked puzzled. "The president. Alex. The First Lady. Lynn, a staff member. And the plane's crew."

"Who told the assassins?" The general stepped into deeper waters than he had expected to.

"You think I was the prize? I think you're wrong." He told him Mickey's story. "If you ask me, they were after him. Except for Mariah and Mickey Logan, no one knew I was going to the Ice Sheet."

"Did you tell Dimitri Bakov you were going to Greenland?" Tex shook his head. "You're sure?" Tex nodded. "You meet with a Russian one day. The next day, you and Logan are nearly murdered by folks I think were Russians or were hired by Russians."

Tex leaned against the elevator wall. "If Bakov knew, Alex Sullivan told him."

The general hit the elevator start button. "This stays between us. Understood?" Tex nodded. Together, they walked silently down the corridors. *Yes, Sullivan.*

65

White House
Oct. 22, 2016

INSIDE THE CONFERENCE ROOM, the general pulled up a chair. Together with Tex, he scanned the email that had arrived just before they went to the Situation Room. The general put on his glasses and leaned forward. What he saw gave him goose bumps. Instantly, he was like a porcupine with its quills raised.

"I'm sorry about the young woman. If you don't act, many others will die as well."
—*Zhivago*

General Mason texted Emma and Dave. "Get down here, now!" Emma, in particular, was a master profiler. Before they responded, he wanted their input about Zhivago.
Too late. Tex hit the send button.

"Someone tried to kill me on the Greenland Ice Sheet. Why? Who? Is there a Pakistan connection?"

"Cassidy!" If the general's single word had been a bullet, Tex would be bleeding out. "I'm in charge."
General Mason felt his mobile device vibrate. He read the confirmation text from Emma. When he turned back, Tex was hitting "send" again.
"I meet with the president in twenty-four minutes. Give me something concrete!"

Thousands of miles away, Zhivago sat in his old stuffed chair. Tex's e-mail had set a forest fire raging in his mind. *Who ordered that at-*

tack? *The prime minister? Someone on the Centennial Committee? The Quartet? Sukirov!*

Zhivago rubbed his thick beard. *I've given you enough!* He tried to concentrate. He saw himself as a boy, watching his father being pistol-whipped and hauled away.

"*Tell me what you think is true.*"

Tex turned to General Mason. His eyes said, *I've got him. Let me keep going.* The general's face was frozen, until he nodded. Instantly, Tex typed:

"*For Russia, climate change is a benefit, if not a blessing. She'll go after Arctic hydrocarbon reserves. Yes?*"

Zhivago answered:

"*Go further.*"

Emma and Dave burst through the door. They read the exchange. They saw the general muscle Tex aside and write:

"*For God's sake, just tell me!*"

Nearly five thousand miles away, Zhivago swallowed two pills: one to quell the pain and the other to quiet his nerves. His father had been betrayed by a neighbor for a loaf of bread.

"*I can't,*" he typed. But just as his finger honed in on "send," he replaced those two words with four others.

"*Iran-Contra. Russian style.*"

"Iran-Contra!" In the White House conference room, four different people had the same dumbfounded look. "That was a thousand years ago!"

"It was an arms-for-hostages deal?"

"Nobody's been taken hostage, have they?"

"Are the arms the snukes?"

Tex grabbed the keyboard. "He's crossed a line. Let's see how far."

"*Pakistan? Is Russia responsible?*"

Zhivago looked around. His eyes started to float in their sockets. Once, twenty-six years ago, he had been in a submersible. The oxygen system failed. He had been disoriented and nearly died just before reaching the surface. This felt like that. But worse, he was overcome with a dying man's morality.

"Russians. Not Russia."

"Oh, my God! Is he saying what I think he's saying?" It was dawning on Dave and the others.

Tex speed-typed:

"If Russia has its own Iran-Contra, is the goal to get the oil and gas, no matter what?"

He pounded the table when the e-mail unscrambled.

"The goal is what the oil and gas gets Russia."

Tex quickly typed:

"Which is what? I meet with the president in thirteen minutes."

Eight minutes later, nothing. Not a syllable. They all put grooves in the rug, making up reasons.
"He's gotten cold feet."
"Maybe he's been arrested."
"They could have killed him."
Tex nearly smashed the screen closing his computer. "Let's go. We're done here." This time, he outpaced General Mason. Mid-corridor, a new thought popped into his brain. He knew the "who": a small band of Russians. He knew the "where": the shifting Arctic. He knew the "what": Arctic energy reserves. He knew the "when": now, or damn soon. But the "why?" His new thought was so unimaginable that he whispered it to the general, adding afterward, "That couldn't be what they're up to, could it?"

66

Thule Air Force Base, Greenland
Oct. 22, 2016

"YOU'RE PROBABLY PICKING UP the cake," Dr. Pieter Skov spoke happily into his wife's answering machine. And loudly. The patient in Room S was comatose. Pieter was a Danish doctor who contracted to work at Thule Air Force Base while his family lived in Ilulissat. "But call me back so I can tell you when to meet me." He glanced over at a wall calendar. Tomorrow, after two long weeks away and that awful experience trying to save the US president's daughter, he would be home for his son's eleventh birthday party.

Pieter checked the patient's IV. Then he checked the device that monitored his vitals. *Looks good.* Heart rate: 58. Blood pressure: 138/70. Percentage of oxygen in the blood versus normal amounts of oxygen in the blood: fluctuating between 80 percent and 95 percent. When it sank below 88 percent, as now, the beeping alarm sounded. *Probably the anesthesia still in his body.* The man had been brought in unconscious, and doctors had removed the bullet from his lung. Before stepping into the hospital corridor, Pieter boosted the oxygen flow through the tube in the man's nose. *Let's make sure the levels stay high.*

"Your job can't be as boring as mine," the solitaire-playing National Guardsman outside Room S joked. Born and raised in the Mississippi Delta, he had never gotten used to his assignment on Thule Air Force Base, "north of everywhere."

"Depends on whether I've got somebody to annoy," Pieter responded, placing the queen of spades under the king of hearts. Then he entered the ward's empty break room to microwave his dinner.

Meanwhile, in Ilulissat, Pieter's wife hadn't heard the phone ringing because her son had the stereo up a few decibels beyond ear-shattering. "Honey," she screamed and waved her arms, "turn that down." Naturally, the boy didn't hear his mother. And in this small Greenland town where a door-lock salesman couldn't earn a nickel, neither of them heard the two men in ski masks entering the house. What they finally did hear was, "Sit on the couch. Now." Shocked and scared, they sat obediently, while their hands were tied, blindfolds were placed over their eyes, and a thick, wooly sock was taped inside each of their mouths.

"We won't hurt you, if you, Mama, obey our command." When she nodded, the man undid the tape. "Now, listen to this message. Repeat it twice. Screw it up, and your kid will never hear another piece of music."

Eating his dinner in the break room, Pieter grabbed the ringing phone. "Hey, sweetheart, I'm desperate to see both of you. Listen, can you pick . . ." Slowly, he pushed the food aside. His whole body shook. "I love you, honey. It'll be okay. Tell them I need fifteen minutes."

Instantly, Pieter headed back toward Room S. The guard had never seen him move that fast. "A pack of smokes says he never knows what day it is." When Pieter didn't respond, he asked, "You okay, Doc?"

"Just anxious to see my family." He walked into the room and stared at the comatose man. *Who are you?* Then, hands shaking, he unlocked the window latch, raised it an inch and, as a signal, knocked the snow off the sill.

As he turned to leave, Pieter heard the unconscious man babbling. He looked at the window. He looked at the bed. He looked at the window again. Nothing yet. Then he leaned over the bed railing. He felt the man's breath on his ear. *Come on! What are you saying? He'll kill me, too.* But he couldn't understand the words. Was he telling a secret? Was he confessing sins? By the time he heard a creak outside the window, all Pieter knew was that the unconscious man was speaking Russian. Running on his toes, he exited Room S half a second before the intruder entered the window.

"Why don't you do something useful with this boring time like learning Danish?" Pieter distracted the guard's attention. "Here, I'll teach you. Recognize this tune?" As he started singing, "Home, home on the range" in Danish, the guard had no clue that, inside, a man in a thermally insulated suit had climbed through the window, turned the data device power off, and reduced the oxygen flow setting to zero. With no beeping alarms, he then covered every inch of the patient's nose and mouth with his gloved hand for a full two minutes. He turned the oxygen back on, as well as the data-monitoring device. Heading out the window and into the cold night, he heard all the heartbeat, blood pressure, and other alarms beeping.

In the hallway, the guard love-tapped Pieter on the shoulder. "You're all right, man. Thanks for the boredom break." When they heard the alarms, they raced into Room S, where the man had just slipped into permanent unconsciousness.

67

White House
Oct. 22, 2016

PRESIDENT BREEN HUNCHED OVER his desk in the president's personal quarters. His eyes were riveted on a picture of an excited twenty-year-old, fly-fishing, on the edge of both a stream and womanhood. At the time, he had stumbled over his words. She dropped her rod and threw her arms around him. "Oh, Daddy! Yes! Run! You'll be a wonderful Prez. I'm so proud of you."

The president then forced his eyes to the Daily Briefing "Top Ten" items. He got to the second bullet and put his head in his hands. It all seemed abstract, insane. He felt as distant from himself as from those events. He looked over at "November 1st—Election Day" on his desk calendar. In the past, his eyes would have blazed brighter. Today, they glazed over.

"Sir," Alex said on the phone, "Tex is in the Treaty Room." It was where the 1898 Protocol of Peace ending the Spanish-American War was signed. Since then, many presidents, including President Breen, used it as a private study. "Whenever you're ready . . ."

The president passed the open door to the Blue Bedroom. Through the door, he saw his wife standing in the open closet, fingering Mariah's clothes.

A few minutes later, he and Tex talked about Mariah and Ellie. Neither man had anything new to say. Both men spoke from their hearts and ever so slightly eased their bone-crunching pain. Finally, Charley was done, and the president took over. "Your trip was cut short. But tell me what you found." He picked up a pad of paper and pen.

Tex was torn. The president needed to know, but he didn't want to burden his friend. "There's a lot, Charley."

"I'm hurting, Tex. But I'm still the president."

"Bottom line, the climate shifts are barreling down. We're not prepared. The Russians are. We could wake up one day, begging them for a cup of oil."

The president listened impassively. "Five years? Ten years?"

"Maybe sooner." *Zhivago!* Tex wanted to tell him. General Mason had insisted on doing it. "That's what I'll tell the cabinet tomorrow."

"No need to. I called that meeting off."

"Off? What do you mean?" Tex leaned as far forward as he could without falling off his chair. It was as if the president had called off the Fourth of July.

"I mean 'off'! Between now and Election Day, I have one job: reassuring voters that I'm the man."

"Charley, people are out of work. They're broke. They're scared. They want to hear about—"

"They will, after November first."

"You can't do that." Tex leapt up. He started pacing.

"I can't do that?" The president put his hands on the arms of his chair and half rose. Under the surface, molten anger about Mariah's death and every goddamn thing else had found a fissure. "And why not?"

Tex stopped. He leaned forward. He put his hands on the president's desk. If there had been Secret Service agents in the room, he would be lying on the ground. "Because you've got their attention. By Thanksgiving, they'll be back to soap operas and football."

"Damn it! Sit down!"

Tex didn't move. "Charley, there's something else." *Sorry, General.* Zhivago . . . the Iran-Contra message . . . the link with Pakistan: he laid it all out. "Mason will confirm."

The president put his head back and looked up at the ceiling. "Are you crazy? Are you fucking crazy?" He spoke each word distinctly. "There May Be A Rogue Group Within the Russian Government. If you're half right, we're closer to Poland and Pearl Harbor than we've been in fifty years."

"You just told me you're the president."

"I did." He rolled his chair back a foot from the desk. "So, do I call the prime minister? 'Excuse me: sorry to interrupt your dinner. But we just got an e-mail saying your government's being undermined right under your roast beef."

"And if it were reversed?"

"I'd want a little proof, Mr. Pulitzer Nominee. Something that didn't sound like a whacko Internet rumor." Tex backed away from the desk. "If you were me, would you make that call?"

"Charley, this could be the biggest thing since the asteroid wiped out the dinosaurs. And you're worried about sounding stupid?"

The president leaned back and stared at the ceiling. "The prime minister's calling me later. I'll play it by ear. Meanwhile, I'll put the cabinet meeting back on." *Christ, it's a balsa wood world.* He turned back to Tex. "You really think I should talk about these issues because people are tuned in?"

Before Tex could answer, they were both startled by Ellie's voice. "That's not why, Charley." She had come through the partially open door.

"Honey . . ." He walked quickly to her, but she wouldn't let him take her arm.

"That glacier calved because the air and sea were too warm for it not to."

"That's true, Ellie." Tex got a chair for her. "But what are you saying?"

Ellie moved a few steps closer. "It was *Murder on the Orient Express.*" She was referring to the old novel in which the murder of one passenger was committed by a conspiracy of all the others. "It came to me at the funeral. I looked around. Our family, the minister, the police: we all warmed the air that calved the glacier that killed Mariah and the others."

Charley had two hats in his hand: husband and president. "Ellie, you make it sound like mass murder."

"Isn't it? The masses killed them, and they're killing themselves."

Husband grabbed her hand. "Come on. I'll walk back with you, and . . ."

Ellie pulled her hand away. She almost smacked him. She looked him right in the eyes. "Avenge her, Charley." It was the clearest statement of her life.

"Christ, Ellie. I'm only the president. I'm not God."

For the first time since the awful news, she felt terra firma inside herself. "You're her father!" she screamed at him. "And you're the president. Who else can avenge her? Who else can save others?"

Tex's jaw dropped open. "She's right, Charley."

The president . . . the father . . . the husband . . . the friend: they all knew she was right. "Answer this carefully: what would you have me do?"

"Tell the truth, Charley." This time, she grabbed his hand. "Tell it because it needs to be told. If you lose, we'll go home. There are worse things than being a one-term president."

68

The Kremlin
Oct. 22, 2016

As HIS AIDE approached with a tray of the Kremlin's best tea, the prime minister let out a sigh of relief: the report confirmed that Nature had killed President Breen's daughter.

"Sir, one minute till your call." Expressing sympathy was distasteful even when it was to a man he respected. Nevertheless, the prime minister sipped his tea and picked up the phone.

"Mr. President, my condolences to you and your wife on the loss of your daughter. I say that from the Russian people and from me personally."

"Thank you, Mr. Prime Minister. It's been very hard on us. The death of a child is hard, whatever the circumstances."

"Which is why you and I must prevent those circumstances."

"Exactly, sir," the president hesitated. *This isn't the time. Oh, hell.* "In that regard, may I ask why Russia is drilling in the Arctic? You just announced higher renewable energy goals, and the world is moving toward renewable energy."

"The world? Or a few places like western Europe, China and Japan?" The prime minister rolled one hand into a fist. "You and I will be long dead before the world doesn't need Russia's energy." Instantly, he regretted his phrasing. "You're not interfering, are you, Mr. President?"

"No, sir," the president replied. *How could I? Our companies drill all over the world.* "But I do need to tell you that on the very same day my daughter died, there were two attempts to murder my special assistant and a videographer he was with."

The president summarized the notes that General Mason had prepared: the leader of the first attempt was apparently a Swedish citizen who had emigrated from Russia. One of the assassins was the videographer's assistant, into whose bank account twenty thousand dollars had been transferred from a Moscow bank via a Brazilian bank. "And, lastly, Mr. Prime Minister, the man we captured spoke Russian just before he was murdered."

"Are you accusing me, Mr. President?"

"No, sir. I'm alerting you. Maybe warning you. May I tell you something I can't prove?" Delicately, he described the Zhivago messages and the Iran-Contra reference in particular. "What particularly concerns me is that a tactical nuclear device was used in Pakistan. Only the US and Russia made them. We didn't explode it. If you didn't, then either someone outside your government stole or bought the device, or someone inside your government did it without your knowing."

"I will make inquiries. Again, my condolences for your loss, Mr. President." He hung up and slammed his fist on the table. *It must be them!* He rubbed his fingers together, while speaking into the intercom. "Get my car. Right now."

69

Renesse, Netherlands
Oct. 22, 2016

THE PELTING RAIN hit Dagmare in the face. She put her mesh shopping bag into her overcoat pocket and opened her umbrella. Slowly, she made her way down the sidewalk. Every shopkeeper greeted her, though none stopped to talk. Instead, they hurried to bring their displays indoors.

Like everyone in the Netherlands, Zavia's aunt was stocking up on beans, rice, candles, and flashlights. Suddenly tired, Dagmare sat on a dry bench out of the wind. She watched the trees swaying. She heard the crash as a man on a bicycle was blown over. Then her head felt light, and she slipped backward. The owner of the grocery store raced over and kept her head from banging into the brick wall. He carried her to his delivery van and drove her home.

Within an hour, two neighbors and three relatives had brought soup, flowers, and the local doctor. One relative, Ingrid, slipped downstairs and dialed a US phone number. "Zavia, it's about Aunt Dagmare. I don't want to scare you . . ." She sat cross-legged and spoke with a quivering voice. "No, she wasn't hurt. . . . The doctor thinks it was a minor stroke that. . . . No, we won't know how much damage until . . ."

At the other end of the line, Zavia was shell-shocked. *I just saw her. She looked great.* "I'm so glad you called. Let me know if she gets any worse, okay?" Then Zavia remembered something. "Different subject, honey. The Pakistan explosion? Aren't you doing something with glaciers?"

Ingrid uncrossed her legs and walked out onto the porch. One of the neighbors had left a pack of cigarettes on the railing. "With my friend, Christian. We're writing software . . . to activate cameras . . . but nothing in Pakistan." Zavia's question was like a stick of dynamite. Ingrid took a cigarette out of the pack, but put it back in. Her lips trembled. Her mouth dried up. For two days, Christian hadn't been at work. No calls. No e-mails. No little gifts tied to her handlebars.

Plus, she wanted to tell her cousin the Big Secret. *Not now. This isn't the time.*

"Ingrid, is something wrong? Are you all right?"

"I'm just busy. It's been a cram course in geography." Ingrid sat on the railing. It was still wet from the afternoon rain. "But everything's fine, and our boss is happy."

Zavia broke out in a sweat. She heard Ingrid's voice. She recognized the crack, the distance, the worry. "Well, your dad must be very proud of you. Listen, back to Dagmare. Is she lucid when she's up?"

"She's not dying if that's what you're asking. But you might want to come over in the next few weeks."

"Let's see how she does. By the way, what's the weather? I heard there were big storms." Zavia surfed a travel website while she talked. She now had two family reasons to go.

"Yeah, one last week. A big storm today." She looked up at the clouded sky. "Maybe another one tomorrow. Winter on the North Sea coast."

"Your father? Is he worried?" *There are cheap flights. Good.*

"You know what a worrier he is. But things seem normal. Just some routine maintenance on the barrier."

"Well, give him my love, okay? If I'm there in a few weeks, let's go shopping and hang out. I really want to hear what's going on with you."

Zavia hung up. She sat still for a few minutes. *Dagmare may be dying. Ingrid's hiding something. It's way too early for that much rain.* Her stomach rumbled, and it wasn't lunch. Finally, she went back to her White House presentation.

70

Moscow
Oct. 22, 2016

"**I**VAN, YOU LOOK LIKE you've seen the ghost of Stalin."

The prime minister wandered around the Arctic researcher's small Moscow apartment. He looked at photos and even stepped into Fyodorokov's bedroom and bathroom. Fyodorokov had leased the apartment seventeen years ago, when he spent substantial time in the Russian capitol. "You haven't redecorated since I was last here, a decade ago." The prime minister slapped the old couch. "Of course, you haven't invited me over since then. You're not smuggling weapons, are you?" He opened a silverware drawer and pretended to be looking for a weapons cache.

"Do you want this apartment when I'm dead? Is that why you're here?" Fyodorokov looked at the wall clock. It was just after ten.

"I'm not sure why I came." The visitor got himself a glass of water and looked in the bare food pantry. The sink was cluttered with pills, gels, and liquids.

"You're worried about the committee?" Fyodorokov's legs were giving out. He leaned on the arm of the couch and eased himself down. *What does he know?* Then he coughed for a full minute.

"I'm sorry the cancer is killing you, Ivan."

"If we'd been as careful as the Japanese or the French, for God's sake, I'd outlive you." Ivan coughed again. This time, it was deliberate. *The laptop! It's open! The e-mails with the American!* There was a vial next to it. Fyodorokov stood up again and moved toward his desk. "I need a pill." He gripped the back of a tall chair and swiveled it in the hopes of blocking the prime minister's view.

The prime minister watched him navigate both the room and the conversation. "Have you ever thought about the ten worst mistakes human beings have made?" This time, he read book titles on the wooden shelf, or pretended to do so. "The Inquisition? The gulags? Fast food?"

Fyodorokov looked puzzled. "Maybe a floating nuclear power plant in the Arctic?"

Fyodorokov grabbed the end of the desk. His eyes were like flame-throwers. "A Chernobyl up there? It would be hundreds of times worse than Hiroshima." Using his indignation as a cover, he closed his computer. Then he made his way back to the couch and nearly fell into it.

"Is that what I think it is?" Across the room, over the table with the computer, the prime minister saw an old, yellowish framed document. He walked over and stared at it. "It is." Thirty years ago, Ivan had been named a Hero of the Soviet Union. "Did you know I nominated you?" He leaned against the table and put his hand on the computer.

"Mr. Prime Minister, I need to sleep." He felt like a mouse being toyed with by a large cat with sharp teeth.

"Yes, yes. But first: President Breen. A good man, but naive. Anyway, do you know what he said?" Fyodorokov's eyes drooped. "Someone tried to murder his special assistant in Greenland. Would that make your 'crazy' list?"

"Who did it?" Fyodorokov felt sick to his stomach. *Sukirov.*

"Evidently Russians. Any idea which Russians?"

"I'm not feeling well, Mr. Prime Minister. May I call you in the morning?" His next coughing fit was genuine, and he was thankful for it.

"I'll send a car at seven. Then we can have a longer chat. As long as we need." Stepping into the hallway, he spoke to three men in suits with drawn weapons. When the prime minister returned, he leaned right into the sick man's face. "You'll be dead by the end of the year. I've already ordered a state funeral for you. But if you've betrayed me, I'll cancel it."

Once again, Fyodorokov coughed, as sleep overcame him. "Cancel it anyway," he mumbled. "Save the state some money."

The prime minister nodded to his bodyguards. They made less noise than you would hear in a Trappist monastery. They didn't lay a finger on the sleeping man. They just unplugged his computer and carried it away.

In the morning, Ivan awoke and saw that the computer was gone. Shaking, he heard footsteps racing up the stairs. The pounding of his heart echoed the pounding on the door.

71

Washington
Oct. 23, 2016

TWO HOURS BEFORE SUNRISE, the First Lady wrapped her bathrobe around her and came into the Oval Office. "Come back to bed, Charley. Another hour's sleep will do you good."

He swiveled around and looked at her. Even after thirty-two years of marriage, even though she had been gutted and filleted, he still found her beautiful. "I can't sleep, sweetie . . ."

She came up behind him and rubbed his shoulders. *They're tighter than rebar.* "What are you thinking about?"

"Nothing as good as this feels." He closed his eyes and concentrated on the sensations.

"In the cabinet meeting, today, I want you to remember something, okay?" She reached down and put her hands over his heart. "I'll be here with you. And so will Mariah."

Several hours later, the early sunlight filled the Oval Office. It was 7:35. The president and Tex hunched toward each other with coffee cups in their hands. Their suit jackets were on the backs of their chairs.

The president looked over at his best friend. "Just between us: this cabinet meeting? I'm not sure what I want out of it." Then he glanced at his watch. "Tex, one other thing. I've saved it till now, because I didn't want it to color—"

The northwest Oval Office door opened. From the main West Wing corridor, Alex Sullivan escorted in the "one other thing." Zavia Jansen strode like a lioness toward the president. She wore a single strand of pearls that offset her dark-blue dress and matching heels. But before her outstretched hand grasped the president's, she heard, "What the hell are you doing here?"

Zavia turned, saw Tex, and squared her shoulders. "Exactly my sentiments."

"Please, sit." The president shook his head in disbelief. "There are two things." First, he reviewed the meeting. "Don't be intimidated. I need you to be as objective as you can, and right up in their faces."

Then he looked intensely at Zavia and Tex. "Both of you: I mean this. No barking and scratching. This is too important. Do you understand?" They nodded. "Good, can you bury whatever you have to bury for the next two hours?"

They were both silent. Finally, Zavia spoke. "I can, sir."

"I can, too."

"Well, you'd better. For today, at least, you're teammates."

Zavia stuck her hand out. Tex took it, shook it, and to his surprise, he liked the feel of it.

"Right," the president said, "let's go shake up the cabinet."

72

White House Cabinet Room
Oct. 23, 2016

AT 7:55 a.m., the cabinet secretaries and military officers whispered tensely among themselves. "What shape is he in? Do you think he's going to . . . ?"

Of the twenty-two people in the room, secretary of state Jane Harkle was the most steely. She had charmed Mahmoud Ahmadinejad and threatened Kim Jong-Il. This morning, in her limo with the secretary of defense, she confessed, "Forty-two years ago, I was a White House aide when Nixon resigned. This morning, I'm having déjà vu."

At 8:00 a.m., two marines swung open the Cabinet Room doors. The tension tripled, as everyone rose and the president walked quickly to his center-table leather chair. "Ladies and gentlemen, in the last four years, we've made tough decisions. Today's will be even tougher. And by the way, I'm not resigning."

If the human ear could hear sunlight, the sunbeams would have been audible. Finally, sitting directly to the president's right, the secretary of state spoke up. "Are you serious, sir, about this tough decision, with no warning and no preparation?" *You may not be resigning. But we may still ask you to.*

"Trust me, as serious as I've ever been." For the first time in four years of cabinet meetings, he stood up to say something. "Here's the decision I'll ask you to vote up or shoot down: very soon, this week or next, definitely before the election, should this administration mobilize against the situations you're going to hear about now?"

Meanwhile, Zavia sat behind the conference table near the windows looking out onto the Rose Garden. Her crossed leg swung up and down. She accidentally kicked Tex, who was sitting next to her. *This is the United States cabinet!* Her leg swung even more when the president introduced her as a world expert in climate impacts.

Zavia stood up. She steadied herself as best she could. "Ladies and gentlemen," she spoke through parched lips, "good morning. In terms of climate change, here's what we know."

Zavia looked at the cabinet. She barely saw them. "The Arctic is the canary. But don't picture one canary: picture a sky full of them. For example, here's a photo I took a year ago." She heard and hated the tentativeness in her voice. *Don't be intimidated.*

On a screen that had been set up, the cabinet saw hundreds of thin-ribbed, dead, or near-dead Australian cows lying on the hard-baked land. "The whole continent's in a fifteen-year drought."

She showed the next photo: a Canadian forest. "Looks healthy, doesn't it? But it's a canary, too, because it's migrating north." This time, she heard more confidence in her voice. *I want you right up in their faces.* At the rate of one-a-minute, she rattled off a half dozen other impacts. "I've seen them all. This one makes me cry." She showed photos of the Maldives. "I could list a hundred more."

Fourteen minutes into her presentation, her tone was "This is the captain speaking." Not one cabinet member had drawn a single doodle. "Now let me outline the next wave of impacts; the ones predicted by scientists."

For the last few minutes, the secretary of the Treasury had stared at a chandelier hanging from the eighteen-foot ceiling. He deliberately dropped his pen onto the pad in front of him. "Speculated by scientists. Isn't that more accurate?"

Zavia eyed him like one gunslinger sizing up another. Then she walked right up and stood between two cabinet officers, staring at him across the table. "Sir, the Federal Reserve makes economic projections. Do you call them speculations?" The secretary didn't answer. "In both cases, we're dealing with predictions that are extraordinarily complex. The scientists' models are no less speculative than your economists' models, and, these days, no less important."

Zavia turned to the full cabinet. She glimpsed General Mason reading a text message. What she didn't see was the secretary of defense pass a note to an aide, who passed the note to Jane Harkle, sitting on the other side of the president. "Those scientific projections will impact every part of the country. Any of you from a Rocky Mountain state?"

"Colorado," the interior secretary said. "I know, I know. If the snow pack keeps dropping, the ski industry will collapse. And so will the local communities."

"Different states, different impacts, different industries, same story. But let me focus on the one I know best: coastal flooding." She had given so many talks to people with power who didn't care and to people who cared but had no power. But these people? They cared about their country, and they could sure as hell set things in motion.

She was heading into her home waters. Tex noticed that her legs were as steady as pillars. "Do you know the Delta Works in the Netherlands?" Most didn't. "In my opinion, it's the gold standard of dikes and storm surge barriers in the world. I was very lucky to work there for six years. Most others aren't worth the concrete they're built out of."

The secretary of defense took his glasses off. "What about ours?"

"Close to worthless, sir." She felt like a guy in a body shop telling a customer his car was totaled. "You can shoot missiles down. Thank God for that. But honestly, can you stop rising tides?"

"Mr. President," Secretary Harkle turned slightly to her left, "these rising tides are decades away. In the meantime—"

"Decades? Maybe."

Tex turned to look at Zavia. Spitfire! She stepped right into the middle of the secretary of state's statement.

"Maybe only one decade. Maybe half a decade. Maybe tomorrow. Sometimes, awful things happen with no warning. Look at what happened to . . ."

The room froze. No one inhaled or exhaled. If Zavia could have transported herself through a wormhole to Pluto, she would have. Immediately, she turned to President Breen. "I'm so sorry, sir. I'm so sorry."

Every cabinet eye turned to the president. Would he cry? Crack? Crumble? The president just arched his eyebrows. "Finish your sentence."

Zavia hesitated. "Look at what happened when the glacier calved."

"Your exact sentence."

Zavia took a deep breath. "Look at what happened to the president's daughter."

Dead silence hardly described the next thirty seconds. The secretary of defense stared hard at Secretary Harkle and mouthed, "Now!"

"Mr. President," the secretary of state turned again to the president, "the climate is important. We all know that. But compared to who set off the Pakistan explosion? Or whether you should finish this campaign?"

The air was charged as if lightning had passed through it. The president's eyes circled the table, looking at every cabinet member in turn. "If you ask for my resignation, I'll give it. But be clear. This meeting isn't about the climate. It's about our security."

73

White House
Oct. 23, 2016

THE CABINET SAT in stunned silence. The president turned to Zavia. "Dr. Jansen, thank you. I don't know if you've scared anyone else, but you've scared me. What's even scarier is how it fits in with the Russians."

"The Russians?" Jane Harkle simultaneously gasped and spoke.

"Yes, the Russians. Bear with me." The president introduced Tex as his longtime friend and new special assistant. "He's also my daughter's godfather. He was there the day Mariah was born and the day Mariah died." The president's voice caught, but not enough to make him an ex-president.

Tex stood and walked closer to the oval conference table. His heart sped up. His palms weren't sweaty, but they weren't dry either. For his entire life, he had felt galaxies away from any seats of power. Now he was in the inner sanctum. "Let me describe a few things, and we'll see how they fit together."

First, he detailed quickly what they knew. "The world's demand for oil is rising while the world's supply of oil is falling. The US still depends on Canada, Saudi Arabia, Venezuela, and other foreign countries for well over 30 percent of its oil."

Then he told them what they didn't know. "In the next few years, the US could be at the mercy of Russia. They've got a lock on the Arctic oil and gas. In fact, they're already extracting it."

Tex looked over at his friend and his president. Both personas nodded to him. Then, like a magician making a rabbit appear, Tex connected this morning's dots and made a conclusion appear. "The changing climate will reinvent Russia. They'll be a world power with power over the world."

The cabinet looked stunned. Was this guy out of his mind? Was the president out of his mind? They came here to evaluate his sanity, and they were being told this cockamamie story about a has-been nation's plot to bring the United States, Europe, China, and everyone else to their knees? Before any of them could speak out, freak out, or walk out, General Mason leaned forward and raised the temperature in the room. "Mr. Cassidy. The attacks on the Greenland Ice Sheet. Tell them."

Tex took a deep breath. "This may be hard to believe." Then he described the predators on snowmobiles; Mickey's screams; Mac's betrayal; the armed skiers; the battle in the crevasse; and the rest. "Without the helicopters, we'd have died on the ice."

The cabinet swiveled their heads toward each other and then toward the president.

Why didn't we know?

There's obviously more to worry about than the president's mental health, but what?

Before they could swivel back, General Mason jumped in. "We think the woman who led the first attack was Russian. And we think the soldiers in the second attack were either Russians or worked for them."

Zavia was stunned. She didn't know any of what had happened on the Ice Sheet. *That call on the train from Dimitri Bakov? Was it really about Tex and not about the contract? Was Emma Wolfe right about 'no coincidences'? Who the hell is Tex? My God! This is a different guy from the yo-yo in college who couldn't relate his way out of a paper bag.*

Jane Harkle was also stunned. In a different way. "You think, General?" She had stiffened up faster than instant concrete.

"Just confirmed it a few minutes ago. Plus, Pakistan: the nuclear device wasn't one of ours. Had to be Russian."

Jane Harkle wasn't thinking about the president's resignation. She was thinking about hers. "Everything you've said is circumstantial. I'd be embarrassed to call my counterpart in Moscow."

Tex opened his mouth to speak. Mason had covered his ass. Now he would cover the general's. "There's something else you should know." He walked them through the Zhivago e-mails and the Iran-Contra warning. "If Zhivago's real, so is the Russian threat."

Secretary Harkle could barely speak. "Mr. Cassidy . . ." She just stared at him. "You're either highly gullible or highly imaginative." Then she turned to General Mason. "In forty years of diplomatic work, sir, this is a low point. For God's sake, you are the national security adviser. Show us. Tell us. Where is the intelligence? Where is your intelligence?"

The general didn't hesitate. "It's in the logic, meaning: the climate warms. The oil and gas are accessible. The Russians control the reserves. Then they control everyone else." The general paused, as the logic sank in. "In other words, they win."

"Win what?" The secretary of state's voice would crack if it were any tighter.

"The energy game. The power game. The world game."

No one said anything. Finally, the president spoke. "Come on, folks. Who ever thought we'd walk on the moon? Is it preposterous to think the Russians are plotting world domination? You bet it is. But what if it isn't?"

"Mr. President," the secretary of defense faced his commander in chief, "with all due respect, sir, your child has just died. Are you really clear-headed about this?"

"I believe so, though you will have to decide."

"And," the secretary of defense pressed him, "if we mobilize, as you put it, are you strong enough to ride in front?"

"I am." His voice was clear. He sat straight up in his saddle. "But we do it as an administration or we don't do it."

Tex counted more than enough votes.

"And how do we decide that?"

"Unanimously, or we drop it until after the election."

74

Moscow
Oct. 23, 2016

THE PRIME MINISTER read the "Fyodorokov Computer" report. Treason. Seconds later, he screamed at his intelligence chiefs. "Get them! All four of them!"

Four black vans sped through the Moscow night. In each, the order was "Keep them alive if you can." At their separate destinations, three teams raced up stairs. They pounded on doors. They shoved their aging quarry into the vans.

The fourth team broke through the door into an empty apartment.

As the sun rose, Dimitri Bakov, General Valikovsky, and Ivan Fyodorokov sat in separate interrogation rooms. They were in various stages of stubble and clothing as Fingers visited them.

First, the prime minister sat across from Bakov, whose fat body was strapped tightly to the arms and legs of a skinny chair. "There's no sense denying anything, Dimitri. If you think there is, I'll have someone prove you wrong." *You only wanted the money.* His disgust subsided only slightly as Bakov, in a quaking voice, confirmed the Quartet's identities, plans, and purpose. "Pakistan was just the beginning." His hands trembled under the ropes.

Next, he confronted Ivan Fyodorokov. The Arctic researcher looked like a once-mighty glacier reduced to an ice cube. "Of the four of you, your betrayal cuts the deepest." The prime minister liked Ivan. He may have been a traitor, but at least he did it for Russia. "You can die in your bed. But I'll need to know all the field operatives running the operation." He was surprised to hear that just two men had run the whole plan.

Finally, the prime minister leaned over General Valikovsky. He trusted that the general's highest value was making Russia ever greater. "I won't have you killed." The general's one good arm was strapped to the chair. "But if I were you, I'd give me the exact location of the other snukes," he said, placing his hand around the general's right knee. "With just your right arm and your left leg, you'll have a terrible time keeping your balance in prison."

None of the three conspirators knew where Admiral Sukirov was. As General Valikovsky put it, "We betrayed you. He betrayed us."

By lunchtime, the prime minister had answers and a plan for stopping Sukirov. "Any questions?" he asked Fyodorokov, Bakov, and the general. "Betray me again, and you will beg me to die."

75

White House Cabinet Room
Oct. 23, 2016

"Here's the one ground rule." The president looked at each cabinet member. "We're all in, or we're all out."

Steam poured out of Tex's ears. *You just undercut the country and Ellie's plea to avenge Mariah!*

"Mr. Secretary, let's start with you." The president strategically chose the head of defense. He was as much a political heavyweight as a physical one. "Yes or no? State of the Union before the election?"

The secretary sat still. Finally, he spoke. "Yes."

In the next ten minutes, the president called on each cabinet secretary. With each "yes," the mobilization became more likely and weighed more heavily. Finally, one more cabinet member. "Madame Secretary, yes or no?"

Jane Harkle turned her steely eyes toward the president. "Absolutely not." The room fell as quiet as deep space. Tex's eyeballs did a roll. Zavia didn't know what to make of the secretary's vote.

"Why not?" the president snapped at her. He was mad. He didn't want a war. But he wanted a war-footing.

Secretary Harkle shot back at him before he had drawn another breath. "Because you're betting the national ranch. On what? A plot you can't prove and a motivation you can't confirm."

"What proof would it take?" He knew she was right. Everyone did.

"Find Zhivago."

Tex bit his lip. Zavia covered her eyes with one hand, as if she were trying to retrieve a neural diamond that had fallen down a mental well. "Prove that he or she isn't a Russian hack. Or a vengeful Georgian. Or an oil executive with an agenda. Or maybe even someone—"

"My God!" Zavia stood up. Her eyes were wider than the Pacific. "He called me Lara. In *Dr. Zhivago*, the main female character is named

Lara."

"Who did?" The question vaulted out of the president's mouth.

"Ivan Fyodorokov. On the harbor tour in Murmansk."

"Fydorowho?"

While she explained, Tex grabbed his laptop and sent a coded e-mail.

"The ball is rolling fast. The stakes couldn't be higher. Are you Ivan Fyodorokov?"

After his interrogation, Ivan had been escorted home. The cancer was devouring his liver. He could barely swallow two painkillers, never mind get his old computer out of the closet, boot it up, see the encrypted message and respond, before the drug fog crept in.

Tex stood up. "Excuse me. I've asked Zhivago to confirm or deny that he's Fyodorokov."

The cabinet stopped. They sat, waiting. But with each unanswered minute, the people got edgier. Finally, Zavia snatched the computer from Tex. "Let me try something."

"Zhivago, this is Lara. I remember you from the Murmansk Harbor tour. Remember me?"

Fyodorokov had seen Tex's e-mail. He leaned against his window and watched people. They had what he didn't: a life ahead of them. *Can you feel sunlight when you're dead?* Then he stumbled back to the computer. This time, he saw the Lara e-mail. He typed:

"I am Ivan Fyodorokov. I remember you, Lara."

When the message appeared, the cabinet broke out into shortlived smiles and pumped fists. "Tell him to prove it," the secretary of state said.

Prove it? How? It would be like proving God or gravity. None of the cabinet had a clue. But Zavia did.

"Zhivago, what did Lara tell the prime minister?"

Her message pinged out. No one breathed until Zhivago's message pinged in.

"I don't remember. Tell me. Maybe it will jog my memory."

"He doesn't remember?" The president was enraged. Zavia started typing a clue, but the general grabbed her wrist. "Can't do that."

"Damn it." The president stood abruptly. "This meeting's over." He pushed his chair back and headed for the door, when they all heard the pinging sound.

"If the climate continues to warm, Murmansk could be the Russian New Orleans."

"That's it!" Zavia screamed. "That's what I told him!"

"Dr. Jansen," the president looked over pointedly, "if we proceed, the future may be a game of pick-up sticks. Are you as certain of this as you are of your own name?"

"Give me a minute, sir." Zavia flipped open her computer, found her "Murmansk Notes" file and highlighted: "I told them that if global warming continues, Murmansk could be the Russian New Orleans." Then she projected her notes on the screen.

The president turned to his secretary of state. "Convinced?"

"Scared." Even with all her makeup, Jane Harkle's face was as pale as a circus mime.

PART FOUR: ORANGE

76

White House
Oct. 23, 2016

For the first time since Mariah's death, the White House mood was north of morbid. People stopped updating their résumés. It was October, but it felt like spring.

One hour after the cabinet meeting, Alex, Tex, Zavia, General Mason, and several aides sat with the president in the Oval Office. The president sounded upbeat rather than beat up. "Alex, we're invoking Article II, Section 3 of the Constitution: the president's right to convene a State of the Union. Brief the congressional leadership, let the networks know, inform the usual heads of state.

"Tex, draft me a speech that lays out the climate/Russia/oil/national security story. And get me three versions: low, medium, and high mobilization. The front and back can be the same. My staff writers will help. But you're on point.

"Zavia, work with General Mason. Build the 'climate-change-is-a-national-security-threat' section."

Ten minutes later, the president walked quickly to his quarters. In their dining area, he saw Ellie sipping soup, mindlessly watching the muted news. She had lost six pounds since Mariah died. Sometimes, she obsessed about Mariah's wedding, her grandchild's first day of school, and other events that would never happen. Other times, she thought about life after the White House. Could she and Charley get back to the rhythm of the relationship that had carried them for thirty-plus years?

Charley sat next to her and stroked her hand. "Ellie, I'd love it if you'd be up in the gallery."

Ellie looked as if he had asked her to cross the Himalayas on a donkey. "I'm still pretty raw." She didn't want to talk. She turned back to the television and saw an image of them stepping out of the limo at Mariah's funeral. Charley was in the forefront, looking ghostly and lost. Under the image, the caption read: "Can He Govern?"

"You better hear this." She undid the mute. For the rest of the thirty-second spot, they listened as the voiceover cited the *LA Times*' "Can He Govern?" editorial. At the end, they heard a different voice. "I'm Governor Wilton, and I approve this ad."

"That son of a bitch!" Ellie stood up. Her hands were on her hips. "It's politics. But it's disgusting. Whip his ass, Charley. Whip it hard. Damn right, I'll be in the gallery."

77

Oosterschelde Barrier, Netherlands
Oct. 23, 2016

WHILE BETA CLEANED his gun, Alpha drove south along N-57. After the Delta Works Orientation, he had arranged for the positions they wanted. "Check the package," Alpha ordered.

Reaching back, Beta pushed aside the cardboard boxes that camouflaged the snuke. Then he pulled back a corner of the painter's tarp and tugged on the nylon ropes. *Secure and out of sight.*

Ten minutes later, Alpha turned onto the access road. He scanned the sixteen-gate structure they had toured. "There's the project office." Beta aimed one of his large fingers at a trailer. The foreman was in front, waving.

Alpha guided the van toward him. "Right on time. I like that." Alpha stuck his hand out for the foreman to shake. Meanwhile, Beta held a syringe, just in case.

"Where's the regular crew?"

"Taken away, unexpectedly," Alpha said smoothly. "But we'll cover for them."

"You've done this kind of work before?" the foreman asked. When they nodded, he resigned himself. "Okay, grab your hard hat. I'll show you where to start."

78

Washington
Oct. 24, 2016

THE PRESIDENT SAT at his Oval Office desk. He put on his reading glasses and skimmed the three mobilization levels Tex had drafted. "Low" would bring the world's attention to the Arctic changes and the Russians' activity. "Medium" would challenge the Russian prime minister to "cease and desist." "High" would announce the United States' actions and call on the world's leaders to do the same.

"First read looks good. Give me an hour to make edits." He glanced over at Tex and Zavia. "Take a walk. Sit in a café. Have a life. I'll live vicariously through you."

As they passed through the White House gate, Zavia didn't notice the Russian commercial officer taking pictures of her. "Heck, we were like Fred and Ginger in there," she joked.

A few blocks away, they snagged a table at an outdoor café. They leaned forward to hear each other. With the traffic, it was like carrying on a conversation at a heavy metal concert. The street crowd wasn't any quieter. From near and far, folks were pouring in for the Big Event that night.

Tex and Zavia quickly ran out of "speech" things to discuss. Then they awkwardly sipped coffee and watched a large moving van circle the block for the fourth time. On the side, "Can He Govern?" had been painted in three-foot letters over a droopy headshot of the president.

Oh, what the hell. "Are you feeling as weird as I am?" Zavia asked.

"Probably more so." He swished the remaining coffee in his cup.

"Well, how about clearing out a few cobwebs?"

Warily, Tex nodded. He also pointed at the moving van circling again.

"It's ancient history, but whatever happened to us? Was it Katie?"

He shook his head. "We were great in bed and terrible out of bed."

They were quiet again. Like most men, his strong suit was silence.

Finally, she asked, "This'll be over in a few days. What will you do then?"

"Go back up to the lake, chop wood, maybe write an article, maybe not." He turned again toward the street scene, eyeing a few more folks carrying protest signs.

"And Katie? What will she do?"

Tex felt like the moving van had just him run over. *She doesn't know! I don't want to talk about it.* He threw a twenty-dollar bill on the table and bolted. Zavia bolted after him. She nearly lost an eye on a protest pole. "Tex, what did I say? Are you not with her anymore?"

At the corner of 17th and K, Tex whirled and banged into a man with a stenciled "Can He Govern?" T-shirt. "Katie's dead." He took off again, wanting to disappear off the planet.

At 16th and H, he stopped on the curb. Out of breath, Zavia grabbed his arm. "I'm so sorry. I didn't know." Tex looked at the traffic light countdown signal instead of her. "Tex, I didn't know! Damn it, talk to me. When?"

"Six days before Charley Breen was elected." The traffic light shifted. Along with a crowd of pedestrians, he crossed the street. Halfway there, she grabbed his arm again. "How?"

Standing in the middle of the intersection, everything in Tex told him to keep his mouth shut and his legs moving. Meanwhile, the light shifted. Traffic approached. "Human stupidity." He looked around at her clothes, the air, the traffic signal; all the normal things chock-full of toxins.

A big SUV stopped a foot from them. The driver leaned on his horn. Tex tossed him the bird, kicked his bumper, and headed to the sidewalk. Zavia's high heels couldn't keep up with his cowboy boots. When she finally got to the White House front gate, she bumped into an overnight delivery guy checking in a package. But Tex was already upstairs, knocking on Alex Sullivan's door.

79

White House
Oct. 24, 2016

"COME IN, TEX." For once, Alex Sullivan didn't treat him like a virus. "If we get four more years, you may be recruited to write speeches." The chief of staff tossed a folder across the desk. "Just a few edits. He's happy. But you may not be. He wants you on another plane."

Tex got up and headed for the door. "Sorry. Mission's over."

Alex was putting his computer to sleep. "This time, it was my suggestion."

"Even more reason to pass." He looked at Alex very suspiciously, as he placed his hand on the doorknob.

Alex stared at Tex. "What's up with you? This time, you're the right man. Maybe the only man." He then laid out the few brush strokes he knew about a US-Russian conference. "It's a sliver of light. But the prime minister didn't snuff it out."

"What did you tell Bakov about me and Greenland?" His tone was as cold as the Ice Sheet.

Alex made sure the door was closed. "Tex, what are you doing?"

"Finding out what you did."

"I don't like you. But I didn't do anything to hurt you. Now, will you get on that plane?"

"The election's getting to you. They won't listen to me."

Alex pressed his intercom. "They won't. But they'll listen to her."

Jane Harkle, the secretary of state walked through the door. "Mr. Cassidy, I understand we may be working together."

80

Moscow
Oct. 24, 2016

LIKE IVAN FYODOROKOV, Dimitri Bakov kept a Moscow apartment. But Bakov's was the penthouse in a lavish high-rise on the north bank of the Moscow River.

Standing in his living room, Bakov called and verified that the private jet was fueled and ready to go. He checked on his computer that the international bank transfers had been completed. And finally, he carried his two packed bags out of the bedroom and placed them by the front door.

Bakov walked onto his deck. In front of him, he looked out into the distance toward the city lights he would never see again. Behind him, he listened to a knock on the door and a voice he had never expected to hear.

"May I come in, Dimitri?" General Valikovsky stood in the doorway.

"Of course, but I just have a few minutes." The general saw the suitcases. "Is there a change in plan?"

"Several. Why don't you start?" Bakov's face went from puzzled to frightened. "It all comes down to one word, doesn't it? Winnipeg."

The general walked over to the liquor cabinet. "May I? You'd better have one, too." He used his good arm to pour aperitifs. Then they walked out onto the deck. "For starters, the apartment on St. James Street. It looks very nice. Worth paying cash for. And you won't have to worry about coastal flooding in Winnipeg, will you?"

Bakov nearly dropped his drink. "I'll be in Canada a lot once the ice is gone and the shipping traffic to Churchill picks up. I wanted a place of my own. "What's wrong . . . ?"

"Dimitri . . ." The general stood up and stared down at Bakov. "The prime minister knows about the Canadian bank accounts and all the rest, including your two calls with Sukirov in the last few days." Bakov's face went from frightened to terrified. "I'm afraid that to get back in his good graces, I volunteered to give you the bad news."

"General, we've been part of . . ."

"Save your breath. Enjoy your breath. You've only got a few left." The general watched Bakov's mind search for an exit. "You can kill me, but that won't do you any good. Basically, the prime minister's given you two options. Want to hear them?"

Bakov wondered if he had five breaths left or fifty; certainly, not five hundred. He used one of them nodding to the general.

"You can't see the vans down on the street. But they're there. And," he looked at his watch, "in four minutes, some very unfriendly men will take you away. If you remember, the prime minister promised that if we betray him, we'll beg him to die."

Bakov was now really terrified. "The other option?"

The general patted the metal railing. "Throw yourself over." Bakov looked at the general, his face pleading.

"I'm sorry, Dimitri. I've got to go. Good luck with your decision."

81

White House
Oct. 24, 2016

IN THE OVAL OFFICE, the president vaulted out of his chair. "Thank you. Great work. You're a great team. Someday, maybe we'll open a restaurant together."

Tex, Zavia, Alex, and a dozen others laughed. Then they headed for the door, pumped up about tonight's address. Tex looked over at Zavia, conveying with regretful eyes that he was sorry. She wouldn't meet those eyes. Instead, she stared at the president's gray-haired secretary, bursting through the northeast door into the Oval Office. "Sir," she was out of breath from her ten-yard dash, "Ms. Dean, your political director, she says to turn on the news."

"Why not? How bad could it be?"

"This looks really bad for the president." Philip, the news anchor, thinly masked his thrill at having a developing story with his tone of concern. In the background, live photos showed the US Capitol with a crowd of twenty-five thousand people in front of it. They weren't easily characterized as the "angry majority" that loved a good rant. Some looked like librarians who loved a good book. Mostly, they were white. But a smattering of black, brown, and yellow faces gave the crowd a rainbow tinge. Collectively, they seemed like sharks waiting for an injured surfer to fall off the board.

The folks in the Oval Office all looked to the president. Their faces were ashen, as if they had just walked into their kitchen and found a bloodied loved one on the floor. Tex was probably the only person who saw the slight nostril flare that Charley used when he was choking back pain or rage. Even when a twenty-something punk leaned into the camera's view, exposing a sign that had a picture of Mariah and the words "Melt and Hit Victim," the president's face looked as if it were carved on Mt. Rushmore.

"Enough." The president dismissed the others with a wave of his hand. "Tex, walk with me."

Together, they entered the president's private quarters. "Don't lie to me, Charley. You look terrible."

The president pulled up two chairs. "I am terrible. But forget that. I need to say something to you. No expectations, okay? Just fifty years of Frank and Jesse." Tex could almost feel his friend's breath. He could definitely feel his pain.

"Remember when I decided to run?" His eyes drifted to a time when he believed a President Breen could accomplish good deeds. "I thought I understood all the forces on a president. I was naive."

Everything in Charley, his look, his voice, his posture, spoke of conversations and threats and realities that even Ellie hadn't heard about. "So, just know: for reasons I won't explain, I may call for the lowest level of mobilization. If I do, go home and wrap your pipes." Then his voice dropped to a whisper. "But if I strap on my holsters, it could get dangerous. Very dangerous. Will you be my deputy?"

Tex looked straight into his friend's ocean-blue eyes. For a long time. When he finally spoke, the words mirrored his look. "To the end of the line. You have my word."

82

Washington
Oct. 24, 2016

Z AVIA RACED HOME. She put on an apron. Then, like a TV chef, she bustled around the kitchen and made her world-famous eggplant parmesan. It felt good to bring the entrée so her friend, Trish, only had to make a salad. Together, they would have dinner and watch the president. It also felt good to bring a new Transformer toy over to Trish's son, Dalton, age nine.

    The president's speech was two hours away. Zavia was scooping the eggplant into a large plastic container when the phone rang. "I'm so glad I caught you. Dalton fell off his bike. I'm taking him to the doctor. I'm really sorry . . ."

    Zavia sat on the couch. Tears filled her eyes. Sure, she knew how to be alone. But the hardest times were always the most meaningful ones. *Christ! The president of the United States is speaking, and I wrote sections of his speech!* She called three other friends but got voice mail. Ouch! Just then, the phone rang again.

    "Zavia, don't hang up. Please. I'm really sorry." Tex got right to it. "I've got a lot of raw nerves. You hit the rawest of all."

    Zavia just stood there. She had gotten boatloads of apologies from men, but never so genuinely. "I understand, Tex. Now you understand something. Treat me that way again, and we're done. Finito. Forever. I swear to you: you'll be a permanent resident in my emotional graveyard."

    Before his years with Katie, Tex might have made a joke to lighten the moment. But he had learned to take a woman seriously and to take himself seriously. "I understand. I will not treat you like that again. If I do, I deserve the graveyard."

    Zavia listened. Her bullshit alarm didn't sound. "Okay, Tex. We'll try again."

    "How about later tonight? I'd love to watch the speech with you. But Mason's got me with the analysts." This time, he paused. "Can I take you for a drink afterward?"

"That's not a good idea."

"Because it's me?"

"Because I'm watching by myself. That feels bad to me. I doubt I'll want to be with anyone."

Tex took a few moments to respond. "How 'bout this? I'll call you after he's done. We can decide then. Either way's fine with me. Deal?" Zavia agreed, feeling softer. "In the meantime," Tex continued, "why don't you check out the protest? It'll be high theater. You can watch the president on one of those large televisions. At least you won't be alone."

"My stomach's not that strong. But thanks for the suggestion." When they hung up, Zavia poured herself a glass of wine, turned on the TV, and watched the pre-speech drivel. Her heart beat faster. Unlike the rest of the world, she knew whole sections of what the president was going to say.

At one point, the camera switched to scenes at the ever-growing protest. Zavia saw the massive crowd and all the anti-Breen signs. She put the food away, left her apartment, took the Metro, and walked to the Capitol grounds. *If I can't watch him with a friend, I'll watch him with tens of thousands of strangers.*

83

Outside the Capitol Building, Washington
Oct. 24, 2016

WALKING A SHORT DISTANCE from the Capitol, Zavia continually banged into arms and shoulders. In the distance, she saw police moving wooden barriers back to accommodate the ever-growing crowd. Off to the side, she saw a parking lot jammed with buses with Wisconsin, Texas, New Hampshire, and other license plates. She heard snippets of conversation from the protestors:

"You can't have an unstable president."

"Isn't it great? There are protests from Sacramento to Boston."

"I'd have voted for him. He's a good man. But how can we trust his judgment?"

When Zavia turned a corner, she saw the back of the massive crowd. *Oh, my God!* Protest signs everywhere, reaching up to the sky. People were elbow to elbow. Many screamed a mocking two-part chant in a derisive singsong tone.

"Can He Govern?"

"No, He Can't."

Finally, she scooted up an elevated grassy area. From there, she watched a protest organizer on a platform speaking into a microphone. "Testing—1, 2, 3—testing." Zavia's face turned from curiosity to disgust: at the back end of the platform was a twenty-by-twenty image of the ravaged president that Governor Wilton had used in his TV ad.

Zavia looked for a place to stand. She saw people sitting on blankets watching one of the many large-screen monitors that had been set up. Nearby, she saw a stone statue. Since there was room to sit on the statue's raised base, Zavia headed there. Seconds ahead of her, a young man in sweatpants took the spot. Zavia saw a little room next to a young woman with headphones, who had saucer eyes, wore a bulky sweater, and moved stiffly with her arms at an odd angle. A balding man next to the young woman reached down. "Give me your hand. We'll make room."

"No, thanks. I'll go over there." Quickly, Zavia got to one of the few open spots by a tree. Once settled, her eyes focused on the woman sitting on the statue. Who is she? She wasn't yelling. She didn't look angry. Zavia followed the woman's eyes, as they watched first a trailer truck deliver two dozen more portable toilets and, a moment later, even more armed police with shields jumping out of vans. To Zavia, the woman's eyes were beautiful, but hollow, like people she had met in Africa who had survived their towns being raided and their families being butchered.

As the crowd grew and the noise rose, Zavia watched the woman very carefully reach into a sweater pocket and pull out a small bag of carrot sticks and a container of hummus.

What Zavia didn't know was that, in the young woman's mind, the sixtyish man standing next to her had already had a long life. The twentyish woman with a pink blouse and cleavage was probably a lost soul. And, now looking directly at Zavia, the fortyish woman with wild red hair was just in the wrong place at the wrong time.

Zavia also didn't know that, through the woman's eyes, the limos, the police vans, the toilets, the large-screen televisions, the tight pants, the short skirts, and the crowd full of women, were all alien rituals of a devilish cult.

Nor did Zavia have a clue that, as the president's car approached, the young woman's heart skipped a few beats. She saw the woman's body stiffen as she reached into her right sweater pocket. A second later, her body relaxed as she removed her hand and ate a carrot.

84

Congressional Chambers, Washington
Oct. 24, 2016

T HE SOUNDS OF SOFT LEATHER SHOES on hard tile floors filled the corridor, as the president's entourage marched toward the House Chamber. As they did so, the president suffered from Decider's Remorse: the doubt that eats away at one's confidence like termites at a two-by-four stud. *Ten minutes ago, in the Green Room, I put American pilots, sailors, and soldiers on alert. And now I'm about to set off World War III or worse.*

Entering the chamber and seeing the United States' leadership, the president stepped more purposefully. Reaching the podium, he sipped a glass of water. He nodded to Ellie in the gallery. Then he looked into the cameras and out to the billion people who were watching. *God help us. Here we go.*

"Members of Congress," the president began his opening litany, ending it with "my fellow Americans and those of you outside America." A minute later, "America is part of a deeply interrelated system of nations. If that system goes down, all nations, including America, will, too."

Down in the White House Situation Room, Dave Dunn gave Tex a cuff on the shoulder. "Nice opening."

"Now, if I were you," the president said, "there are three questions I'd want answered. First: am I resigning or withdrawing from the campaign?" He let the question hang. "No, I'm not."

Outside the Capitol, Zavia covered her ears as protestors screamed, "No! No! No!" The son of a bitch had killed their hopes three minutes into his address.

"The second question is can I govern? You decide after you hear what I say."

The TV cameras cut to a bar, where a packed crowd watched the president. You could hear the ice cubes melting.

"And the last question: what about the very real threats to our national security? That's what I want to talk about tonight, because it is insane to lie on the tracks while the train whistle gets louder. In that regard, let me say this: my daughter's death grieves me deeply, as it does the First Lady. But the needlessness of all the deaths that day is like jet fuel in my engine. So, hear me clearly: we will reverse the threats of climate change and of those who would destroy us to capitalize on climate change."

In the chamber, America's leadership flipped a switch. They weren't here to bury Breen. The president was here to rally them. Up in the gallery, Ellie beamed and felt Mariah with her. Down in the Situation Room, Tex's shoulders relaxed. He checked the other monitors but couldn't keep his eyes off Charley. *He's swinging for the fences.*

"As you well know," the president said, "eight years ago, credit dried up. Businesses closed. Millions of you lost your homes, your jobs, your hope."

In Moscow, it was several hours before dawn. Sitting in his apartment, the prime minister was tight-lipped and tense. He stopped his exercise bicycle. He just sat on the seat, watching and wondering.

"Was the financial system breakdown, or, 'meltdown,' as it's often called, a matter of national security?" The president looked right into the cameras.

"If our economy collapsed, if the economies of Europe, China, Japan, Brazil, India, and other countries collapsed, if the levels of world trade dropped through the floor and global unemployment rose through the ceiling, if there were riots in countries where we manufacture and in countries where we sell, if there were dramatically fewer funds for civic services, if it took dramatically more funds to support military action in more places around the world where America has interests, if, if, if . . . then I can't possibly view that financial meltdown as anything but an arrow speeding toward our national heart."

In his hotel room on the outskirts of Amsterdam, Admiral Sukirov nursed both his drink and his rage. He made a secure call to a waiting Alpha. "Contact your operative. Tell her ten minutes."

"Yes, sir. She's there, waiting."

"One more thing." Quickly, the admiral gave a second order. Surprised, Alpha repeated it to confirm it.

"You heard me. Do it before you call her."

Meanwhile, the president pushed forward. "But, in retrospect, was the meltdown caused by a handful of people and organizations that took mega-risks? Of course. But we were all complicit. We bought the idea that debt is good, and we bought beyond what we could afford, which brings me to the heart of this address."

In a New York news studio, Donna Dean, the president's political strategist, studied the real-time focus group results. Nine of the ten groups had her thinking about her inauguration dress.

In front of the Capitol, Zavia listened to the nonstop groans and boos. They were intense. She was scared. This had all the earmarks of a lynch mob.

On Sanibel Island, Mickey and Elena were munching on fish tacos as they watched the president. Suddenly, they nearly choked. Behind them, they heard a loud noise that sounded like a gas main had erupted. They swiveled their chairs. On the Greenland monitor, they saw huge plumes of snow and ice rising into the cold, wind-blown night sky. "Holy shit!" Mickey said out loud. A moment later, exploding snow covered the camera lens. But they heard the unmistakable sound of glaciers breaking off.

Meanwhile, in the White House Situation Room, Tex punched the air. *Go for it, buddy!* Then his phone rang. He was pissed, but happy to see who it was. "Hey, Mick, you watching?"

A moment later, Tex turned to Dave and Emma. There was no blood in his face. "Bring up Greenland."

After a few key clicks, they all saw the ice explode and the glaciers plummet. "Mickey said it could be an earthquake."

Dave logged into a seismic activity database. "It's not. Let's check radiation. Holy shit! Lots!"

Emma drummed her fingernails on the desk. "The general's inside the chamber. He won't even look at text messages till the president's done."

Instantly, Tex was standing. "I'll go. Keep watching."

Emma grabbed his arm. "You'll never get in." She made a call. "Sir, we've got an emergency." Crisply, she informed the secretary of defense, who was the designated cabinet member absent from the president's talk. He would broadcast the alert to every military base and civilian area. Dave and Emma then raced outside and commandeered a security vehicle. "Get us to the Capitol," she ordered. "Now."

Minutes later, the security vehicle reached the edge of the protest. Dave lowered the back window, and they heard the president on one of the monitors. "If we thought the financial system melting down was a threat, imagine the consequences when the natural system, what we call 'Nature' breaks down."

The car inched forward. Suddenly, a few dozen protestors surrounded it. They banged hard on the roof with their hands and their signs. They didn't know who was in the car, but they screamed at them anyway. Emma and Dave could barely hear the president say, "In military jargon, the changing climate is a threat multiplier. It is a grave danger by itself, and it multiplies . . ."

Dave called Tex on his cell phone, "Tex, we can't—" He couldn't finish the sentence. He was tossed sideways, as the crowd tipped the car over. Dave smashed up against Emma, who smashed up against the window. Blood poured from her temple and down the window. Dave's broken arm flopped, as he strained with his other hand to reach where his cell phone had fallen. "Tex, get . . ." Dave's voice was lost, as some guy yanked the two of them out of the back and yelled into the phone. "Whoever you are, get your ass over here so we can kick it around."

Tex raced down the corridor. He had the phone to his ear, yelling, "You motherfucker!" Then he was out the door, racing down the path toward the front gate. He waved off the guard, turned onto Pennsylvania Avenue, raced to the end of the block, and scrambled across the street between oncoming vehicles. One of them was a slow-moving motorcycle. Tex grabbed the handlebar and squeezed the brake. "Sorry. I need your bike. Emergency." Then he dragged the guy off his bike. He sped off toward the Capitol. He weaved in and out of the traffic. He caused four fender-benders. He almost hit two pedestrians. Charley!

Finally at the crowd's edge, Tex slowed the motorcycle. Out of the corner of his eye, he saw someone waving wildly at him. *Zavia! Shit! I don't have time to tell her.* He dumped the cycle and ran toward the Capitol, veering around people as if they were trees in a Colombian jungle. One big guy threw a punch at him. Tex caught his fist, twisted it, and put him on the ground.

As he pushed and shoved his way through the crowd, Tex could only hear snippets of the president. ". . . millions of eco-refugees that overwhelm our allies . . ." And then he heard the terrible noise. Tex stopped in his tracks. From the sound alone, he knew it was a plastic explosive.

As soon as the saucer-eyed woman had hit the detonator, her own body was blown apart. The explosion shredded those closest to her. It sent the statue's stone flying through the air.

A twenty-pound hunk of stone crashed into the elm tree Zavia was leaning against. A volley of shrapnel flew by her. A few pieces sliced her forehead and cheek. Another piece ripped the left sleeve of her blouse. Instinctively, she dropped to the ground. She heard screams everywhere. Then the sirens filled the night as police vans, fire trucks, and ambulances descended.

Tex looked back. *Jesus! The bomber was close to Zavia!* He saw EMTs racing toward her location with medical bags and stretchers. Tex took a few steps toward them. *I can't!* Then he sprinted toward the Capitol. He crashed into three protestors and knocked them over. With the crowd behind him, he reached the Capitol steps and took them two at a time. His lungs ached as much as his legs. Near the top, he heard bullets ricochet off the steps he had just left. A Capitol policeman was firing first and asking questions later.

Finally, panting, Tex reached the top step. He willed his legs forward and headed straight for the Capitol doors.

85

Congressional Chambers, Washington
Oct. 24, 2016

INSIDE THE CAPITOL, the Protection Unit head picked up the phone on the first ring. "Yes, sir, I'm listening."

At a Midwest military base, the secretary of defense was sweating profusely. From China to Israel, the world's nuclear nations had ordered their weapons to be aimed, though they weren't sure where to aim them. From Australia to Spain, borders were shut down, cities were locked down, and suspects were being hunted down. Within minutes of the Greenland blast, Internet bloggers announced "the ultimate October Surprise"; accused "the imperialist fanatics"; skewered "the Muslim terrorists"; and put forth every known conspiracy theory and a few new ones.

"This is a Red Alert," the secretary told the Secret Service agent at the Capitol. "If I get one more piece of evidence, you will evacuate the president and everyone else. Meanwhile, you are authorized to take down any suspect for any suspicious behavior."

The Protection Unit head immediately sent additional agents to the front of the building. Just as they arrived, Tex pushed his way through the front doors, yelling, "I'm the president's special assistant! You've got to tell him a nuclear bomb was set off in—"

Instantly, three agents shoved Tex's face into the floor and bent his arms behind him. "Shut up and don't move."

An agent got one handcuff on Tex. But he rose up on his knees and screamed, "Damn it! Tell the president!" When they wrestled him down again, he crashed the handcuff into the agent's face, breaking two of the man's teeth. He got to his feet and ran down the corridor with his shirt ripped and blood oozing out of his left eye.

Behind him, an agent aimed his gun at Tex's back. Suddenly, from down the hall, a different agent yelled in a grating New England accent, "Don't shoot! He's the president's friend!"

Tex recognized the man who had slept outside his home the night before he had met with Charley. He stopped, turned, and announced, "The president's got to know!" Seconds later, both men ran at full speed toward the chamber doors.

86

Congressional Chamber, Washington
Oct. 24, 2016

WHILE TEX AND THE SECRET SERVICE AGENT raced through the corridor, America's leadership inside the chamber was hopeful. The cabinet was ecstatic. Hell, the secretary of state even pumped her fist when the president said, "The climate isn't waiting. The Russians aren't waiting. And neither are we. As of tonight, I am ordering a war-level implementation to end this threat to our country."

Up in the gallery, Ellie clasped her hands tightly, anticipating the part of Charley's speech that linked what killed Mariah with what could kill America. That was when she saw a side door open and a Secret Service agent walk quickly toward the Speaker of the House. Next, she saw what everyone in the chamber except her husband saw: the agent handed the Speaker a note and whispered in her ear.

"The financial collapse and the climate-related national security threats: what do they have in common?" the president asked, unaware of the activity behind him. "For sure: they result from the destructive acts of a few people. But they are also the consequences of small acts from you, me, and the other seven billion of us."

In Moscow, in the middle of the night, the prime minister moved from his exercise bike to his favorite chair, as the president continued. "Because if there is an enemy, it is not a particular nation. It is a particular way of thinking." The president looked out at the chamber. "That way of thinking sees black versus white, good versus evil, us versus them. Now, sometimes, it is absolutely like that. But often, it is not. And it is always more complex than we think."

In bars and living rooms, new thoughts slipped through old mental frameworks. "Think about it," the president said. "The entire world economy: how many moving parts does it have? And how many points of vulnerability?" He paused, milking the moment. "No generation has ever lived in a more interconnected world. For America to be truly secure, the whole system of nations must be secure."

Inside the Capitol, Tex and the New England agent raced down the corridor. When they passed a monitor, Tex heard the president's voice. *Three minutes, at most.* He knew Charley was getting to the section of his speech where he would talk about stopping those who would threaten the world. *Charley, you can't say that!* If the president did say it just minutes after the nuclear detonation in Greenland and the suicide bomber on the Capitol Mall, he would look as out of touch as people feared.

Panting for breath, Tex and the agent reached the chamber doors. "Don't move, Cassidy. Let me handle this." The agent huddled quickly with the unit protecting the doors. Tex heard the president, who was now less than ninety seconds from losing the election and, by allowing Wilton to win the election, allowing the Russians to move forward.

Tex banged into the huddling agents. "There's no time! Don't you understand! There's no—"

Just then, the New England agent grabbed Tex and landed a powerful fist in his stomach. "Shut up!"

Doubled over, Tex saw the chamber door through the huddled agents' arms. He took a deep breath. He raised his body. He contracted his leg muscles like a fullback heading for the end zone. But before he could move his legs, two agents hauled him up to a standing position.

"The Speaker of the House already has a note. She'll hand it to the president," one of them said. "We want you just inside the chamber doors, so the president can see you. But we don't want an incident. Can you just nod if the president looks at you?"

Tex moved his head up and down. His ribs hurt badly.

"You look like shit," the agent said, taking off his suit jacket and giving it to Tex. "You'll probably be on TV, and we don't want to scare people any more than we have to." The agents let Tex's arms hang loose, so he could put on the jacket. When he was done, he stood there in cowboy boots, jeans, ripped shirt, cut eye, mussed hair, and dark-blue suit coat.

Tex was ready. Then the agents grabbed Tex's arms and inched him forward. As the doors opened, Tex stood on the top step of the chamber. Below him, he saw the seated members of Congress, the Supreme Court, military leaders, and others. He saw the president standing at the podium, no more than thirty seconds from the critical section of his speech. Tex sighed in relief as the Speaker of the House stood up from her leather chair and stepped forward.

But then, visibly nervous, the Speaker abruptly took a step backward and sat down again.

A wave of anger welled up in Tex. He yelled as loudly as he could, "Mr. President! Nuclear explosions in Greenland!"

Every head turned. The First Lady froze as she saw Tex being dropped to his knees. The TV cameras turned toward the intruder. At the podium, the president stopped mid-sentence and looked out at Tex, who was sprawled on the ground with guns pointed at him. "Let him up," the president said tersely. "He works for me. And he's my friend."

The agents jerked Tex up by the armpits. His head hurt, and he spoke, out of breath. "Mr. President . . . it's like Pakistan; Greenland glaciers were just nuked."

"Three explosions." General Mason stood up and spoke out, after reading his text messages. "And a suicide bomber outside this building minutes ago. Fourteen dead, so far." Tex winced when he heard the death count.

The chamber was silent. Every eye and television camera swiveled back to the president. "Ladies and gentlemen," the president spoke slowly, "whether you are in this room or outside it, these events reinforce what I've said. I am calling upon the prime minister of the Russian Federation and other world leaders to immediately convene a meeting, while we track down those who would endanger us all."

As the president headed down the podium stairs, the Speaker of the House slammed her gavel three times, officially ending this State of the Union Address.

PART FOUR: RED

87

Washington
Oct. 24, 2016

It was 9/11 all over again. The US airspace was shut down. Sirens and flashing lights crisscrossed Washington all night long. Strangers held one another on the street. People knelt, prayed, and screamed.

After being treated for her cuts and bruises, Zavia made her way back to her apartment. A few inches more to the left or right, and she would have been in the morgue. She saw herself in a mirror. *I'm lucky to be alive. I look awful.*

Still quaking like an aspen leaf, Zavia turned on the television. She watched armed soldiers jumping off transport trucks to surround the White House, the Pentagon, the Capitol, and other seats of government. She stared at scenes of chaotic Washington streets, where EMTs carried off the dead in body bags and police officers interrogated drivers. She could barely listen to the Greenland stories. "It's now been confirmed," a reporter in a thick fur hat and parka spoke from a small town on the Greenland coast, "that three nuclear devices were detonated; two along the western coast of the Ice Sheet and one along the eastern coast." Behind him, videos displayed images of glacial debris in the water, commercial vessels fleeing the area, and military planes taking off from aircraft carriers. "Radiation levels are being monitored," the reporter read from a clipboard he was holding. "So are tidal and tsunami activities."

Zavia muted the television. Then she stared at her rugs, wine glasses, and leather couch. They felt like props in the safe little world she had constructed. She could almost hear the ticking bomb that threatened to blow up everyone's safe little world.

The bomb ticked louder when the phone rang. "Oh, God, Tex, you're alive." Her shoulders relaxed a little bit. "I saw you. And then—"

"Zavia," he interrupted her and summarized what had happened in the Capitol. "Help me understand what those detonations mean."

Zavia took her portable phone. She walked across the room to a cabinet where she kept what little liquor she had. "You understand, Tex, this has never happened before. I don't know for sure. Nobody does." While she listened to Tex pleading with her to make her best guess, she poured a glass of wine and looked out at the sky, bizarrely lit from all the emergency lights.

"If it's just the three detonations," she said, "sure, there'll be some coastal flooding. But there won't be too much damage. Longer-term, more ice will be exposed, so it'll melt faster, which will affect the ocean currents."

Tex listened closely to each word. "And if there are more detonations?"

Zavia took a sip of wine. "You know the story about Noah and the flood. Well, it's not just in the Bible. Just about every culture has its own flood story. That's no coincidence . . ."

Tex waited for her to finish. When she didn't, he asked, "Then what do you believe?"

Zavia hesitated. She knew that what she was about to say might get her laughed out of her profession. "It goes back ten thousand years, when the Ice Age ended and the glaciers melted. The flooding would have been gradual . . . cumulative . . . unimaginable . . . and monumentally disastrous."

"And if massive flooding happened now?"

"With all the coastal buildup, it'd be worse." Zavia put her glass down and sat down. Then she rattled off a slew of likely impacts. "Millions could die, Tex. Maybe billions. And most of the living would just be surviving."

Minutes later, they both said good night to each other, differently than they had said it to anyone in a long time. What they didn't say was that given the snukes and the storms, they might never have a good night or a bad night or any night together.

Zavia put the phone down. She went into her bedroom, where a blinking light caught her eye. "Eleven messages." She listened to the first ten. Skip . . . skip . . . skip. . . . The eleventh was an old, dear friend. "Zavia, it's Lars. I just heard about the bombing. Are you all right? Please call me. Also, Dagmare's worse. You should probably come over. And I need to talk with you about the Delta Works. There are some things you know better than I do."

Zavia pushed pause. She sat on the edge of her bed but wanted to crawl under it. Tears and fears swept through her. She doubled over as sobs wracked her body. *I'm worn out. I don't want to go all the way back there. I hate that I don't want to go. Of course I'm going.*

88

The Kremlin
Oct. 25, 2016

THE RUSSIAN PRIME MINISTER looked halfway up the optic nerves of his intelligence officers. "Find Sukirov. Preferably alive. But dead is fine." As they left, the younger Centennial Committee members entered. The prime minister revealed the Operation Noah plot and reassured them that their market-based approach to world power was still in play.

Finally, the prime minister put in a call to the White House. It was a call he had to make. While he waited, the prime minister received a call he had to take.

"Admiral, it's over," he wasted no time. "I know about the Quartet and Operation Noah."

"What's over is your selling out Russia," the admiral hissed like a viper. "Listen carefully." He then laid out the situation. Two years ago, the Antelopes buried the first snukes in Tibet. Within weeks, the Bears did the same in the Italian Alps. The Cheetahs took care of the Andes. Today, the Quartet was more than midway through the alphabet. That meant that five dozen snukes were set to go one at a time or all together. "Follow my orders, and the world will bow to Russia. Defy my orders, and the world will fall apart, including Russia."

"Admiral, you're insane."

"Thirty minutes." The line went dead eight seconds before it could be traced.

90

President's Private Quarters, White House
Oct. 25, 2016

THE PRESIDENT'S ADVISERS pulled an all-nighter. The president himself was looking at one. There was no way in hell he could sleep. Instead, he opened a beer bottle and tossed one to Tex. "Tell me about Prago." Behind them, the door opened. Ellie couldn't sleep either. She joined them, carrying a small box in her hands that she placed on a side table. "If you've got the stomach for it, Tex is telling me about a Russian psychopath."

Ellie sat on the arm of her husband's chair. Charley rubbed her back. Tex sat low in his chair and stretched his legs out. He took a long swig, gearing up for his unpleasant tale. "I've had three contacts. The first was in a Palestinian bomb factory." Tex then described his interview with the Russian adviser to the Palestinians.

"Second time," Tex continued, "was three years ago in Colombia." He described the gruesome killings, especially the crucifixion in the church. "You know me, I'll eat the warm liver out of a dead deer. But this was..."

"You don't have to do this, Tex." Ellie knew he was swimming in dangerous waters.

"I do." He turned to the president. "You've got to know, Charley. You deal with crazies. He's a different breed."

Charley raised his bottle, indicating for Tex to continue.

"The last time was just two weeks ago." Tex told them about talking to Prago, while tied up in the jungle. "I was pretty sure I'd be dead."

As Tex relayed the rest of the story about Carlos, Juan, and his escape, Ellie took an emotional dive. Even before Mariah's death, she was up to her eyeballs in suffering-and-death stories. God bless him: Charley's skin had gotten tougher than a goat steak over the years. But hers had thinned. Finally, she got up to go. "Sorry, Tex. I walk out of movies, too."

Ellie headed toward their bedroom. "Oh, before I forget, this came for you." She handed Tex the box with a note on top. "For Tex Cassidy. Arrived by special courier. Cleared by Secret Service for delivery."

Tex picked up the very light box and shook it but heard nothing. Tearing away the tape, he saw a torn-off label from a can of industrial-strength rat poison. Under it was a sheet of paper. When Tex turned it over, he shuddered. He felt evil in the room. He saw a photo of Katie and the words: "You're next, amigo. As they say, revenge is best served cold. P."

Twenty minutes later, Tex paced in the Lincoln Bedroom faster than most people jog. *Revenge? For what?* He kicked over and broke an antique Victorian sofa. He stuck his head under a cold-water shower. Then he stopped in front of the mirror. His eyes morphed into Prago's eyes. *If I get my hands on you, you're a dead man.* Suddenly, Prago's image was gone. His own eyes were more intense than he had ever seen them.

91

Washington
Oct. 25, 2016

THE SUN WAS UP. Zavia was on her deck. The tremors still coursed through her. The cuts still stung. The explosion still echoed in her mind. When she returned inside, she went to her computer and booked her ticket to Amsterdam. Then she put on the television. Tex! There he was, looking dreadful, yelling to the president. She was glad she would see him on her way to Dulles.

An hour later, Zavia laid the "just in case" black dress into her traveling bag. Feeling half-human again, she brushed her hair, put on mascara, and applied the deepest red lipstick she had worn in years.

At the White House, Zavia was escorted to a sitting room. Tex had gotten maybe an hour of shut-eye, obsessing about Prago. Now, he alternated between reading Sukirov reports and glancing down the hallway to see if Zavia had arrived. "I'm so glad you're okay." He practically ejected himself out of the chair. He hugged her and touched her facial bruises gently.

For the next hour, Tex told her what he could about the prime minister's call, Alpha's present, and Katie's death. She told him about her unhappy marriage and her interactions with Sukirov.

Behind them, the First Lady entered quietly. "You must be Zavia." There was a smile on Ellie's face as she walked right up to Zavia and stuck out her hand. "It's so good to meet you."

"Mrs. Breen!" Zavia's tears filled her eyes as she took the outstretched hand. "It never crossed my mind that I would meet you."

"Call me Ellie, please." The two women connected right away, as two women can.

"I'm so sorry about Mariah." Without thinking, Zavia hugged her and held her for a moment.

Ellie was startled. White House staffers had personally offered their condolences. Members of Congress sent notes or flowers. A few stopped by the White House to offer kind words. But to all of them, she was the First Lady. Tex and Charley treated her like Ellie. But this was the first time someone else did. Her mountain of pain eased ever so slightly. She had lost her daughter. Maybe she had found a sister. "I don't mean to interrupt." Ellie stepped back and looked deeply at Zavia. "I'm in the middle of something, anyway. But I just wanted to say hello." Ellie then excused herself. "I hope we'll see each other again."

"Wow!" Zavia couldn't speak. She had been touched as well.

"You just gave her something, Zavia. I can tell." Tex had a tear in his eye. He knew that deep connection with people was like manna from heaven for Ellie. It had always been rare. It had gotten even rarer when she became a title.

Zavia stopped staring at the door through which Ellie had left. As her eyes moved back to Tex, she noticed a clock on the table. "Oh, God, Tex. My flight . . ." Zavia gathered up her purse.

"Who's picking you up at Schiphol?" Tex walked her downstairs.

"My cousin, Ingrid." She described what Ingrid was doing with Climate Trackers; who Lars, Ingrid's father, was; and how Lars had mentored Zavia at the Delta Works. "They're dear people. My whole Dutch family's that way."

Outside, heading toward the White House gate, Tex stopped in his tracks. "Look, Zavia, obviously something's going on between us." Uncharacteristically, he shuffled from one foot to the other. "The world's pretty crazy right now. But if you're game, I'd like to see where we go from here."

Zavia looked into his eyes. Inside herself, she couldn't stand the push-pull feeling. *Go slow. Go fast. Go toward him. Run away.* "I would, too."

"I hate that you'll be across the ocean." Unspoken was their shared fear that the world would fray apart while they were so far apart. "I'll call you. Call me anytime for any reason."

At the White House gate, he hugged her again and kissed her on the cheek. "Safe travels," he said. He almost added "sweetheart," but couldn't quite form the word.

92

Oosterschelde Barrier, Netherlands
Oct. 25, 2016

OUTSIDE THE PROJECT TRAILER, the foreman walked through the light rain with a cigarette dangling from his lips. He found his two contractors wearing thick goggles and fine-particle respirators. Before repainting one of the sixteen gates' cylindrical arms, they were blasting off the old paint with an air compressor and a metallic abrasive. In keeping with Dutch law, the contractors captured the abrasive for reuse. They also captured the old paint for disposal, as it contained lead, zinc chromate, and other highly toxic materials.

Given all the noise, they didn't hear the foreman. But they saw him waving. They returned to the access road in the mechanical bucket that allowed them to move up, down, and sideways.

"I've got a meeting up at the Maeslant Barrier. Will you be okay by yourselves?" Alpha gave him a thumb-up, as he and Beta dumped the captured abrasive into a large fifty-five-gallon drum and the waste paint into another. The foreman then walked off toward his car, tossing his cigarette into the water below.

Minutes later, Beta placed the specially hinged lids on the containers and rolled them aside. He then drove their van onto the access road to the three structures covered with tents to facilitate maintenance. After making sure no one was around, they lifted the snuke out of the van, placed it in the mechanical bucket, and lowered themselves down to the hydraulic gate arm within the middle tented structure. A few minutes later, they had tied the bomb between the hydraulic arm and the gate itself with a nylon rope.

93

Amsterdam
Oct. 26, 2016

Z AVIA LEANED BACK against her window seat. It was an overnight flight, and her brain was working overtime. *Dagmare, the end of her life? Tex, the start of my new life?* Her thoughts all felt like rocks in a tumbler.

An hour before landing, the captain announced, "There are some storm clouds up ahead, so our descent may be bumpy." Bumpy! Wind and rain pounded the plane. Lightning danced along both wings. Zavia and half the other passengers gripped their seats, until the wheels touched down on the slick runway.

Finally in the airport, Zavia stepped into the cavernous Schiphol terminal and froze at the sights and sounds of wall-to-wall people.

Thousands of human bodies were crammed together. They were hot. They were mad. Half of them were yelling into cell phones. Virtually every child cried. The line in the men's room was out the door and around the corner. The line in the women's room extended to Belgium. A man at the rental car counter offered to pay ten times the fee, but there wasn't a car available. People queued up to stand on trains headed inland. It was a pickpocket's heaven. With no food or drink left in any shops or restaurants, it was a passenger's hell.

As Zavia elbowed her way into the crowd, looking for Ingrid, she got pushed forward, backward, and sideways. Finally, she saw Ingrid standing on a chair, waving her arms like a merchant marine officer with semaphore flags.

"Jesus, Ingrid." She gave her a huge hug. "Is the airport shut down?"

"The whole country's shut down. Your flight was one of the last ones in or out. You haven't heard?" She pointed to a large-screen TV.

"Two hours and six minutes ago," the announcer said, his voice trembling, "another small nuclear device was detonated." He then described the explosion on a glacier at the Qinghai-Tibet plateau. The area is the headwaters of the 3,900-mile Yangtze River, which is the longest river in Asia and a major source of Chinese irrigation and hydroelectric power. "This is a lot like the recent Pakistan explosion. An entire watershed is demolished. Hundreds of villages are swept away in the raging waters. Tens of thousands of people are already dead."

"Heaven help us," Zavia whispered. The announcer continued on, sounding like the foreman of a jury reading a verdict. Behind him was stock footage of the plateau, Chinese wheat fields, and crowded city scenes in Beijing and Shanghai. "Authorities around the world are thinking the unthinkable: what will this terrorist act mean to the world's economic engine and the 1.2 billion people who drive it?"

"Oh, my God!" Ingrid's whole face puffed up. "We put a webcam there. Christian inputted the coordinates for it just before . . ." She stopped, realizing that Zavia was too glued to the news to really take in her news.

Fifteen minutes later, they had made their way through the garage to Ingrid's car. "Thank you so much for taking me to Dagmare's." Zavia felt distant and still in shock. "If you hadn't . . ." Suddenly, Zavia heard Ingrid sobbing with her head on the steering wheel. The small car shook along with her body. Zavia put her arm around Ingrid's shoulders. "It's scary, Ingrid. It scares the hell out of me, too."

"Somebody murdered Christian." The awful news just sprang out of her. "They found his body in a dumpster. I had to identify him." Zavia stroked her young cousin's head. Ingrid broke out in sobs again. "Can I tell you something else? But you can't tell Dad." Zavia nodded, not liking this promise but knowing she had to make it. "I'm pregnant. It's Christian's baby. He asked me to marry him five days ago."

As the next wave of tears flooded through Ingrid, Zavia held her until the grief and pain had run their course. "Zavia, the funeral's at ten o'clock. Just drop me off and take the car. One of Christian's friends will take me home."

Ingrid pulled onto the highway and headed toward Zorgvlied Cemetery. The rain slowed to a misty drizzle. "We can go to Dagmare's later," Zavia said. "I'll stay with you at the funeral."

They slowed, entering the cemetery gates. "Thank you. But I'd rather be here with just his family and friends." In the distance, a hearse pulled up, along with several cars for Christian's family.

"That's fine, sweetie. But let's talk tomorrow about the baby, okay?"

Ingrid drove along the narrow cemetery roads. As they turned a corner, Zavia leaned her head against the window. What would she say to Ingrid tomorrow? How could she not tell Lars today? Through the misty rain, she saw the cemetery buildings. She saw a large, square-looking man standing with his head bowed, hat in hand, staring at a headstone. She saw the rows of headstones. She saw an elderly couple laying flowers on a grave.

Suddenly, Zavia snapped forward. "Turn around! That man we just passed..." Ingrid was flustered and upset. She could see the minister starting Christian's service. "Ingrid, I'm sorry. But you've got to go back!" Annoyed, Ingrid made a U-turn and drove past the man faster than Zavia wanted. "Slow down. Drive on the opposite road, so I can see his face." Just as they were in position, he turned and walked away, heading toward a dark-blue Citroën. Ingrid looked harshly at Zavia. She needed to get to her fiancé's funeral. "Drive around..." Then the man turned for one more look at the gravesite. *I was right. It's Sukirov.*

94

White House
Oct. 26, 2016

At 7:35 A.M., the president passed through his private quarters. He looked at his wife, still in her bathrobe, mindlessly eating a bowl of cereal. He watched her reach for the Washington Post and pull her hand back. Instead, she thumbed through a clothing catalog.

A few minutes later, the president talked briefly with his chief of staff. "What's the political fallout, Alex?"

"According to Donna Dean, every state is a swing state, sir."

As soon as Alex left, Tex was ushered in, and they returned to the Situation Room. Tex moved to a seat along the wall. The president sat at the head of the long table, facing his military and civilian advisers. He took a sip of coffee that had been placed next to him. "Okay, ladies and gentlemen, you know the threats. What do you recommend?"

"Sir," the secretary of defense started right in, "the planes we launched last night just before your address? We think we should add another squadron and deploy them to Greenland, the Alps, and other major glacial areas, including Alaska."

The president wasn't impressed, but he nodded. Can't hurt. Might help. Then the secretary made his recommendation in regard to Sukirov's demand that the US blow up the Trans-Alaskan pipeline. "We think the best way to go is to plant dummy explosives."

The president just looked at the secretary. "Is he that stupid?"

"No, but it'll buy us time to find the other snukes. Or, better, to find the launch-code site."

The president shrugged. "Let me hold any decisions until I hear all the recommendations." The president jotted down a few notes.

"Mr. President, if I may speak next." General Mason leaned forward. "We've already set in motion a very large manhunt. I recommend we expand it immediately."

The president looked up. "What does 'expand it' mean, General?"

"We'll show pictures of Sukirov and Alpha to every police officer, airline steward, hotel front desk staff, and cab driver in the world's major cities."

The president sighed. His voice was angry. "Are you saying we're not doing that already?"

"We are, sir. In fact, we've gotten 1,183 leads, but none have panned out."

"Well, maybe number 1,184 will be lucky. What else? Then you can all get some sleep."

"Sir," the director of Homeland Security spoke up. His eyes were red, and his voice was hoarse. "We just met with FEMA in Wilmington, North Carolina. State emergency coordinators were there, too. If and when you give the word, we'll evacuate all the coastal communities along the east and Gulf coasts."

The president made a few additional notes, more to cover the deep disappointment he felt than to have a record. *Those recommendations are lame.* Then he looked up. "Let's go with what you've laid out." He then stood up, signaled for Tex to follow, and strode out of the Situation Room.

Followed closely by two Secret Service agents, they headed up an inner White House staircase. "Just between us," the president half-whispered, "we're in deep shit."

As they reached the president's private quarters, Tex put his arm around Charley. "We'll catch a break. Why don't you catch some sleep?"

The two men went in separate directions. Back in his White House room, Tex sat on the edge of the bed. He couldn't get Sukirov or Prago out of his mind. He was also consumed with this thing with Zavia, but she was across the damn ocean. Suddenly, his cell phone rang. "You're reading my mind," Tex said, leaning against the headboard. "I was just thinking about you."

"Tex, listen to me." Zavia was driving southwest toward Dagmare's house and the Delta Works. "I just saw him. Sukirov. He's here in Amsterdam." She described everything from Christian's murder to the admiral's mourning. "By the time I dropped Ingrid off, his car was gone."

Tex lodged the cell phone between his ear and shoulder. Meanwhile, he stuffed a few clothes into his pack. "Call me when you get to Dagmare's. I'm on my way." Racing into the corridor, he didn't fully close his door. Nor did he take the time to turn and shut it.

"You can't come," Zavia yelled into her phone. "Everything's shut down." The rain was picking up again. The windshield wiper on the driver's side was older than she was.

"Keep your phone on." Tex burst through General Mason's office door. The NSA was going over notes with Emma Wolfe. Tex relayed Zavia's message.

"He could be visiting his son's grave," Emma said. "We think he died in Amsterdam."

Seconds later, the general called his Dutch counterpart, who ordered a military and police dragnet. The general then rose quickly. "I've got to tell the president." Even more quickly, Tex blocked the door.

"First, get me to Amsterdam. You gave your word: wherever I want to go."

"Let the Dutch handle this."

"If Sukirov's there, Alpha probably is. I'm the only one who knows what he looks like."

"The country's closed, Tex."

"Then drop me off in Brussels."

"Planes aren't flying there."

"Fuck planes. I want a military jet."

I don't have time for this. The general made a terse call and kicked Tex out. In less than an hour, Tex was at Andrews Air Force Base. As fast as he could, he put on a flight suit, climbed into the seat behind the pilot, and put his oxygen mask on. The hangar doors opened. Within minutes, he was traveling nearly twice the speed of sound, heading east at fifty thousand feet.

95

Amsterdam
Oct. 26, 2016

INGRID OPENED HER UMBRELLA, buttoned up her raincoat, and stepped quickly toward Christian's funeral. She didn't see Admiral Sukirov's dark-blue Citroën pull alongside a white van at the end of the cemetery road. Nor did she see her boss, who had come to the cemetery to allay suspicions that he was involved in Christian's murder. In his Dutch disguise, Alpha stood in the rain and tapped on the Citroën's window.

Finally, the admiral lowered his window. Alpha leaned down. "Sir, you were spotted. By Zavia Jansen, the hydrologist." He described what he was doing here and what he saw.

The admiral squinted as if he were trying to take in what he just heard. "How do you know it was the American?"

"Beta and I sat through her lecture at the barrier orientation."

The admiral looked past Alpha to his son's headstone. He had done his best to teach Anton about why Russia was the best of nations. But Anton had been infected with a powerful strain of the individualist virus. And of all the places in the world, he had come to Amsterdam: the most decrepit, individualist city in the world. He had once described Amsterdam to someone as "the modern Sodom and Gomorrah." As long as the admiral lived, he would never forgive either Anton or the Dutch for his son's love of heroin.

The admiral closed his thick fist, making it look like the head of a sledgehammer. "Let's hope we see her again. In the meantime, make sure the launch codes are complete. Then let's meet in the barrier parking lot." He rolled up the window and drove through the misting rain. Some of the wet street splashed onto Alpha's boots. Alpha shook it off and walked toward the funeral.

"The Lord giveth, and the Lord taketh . . . Dust to dust." The minister was a fountain of clichés. In between them, he saw one more griever approaching.

Ingrid's boss mouthed, "I'm so sorry," and put his arm around her grieving body. Ingrid leaned her head against his protective shoulder. "If you don't have a car, let me give you a ride home," he whispered gently.

After the service ended, Alpha escorted Ingrid into his van. "I saw someone drop you off. Is she a friend?"

"My cousin, Zavia. She's from America." Alpha's eyes narrowed. Lightly, but purposefully, he pressed Ingrid for more information. "She's here because our aunt is dying. And besides, my father's the chief software programmer at the Oosterschelde Barrier. She's going to help him."

"Oh, so that's where you get your skill." He touched her arm gently and noticed how pretty she was. "I'll bet your cousin's very proud of your work with Climate Trackers. Have you told her much?"

"Just a little." Alpha stopped at a red light. "Would you mind if we go to the office first?" Ingrid asked. "I'd like to get Christian's things and double check the codes."

Ten minutes later, Alpha stopped in the middle of the street in front of the Climate Trackers office. There were no parking places, and he didn't want to delay his task. "Tell you what, Ingrid. I've got to do an errand. I'll pick you up in an hour. Is that enough time?" He watched Ingrid; her young woman's body stepped quickly through the rain and up the stairs. Then he drove quickly to his hotel. After checking that the single hair he had placed from the bottom of the door to the doorframe was still in place, he went inside, unlocked his pack, and took out a small device that Beta had built for him the day before.

At precisely one hour, Alpha entered the Climate Trackers office. He saw Ingrid hunched over her computer. Her black dress was two inches above her knees. When she started to verify the location of each camera on each glacier, he listened very, very closely. Finally, satisfied, he said, "Excellent work. Come on, I'll take you home. The rain's pretty gnarly."

In front of her apartment, Ingrid felt she owed him something. "It's so damp and nasty. Would you like a cup of tea?"

While she went up to boil the water, Alpha made a quick phone call from his van. Then, walking upstairs and entering her apartment, he saw her standing by the stove in her stockinged feet. "The water will boil in another minute." She leaned into the refrigerator to get cream and a few pastries. She felt him behind her, pressing himself against her. Instinctively, she stood upright and stepped to the side. "Don't do that. Please don't do that."

Alpha grabbed her left arm. With her right arm, Ingrid picked up a small frying pan and swung it wildly at him. Alpha easily stopped her with his other hand. He held her there, holding both her hands in the air.

"You know," he said, looking into her eyes, "Christian struggled a little bit, too. I like that." Then he threw her onto the bed. Ingrid tried to fight, but Alpha spread-eagled her arms and legs, tying them to the bedposts. He stuck a washcloth in her mouth and taped it in place.

Ingrid lay there, shaking, tears flowing down her cheeks. She shut her eyes so tightly that they hurt. As she tried in vain to bring her legs together, she felt the terrible, helpless feeling that her boss was undoing his pants. Thirty seconds passed. A minute passed. She didn't feel him even touching her. Terrified, she opened her eyes and saw him filling a hypodermic needle from a small bottle. She tried to scream but couldn't. She tried to hit him but couldn't. Then, almost gently, he bent over and injected the sedative. By the time, he put the vial and needle away, she was slipping into a very deep sleep.

In another two minutes, Alpha took his shoes off and placed them by the front door. Then from his pack, he carefully pulled out the small metal box that Beta had made for him. He placed a pillow next to Ingrid. As he ever so carefully laid the box on top of the pillow and connected two wires, he looked over at Ingrid's unconscious face. Finally, very deliberately, he tiptoed out of the room, making sure that his steps didn't activate the mercury-switch bomb.

96

Outside Amsterdam
Oct. 26, 2016

Zavia CLENCHED HER TEETH and the steering wheel. The rain was pelting Amsterdam. The traffic was bumper-to-bumper. Finally, she turned onto the N-15 highway, got the car out of second gear, and sped down toward Dagmare's house and the Delta Works. She leaned forward to see through the wipers, but the sheet of water blocked the road. Suddenly, the car fishtailed badly. Zavia turned the wheel, but the tires slid over into the oncoming traffic. She screamed when she saw a government evacuation truck full of scared, fleeing people heading toward her. Thankfully, the driver had slammed on the brakes as Zavia skidded within an inch of the truck's bumper.

    Zavia was still shaking. She righted the car, pulled off the road at the first highway turnout, and turned on the radio. *Maybe a little music will calm me down.* At first, she slammed the seat in disgust because she thought the station was replaying a broadcast from several days ago. Then, as the realization spread through her, so did the fear.

    According to the news report, three more snukes on the coastal edge of the Greenland Ice Sheet had just blown ice, snow, and radiation sky-high into the atmosphere. Simultaneously, the detonations sent glacial calves hurtling down into the sea, where they splintered into icebergs of every size and shape and sent violent tremors rippling outward through the sea. "No one knows who did it, or why. According to the authorities, if you live near the coast, you'd better evacuate. They can't tell if the turbulence will drive the water all the way down to the Dutch coast, but it might."

    Zavia sat still. *Dagmare lives on the coast.* Then her eyes teared up. Oh, Jesus! Oh, no! Twenty minutes ago, she had called Ingrid, who had said, "The funeral was beautiful. My Climate Trackers boss drove me home. In fact, he's coming up for a cup of tea before he activates the cameras." *Cameras on glaciers. Snukes on glaciers!*

Zavia dialed Ingrid's number. No answer. It rang a second time. No answer. After the fourth ring, she heard, "Hi, this is Ingrid. Leave me the usual." Zavia couldn't see straight. "Ingrid, it's Zavia. Pick up. Please pick up." A few seconds later, she added, scared, "Call me as soon as you can. Okay, honey?"

Heavily sedated, Ingrid didn't hear her cousin. But her boss did.

Zavia cranked the engine but didn't move. *Do I go back to Ingrid's or go on to Dagmare's?* She started to head north but stopped. She started to head south but stopped. Then her cell phone rang.

"Ingrid?" She got it on the first ring.

"Sorry, it's Top Gun," Tex said. "If reincarnation is real, I'm coming back as a military pilot." Despite the time difference, it was still daylight when he had descended through the storm system that socked in the north Atlantic and northern Europe. "I'm on the outskirts of Amsterdam. Where are you?"

"Tex, you've got to find Ingrid."

"I can't. I need to find Sukirov. And the codes." He paused for half a second. "What's going on, Zavia? Where's Ingrid?"

Zavia was close to flipping out. She relayed what Ingrid had told her about webcams on glaciers. "They didn't do Pakistan, but they had codes for Tibet and Greenland." She also told him about Christian's grisly death and Ingrid's boss.

Prago. "Give me her address." Tex saw a closed Jeep coming for him. It was a quarter mile away. "Call the White House. Tell Mason everything." Before she could respond, he was running in the rain to meet the Jeep.

97

Amsterdam
Oct. 26, 2016

WHILE ALPHA WAS TAKING care of Ingrid, Admiral Sukirov had his own work to do in a different part of the Netherlands' capital.

By 3:35 p.m., he had walked along many of the city's sixty miles of canals, ninety islands, and fifteen hundred bridges. At one point, he leaned on a railing and looked down the Prinsengracht, one of the four main canals dating back to the seventeenth century. *I've seen enough.*

Like a medical pathologist about to conduct an autopsy, he had surveyed the body of Amsterdam. A thin smile crossed his face. He remembered a 1632 Rembrandt painting, *The Anatomy Lesson of Dr. Nicolaes Tulp*, that seemed particularly appropriate since it portrayed an autopsy that was considered at the time a public social event as well as a medical one.

The admiral spat into the canal. *It's time.* If he could, he would spit on the whole city. It was decadent. It killed his son.

At 3:45 p.m., the admiral drank espresso in an outdoor café on the Oudekerksplein—the plaza in front of Amsterdam's oldest church. He reached into his pocket and pulled out the small detonator. Then he watched people passing by and chattering away. They had no idea that their expectations about life, along with their world, were about to explode.

"Anything else?" The waitress had four rings on each ear, as well as one in her nose and tongue. She was already clearing his cup and wiping down the table. In this high-tourist area next to the red-light district, the faster she turned the tables, the more tips she would get.

"Just the check." The admiral paid the bill. Then he walked a short distance. In the plaza, he saw tourists gawking at the sculpture of a man's hand fondling a woman's breast. Right in front of him, other tourists took photos of Belle, the bronze statue of a full-breasted woman with her feet apart, standing in a doorway. This time, the admiral spat on the plaza. In a country where prostitutes were legally self-employed, Belle was meant to honor millions of "fee-for-service" workers around the world. *Only a whore nation would honor whores.*

At exactly 4 p.m., the admiral quietly said, "For you, Anton." Then he entered the detonator code.

A moment later, the admiral looked up. The gawkers were still gawking. They didn't hear the massive explosion on the Greenland Plate, maybe a thousand miles closer to the North Pole. They didn't know that the explosion point was part of the much larger North American Plate, which was one of the largest tectonic plates making up the earth's crust. Nor did they know that Alpha and Beta had planted the snuke up there, right under the seabed along a major fault line, when they had accompanied the admiral to the submersible drilling rig's ribbon-cutting ceremony.

At 4:35 p.m., Admiral Sukirov drove out of Amsterdam. By now, the streets were full of shocked people. As yet, they didn't grasp the news reports that someone had intentionally created an underwater earthquake; that the earthquake would set in motion a giant tsunami; and that the giant tsunami would roll through the oceans down to the coast of the country where they were so innocently living out the last day of their normal lives.

98

Amsterdam
Oct. 26, 2016

As WORD OF THE EXPLOSION and tsunami spread, people fled the coastal areas. They drove like Italians, but without the skill. Soon, there were pileups and abandoned vehicles everywhere. Tex's driver wove in and out of the traffic. Several times, he put two wheels up on a narrow sidewalk in order to pass a car. He took every shortcut and drove the wrong way down one-way streets to save a few seconds. For the last mile, he drove down a wide, rainy thoroughfare next to a canal. Finally, he turned onto Ingrid's street.

"There it is." The driver pulled over, two blocks from Ingrid's building. Tex looked at the nineteenth-century three-story home. Sometime in the last hundred years, it had been converted into small apartments. Tex also surveyed the deserted street. There were some parked cars and no people. "I've got to get back to the base, sir," the driver said anxiously and then left.

Tex darted from one car to the next, making his way down the block. He looked up at the closed curtains in Ingrid's third-floor apartment. *Is Alpha behind them, watching me?* He stood up, put his head down, and walked nonchalantly toward the building. Then he raced up the steps and into the front hallway, where half a dozen bicycles were stored. The only weapon he could find was a featherweight bicycle pump. Useless. Then he took off his cowboy boots and climbed the squeaky stairs in his stockinged feet, until he was in front of her apartment.

Down the hall, Tex heard a television. "The underwater earthquake has sent Arctic seas barreling toward our coast. It's reinforcing all the other water from all the other Greenland explosions." Then, with the precision of a safecracker, he turned Ingrid's door handle until the latch disengaged. *If Alpha were inside, he'd have fired by now. Wouldn't he?* Tex nudged the door open and saw the hallway with jackets on hooks and a

Van Gogh *Starry Night* poster on the wall. Pushing the door farther open, he saw the small kitchen and living room. He also saw the exposed water pipes and the upstairs drainpipe that ran just under Ingrid's ceiling. Then he saw into the bedroom, where there was a dresser, a chair, and a young woman on the bed who was drugged, bound, and gagged.

Without making a sound, Tex entered the apartment. He didn't think it was Alpha's MO to hide in a closet or bathroom. Nevertheless, in the kitchen, he picked up a chopping knife and a rolling pin, as he inched his way forward. The bathroom door was ajar. From the angle of the mirror over the sink, he could see that Alpha wasn't behind the door. Crouching, he reached the closet just outside Ingrid's bedroom. Quickly, he designed a plan: he would yank open the closet door while diving onto the floor just past it. As he contracted his muscles, ready to leap, he glanced into the bedroom. His eye caught the metal box on the bed right next to Ingrid. At the last possible second, he stopped himself from moving.

It's a bomb! Memories from his Ranger training came flooding back. The first memory was: leave bombs to the experts. But that wasn't an option. Already, he could hear slight murmurs from Ingrid as the sedative wore off. Soon, she would be awake enough to move and to blow them both up.

Tex stared at the bomb. *It must be motion-activated.* He smelled the air. *Plastic explosive, probably C-4.* Standing as still as he had ever stood, he remembered that, unlike nitroglycerine, it was a relatively stable secondary explosive that required a small, violent explosion to trigger the C-4. That meant there would be a blasting cap inside. And since Alpha seemed to prefer playing some kind of game to murdering Ingrid outright, the bomb was probably set with a mercury switch. If Ingrid stirred on the bed, or if he himself stepped too hard trying to reach her, the mercury would move and close the circuit between two electrodes, setting off the blasting cap, which would set off the C-4. *How the hell do I defuse it?*

Before doing anything, Tex pulled out his cell phone and took out the battery. If someone called, the cell signal might detonate the bomb. Just as he put it back into his pocket, Ingrid's landline phone rang. *Is it Zavia?* Then he heard a deep, deathly voice speak into the answering machine. "Our paths keep crossing, Cassidy. Maybe we should have lunch sometime. In the meantime, look out the window. But be careful not to trip the motion sensors."

Barely breathing, Tex pivoted and opened the curtain. He saw Alpha two blocks away, in the middle of the street, straddling a bicycle and laughing aloud. Alpha waved good-bye and pedaled down the street.

Ingrid stirred a little more. Tex figured he had two or three minutes. Suddenly, he had an idea. The odds were that the motion sensors were aimed down and toward the door to Ingrid's room. Alpha had probably gone down the fire escape through her bedroom window. If he could get on the other side of the motion sensors, maybe he could defuse the bomb. *But how? That's how!*

Moving ever so carefully, Tex stepped onto the chair right outside the door of Ingrid's bedroom. Then, stepping onto his tiptoes and leaning as far forward as he could, he reached under the door opening and put his hands around the drainpipe that ran under the ceiling. After taking a deep breath, he pulled his knees up, pushed his body forward, and swung himself over the motion sensors. With his arms straining, he shimmied his hands along the pipe until he was past the bomb. Slowly, gently, he lowered himself down, at the same time that Ingrid's eyes started to flutter.

Next, Tex stepped gingerly toward the bomb. He reached down from behind it and lifted off the top of the box as gently as he had ever done anything in his life. As he put the top down on the floor, he heard Ingrid's breathing grow stronger. For a second, he stared at her. "Ingrid . . ." he said as soothingly as he could. Then he decided that the presence of a strange man would startle her and set off the bomb. Instead, he reached over to the bomb again. He saw the blasting cap affixed to the C-4 brick. He moved his hands into position. With his left hand, he steadied the box. Then, taking a deep breath, he guided his hand over to the blasting cap and pulled it out, half a second before Ingrid, still tied down, rolled her body around within the limited range she had.

99

Amsterdam
Oct. 26, 2016

TEX UNTIED INGRID and removed the washcloth. She was still doped-up and groggy. He rifled through her purse, looking for a "Climate Trackers" address. He found a check, but the address was a PO box. There was no listing in the phone book. He dialed telephone information. But with the floodwaters getting closer, the service had been abandoned.

Tex picked up the washcloth from the floor, wet it down, and rubbed it hard across Ingrid's forehead. "Ingrid, wake up!" Ingrid stirred but was still out of it. Finally, he pulled her into a sitting position and slapped both sides of her face. "Ingrid, wake up! Wake up!" This time, slits appeared. "I'm a friend of Zavia's." He put his hands on each of her cheeks and shook them up and down until he could see her doped-up eyes. "You're okay and you're safe. Talk to me: what did you and Christian do for Climate Trackers?"

Slowly, she formed her words, telling him about the codes. "Thirteen different glaciers." The latitudes and longitudes were public information. But the exact locations in degrees, minutes, and seconds had to be inputted.

"Where's the computer with the codes?"

Ingrid struggled with her mind. When it cleared for a moment, she described the laptop in the back office. But the next moment, her mind was shrouded in fog.

"The address? What's the address?" She was going inward, and Tex yelled at her. "Ingrid, the damn address?" Suddenly, her body shook loose waves of tears. He didn't have time for her to stop sobbing. He yelled at her again. "Ingrid, where's the office?"

"I can't."

"You have to." Anger welled up in him.

"He said he'd kill me . . ."

Tex wanted to slap it out of her. "Ingrid, you were lied to. Those codes were for nuclear bombs, not cameras. I know your boss. He'll kill millions. I'll protect you. Damn it: where is the fucking office?"

Ingrid's pale skin grew three shades paler. "On some of those glaciers, there were two or more . . ."

Then she started to go into a stupor. Tex grabbed her and yelled at her. "Stay with me, Ingrid!"

Seconds later, another wave passed through her. This wasn't fear, but morning sickness. She started to sit up, shaking her head to clear it. "Near the Melting Pot coffeeshop, four blocks from here. It's getting dark. And there are shortcuts. I'll take you."

Three minutes later, they moved through the rain. At first, Ingrid stumbled. But as her head cleared, she walked fast. Finally, she was running down one alley and then another. They emerged onto the Gravenstraat. The office building was half a block away. The fear gripped her again, but she pointed to an open window on the fourth floor. "That van in front. It's his."

"Find a hotel. Call the police. Keep your cell phone on." Then he darted to the alley. He picked up a rock, passed through the back entrance, and climbed the stairs. Opening the fire door into the corridor, he saw "Climate Trackers." The glass door was ajar, though the blinds were drawn. Using his elbow, Tex pushed the door open. Inside, he heard voices and background music. On the wall, he saw maps and photos of glaciers and a "Quick Facts" checklist: "If all land ice melted, the world's seas would rise approximately 230 feet." Inching his way toward the wooden door leading into the back room, Tex put one hand on the doorknob and gripped the rock more tightly in the other. Then, taking a deep breath, he crashed into the darkened room, prepared to take on a psychopath that wasn't there.

As his eyes adjusted, he heard the sounds and music repeating, exactly as before, from a computer on the desk. *No booby-trap wires or explosives.* As if opening Pandora's Box, he raised the top of the computer and saw the looped movie trailer from one of the *Halloween* horror films. "Now the Nightmares" appeared on the screen, followed by "Will Become Reality."

There wasn't another fucking thing on this computer, certainly not the codes. The only other thing in the room was the fragmentation grenade that came through the open window a split-second later. He knew that if he was lucky, he had four seconds before it exploded. He dove through the open door and slammed it closed, just as the shrapnel flew toward his body.

Racing to the window, Tex saw the white van. Alpha was leaning out the driver's side window, looking up. Tex saw that he was surprised but smirking. Tex descended the stairs. Racing into the street, he saw the van turn down a narrow street along a canal, crashing into tables, chairs, and bicycles.

Quickly, Tex jumped over a fire hydrant and turned west over a narrow bridge. His legs were like pistons, but he was losing ground. Then he picked up a bike and pedaled through alleys and down the slick streets, guessing where Alpha was going. Finally, he emerged onto a main street and saw the white van slip between evacuating cars of frightened people, crashing into the sides of some of them, heading for one of the highways that ringed the city, connecting it with the rest of the country. Tex pedaled even faster. His legs burned. His lungs burned. He had close encounters with three different vehicles. Now, as close to Alpha as he had been on Ingrid's street, he memorized the license plate.

Tex looked up. In the side-view mirror, he saw Alpha. Then he saw his torso, the arm, the hand lean out the window, and he saw the second grenade hurled at him, hit the street, and roll toward him. Tex swerved the bike in front of a car, sliding behind the front tire, just enough to shield himself from the shrapnel that cut into the car's frame, slit a tire, and cracked the windshield. With his clothes ripped from the fall, Tex jumped up and watched helplessly as the white van turned onto a ramp and sped down the highway.

Where's he going? When's the next detonation? Where will it be launched? Tex dialed the police emergency number and gave them the license plate number. "He's armed and extremely dangerous. Stop him at any cost." Then off to the side, he saw an abandoned car. He ran over to it. The keys were in it. Seconds later, he was speeding down the highway.

Suddenly, Tex slammed down on the brake pedal. Behind a greenhouse just off the road, his eye caught a half-hidden white van. The license plate matched. Alpha wasn't inside the van, but the smell of gunpowder hung in the enclosed air. The well-dressed driver's gray suit and blue tie were stained with his own blood. His breathless body was still very warm. Tex rifled through his clothes but found no identification. Tex slammed his fist against the side of the van. There was no way to know what car Alpha was now driving or in what direction he was now heading.

100

Oosterschelde Barrier
Oct. 27, 2016

Zavia barely slept. She tossed. She turned. She worried. She cried. On top of everything else, her stomach turned like a cement mixer whenever she looked at her unconscious Aunt Dagmare.

Now, in the early dawn, she raced around Dagmare's house, duct-taping a large "X" on every window to protect them from the storm. Then, fighting the wind and rain, she locked the shutters. The activity blocked out all her questions about Ingrid, the admiral, Tex, the suicide bomber, and everything else for the moment.

"It's too wet for ducks out there," one of Zavia's cousins philosophized. Zavia looked down at her comatose aunt, while the cousin wrapped a blanket around the elderly woman. Then he carried her like a precious vase down the stairs and across the muddy ground. He laid her on the backseat of his truck and kept her warm with more blankets. "I'll get her to an inland hospital."

In the distance, Dutch authorities with bullhorns bellowed instructions over the storm. With the tsunami pushing even more water toward the coast, people were jammed into any vehicle with four wheels and gas. The evacuation caravan was six miles long. Twenty-two cars and trucks passed before someone let the cousin turn in and join the caravan. Shortly afterward, the other relatives pleaded with Zavia. "Come with us. You'll be safer." Instead, she drove Ingrid's car toward the barrier. On the way, she checked her cell phone for the millionth time. There were three more messages from Lars, each shorter and more urgent than the last. Also, Ingrid had called from a hotel lobby. "Your friend saved my life. He's gone after my boss, someone he called Prago." End of messages. *Oh, God, is Tex even alive?*

Ten minutes later, Zavia exited the highway and drove toward the North Sea Beach and the Oosterschelde's control room. Her heart beat a hundred times a minute. *I need five minutes*. She pulled into the deserted beach parking lot. She looked around. To the south, she saw the high dunes and the broad beach, where even the crabs had gone underground to get out of the weather. To the north, she saw the funneling landmass intensifying the tides that normally ran under the barrier's raised gates. In both directions, she saw the half-dozen modern windmills shut down by the storm.

Zavia leaned her head back against the car seat. She remembered a time, a few years ago, when she had picnicked under a windmill near Amsterdam and had lifted her wine glass to the symbol for both "old Holland" and also "the new world of energy." It had been Tex, in Peru, who had pricked her balloon. She remembered sitting with him in the conference center restaurant when he said, "Not that simple. For example: what about all the copper in them? Is it virgin or recycled copper? If virgin, where's it mined? What does the mining do to the ecosystem and to the miners?" *Tex* . . .

As Zavia moved the car forward in second gear, she also thought about the one consistent love in her life: water. In this case, it was the rain pounding the windshield and the North Sea pounding the coast. On another day, it could just as well be a dripping faucet or a puddle in the road. As an eight-year-old, Zavia had played in the bathtub with dolls. But it was the water's vortex going down the drain that captured the young girl's imagination. Eventually, it set her on a life path that overshadowed finding a man and raising a family. It was now far easier to see why her life revolved around her career rather than a marriage. Another reason, of course, was the men themselves: like her ex-husband, most had the relationship skills of a slug.

"Tex, are you alright?" She nearly burst into tears when the phone rang and she heard his voice.

He gave her the short version, ending with, "I had that motherfucker Prago—twice!"

Suddenly, a terrifying thought popped into her mind. "Tex, tell me he's not about six foot three, built like an armored tank, with a scar on his right cheek."

"That's him. Why?"

"He was in the orientation I gave." Her voice rose in pitch and paranoia. "He knows the barriers inside and out." Zavia gasped. "Oh, Christ . . ." She told Tex what Lars had said about an older Russian visiting the Oosterschelde Barrier and asking questions. "It must have been Sukirov. I've got to get there."

"Zavia, call Lars. But don't go there. Do you hear me? Don't go there."

She backed up the car and turned toward the control room. "I'll be there in three minutes."

"Zavia . . ." Tex might as well fight the wind. "Give me directions to the control room." A minute later, he drove far too fast down N-57 toward Zeeland and South Holland. He passed a dozen crews laying sandbags. He swerved in and out of the cars, pickup trucks, and tractors fleeing the water that was moving toward them faster than they were moving away.

Meanwhile, Zavia made her way through the storm. *Were the Russians here? Was this the launch site? If yes, why here?* Finally, she pulled into the large parking lot with only a few cars in it.

"Dr. Jansen, thank God you're here," the control room receptionist greeted her. "Lars comes down every five minutes looking for you."

Zavia climbed the open stairs to the second floor. She greeted Lars's assistant, a perky man in his thirties. Then she hugged Lars and felt him shaking. "Let's go into the conference room."

For the next half hour, Lars sat elbow-to-elbow with Zavia, poring through reports. The phone rang incessantly, but Lars had nothing he could say with certainty to the ministry. From time to time, he drew equations on the whiteboard. At one point, he erased the equations and drew a stick-like figure of the barrier in the bottom right corner. Then he drew wiggly lines to indicate waves at the top left.

"You better add more waves," Zavia said. "A lot more, after the detonation along the tectonic plates."

While they reviewed the data, Lars compulsively walked to the window and stared out at the storm. He measured the seawater's rise by the rise in his own fear. "It's not just the calving, Zavia. This is also the spring tide. And the Weather Service says it's the biggest storm in thirty-five years." Then he turned to her. "Tell me the truth." He looked over at the rows of wave images. "I closed the gates. Could all that water damage them?"

Zavia shrugged her shoulders. "I don't think so. The calving glaciers are too far away. They'll move a lot of water, but not enough to harm us."

"The tsunamis. From the tectonic plate earthquake. Can they harm us?"

Out of the corner of her eye, Zavia saw the barrier's security guard posting a police flyer on the bulletin board. "If any were set off. And depending on how big they are." Her words trailed off. Her face was whiter than the snow that would soon cover the ground. Gently, she took Lars's hand and walked him over to the flyer with Admiral Sukirov's picture on it. "Is that who visited here a while ago?" Zavia felt him grip her hand tighter, as if he was applying a manual tourniquet.

101

Oosterschelde Barrier
Oct. 27, 2016

WHILE ZAVIA AND LARS were evaluating whether the closed barrier would hold, the admiral and Beta turned into the far corner of the control room's parking area. The admiral was calm. He had said goodbye to the son he had loved but never respected. The detonations were progressing. Breen was meeting his demands, at least on the surface. And, in the next few hours, Operation Noah would culminate in the world's capitulation to Russia.

Five minutes later, an approaching Mercedes flashed its lights twice. Beta put his gun away, as Alpha slipped into the backseat. He was wet from running between cars.

A moment later, they moved the car closer to the control room. Suddenly, the security guard exited the building and ran through the rain toward his small drive-around vehicle. Beta gunned the car, and the Citroën hit the guard. The young man's body cracked in several places, as he fell forward onto the hood of his car.

"Move!" Sukirov ordered Alpha and Beta out of the car. In an instant, they burst through the front door. Alpha put a bullet through the receptionist's head and raced up the short flight of stairs, before either Zavia, Lars, or his colleague identified the sound of the firing gun.

"Don't move. Don't even breathe," Alpha ordered.

"Well, if it isn't Mr. Software Engineer." The admiral entered the room. "Nice to see you again." He stuck his nose right up against Lars's. "You lowered the gates. Now open them."

Lars stared at the admiral. "I can't do that. It's too dangerous."

"You're probably right." He then pointed first to Alpha and then to Lars's terrified colleague, who sat with his hands as high over his head as he could get them. Alpha calmly fired, putting a bullet through the man's right temple. Zavia screamed at the admiral. "You sadistic son of a bitch . . ."

"But then, again," the admiral smirked and looked back to Lars, "maybe you'd reconsider if you don't want the dear doctor to be a dead doctor." He grabbed Zavia by the neck. His powerful hands could snap it like a twig.

"Lars, no!" Her words constricted, sounding like gravel.

Lars shook. He couldn't stop. He didn't know what to do. Save his country? Save the woman who was like his own daughter? He sat down. He turned on his computer. His fingers shook so much he kept making mistakes keying in commands. Finally, he looked up. "It'll take a minute. Now, let her go."

Zavia went limp as the admiral released her. She knelt on the floor and imagined her grandmother smashing up against a car in the 1953 flood. She saw more bodies than she could count, including her extended family, floating away as these waters, today, drowned both them and their country. *For what? So I can live another minute?*

The admiral walked to the window. Through the rain, he saw and heard the massive steel gates rising. "Nicely done. We could have blown up a couple of them ourselves. But thanks to you, all sixteen are open."

For an instant, Alpha and Beta followed the admiral's eyes and watched the rising gates. In that instant, the software engineer grabbed a fire extinguisher and smashed it hard onto Beta's shoulders. He turned and swung it at Alpha's head. But the psychopath grabbed Lars's wrist and snapped it. Lars fell to the floor. With a smirk on his face, Alpha aimed his gun and put a bullet in Lars's stomach. "Like the gates, your death will take a minute."

Zavia knelt down. She held her uncle. Her tears mixed with his blood, soaking his shirt, even covering the cell phone in his pocket. It now covered her hands, pants, blouse, coat, and shoes. As his eyes closed, he mouthed his final words to her. "Watch the gates."

Zavia gently lowered his lifeless body. If she could, she would rip out their eyes, their fingernails, their testicles, and their teeth. But, in the next moment, she felt a different kind of revenge. Maybe a better kind, especially when she saw Sukirov's face expand like a puffer fish about to explode. As they all stared out the window, they watched the gates reach their fully open position. They held there for a minute. Then they reversed direction, heading back down toward the sea.

102

White House Situation Room
Oct. 27, 2016

"All right, General... the latest." The president put his glasses on.

"Let me warn you, sir: it's pretty ugly." For starters, he showed satellite images of Murmansk, where hundreds of trucks, buses, and vans carried thousands of scared people inland. Then China. "Let's be thankful it's not Miami," the general said. The image showed mile after mile after mile of evacuation queues in Shanghai and other coastal cities.

"Enough, sir?" General Mason didn't want to bombard the president.

"Keep going." For the next ten minutes, the president watched the horrific consequences of human stupidity. In Bangladesh, a country largely below sea level with very few remaining natural barriers and very large annual floods, masses of people slumped down dirt roads. Along the northeast coast of Canada and the United States, people hugged their neighbors and glanced back at their homes, expecting to never see either again. In Europe, citizens everywhere crawled along crowded highways toward Switzerland, Hungary and Romania: all landlocked countries that would be devastated later on as the economic dominoes fell.

"Okay, that's enough," the president finally said. Stoop-shouldered, he headed up the back staircase. For the first time in years, he used the railing. Walking down the corridor of his private quarters, he remembered a biologist he had once met. She had waxed on about there being only two species out of thirty million with the power to alter evolution. "Bacteria were the first," she had said. Billions of years ago, they gave off so much waste oxygen that they altered the atmosphere's chemistry and shaped the emergence of life. "And, God help us, we're the second."

The president reached his private office and sat down. Like his mind, his breathing was disturbed.

"Are you okay, Charley?" Ellie sat beside him and clasped his hands in hers. He noticed their wedding rings touching.

Charley spoke very softly to his wife. "Last week, when you were with Mariah? I had a dream." His skin turned pale as he described the inundated coasts, panicked people, runs on banks, and all the rest. "Was it prophetic, Ellie?"

"Could be." Over the years, Ellie had studied dreams, especially her own.

Charley sighed and shook his head. "I enlisted when I was eighteen, Ellie. I've been in the military or the government ever since. I can't believe in that hocus-pocus. But I do."

Ellie just smiled. She stroked his hands ever so gently, only removing her hands when the priority phone line rang.

"Tex! Where are you? Have you located the codes?" Ellie looked at her husband, who was listening to their oldest, dearest friend. She watched his pale face turn paler. As she caught the gist, she herself looked ghostly.

Tex drove through the squall, gripping the steering wheel in one hand and his cell phone in the other. "Charley, listen to me. Those planes you launched before the speech? Fire those missiles! Blow the Oosterschelde Barrier up before Sukirov blows everything up." He saw the barrier a quarter mile ahead. Earlier, he had nearly broken the radio dial, searching for news of the Big Bang explosion, when Sukirov would set off all the snukes on all the glaciers. There wasn't any news about that. Maybe there was still time.

"Turn around, Tex. Get out of there."

"I can get Sukirov. And Zavia's here . . ."

"Tex . . ."

"Do it, Charley! If I can't get Sukirov, the missiles are our last hope."

Both men allowed two seconds of silence. It was the deepest two seconds of their lives. "If I get him, I'll call—"

Suddenly, the line went dead. So did the radio. The storm had taken out every line of communication. Tex knew that Charley knew the consequences. The missile attack would kill Tex and Zavia. It would also destroy much of Europe, as the flooding collapsed the economies that supported more than half a billion people. Tex couldn't imagine his friend, Charley, giving the attack order, but he hoped his president could.

103

Oosterschelde Barrier
Oct. 27, 2016

FOLLOWING ZAVIA'S DIRECTIONS, Tex turned off the highway and headed down the long driveway toward the control room. As he parked, he saw the driving rain in the glow of a parking lot light. Then he turned his headlights off, grabbed his knife and gun, and pulled his jacket and cap tightly around his ears. He got out of his car. Crossing the parking lot, he saw the security guard sprawled across their vehicle. The rain soaked the portion of the man's spine that had ripped through his skin.

Tex almost threw up. Instead, he ran toward the lit building. He peeked over the front window and saw the receptionist slouched on the floor. He looked up the open staircase and detected movement, though he couldn't tell who was there or how many. *Must be another way up there.*

Tex raced outside and moved along the sea side of the building. In front of him was a metal cage that protected the outdoor staircase leading up to the second floor. *Locked!* Tex shook the cage, but the only thing that opened was a cut on his left hand.

The guard. He'll have keys. Tex retraced his steps. In the open parking lot, he was nearly knocked to the ground by the roaring wind. Finally, he stumbled the last fifteen feet to the guard, where he found a ring of keys. Then Tex saw the blue Citroën. *Who's in it? What's in it?* He crouched low. Seeing no one in the side-view mirror, he flung the front door open and stuck his gun inside. *Empty.* But sticking out from under the seat, he saw a manila envelope with maps, passports, and five different currencies, two of which he couldn't identify.

Tex then pulled out his knife, lay down on the wet ground, and reached underneath the car. A minute later, he was back at the staircase cage, opening it with the key. Soaking wet, he took the stairs two at a time, finally squatting on the grated platform in front of the control room door. Using the storm to cover his actions, he inserted different keys until he felt the bolt move. He leaned over and looked in the window.

Inside, he saw Lars and his colleague. They didn't move and never would. When he confirmed that nobody else was there, he opened the door, just as a door down below closed.

Tex ran down the inside stairs and nearly tripped over the dead receptionist. He stood along the wall by the front window. Slowly leaning out, he saw the blue Citroën pull up in front. A man was carrying a woman over his shoulder, apparently sedated. He put her into the back of the car. *Zavia!* Her red hair blew in the storm. *She's alive, or they wouldn't be taking her.*

104

White House
Oct. 27, 2016

PRESIDENT BREEN CHECKED HIS WATCH. Twenty-nine minutes until he met again with his full set of advisers. He picked up the phone in his private quarters and gave two orders. "As soon as they can."

Three minutes later, the president sat with his feet up on his Oval Office desk. His tie was undone. He held a glass of scotch. It only had one finger's worth, but it was helping. He leaned back in his chair, worried about Ellie, scared for Tex, terrified for the country, and horrified about the choice he had to make.

"You wanted me, sir?" General Mason entered.

The president moved to a couch and had the general sit opposite him. He held up his glass. "Want one?"

"No, thank you."

"Good. Because I'm looking for some good off-the-record advice, General. Before we go back downstairs. You're here first. Let's start."

The president took a sip of scotch. "I talked to Tex Cassidy." He summarized what he had told him. "Those planes in the air? He wants me to send them toward the Dutch coast, and he wants me to order them to blow up the barrier."

"Is he there, sir?"

The president nodded. "So is Zavia Jansen."

"You know what that means?"

The president nodded again. "Here are the three choices, as I see them, stripped to the bone." He leaned forward a little more. "Number one: We don't blow up the barrier. Tex stops Sukirov. The world survives another near-meltdown, and we go back to mundane things like winning elections and getting sleep."

He held up two fingers. "We don't blow up the barrier. Tex can't stop Sukirov. Sukirov blows up the barrier, along with a dozen of the world's largest glaciers."

The president breathed in a roomful of air. And he took another sip of his drink. This time, he held up three fingers. "We blow up the barrier. In doing that, we flood the Netherlands, devastate Europe, and set the world economy back about five hundred years. Hell, it might even set us back about five hundred years."

The president looked more intently at the general. "Does that sound about right?"

"I don't see a number four."

"Okay, national security adviser, advise me."

After four years in his job, the general rarely slept well. The threads that held nations together: he knew how thin they were and how easily they broke. From time to time, his shoulders had sagged from the weight of it all. *How is the president holding up? He looks ravaged.* He leaned forward and looked his commander in chief in the eye. "If I were in your shoes, sir, here's what I'd do." He laid out the option he would choose and why.

The president listened. His face was stoic. He made no comment. "Thank you, General. I'll meet you downstairs."

At that moment, the chief of staff knocked and entered. He needed a shave and a year at the ocean. "You wanted me, Mr. President?"

"Sit down, Alex. I'm collecting opinions on impossible situations, and I wanted yours." With each step Alex took toward them, the room temperature dropped ten degrees. "General, you might as well hear this, too."

"Sir, I think it'd be better if I go." He looked over at the chief of staff. Frosty would hardly describe the cold look he gave and got back.

"Gentlemen, I feel like I need a sweater. What's going on?" He looked at his watch. "The short version."

Both men hesitated. Finally, Alex spoke. "He thinks I set Tex up to be murdered. That day on the ice sheet."

The president nearly dropped his scotch. He looked over at his national security adviser, incredulous. Before he could speak, the general turned toward him. "Tex going to the ice sheet? Sir, somebody told the Russians. Only your daughter, Mickey Logan—who was nearly murdered—and Alex knew. Alex set up the meeting with Bakov. Years ago, Bakov bailed Alex out with a bundle of money."

"Is that all true?"

"It's not the whole truth." Alex wiped the sweat off his forehead. "Bakov defected to the UK in the seventies. He came to work for my company. I liked him. I liked his guts in leaving. So for three years, I took him under my wing. I taught him business. How to make money. Pretty soon, he had his own companies."

"But you did owe him for covering your debts?" The general was no less frosty than before.

"He felt he owed me for teaching him the ropes. 'We're even,' he joked one night. But it wasn't a joke. It was a statement of accounts and a statement of honor."

The three of them heard a knock. An aide entered, handed the president a note, and left. The president held the note. "Is there more?"

Alex took a deep breath. "I asked Bakov to give Tex information. That's true. But I also asked him to look out for Tex if he could."

"Why?" The president put his hands in the air. The note almost flew out of his hand. "You couldn't stand Tex?"

"Because he was your special assistant and your friend. But bottom line, sir, I didn't tell Bakov about Tex going to the ice sheet."

The president looked at his watch again. Four minutes. Then he looked at the note. Instantly, he jumped out of his chair and went to the intercom on his desk. "Yes, put him through."

"Tex, you're on speaker. The general and Alex are here. Where are you?"

"On the barrier. Prago and Sukirov are here. Have you launched the missiles?" His voice was tight. He sounded alert but exhausted. They could all hear the storm in the background. Sometimes, it made it really hard to hear Tex.

"Not yet. Planes are on the way. But, listen: the Russians? How did the Russians know you were on the ice sheet?"

"Jesus, Charley..."

"Five seconds, Tex. Any idea?"

"Launch the fu—" Suddenly, he saw an image. A woman kneeling, gathering papers, reaching under a chair. *A transmitter!* "Charley, best guess: the attacker. Bernice Johnson. She was on the *Pilgrim*. Now, launch the missiles!" There was a click as Tex hung up.

The president swung out from behind his desk. "You two okay?" They shook hands quickly. "Let's go. We've got a decision to make."

105

Oosterscheide Barrier
Oct. 27, 2016

As THE CITROEN PULLED away with Zavia inside, Tex burst out of the building. He jumped into his car and followed them with his headlights off. At the edge of the access road, he pulled over. The roar of the sea was so loud he could barely think. Then he saw the size of the wild waves. They looked like they would knock down the Alps.

Just below him was a field of very large boulders. Tex crouched and moved from one to the other, each time getting closer to the edge of the barrier. He calculated that if he scurried along the rocks, he could climb over one of the large hydraulic arms that moved each gate. Then he could make his way along the cement parapet and come up right next to the tented gate structure where the Citroën was parked.

What he hadn't calculated was that Alpha had seen him race out of the control room. As the Citroën turned a corner, Alpha had jumped out. Then, like a leopard hunting its prey, he had followed Tex, who now felt cold metal pressed against his head.

"Do you have any aspirin?" That was the last thing Tex heard before his head stopped the forward motion of Alpha's gun.

106

White House Situation Room
Oct. 27, 2016

THE PRESIDENT, ALONG WITH Alex and General Mason, raced downstairs to the Situation Room. His top advisers, including half the cabinet, would have gladly taken a glass of scotch. They were stymied. They felt like seventeenth-century castrati. "Shape up, ladies and gentlemen. I need your best thinking."

In the next eight minutes, they threw out options. Most were piss-poor.

"Time?" The president turned to the secretary of defense.

"Thirty-one minutes, sir: the planes will be in range. Once the missiles release: six minutes and nine seconds to target."

"Jane, what about the Dutch?"

The secretary didn't see a way out of this mess. She didn't sound steely. "They're sending troops, who won't get there in time. And they won't blow up the barrier even if the weather clears. 'We won't commit national suicide,' is how their prime minister put it."

"You told him we might blow up the barrier?"

"He screamed at me in Dutch, then slammed the phone down."

"And the others?" A moment later, on a large screen, they saw the heads of state of the UK, France, Belgium, Germany, Sweden, Ireland, and nine other European Union countries. They looked like Inquisition judges. "Ladies and gentlemen..." He explained the circumstances. "Will you help us?"

"Mr. President, you made that speech. You didn't ask us about it. Now you want Europe to cut out its heart? Please . . . on what basis? Phone calls from two Americans?" The German prime minister spoke for the group. "If they're right, there won't be any more European Union. But there won't be any more United States either. Or any China. Or any Russia. We'll all be using hand tools and reading by candles." He shook his head, disdainfully. "Excuse us, we've got people to evacuate."

The Situation Room was a tomb. Finally, the defense secretary spoke. "Nineteen minutes, sir." They all stared at the plane icons on the wall, streaking toward northern Europe. "And the prime minister is on the speakerphone."

The conversation was very short. "If I learn anything, I'll call immediately."

"Likewise, sir." The president stared at the plane icons. *What have I done? What have we all done?*

107

Oosterschelde Barrier
Oct. 27, 2016

I<small>F ALPHA WERE IN CHARGE,</small> he would have held Zavia over the railing by her ankles. Then, after she had begged and cried and screamed, he would have dropped her into the roiling water as if he were dropping an egg into boiling water.

The real fun would be Cassidy. He would turn him into a human carving board, inflicting enough cuts and snips and pain to feel a measure of revenge. Then he would flick him into the sea like the foreman's cigarette butt.

But the admiral had his own plan for torturing and killing the Americans. He stood inside one of the dry tented structures. "Strap them down. Let them drown."

The two elite murderers each tossed an unconscious body over their shoulder and stepped along the barrier's long, wide, cylindrical hydraulic arms. In the fierce wind, they struggled to keep their balance. Finally, they got the nylon ropes around the cylindrical arm and tied them around Tex's neck, abdomen, and ankles. Then they did the same with Zavia. In the end, the two Americans couldn't move. They were soaked to the bone. And a wall of water, far higher than Zavia had imagined or Lars had feared, rushed toward them.

Moments later, Tex was groggy. But suddenly, he heard "Tex." The voice was weak.

"Zavia!" He raised his head slightly. But a surging wave shoved his head back down onto the hydraulic arm. Pain swept through him.

So did terror. Every cell remembered being trapped underwater at Mackenzie Point.

And so did a memory. He and Charley maintained their families' boats. Charley's father had warned them: "Be careful with nylon rope. If it's wet, it stretches." *Were these ropes nylon?*

The hydraulic arm was slick. Tex could wiggle his fingers. First an inch. Then three inches. Then he could wiggle his whole left hand, until it slipped free. Then his right hand. He got whacked in the face with a wave. Two waves. Three waves. But he got the ropes off his chest. Then off his legs. *If I can just stand up and climb over to the cement parapet.* He struggled to his knees. Then, wobbly, he rose up. *Not enough traction to jump onto the parapet.* He wouldn't make it with the sun shining, let alone with these gale-level winds.

The only way out was down. He remembered the Cacua River. It was like a water park compared to this. He would have to catch the breaking wave. But the rocks were huge. They were covered with sharp barnacles and wet algae. If he didn't smash every bone in his body, he could lose his balance, slip back into the waters, and be carried out by the receding waves.

"Zavia? Can you hear me?" Her response was low, but he heard her. "I'll be back for you. In a few minutes." Finally, with more reason to live than he had had in years, he plunged into the cold, deathly water below.

108

The Kremlin
Oct. 27, 2016

THE PRIME MINISTER STARED out at the stars. As his hopes faded for restoring both Russia's stature and his own legacy, his feelings felt as distant as those stars.

Suddenly, through the intercom, he heard, "Admiral Sukirov is calling, sir."

At hyper-speed, the prime minister was pulled back into the present. "Tell him I'm in a meeting. You'll have to get me."

The prime minister then did something bizarrely out of character: he closed his eyes. *I've made a million mistakes. But this is the first time I've been wrong.* He sat there. He barely moved. He came to terms with the truth: he had bought the admiral's view that Russia must hold a samurai sword over the necks of nations. But this was a new era.

Eyes wide open, he gave a new order over the intercom. "You heard me. Make that call. Now!"

Two minutes later, the president, along with his chief of staff and NSA raced down the stairs to the White House Situation Room. They arrived just in time to hear the prime minister take the phone off hold and say, "Boris, we know you're in the Netherlands. What are you doing?"

The admiral had moved to another tented gate for privacy. "Completing what you and I started five years ago."

"Do not detonate those bombs. Do you understand?"

"Do I understand? Let me tell you what I understand." The prime minister felt venomous fangs breaking his skin and breaking his heart. "I understand that the world is cracking apart, that Russia's waited a hundred years . . ."

"Boris, it'll happen, but not the way we thought."

". . . that if the world interferes, the world must suffer." The admiral was talking, not listening.

"But your demands are being met."

"Really? According to an old crew member, you couldn't blow up a snowball with the explosives the Americans placed along the pipeline." Just then, he saw Alpha signal. The rain and seawater were wiped off the snuke. "My last words to you: Trotsky and Khrushchev were traitors. So was Gorbachev. But you're the worst."

The admiral hung up. The line was as silent as outer space. Finally, "President Breen, are you there?"

The president unmuted the phone. "I am, sir. You did what you could." He told him about his call with Tex. "I was about to call you. The planes are less than twelve minutes away."

109

Oosterschelde Barrier
Oct. 27, 2016

S INKING BELOW THE ICY WATER, Tex felt eerily calm. He saw Mariah and Katie. He prayed he could save Zavia.

As he bobbed to the surface, he saw the very large rocks in front of him, just as a wave, like a wet tornado, tossed him in the air. Miraculously, it flung him down between two of the biggest rocks—either of which would have smashed his skull into bonemeal. When the water retreated, he stumbled to his feet and crouched as low as he could behind a rock until the next wave passed. Then he crawled over the other rocks and onto the staircase leading to the cement parapet.

Tex raced along the parapet until he stood about eight feet from Zavia, almost directly over her. She had wiggled out of the ropes. But the water was now too high for her to even sit on the hydraulic arm. Forced to stand, she was barely keeping her balance. The movement of her head to look up at Tex nearly pushed her down into the water.

Tex yelled, but the water was louder than a jet plane. With his arms, he gestured wildly. "Throw me the rope!" In the fierce wind, it took three tries to get the rope even close to Tex. On the fourth try, he leaned over the railing, stretching just far enough to grab the end and tie it to the railing.

Then he stopped for a moment. No gestures. No words. Looking into his eyes, she understood the abyss she had to cross. Water had been her life. It would likely be her death. She bent her knees as much as she dared. Then she pushed off as far as she could. Hanging in midair, midstorm, her hands burned on the rope. Her shoulders were at the edge of their sockets, as three inches by three inches, Tex hauled her dead weight up. She felt his flesh on hers, grabbing her wrist so tightly as to nearly break it. Then she felt a sharp pain in her calf, as it hit the top of the railing. A blessed second later, she was flat on her back on the parapet. Landing on cement had never felt better.

"You all right?" he screamed over the wind, helping her to sit up, holding her, sheltering her with his body against the squall. *Nothing's broken.* When she nodded, he ordered her back to the car. "I'm going after them."

"The hell you are, not without me!"

Tex looked at her wild red hair blowing in the wind. She had that "don't mess with me" look in her eyes. *Spitfire!* He took her hand in his. Together, they kicked up water, running down the access road toward the tented towers.

110

Oosterschelde Barrier
Oct. 27, 2016

THE ESCAPE PLAN WAS SIMPLE. Activate the snukes, including the Oosterschelde one. Get the hidden car. Follow the evacuating hordes inland. Drive to Frankfort or another airport where planes were still flying. Then scatter: Alpha to Uganda, Beta to Canada, and Admiral Sukirov to Chile. For the two operatives: collect the balance of two and a half million dollars due each of them. For Admiral Sukirov: enjoy the sunset and the apocalypse. Afterward: learn to fish? Paint seascapes? End his life? He didn't much care.

"To Russia!" Admiral Sukirov toasted his comrades with his cell phone. He then input the activation codes and saw a countdown of thirty minutes begin. The flashing red light confirmed the countdown mode. He imagined the flashing red lights on Mt. Kilimanjaro, in Glacier National Park, the Alps, all along the edge of the Greenland Ice Sheet, and half a dozen other hostage sites.

"Let's go." He got into the front passenger seat. Alpha turned the ignition, but it didn't turn over. He tried it twice more, before the admiral ordered Beta, "Quick. Find out what's wrong!"

In the wind and rain, Beta opened the hood. Nothing obvious. Then he knelt down, looked under the car and saw gas dripping from the severed gas line. He also saw something move out of the corner of his eye. "It's the Americans," he told the others. "Get another car. I'll take care of them."

Alpha wanted to feel Cassidy's flesh in his teeth. But the professional took over. He and the admiral made their way back down the access road to the parking lot. Beta, meanwhile, followed Tex and Zavia into the tented structure two towers away. Licking his lips, he pulled out both his gun and his knife.

Inside, Tex pointed to a large hanging tarp that Zavia went behind. He then positioned himself on a section of scaffolding, right above the entrance, with a scaffolding pole in his hands. He remained as motionless as the wood he stood on. But when he shifted his weight slightly to fling the pole, the board creaked. Beta dived. The pole clanged onto the floor.

Tex moved quickly between barrels and boards, using them as shields against Beta's bullets. Zavia, meanwhile, had snuck out and gone up onto the access road. Looking down, she saw Beta toss his empty gun away and rush Tex, flailing at him with his knife. Zavia grabbed a gallon can of new paint, raised it over her head with both hands and threw it. But with the wind howling in her face, it sailed by the Russian.

Seconds later, Tex took a thick-booted kick to the chest that nearly sent him over the railing and into the North Sea. Beta pounced on him, barely missing with his knife as Tex landed an elbow in the man's face. But Beta, with his nose broken, landed one of his powerful fists into Tex's rib cage. Tex fell to the cement facedown. Beta stood over him with his knife poised. As he started the blade down toward Tex's spine, he felt his own back cracking somewhere between the third and fourth vertebrae, as Zavia, standing in the metal bucket, put the throttle up as high as it would go and smashed the bucket into the Russian. Beta fell forward, passing right over Tex and right over the railing. "That's for Lars, you son of a bitch!"

Tex nodded at her, acknowledging that she had saved his life. Then they raced toward the tented tower, where the Russians had been. Thirty seconds later, they stared at the nuclear bomb and the flashing red light.

"Can you disarm it?" she asked.

"We need to get the detonator." They moved quickly back down the access road, when, in the darkness, an accelerating car turned on its lights and headed directly for them. Tex shoved Zavia to the side. Then, in one motion, he grabbed his knife, dove onto the ground, rolled over, and shoved the knife into the passing right front tire. The car swerved and hit the guard rail. Alpha lunged forward and hit the windshield.

Seconds later, Alpha was out of the car. He had two gashes on his forehead but only one thing on his mind: Cassidy. He now wanted him more than he wanted his money.

Alpha pulled out his gun. He saw Tex crouch behind the hinged fifty-five-gallon paint barrels. He saw Zavia huddle behind the construction trailer. He fired a few shots at Tex that ricocheted off the barrel. Then he grabbed Zavia around the neck, put his gun to her head, and pulled her out into the open. His eyes smiled when he saw Tex step out from the barrel with his hands in the air.

"Let her go." Behind Prago, Tex saw the admiral exit the crashed car and make his way back toward one of the tented structures.

"Is she Katie's replacement or just a whore?"

Tex was drenched. He was also stunned. *Katie's replacement?* "What are you talking about?"

"An eye for an eye. A tooth for a tooth. A woman for a woman." His forearm pressed harder against Zavia's windpipe.

Tex was twenty feet away. He knew that if he rushed Prago, Zavia would die. He himself would probably take a bullet, followed by a horrifically painful last few minutes before Prago killed him, joined the admiral, and nuked the world's glaciers and economies. But if he stalled Prago, maybe the missiles would blow all of them to kingdom come. *Christ! Where are they? Did Charley launch them?* "What are you talking about?" he screamed over the wind.

"I'm getting us even." With her eyes, Zavia tried to tell Tex to get away, find Sukirov, and abort the snukes.

"You're a crazy motherfucker, Prago. Get us even for what?" Tex was confused. Tex had escaped Prago's men and Prago's attempt to kill him directly. Prago wouldn't like that. But those were the breaks in combat, not a motive for revenge.

The smile left Prago's eyes. They were now deathly intense. "Bernice Johnson was my baby sister."

111

Oosterschelde Barrier
Oct. 27, 2016

TEX JUST STOOD THERE, soaked and flabbergasted. Instinctively, his eyes moved upward, looking for missiles. *When will they get here?* In the meantime, he had to save Zavia, find the admiral, and deactivate the codes.

Probing for any advantage, Tex went fishing. "Well, hallelujah, you just made a great night even better."

Prago repositioned his gun against Zavia's head. "Meaning . . . ?"

He's nibbling. "Bernice was so damn sexy!"

"Don't be a smartass, Cassidy."

"And horny . . ."

Prago was biting harder on the hook. As the rain increased, Tex went on and on about later seeing the knife in the night table drawer. He described Bernice's upset, right after they had showered together, when he said he had to leave to meet President Breen's daughter.

Prago's hand shook like he had Parkinson's disease. Zavia felt every tremor. She could hardly breathe. She could hardly believe what Tex was saying or that he was saying it. "I fucked her brains out. Then the next morning, I blew her brains out."

Inside Prago, something snapped. Tex knew he only had seconds. Out of God-knows-where, he remembered what Zavia had told him about Ingrid. "By the way, the US Army doctors did an autopsy. Did you know she was pregnant?"

Prago's eyes looked like double-wide trailers. He put one handcuff on Zavia's right wrist and the other around the railing. "Enjoy the show. You're next."

Now, as the the two men stood just three feet from each other, Alpha's eyes were more intense and rigid than they had ever been. But in Tex, he saw his own intensity mirrored back. All Tex's frustrations with the world, all the death-related sorrow, all the stupidity in how people thought and what they did, all the suffering he had inflicted on others and on himself; suddenly, in that moment, they were directed from his eyes into the eyes of the man in front of him.

As the rain poured over them, Alpha crashed the butt of his gun into Tex's raised arm, sending waves of pain through him and knocking him backward. Tex steadied himself. *Charley! Where are the damn planes?* He looked Alpha right in the eyes and said, "She was a great fuck, Prago." Then he took off running down the access road. He couldn't outrun the Russian. But he could give those missiles another minute to get there.

As the two men raced off, Zavia slumped down against the railing. Her wrist was cut by the handcuff, and it hurt.

Up in the open top area of the middle tented structure, Admiral Sukirov watched Alpha chasing the American. The windblown water whipped against his face and made it difficult to see the countdown clock that now read: "14:12." He knew it was too late to escape. Nor did he want to. As an officer, he was prepared to go down with his ship, whether his ship was a naval vessel, the ship of state, or the global ship that had carried civilization out of the dark ages.

Meanwhile, on the access road, Tex was fifteen feet from the construction trailer. The door slammed back and forth in the wind. If he could get inside, he could lock the door and buy extra time. If he couldn't, outside, scattered everywhere by the storm, were pipes and poles and cans and buckets that he could use to slow Prago down. Now, five feet from the door, he stretched his body, intending to dive inside the trailer, when his foot stepped on a piece of iron scaffolding lying horizontal on the ground.

Tex went flying onto the wet road, landing on his bruised arm. As Prago was about to pounce, Tex grabbed the end of the scaffolding pole, raised it, and held it as firmly as he could, perfectly angled at Prago's throat. But Prago shifted his weight just enough to have it only graze his neck, drawing a small stream of blood as he hit the ground, barely missing his prey.

Both men got to their feet. As Prago lunged, Tex sidestepped his punch and landed a combination to Prago's head and body. The soldier recoiled but remained on his feet, smirking at Tex's pitiful best shot. Tex's arm really ached now. The pole was too far away.

Suddenly, Tex heard rain on metal behind him. Turning quickly, he saw the two fifty-five-gallon drums labeled "Recycled Abrasive" and "Toxic Materials." He dived toward the "Recycled Abrasive" drum. At least he could use it to shield himself from Prago. But if he could lift the drum, he would toss it at Prago's feet and take off again, gaining another minute for those missiles.

Tex heard Prago laughing. In a moment, he knew why. The drum was two-thirds full. *It'd take a goddamn bear to lift it.* Tex noticed the two hinges holding the top down. They were like the bear-proof garbage cans he had seen in Churchill. Instantly, he undid one hinge, reached inside, and grabbed a fistful of the abrasive shards. A second later, he stood, reared back and heaved them, trying to scratch Prago's corneas or at least distract him.

As the shards headed through the air, Prago couldn't stop them. All that intense staring had reduced his blinking response time. But given the squall-like wind, a few shards landed harmlessly on his nose, cheeks, and forehead.

Madder than ever, Prago covered the ground between himself and Tex. He stood over the crouching American, removed the other hinge from the drum top, and raised the heavy lid over his head. By the time, he brought it down, Tex had dived behind the other fifty-five-gallon drum. Quickly, Prago moved toward Tex and landed two punches that sent Tex sprawling across the access road.

Prago came in for the kill. Tex grabbed the drum top that had fallen alongside him. He flung it into Prago's knee. It stopped the Russian just long enough for Tex to dive back to the "Toxic Material" drum. As before, he undid a hinge and reached in. This time, he grabbed a fistful of material that contained lead, chromium, oil vapors, epoxy adhesives, and other industrial toxins. This time, as he arched his arm to heave them, he felt the wind and adjusted his toss ever so slightly. This time, the wind carried the materials directly into Prago's eyes. As the psychopath instinctively raised his arms to clear out the stinging debris, Tex found the scaffolding pole and swung it as hard as he could against Prago's knee, smashing the bone and sending Prago stumbling backward against the barrier railing. Tex charged him, and, using every ounce of strength, he forced the Russian over the railing, where he fell eight feet down and cracked his head open on the gate's cylindrical arm.

A moment later, Tex climbed down and stared at Alpha's body. The Russian's eyes were wide open, filled with blood. Pieces of skull lay close by. Tex didn't even bother to check Alpha's pulse; instead, he retrieved the handcuff keys from Alpha's pocket. As he raced back down the access road to free Zavia, he heard a loud whistling. *It's the missiles! No, thank God, it's just the wind!* For the first time, he hoped they weren't coming.

112

Oosterschelde Barrier
Oct. 27, 2016

GIVEN THE STORM, Tex moved down the access road as best as he could, given the storm, the wind, and his mop-like arm. Zavia was following behind him. But any minute, he and Zavia could be dead from either the detonated nuclear device or the missiles.

Tex's mind raced much faster than his feet. *Sukirov could have driven away and detonated the bombs. Instead, he went back onto the barrier. Why?*

Seriously in pain, Tex passed a dozen gate towers until he reached the three tented ones. The snuke was in the middle of the three. The rain pelted his eyes as he looked up and saw the admiral, standing on the stormy, unprotected platform at the top of the tower. With one hand, he held the detonator with its countdown clock. With his other hand, he held a gun pointed directly at Tex.

"Such big waves, Mr. Cassidy," the admiral yelled down, looking at the clock. "In 03:16, they'll wash us away."

Tex inched his way toward the staircase. He counted fourteen steps. The problem was the in-between landing, where they reversed direction. *That'll slow me down.* "Admiral, there are missiles on the way . . ."

"They'd better get here soon." He looked again at the clock.

Tex used the look to inch forward.

"Only two minutes and fifty-seven seconds left. Not a lot of time to save the world's glaciers. Wouldn't you agree, Dr. Jansen?" He saw Zavia, drenched and bedraggled, catch up to Tex.

Quickly, Tex calculated. *I need to get at least four steps closer.* "Why are you doing this, Admiral?" *Can I rip the wiring out? Will that stop the detonator or set it off?*

"At first, I did it for Russia. But now it doesn't matter. With the world's inertia, the world would have melted down anyway."

Tex wiped the rain from his face, using the motion to take two baby steps. They all heard the deafening sound. The waves in front hit the barrier, tossing fountains of water over the tower and drenching the three of them, as they stood, dwarf-like, before this force of Nature.

"Maybe the world will figure it out," Zavia yelled. She saw what Tex was doing. "Maybe Russia will still be what you want her to be." A moment later, her eyes had a strange sparkle in them. *Russia? Why not? What the hell is there to lose?* Suddenly, she began to sing the Russian national anthem.

"Russia, our sacred power,
Russia, our beloved country.
Mighty will, great glory,
Your heritage for all of time!"

The admiral smirked at her and said, "Very impressive, but sing it in Russian."

Zavia hesitated. Then she reached into the far corner of her memory banks and began.

"Россия, священная наша держава,
Россия, любимая наша страна.
Могучая воля, великая слава,
Твоё достоянье на все времена!"

This time, the admiral was startled, enough so that Tex could creep forward ever so slightly.

"Even better," the admiral said, looking down at the clock again, allowing Tex to move another four inches closer. "But in the next minute and forty-one seconds, I won't be able to teach you the rest."

"It's a pity," she replied, as her mind searched frantically for anything that might distract the Russian. "But tell me: Tchaikovsky wrote two ballets, four concertos, six symphonies, and ten operas. Which piece do you like best?"

"It's three ballets," he corrected her. "*The Nutcracker, Swan Lake,* and *Sleeping Beauty*. But to answer your question: Piano Concerto No. 3."

Tex didn't know a concerto from a symphony. But he knew their body parts would be scattered by the blast and the water that followed. The one blessing in dying this way was macabre: not being around to see the devastation as glaciers worldwide, some ten thousand years old, were blown apart, taking whole economies with them in a matter of days, if not hours. He wiped rain from his face again, using the motion to bend his knees slightly and let Zavia know it was now or never.

Suddenly, Tex bolted up the stairs. As he turned on the landing, the bullet from the admiral's gun landed where Tex had been a half second before. As the admiral aimed again, his eye was caught by the red flashing light that pulsed faster and brighter with fifty-nine seconds before detonation. By the time the admiral looked up, Tex was three stairs from the top. By the time the admiral fired again, Tex banged into his arm. It sent the bullet in another direction, landing in Zavia's right shoulder. Out of the corner of his eye, Tex saw her crumble onto the access road.

As Tex pushed the admiral's square body back against the railing, he saw "00:41" on the detonator clock. He tried to rip the detonator away in the slim hopes of ripping out the wires and interrupting the activation codes, but the admiral gripped it with his powerful sledgehammer hands. Tex kneed the admiral in the balls, but even that didn't work. Finally, in desperation, with twenty-nine seconds left, he did what had worked with Prago: he used every last ounce of strength to push the admiral backward. But the admiral caught Tex's arm and used Tex's momentum to carry them both over the railing and down into the North Sea.

Both men hit the pounding water. They were only four feet apart, and there was less than twenty seconds left. As the waves pushed him upward, Tex filled his lungs and headed down toward Sukirov. With nine seconds left, Tex grabbed the detonator. But with his last breath, the admiral held on as the clock wound down: Four seconds, three seconds...

Tex bobbed to the surface. He looked up and saw Zavia looking down. Their eyes met and locked, awaiting death together. Two seconds, one second, zero. Nothing happened. Five seconds passed. Still no explosion. As a monstrous wave passed over Tex and pushed him down, he saw the admiral still holding the detonator that was corroded by the torrents of seawater that the admiral himself had unleashed.

As the admiral floated away, Tex fought the numbness spreading through his body. He knew he only had a minute or two before he would also drown in the freezing water. In between waves, the wind whipping the water created a crosscurrent that carried him toward the side of the barrier. What he had learned in the furious waters off the coast of Greenland trying to save Mariah he now used in these furious waters trying to save himself. He read the waves. He moved through them. As Zavia watched him from the parapet, he used his last bit of strength to edge his way over to the shore. She then made her way down to where he was lying on the ground with the water lapping against him from his legs to his chest.

With her one good arm, Zavia took his wrist and pulled him a few inches farther onto the land. Then she sat down, raised his head up and turned it sideways, allowing him to violently cough out some of the water in his lungs. Finally, when the spasms slowed, Tex caught his breath and looked up at her face, covered in rain, seawater, and her own tears.

As Tex's lungs cleared, so did his head. "The missiles... cell phone?" She reached into her pocket but pulled out air. Tex forced himself onto his hands and knees. "Control room. Meet me there."

An instant later, Tex ran down the barrier's access road. He passed one gate, two gates, twelve gates. His arm ached. His head ached. So did his ankle. But finally, he stumbled onto the road between the barrier and the control room. *No missiles yet.*

A minute later, he was at the outside staircase. He ran up the slick stairs. He slipped. He crashed his knee into the metal stair. He limped up the last seven steps. He fell through the door and crawled over to the phone, picking it up and listening for the dial tone. There was none. The lines were still down.

Eight feet away, he saw Lars's corpse. Sticking out of his pocket was the blood-stained cell phone. Tex crawled through the drying, sticky blood on the floor to the dead programmer. He flipped the phone open. It started to boot up, but would there be service? The twenty seconds it took to connect felt like an eternity. The signal bars in the upper left were a blessing. Tex dialed Charley's private number and listened. After the third ring, he heard, "The number you have dialed is not in service. Please try again. If you need assistance . . ."

Shit! Did he have the number wrong? Had he dialed wrong? As fast as he could, he hit the keys one more time. If he heard that recording again, he would know it was too late. The first ring went through. The second one went through. At the third ring, he heard, "Who is this?"

"Charley! It's Tex!" Deep in despair at what was about to happen, the president was in the Situation Room with General Mason, the secretary of defense, and his other advisers. The planes were three breaths away from being in range and launching their missiles at the barrier. "Sukirov's dead. The snukes won't blow. Stop the missiles!"

The president started to scream, "Abort!" But the words never came out. Was this Tex? Or was it Prago mimicking Tex?

"Charley . . . !"

The entire Situation Room awaited the order. None came.

"Sir," the secretary of defense broke the silence, "five seconds!"

The president sat rigid. Deathly still. Until he heard, "Jesse! It's Frank!"

As Tex lay on the floor, he heard the president scream, "Abort! Abort!"

In the background, Tex heard someone repeating the order, yelling into a radio.

Somewhere, high in the sky, three F-22 Raptor pilots removed their thumbs from the launch button one breath before they were to push them down.

As Tex lay back with his head on the floor, Zavia came through the door. She held her right arm with her left one. She saw Tex inches away from her dead uncle, giving her a huge grin that she didn't return.

"We've got to go," she said. "Those waves . . . they're peaking . . . they could crush the barrier."

Tex stared at her. *You've got to be kidding.* Then he struggled to his feet. His knee nearly gave out. His arm throbbed. Her shoulder throbbed. They both held onto the banister and made their way down the internal staircase. They went outside. The air was soaked from the rushing water, the spring tide, and the North Sea storm. Tex took her hand, and with their heads down and their eyes nearly closed, they inched their way against the wind until they reached Ingrid's car.

Two minutes later, they turned onto the highway that ran directly over the barrier, parallel to the access road. They were fishtailing all over the road, when, as they passed the eighth gate smack in the middle of the barrier, they heard a loud, piercing sound.

Zavia gripped Tex's hand on the steering wheel. *It's giving way!*

Tex looked through the windshield wipers and pouring rain. *It's one of the missiles.*

Suddenly, they saw two lights heading right for them. Tex swerved to the right, just as the first truck in the convoy of Dutch soldiers passed them, only a few inches away. The truck driver finally took his palm off the horn. *Fucking idiots! What are you doing out on a night like this?*

An hour later, they pulled into a small inland town. They stopped at the local high school, which had been turned into an evacuation center. They were drenched, ravenous, and wounded.

"Let's go in," Tex said.

Inside the gym, aid workers rushed to them with blankets and hot chocolate. "Rough night out there, isn't it? What happened to you?" one of them said in the kindest voice Tex and Zavia had ever heard, as she gently placed Zavia's right arm in a sling. "A doctor will be here in a few minutes."

Exhausted, they sat there waiting. Tex put his arm around her. She put her head on his shoulder, when they heard screams of "Zavia!" from across the room. Zavia jumped up. She ran across the room to where her family was gathered. After a round of hugs and cries of "Thank God," Zavia knelt down next to Dagmare's stretcher. On the wild evacuation trip inland, Dagmare had slowly come out of her coma. Now, weak and paralyzed down her left side, she looked up at her favorite niece.

Zavia stroked her aunt's cheek with her good hand. Then she reached up and took Tex's hand. He squeezed it in a way he hadn't squeezed anyone's hand in four years. She felt it and returned it. "Auntie," Zavia said, "remember that 'one second' you told me about?" Dagmare's eyes cleared. A little color came into her face. A thin smile crossed her lips. Zavia looked at Tex and then back at her aunt. "I want you to meet my friend, Tex."

Epilogue

Amsterdam
Jan. 1, 2017

THE FIRST DAY of the New Year was all blue skies and warm breezes. The million people along the canal parade route, including Tex and Zavia, cheered the bands floating by on barges.

By noon, they were at the conference center in their reserved section. Ellie was there. So were Lynn, Alex Sullivan, General Mason, Dave Dunn, Emma Wolfe, and Jane Harkle from the White House. Mickey Logan had flown over from Florida. And Ingrid was there, too, five months pregnant.

Suddenly, tears flooded Tex's eyes as a Latin man walked toward him with a cane. "Carlos!" Tex gave him a huge hug and introduced him to the others. "This is my dear friend, who gave me back my life."

Carlos shook hands with everyone. When he hugged Zavia, he whispered, "It's you, not me, señora."

At one o'clock, Queen Beatrix of the Netherlands welcomed the two thousand attendees. She led two minutes of silence for those who had died or been otherwise harmed in Pakistan, Greenland, and other places. And she acknowledged this "New Approaches, New Opportunities" conference, "purposefully convened on the first day of both the New Year and the New Era in international relations." Finally, she introduced the conference conveners. The US president and the Russian prime minister shook hands and escorted the queen offstage. The president sat onstage, while the prime minister stood at the podium.

"Ladies and gentlemen," the prime minister looked out at the audience, "what you will hear in the next five days is a way of looking at the world whose time has come. It may be as different for you as it was for me. It integrates the economic, social, and environmental aspects of life that we too often separate."

A few minutes later, the two leaders traded places. For you, Mariah. "Five hundred years ago, there lived the last generation who believed the earth was flat. A generation later, people believed the earth was round. In between, it was a tough transition, deciding which was right, where should money be invested, and how to shape national policies.

"In that vein," he continued, "our generation has also been transitional. Several hundred years ago, natural resources seemed infinitely large, and the human population was infinitesimally small. But today, there are seven billion of us, without the natural resources to sustain us if we continue on as before. May God help us to make the shift to a better way and to a better world."

Later, after the Opening Ceremony ended, Tex and Carlos sat in a restaurant booth. "The best part," Carlos beamed, "is we have a truce with the cartel. And I have my farm back. Will you visit again and bring Zavia?"

"Of course. But trust me, I'm not digging another fish pond."

The rest of the conference was a whirlwind. Tex and Zavia sat through session after session that opened their eyes about what was on the other side of the transition.

In one lecture, they learned that reforesting arid land with mulberry trees could create millions of jobs and provide tough-as-steel silk to the medical industry and other industries.

In another session, they heard about Las Gaviotas, where hundreds of thousands of acres of rain forest were introduced, freshwater was provided, jobs were created, and biodiversity was increased.

Plus, they heard about buildings in London, Melbourne, and Harare that reduced air-conditioning energy use in office buildings by mimicking how African termites control temperature in their twenty-foot mounds. And they took notes furiously about everything from seaweed-based methods for blocking bacterial action to pacemaker alternatives based on the hearts of whales.

On the third day, they took the afternoon off. Tex drove them down N-57. Zavia carried a bouquet of flowers. The day before, she had addressed two thousand people; this would be much harder. Finally, they reached the barrier. The last time they were here, the sea, storm, and spring tide raged around them. Today, it couldn't be calmer. The last time, Lars had been murdered. Today, he would be honored.

Fifty relatives, friends, and colleagues were assembled. The environment minister spoke in praise of "Lars Jaeger's lifelong contribution to the Netherlands, the Delta Works, and this barrier." Zavia spoke about him as an uncle, friend, and mentor. And finally, Ingrid unveiled the "Lars Jaegar Storm Surge Barrier" plaque. Under a relief of Lars, it said: "He Defended Us From The Sea."

At one point, Tex walked to the gate structure where he and the admiral had plummeted into the water. He leaned against the railing and looked north. Then he remembered the comment from Eddie Meeker, the pipeline specialist in Alaska. "The whole country's Prince William

Sound."

That evening, they dressed for the conference's closing dinner. As Tex put on his cufflinks, Zavia walked in wearing an elegant backless white dress with a colorful bird of paradise embossed in the fabric.
"My God, you look fabulous!"

A moment later, the room service waiter rolled in a bucket of champagne and a platter of hors d'oeuvres. Tex tipped the young woman and snuck a piece of shrimp, just as the phone rang. He lifted the receiver, and, hearing the weak voice at the other end, he almost choked on the shrimp. "Mr. Cassidy. It is Zhivago, Ivan Fyodorokov. I'm glad I reached you."

It took Tex a moment to speak. "I'm honored that you called, sir. Deeply honored."

Ivan was in the Murmansk hospital. He had lost another fourteen pounds. "This world conference: without you, there would be no conference, and not much of a world." Tex heard a muffled sob, as he continued. "Sir, someone would like to say hello."

Zavia took the phone. "Zhivago, it's Lara." As they talked for a few moments, Tex let Charley and Ellie in and told them who had called.

A moment later, Zavia gave Tex back the phone. "Good-bye, Mr. Cassidy," Fyodorokov said.

"Good-bye, sir, and God bless you." Tex put the receiver down, took a deep breath, and returned to the others.

For the next few minutes, the four friends chatted away. Some of it was about the conference. Charley, coming off a resounding victory in November, was determined to use the next four years well. Ellie, having regained some new footing in life, couldn't wait for the inauguration hoopla to be over. Tex, meanwhile, filled the champagne flutes and passed them around. He stood and raised his glass. "To a saner world!"

They then sat, laughed, and enjoyed each other's company. At one point, Zavia and Ellie got into a side conversation. Tex seized the moment. "Charley!" he whispered. Tex pulled a small jewelry case out of his pocket and opened it in a way that only his friend could see the ring. "What do you think?"

"It's beautiful, Tex. Tonight?"

Tex was beaming. "The day after tomorrow, when we're back in Washington."

Charley leaned a little closer. "Listen, buddy, I need your help with another small favor. Can we talk tonight, right after the dinner? And maybe Zavia could join us."

Afterword

THE CHARACTERS in this book are fictional. They are not intended to reflect any past, present, or future living person.

The central plot involving the Russians, the Quartet, the detonating of glaciers, and so on is also fictional—at least, I hope it is.

The references to energy statistics, emission levels, climate impacts, nuclear detection planes, "broken arrow" incidents, oceanic flows, and other factual material are just that: factual. They have been vetted by a number of scientists, EPA employees, and others who are experts in the area of climate change.

That said, some material will likely change from the time I began this book to the time you read it. More glaciers may retreat. More energy reserves may be tapped. More impacts may be uncovered, and more solutions may be implemented. Two of the biggest challenges we face as writers, readers, butchers, bakers, and candlestick makers are: (1) to comprehend the degree to which the world is dynamic and interrelated and (2) to develop systems that dynamically integrate the economic, social, and environmental dimensions of life.

Good luck to us all.

CPSIA information can be obtained at www.ICGtesting.com
Printed in the USA
LVOW061247140113

315631LV00005B/15/P

9 780983 964148